HEADLESS

HEADLESS

Robert Blair

The Cloister House Press

ISBN 978-0-9568247-7-6

Produced by
The Cloister House Press

Foreword

This novel, as its title suggests, is about leadership, or more precisely, the lack of leadership that our modern world has spawned in its efforts to immunise its official doings from the threat of human contamination. More than ever before, we see judgement and decision-making being taken out of human hands and encased in the language of rules and regulations. These are undoubtedly useful and necessary tools, but there is a need for vigilance against the danger that they overreach themselves and ride roughshod over their users. Those entrusted with the rules are under constant pressure not so much to use them as to answer to them; increasingly they are constrained to ignore the promptings of their hearts and minds and stick strictly *to the book*. There is growing public awareness of the shortcomings of career politicians, but very little of the dangers posed by other professionals, career lawyers, career teachers etc., people who, only get on in their professions by demonstrating a skill in jiggling in and out through the fine print of *the book*. Leadership seems to have died; its remains are being discretely buried in administrative 'busyness'. The growing breed of manager-leaders deserves our sympathy. In most cases they are good and clever individuals, who have a living to make, but the effects of their increasing neglect of the call of the real world, as opposed to the dictates of the rules, are being felt across the whole of society, most particularly among ordinary working people, who are left to step gingerly among the debris.

Headless and its sequel (*at present nearing completion*) explore this theme as it manifests itself in the field of education and in the justice system. The novel takes the form of a detective story, but does not ask to be judged primarily in the terms of the genre. It often flirts with the tongue-in-cheek and it breaks with some of the standard conventions, not least the unproblematic triumph of good over evil. Hopefully, it will prove a *good read*, the reader will find wit and humour as well as some characters that stick in the mind, and be stimulated to thought by the challenges posed by the '*bad guys*' to the present moral and political consensus.

To my late father, Bobby Blair,
a working man who expected much from education
and just as much from men of education

Chapter 1

"Not guilty? You've got to be joking, 'Not guilty'? He was as guilty as sin. A retina without an eye could see that."

"Not the jury. No, they decided that Patterson was telling the truth, that he was tucked up snugly in his bed sleeping the sleep of the wouldn't-hurt-a-fly-s. That was of course after they'd been serenaded with the full orchestration of '*I'm just a little guy, unloved and blue* ...' Or was it '*It's a big, bad world out there*?' Anyway, it was tear-jerking knee-jerking at its best."

"And the jury bought it?"

"No, not really. But then the defence don't play these little tunes to get believed, do they? They play them to make the jury really hate having to do the authority-figure thing. Usual story, better a good wallow in innocence – and it's all about their own innocence – than getting into a mud bath with a decision that might stick to them. As usual, the judge made it easy for them. You should have heard him. When Bradbury was cross-examining the wife, his Honour made him out to be a real bastard, bullying that poor defenceless woman. And that I'm-the-victim-here story about the car being stolen and used in the burglary, I wonder how much of that the jury would have swallowed if they'd been given a whiff of Patterson's record."

"Ah, but – all men are angels until proven human ... with sticks and stones *they* may break some bones, but with names *we* shall never hurt them. What can you be thinking of? You can't seriously be suggesting that we allow juries to have their minds contaminated with facts that might help them to see things in perspective. Amazing, isn't it? In every other walk of

1

life we're told – with great finger-wagging – always to put things in context; it's the GlaxoSmithKline antidote to obsession and fanaticism. With juries though, it's different. We don't want to contaminate *their* minds with anything dark and dirty; what a horrible thought . . . *the vestal virgins* getting raped by reality!"

"No, that wouldn't do at all, would it? I'll have to chalk it up, I suppose, as another home win for *jurisprudery*, as you call it."

This exchange between Detective Sergeant Colin Smith and Detective Inspector Stuart Stranaghan was a familiar itch-to-scratch for both men. Over the past few years they had been saying more or less the same things every time either of them lost a case in court. But they were getting better at it. They derived consolation in re-working the wording each time, leaning no doubt on the unconscious hope that someday their words would home into the right slots and all would get said, and magically somehow, all would get done.

They were talking in the crowded office of Bedford Street police station and were being judiciously ignored by the shirt-sleeved activity around them. Sergeant Smith was the younger of the two men; he was a young graduate who had been fast-forwarded into his present position above the heads of older and more experienced 'seen-it-all-befores' who, naturally, had not taken kindly to his preferment and had chosen to focus their resentment on what they referred to as his 'speech impairment' – far too many big words ending in '-ations' and '-isms' and long sentences that don't go down the gullet in a bite. Ironically, for much the same reasons, the older man, Detective Inspector Stranaghan had been stood still on the promotion ladder. The powers-that-be were believed to have 'concerns'. They were unable to decide whether his exploring mind was a sign of a genius at work or a child at play. Their safety-first mindset spoke up for the latter. In truth, Stranaghan had probably chosen the wrong profession. He suspected it himself, but his frequently considered 'I-should-have-beens' never came to convincing finishes; wherever they headed, they all tended to end in the anticipation of disappointment, the triumph of imagination over fantasy.

Despite the difference in age and rank the two men viewed each other as kindred spirits and each tended to look to the other to share his frustrations. Stranaghan had not been involved in the case they were discussing, but he was very familiar with it and took a sympathetic share in that feeling of nausea that loss of faith in the controlling powers almost invariably inspires. Sensing that there was nothing more to be said without undermining what had been said, he was about to return to his own office when the phone rang on Smith's desk. The sergeant picked it up, made some receiving noises and then passed it over to the Inspector. It was Superintendent Jacks, or DJ as he was more generally known; he wanted to see Stranaghan in his office immediately.

Such summons from on-high invariably inspired a feeling of insecurity in Stranaghan. It wasn't guilt; there was nothing he needed to feel guilty about. Nevertheless he always had the nagging feeling that there could be something lurking under his fingernails that might expose the naivety of his default innocence, and that somehow this something had come under the prying gaze of eyes that could see what was not on view. When he was a child, his mother had told him the police would get him if he did anything bad. It was clear to him at the time that the police had a special working relationship with the Great Bearded One and he knew all about the Great Bearded One from the rantings of the little bald preacher in the Nissen hut beside the vegetable shop, where his mother used to take him on those long, black Sunday nights that offered no slip roads to take him off the highway to hell. Perhaps it was his rejection of his early faith encounters with the certainties of the gospel hall that had brought him back to a reliance on the dependability of the constabulary – perhaps this was the reason he had decided to join the police force shortly after graduating from university.

Such were his half-thoughts as he made his way towards Jacks' office. His knock on the door produced an instant 'In!' – Jacks was straightforward about entrances; he never tried to relegate an interview to an interruption.

"Ah, it's you, Stuart. Have a seat. I've just had a call from *Somerton Road*. They've asked me to send them someone to take charge of a case that's been giving them a bit of bother. I've recommended you."

A sense of relief immediately registered itself; the all-seeing eye had failed to find what must surely have been there to be lit on. But the minor anxieties of life are in inexhaustible supply and the meaty curiosity that had been awakened in him was already re-configuring itself into the uncomfortable anticipation of being unequal to the task he was about to be entrusted with.

"I understand it involves an attempt on the life of a schoolmaster. What makes the case curious is that a couple of years ago there was a murder at the school. The investigation got nowhere and no arrest was ever made. Obviously, this second incident puts the whole business in a different light. I'm not sure why they can't deal with it themselves, but they insist on having a fresh mind on the case and they're a couple of men down at the moment."

"Do I take Jason?"

Stuart threw out the question without any leanings towards the answer. Jason was his sergeant. He would have preferred to have had Colin Smith, but the protégé had been entrusted to 'sounder' moulding hands than his. There was nothing wrong with Jason. He was a 'goodish' sergeant, though perhaps a bit too much of a procedures man for Stuart's liking. It wasn't that he stuck rigidly to the rules – Stuart himself was usually too much of a coward to jump after his own imaginative leaps – it was that

4

he always seemed to be working with a view to appearing in a positive light in the 'report'. Philosophers call it *bad faith*, but for Stuart it was more like elderly ladies who spot the photographer and make sure they show their best side to the camera, enhanced of course by a conspiring smile. On the other hand, it would be nice to have someone familiar in unfamiliar surroundings, and someone, besides, whose opinion of him was not totally dependent on future outcomes. And there he was, accusing Jason of *bad faith*!

"Do you want to take Jason? I think they want you to work with one of their own men, but I could check that out if you like?"

"No, it doesn't matter."

The image of himself as an old lady making up to the camera had resolved the issue.

"You're expected at Headquarters at 11.00. You're to report to Superintendent Winkworth. He will brief you."

Superintendent Jacks – funny, Stuart only thought of him as DJ when he was in the third person; in the second person he always got his full title, even within the privacy of Stuart's mind – was a man who believed in form. That is what Stuart liked about him. There was something unsettlingly amorphous about the conviviality sponsored by the top brass as the required ambience of the modern force, where each individual supposedly blends into the corporate body and a spirit of buddiness reigns – a myth of course, which no-one remotely believes in, but which everyone is expected to promote in word and spirit; deed was an entirely different matter. DJ – Stuart had now left the office – was nobody's buddy; he maintained a feudal distance in word and spirit as well as in deed. But when things went wrong and blame labels were being stuck on foreheads, Jack's detachment smacked much less of betrayal than the reigning bloke-iness.

At first sight at least, Superintendent Winkworth was an ordinary bloke. His dress was conventional – suit and tie, chosen

5

no doubt by his wife, but with an intention to obscure rather than complement the personality of the wearer. There was something in the way he wore the managerial uniform that demanded that he be considered someone who had gone through the ranks and been thrust upwards into the higher echelons against his will. This insistence on ordinariness afforded him an air of superiority over any superior. Stuart felt himself in the presence of an unassailable ego.

"Stuart, isn't it? You come highly recommended. I asked DJ to send me someone who would feel at home dealing with wordy types. You know the sort – think they understand everything because they have words for everything? Pains in the arse, if you ask me!"

As this did not seem the opening thoughts of an emerging theory of knowledge, Stuart merely intensified his positive smile and the Superintendent continued.

"I've a case that I think should interest you. There has been an attempt on the life of the headmaster of St. Jude's College. I'm sure you've heard of it – it's a posh school for little toffs, up by Meadow Bank. Anyway, the incident happened yesterday. What makes it interesting is that just over two years ago the previous head was murdered. He was shot while he was out for a walk in the grounds of the college. It was at close range with an old World War 2 pistol, but the gun was never found."

Stuart showed the interest summoned, and the Superintendent felt the way clear to go on.

"Our investigation threw up three main suspects. In the first can of worms we opened we found his estranged wife; she had taken it very personally when he threw her out for having an affair with a local solicitor, didn't seem to think he had any right to be so unreasonable ... But she had a cast-iron alibi. At the time of the murder she had been at a concert with her fancy man and we found about half-a-dozen people who got a lot of pleasure out of vouching for that."

The Superintendent was warming to his task.

"The second suspect was a boy who'd been expelled from the school a few weeks before the murder. He'd been caught in possession of drugs and he and the father had threatened violence unless the head changed his mind and reinstated him. Not much was thought of it at the time; a bit of threatening and a bit of calming are as far as these things usually go. Of course, when the head was murdered, that cast a whole new light on the matter, but again, both the boy and the father were in the clear. The boy was abroad at the time of the murder and the father had umpteen witnesses to prove that he was playing darts for the local pub team.

"The third suspect was a bit of a long shot. The head was new to the job; he had been appointed just a matter of a year or so before and had pipped the favourite for the post. This was a very ambitious character – I've forgotten his name, Jones I think. He seemed to take it very badly. There were a few blazing rows between the two men after the appointment. Jones certainly has a fiery temperament and it's not out of the question that he could have lost control. But then there was a fair degree of planning in the murder; the murderer clearly had worked out the habits of the head and chosen his time and place very carefully – hardly a simple case of a lack of control. Obviously, headships are important to these teacher people, but they're hardly enough to murder for. Anyway, there was no real evidence against Jones. He had no alibi, but I really don't think he did it."

"You said you didn't think he did it. Does that mean you were involved personally with the case, sir?"

"Yes, it was just before I was made up to Superintendent. That's why I won't be taking charge this time."

"Why not get another of your own officers to lead the investigation? Why send for me?"

"We're down a couple of detectives at the moment, but in

any case I wanted someone to work with Myles. He was my sergeant on the case and he'll be able to fill you in on the details. Myles isn't the most popular man in the station at the moment. A few months ago he reported a fellow officer for being too heavy-handed with a suspect. It led to the officer being dismissed from the service. He was a very popular figure – emotional, generous, someone who made a good friend. Myles on the other hand … No, I'll leave you to make up your own mind about him. The main point is, he knows the case and most of the people involved in the school. He should be a great help to you."

The Superintendent rose from his seat and extended his hand with a formality that fitted him as badly as the Sunday suit.

"You'll find Myles in the main office. Obviously I am very interested in this case, so I'd like to be kept up to speed."

Stuart had known only one Myles. He had met him at university. He had always connected the name with 'meek' and had been at first surprised and then quite unreasonably outraged when that particular Myles turned out to be a young man of forthright opinions and an equally dogged determination to evangelise those hitherto unfamiliar with them.

On reaching the main office he was confronted by a small group of officers sitting or standing around one of the desks, obviously enjoying an unofficial coffee break. When he asked for Detective Sergeant Myles he was greeted with a wave of interrogative looks ranging from the mildly quizzical to the coarsely challenging. An off-hand 'that's him there in the corner' eventually emerged from what had threatened to remain a hostile silence. The figure in the corner had clearly overheard Stuart's inquiry and was already making his way over to him. Two things about Myles immediately compelled the eye; his tie filled the exact centre spot of his collar, in sharp contrast to the promiscuous meanderings of those of his fellow officers, and then there was his hair; it had a parting as neat as any seen in a photo gallery of fifties' footballers. He greeted Stuart with an outstretched hand and what seemed genuine warmth mixed with a restraint respectful of Stuart's superior rank. The sergeant seemed oblivious of the atmosphere of disapproval that surrounded him and led Stuart into a side office which, he explained, had been made available for them for the period of the investigation.

"Coffee, sir?"

This readiness to call him 'sir', rather than the much used 'guv' or the avoidance of the vocative altogether in their early encounters matched well the tie and the parting. Over the coffee, which was quickly produced, Myles gave an account of the case, which in its coherence and objectivity would have done credit to any college lecturer.

He began with the details of the older case. The headmaster, a Dr. Stevens, had been shot when out walking with his dog in a wood that adjoined the school playing fields. There had been only one shot, which had penetrated the heart causing almost instant death. The gun used was, as Superintendent Winkworth had said, a relic from the Second World War, a Walther P38. There were about a million of them manufactured during the war and veterans had brought them back like rock from Blackpool. Suspicion fell on the wife. She had no money of her own and was unlikely to get much from a divorce settlement, as the marriage had been short – they had only been married three years and she was the guilty party in the break-up. *Guilty party – what a delightfully old fashioned notion! Was it still used in divorce settlements?*

"Stevens had considerable means – teaching seems to have been merely a hobby for him. Mrs Stevens is one of those people who get their strength and forcefulness from feeding off the weakness of others. Stevens, however, was not a weak man, but from all accounts his wife was his Achilles' heel. Her alibi was beyond question, but we did look into the possibility of collusion with her lover, a John Berwin. As a local solicitor he had many contacts with the criminal fraternity. But this proved a non-starter and in fact a few months after the murder the couple split up – hardly a passion big enough then to inspire a murder.

"The father of the boy who had been expelled was a very rough diamond. He had done time for grievous bodily harm on a young fellow on the estate where they lived. And the boy – his name was Robert Snoddy – was very much a chip of the old block. He had been warned several times that he would be expelled unless his behaviour improved. Dr Stevens was a passionate believer in helping children from disadvantaged homes. In fact this is a central plank in the ethos of the school. It is a curious kind of school. It seems to be some kind of mixture between a public school and a grammar school. Most of the pupils pay quite stiff fees, but a sizeable minority pay very little and in some cases nothing at all. The school can afford this for it is heavily endowed. About thirty years ago it received a huge bequest of some millions, with the stipulation that the money be used to fund underprivileged children. In any case, the Snoddies could not have committed the crime; the father had plenty of witnesses to prove where he was and the son had got a job on a farm in the Black Forest in Germany – he had been a star pupil in German and his German teacher had arranged it for him, prior to him taking his A levels.

"The science master, Alistair Evans, was the third suspect. He is a fiercely competitive man and had been the front runner for the headship. The appointment had been made about three years before the murder. Evans clearly set out to make life as difficult as possible for the new man and encouraged a bolshie attitude to him among the senior staff. He was reported to the Board of Governors by Stevens and was told to change his attitude or he would face dismissal. That warning came just a matter of six weeks before Stevens was killed. Evans claimed he was at home at the time of the murder, but he is a bachelor and lives alone, so he had no-one to confirm his statement."

"How did he get on with the second new head?"

"Can't really say. By the time we had given up on the case, no new appointment had been made. The Board had got Stevens' predecessor to fill in. But, clearly, Evans was out of the running for the job after his spat with the Board."

"We'll need to look into that. Now fill me in on the details of the latest development. I don't even know the victim's name."

"Kennedy, sir. His first name is Michael. It happened yesterday and he's still unconscious, so we haven't been able to interview him. He was found, strangely enough, less than a hundred yards away from where the Stevens' killing took place, on the same lane. He had been out riding. It was the horse returning to the stables without a rider that alerted the staff. The stables belong to the school. He had been shot, but the bullet had only caught him on the shoulder and caused little damage. The real damage was caused by the fall. He must have landed awkwardly and banged his head against a concrete fence post by the side of the lane. The doctors give him a better than even chance of recovery, but they don't rule out the possibility of brain damage."

"What progress have you made?"

"Very little, sir. We have the forensics on the bullet; it's from the same gun that killed Stevens. There had been heavy rain and there were some motor cycle tracks visible on the lane. But it's impossible to know if they are connected. Forensics are dealing with them at the moment.

"I assume you checked for tracks last time?"

"Yes, there were tracks, but we thought nothing of that at the time. The path is frequently used by the local scrambler boys. This time the tracks were fresh and that's why I think they might be relevant."

"Have you spoken to Mrs Kennedy?"

"I had a brief word with her, but the woman was too upset for a proper interview. Superintendent Winkworth told me you would be taking charge of the case, so I have sorted out all the old files for you to examine."

"Let's start with the head's secretary. No-one fills in the cracks between facts better than secretaries. Was she Stevens' secretary as well?"

"Yes, sir. Mrs Abernethy. You're right. I found her a great help last time. She doesn't miss much, that lady."

Chapter 2

The school not merely found itself, it imposed itself in the hills overlooking the city. The grounds were extensive with little swathes of grassy rugby pitches emerging brightly beneath a canopy of autumnal trees – a green and pleasant landscape of pastoral promise, until, that is, one's eye hit upon the sickly green astroturf of the hockey pitches and the ill-named tartan of the tennis courts. The main building, neo-Gothic, connived in the pastoral promise and brought you back to nobler times when concrete, glass and tacky colours were unknown to building artists or, if known, spurned. Quite a few other buildings had been added since the original with varying degrees of success at assimilation. The sports hall wallowed in its recalcitrance; it had the stamp of 'local authority' and was a perfect match for the in-your-faceness of the hockey pitches. Behind it another new building was struggling into life – it was too early to say exactly where it would stand in the aesthetic continuum of the school village, but too late to entertain any real optimism.

It suddenly occurred to Stuart that he didn't know who had taken over the duties of headmaster. Myles said he assumed it would be the vice-principal Mr Scott, but he couldn't be certain, and so they were obliged to keep to formal nomenclature and request an interview with 'the acting headmaster'. Mrs Abernethy's smile turned from recognition of past shared experiences with Myles to something more mischievous, but she said nothing and led the two men into the study.

"This is Detective Inspector Stranaghan and Detective Sergeant Myles, Mrs Swanson."

Stuart felt put out. He hated feeling vulnerable to the slur of prejudice. He knew the prejudice involved was inspired by nothing more than the laziness of habit, but he felt potentially defenceless. A second breaker hit him. Could this be a co-ed school? He hadn't checked with Myles. It hadn't occurred to him. He mustn't let on. His ignorance could be quietly put down without anyone knowing of its existence.

Mrs Swanson was instantly takeable-to. She was in her early forties but retained that fresh aura which nature lends to women and, Stuart supposed, to men whom it deems still to be in its service.

"What's the latest from the hospital?"

Her voice had a natural softness to it and threatened none of the unnaturally long vowels of those efficient and intelligent English women who strive to be 'chairs' of committees or boards. It remained to be seen if her utterances would be matchingly jargon-free.

"Nothing new, I'm afraid, Mrs Swanson. Mr Kennedy is still unconscious. So we'll have to manage as best we can in the meantime. If you don't mind, I'd like some background details from you. Can I start by asking if you know of any 'unpleasant-nesses' involving either staff or pupils?"

Where had that word come from? Let those who are jargon-free cast the first stone.

"Mr Kennedy is a very caring teacher. He puts the interests of his pupils above all else. He naturally expects his staff to follow his example and in those cases where they fall short he takes a firm line."

"Have there been any such cases?"

"There has been one fairly serious incident involving a member of staff. The case is currently being considered by the disciplinary committee of the Board and the member of staff in question has been suspended."

Curious, Stuart mused, how the failure to mention the staff member by name raises the tone of what he is being told from the malicious to the professional. Mrs Swanson clearly felt that it was up to him to *drag the name from her*. He duly obliged.

"And who is this teacher?"

"His name is Richard Devine. He teaches history."

"What exactly did he do?"

"There is a whole history. Oh, sorry. I didn't mean to make a pun. Funny, how that happens. No, he has had an unfortunate tendency to ignore the sensibilities of his pupils. This time he went too far. One of the girls in his third form was behaving badly during the memorial service – she was chatting and giggling while the names of the dead were being read out. He grabbed hold of her by the arm in the corridor afterwards and caused her severe bruising. This was clearly unprofessional and totally unacceptable. What made things even worse was that he refused to apologise and became abusive to the head. That's why things have gone so far."

"When you say there has been a whole history, do you mean that it goes back to the time of Dr Stevens?"

"I'm not sure. I was only appointed last September, although I did hear that there had been some minor incidents before Mr Kennedy's time. You should ask Mrs Abernethy. She will have the details. But then surely you would have known all about that when you were inquiring into Dr Stevens' murder?"

Myles was quick to respond.

"Mrs Abernethy told us that it had all been a storm in a teacup and Dr Stevens hadn't even considered it worth documenting. Of course we interviewed Mr Devine and we were quite happy to let the matter rest."

"I am sure you are right, Sergeant. I am sure there is no real harm in the man. He lacks sensitivity and teaching is perhaps the last profession he should have chosen, but I can't believe him capable of major violence."

It was hard to say whether Mrs Swanson was giving her opinion of Mr Devine's propensity for evil or aligning herself with the benevolent forces of optimism. In any case she seemed pleased to have said what she said. It was clearly the right thing to have been heard to say in the circumstances.

"You say you only arrived last September, Mrs Swanson. I understood Mr Scott was vice-principle."

"Indeed he is. The school had two vice-principles, Mr Scott and Mrs Williams. But with the increased burden of administration and the expansion of pastoral provision in the school, the head decided that there was a need for a third VP. The post was advertised and I was appointed. Then the decision was taken to create an official post of deputy head and I was the lucky candidate. I must say I didn't expect to be thrown in at the deep end quite so soon. I've only been in post for a little over two months."

Stuart uttered a ready-made formula of politeness and continued with what in fact was, but would not, he hoped, be perceived as, a *sequitur*.

"What role does Mr Evans have at present in the school?"

There was a perceptible pause before she replied.

"Mr Evans is a very able man. He has a major input into the timetable and he is very successful with his exam classes. I'm sure you know all about his past history in regard to Mr Kennedy's predecessor. At the moment he is not part of the senior management team. I believe he is focusing his energies currently on examination work. I understand he has an important position in one of the examination boards and does consultancy work for QCA."

Stuart was not familiar with the acronym, but forbore to inquire

"How did he and Mr Kennedy get on?"

The question was obviously unwelcome.

"They are both strong personalities. They did have a quarrel, but it wasn't anything serious, between them at least."

"Let us be the judge of that, Mrs Swanson. What was the quarrel about?"

16

"There was an incident in the staffroom a couple of weeks ago. One of the male staff members was abusive to a young female teacher. He had her in tears and the poor girl was advised by her GP to take some time off to recover from the stress that he had caused her. Mr Kennedy took a firm line and demanded that he apologise. He refused and the head issued him with a written warning. The unions are involved and the whole business has got quite messy."

"But how did this involve Mr Evans?"

"He took the side of Mr Ross – that's the teacher who was abusive – and was ... how shall I say? ... rather forthright in his defence."

It was apparent that Mrs Swanson was determined to avoid any Anglo-Saxon and as Stuart was quietly confident that more graphic accounts would be readily on offer from alternative sources, he did not pursue the matter. He asked for interviews to be set up with Evans and Ross; he would also need to speak to Mr Devine, but that could wait until the next morning, as he wanted to view the crime scene and have a word with Mrs Kennedy. On Mrs Swanson's invitation to him and his good sergeant to join her for lunch in the school refectory, he suddenly became aware of an appetite and readily accepted.

The staff ate on a little stage high enough to offer a vantage point to those who wished to keep an eye on proceedings but low enough to avoid the impression of a chimpanzee's tea party. The bell had not yet gone and there was a calm which sat well with the hall, but then so too did the noise which accompanied the subsequent arrival of 'the young people', as Mrs Swanson insisted on referring to them. 'The young people' did include girls! Stuart now felt the same lifting of restraint that he had experienced on his first visit to France as a sixth former once the parameters of 'vous' and 'tu' had been clearly established with the young tutors who were in charge of the course. He and Myles were both introduced to the teachers at the table. There were only five there and these did not include any of those who had thus far been given 'speaking parts' in the case. Mrs Swanson was immediately collared by one of the young woman teachers on the subject of a telephone conversation with a parent. Stuart caught the beginning of the exchange, but was unable to perceive any equilibrium between what was being said and the earnestness on the young woman's face and the pressing tone of her voice. He was glad to be distracted by the middle-aged gentleman on his left who invited him to *expand biographically* on the introductory details given by Mrs Swanson. He was fortunately spared the pain of cutting and editing the wealth of information he had on himself by the intervention of Myles.

"This is Dr Greenfield, sir. He teaches German and was very helpful to us last time. Hello, Dr Greenfield, nice to see you again."

Greenfield smiled warmly and enquired if Myles had followed through on his resolution to take up German.

"I'm afraid not, Dr Greenfield. I'm doing an OU degree course in law. I was told this would be more useful to me in my career."

"That's a pity, but it would seem that that's the way things stand ... or perhaps lie."

Myles seemed immune to the challenge of Greenfield's reply, but Stuart could not resist.

"What do you mean, Dr Greenfield?"

"Oh, I am merely struck by the irony of modern *mores.* We have given up on the big questions of meaning in life. The notion of cosmic purposes is alien to our modern minds and so we channel our need for meaning and purpose into little things such as careers and wealth creation. Previous generations regarded such things merely as means to ends. We seem incapable of making the leap into really modern thinking and justifying our trivial doings in terms of purposefulness rather than purpose."

Stuart was taken aback. Not since his student days had he heard 'talk' like this. The pursuit and development of a thought attempting to form itself into a statement on the human condition was not the stuff of lunchtime exchanges at the station, nor even in the pub at the end of the shift. He was seized by a desire to sign up and offered as a token of his *bona fides* a quotation that had stayed with him from those days of late night musings in the university bar.

"*Il n'y a pas de joie de vivre sans désespoir de la vie.*"

"Albert Camus! I didn't know the law had a head as well as a long arm. You speak French, Inspector Stranaghan?"

"Yes, I studied French and philosophy at university, but I am a bit rusty in both. I don't get to use them much these days."

"Be careful or Dr Greenfield will recruit you into his flock."

Mrs. Swanson had finished her 'surgery' with the anxious young teacher. Stuart had not noticed whether the latter had departed comforted or still racked by anxieties.

"Dr Greenfield is our resident intellectual, Inspector. He runs the *Thinkers' Club*. They discuss all sorts of weird and wonderful topics. What was the one you were considering last month, Bruce?"

"We were exploring the concept of the deserving poor. Mrs. Swanson does not believe in the deserving poor, Inspector. She finds the adjectival element redundant. Come to think of it, she doesn't really like the substantive either. Better the abstract. It's poverty with the capital P that is the enemy. It must be tackled head on. Poor people are only a distraction that shouldn't be allowed to get in the way, isn't that right, Florence?"

Mrs Swanson had clearly no desire to engage with Dr Greenfield on this or, Stuart suspected, any other issue. She contented herself to smile in response. The smile did not lack warmth, but this merely added seriousness to its condescension.

The rest of the meal was passed in the calmer waters of fact exchange. Stuart learned a great deal about the school. Mrs

Swanson assumed the role of narrator, but Dr Greenfield fringed the edges with laconic interjections.

The school had been set up in the late nineteenth century and in the early years had been run as a conventional public school for boys. In the course of time an increasing number of bursaries and scholarships had brought in many boys of humbler origins *who had – mirabile dictu – added greatly to the academic standing of the school.* This process had received a major boost in the late nineteen-seventies when an old boy had set up a trust which enabled the school to accept over fifty extra day pupils who were required to pay either minimal fees or no fees at all, depending on the home circumstances. By the nineties the boarding department had dwindled away and the decision was made to take in girls – '*das ewig Weibliche zieht uns hinan*'. There were still sixty-three boarders, all boys, but it was anticipated that this would be entirely run down in the next few years. The staff of the school had been exclusively male up to the 1950s; but female teachers had been gradually introduced (very reluctantly and in response only to the force of necessity, Mrs Swanson stressed), and of course since the school became co-ed the balance of the teaching staff ... *has been shifting more dramatically ladywards.* At the end of the lunch the two detectives were cordially invited to join Dr Greenfield for coffee in 'the other place'. This, it was explained, was an alternative staffroom which, according to Greenfield, was smoke-filled but gossip-free. It was with genuine regret that Stuart declined the invitation. He would dearly have liked to exchange thoughts rather than facts for a change, but duty called. Mrs Swanson had set up the two interviews he had requested for 3.00 and 3.30, which left Myles and him just enough time to make an inspection of the crime scenes. Coffee and good talk would have to wait for another day.

Whinny Walk was a bridle path which led from the main road along the perimeter of the school grounds, through the adjacent golf course to a little deciduous wood, then past the trout lake to a small road used only by very local traffic. Yesterday's incident had occurred at the point where the lane was leaving the golf course and entering the wood. There was a fairly steep gradient in the direction of the wood. A section had been cordoned off and Myles showed the inspector where the stricken headmaster had been found. There was nothing to indicate to the eye that a human life had come under threat here, but then there was also nothing to indicate that this would have been of any importance. This was a place of nature: how many life-and-death struggles had gone on here unseen and unwept-for by us who are focused on the great human soap opera? Even the concrete post which had been at the centre of the wrong-doing owned up to nothing beyond its presence on the scene. The motor cycle tracks that Myles had mentioned were far from distinct. The path had a clay base but had a thick covering of limestone pebbles. At three of four spots where the pebbles were thinner on the ground and the clay could be seen there were patterns consistent with motor cycle tracks, but just how old these were was a matter for the extra-sensory sleuth-hounds of the forensics department. Stuart hated the amateurism of his crime scene investigations. The mythical powers of observation of the fictional detective from Holmes to Poirot had indeed acquired a reality in modern police work, but it was a reality which had no place for flesh and blood; 'the little grey cells' had long been replaced by electronic bytes. He perked up however when Myles commented on the link between the name of the path and the part played in the incident by the horse. It restored some of his self-respect as an insightful detective to explain that the name had nothing to do with the equine noises but rather with the presence of gorse along both sides of the path, the Scottish and indeed his own native Ulster word for gorse being whin. But Myles was not to be outdone: there was every possibility, he suggested, that the name was deliberately ambiguous.

Investigation of the site of the Stevens' murder proved even

21

more prosaic. This was further down the path and away from the school grounds just before the wood gave way to the trout lake. Here the path had a much more solid base which had yielded no clues as to the murderer's mode of movement. There had been no obvious indication of a vehicle, let alone a motor cycle, having been used, and since the body had not been discovered until considerably after the shot had been fired, the murderer could easily have escaped on foot without anyone seeing him.

"It's unlikely to throw up anything useful, but we'll have to find out if anyone heard the shot."

Stuart had the feeling, which often recurred, less of conducting inquiries than of being conducted by them. But Myles' face brightened.

"I've been to the golf club and got a copy of their tee-off schedule along with names and addresses of everyone on the list around the time of the shooting. We'll need uniform support on this, but I needed your authority before I could get them cracking on it."

Myles was despatched back to the station to get these *futilities* underway while Stuart made his way back through the portals of the school building to the office of Mrs Abernethy, the head's secretary, or, as Stuart could not resist thinking, the now *headless* secretary. Mrs Swanson was required in the classroom, but Mrs Abernethy was a woman who required little direction. She had everything in hand and Mr Ross was due in ten minutes. In Mrs Swanson's absence the head's study was available for the interview. Stuart accepted the offer of a coffee and asked the secretary to join him in the study until Mr Ross should make his appearance.

"How long have you been working here, Mrs Abernethy?"

Mrs Abernethy seemed pleased to be asked this question, mundane as it was. As a secretary she was used no doubt to being the bearer of news and the responder to inquiries, but she never had any ownership of the news or the answers. They were not hers to give.

"I'm afraid I've been here since the year dot, Inspector. Let us say 'more than twenty-five years.'"

"There have been many changes in the school over those years?"

"Yes indeed. It's a very different school now from the one I came to all those years ago. Dr Buchanan was the headmaster then. Wonderful man! He used to do the salaries on the back of his cigarette packets. And he never got them wrong. Mind you, there were few of the staff who would have challenged him if he had made a mistake."

"A bit of a tyrant then?"

"Oh no. Just a man with natural authority. He was scrupulously fair. Everyone respected him, both the boys and the masters. He was also an excellent teacher. Classics, of course. I remember he would have his sixth form Latin class to tea every Thursday evening. It didn't matter what board business was demanding his attention. He always told me to keep Thursday evenings free. The Board was only *about* education, what he did on a Thursday night *was* education. That's what he always said."

"Was he the head who was succeeded by Dr Stevens?"

"Oh no. Dr Buchanan died in the late eighties. He was succeeded by Mr Singleton. He was also a classicist. He was a young man and a great friend of Dr Buchanan. A lot of things were changing at the time and the poor man found it difficult to cope. He struggled on for years but in the end he decided to resign and it was then that Dr Stevens was appointed."

"What became of Mr Singleton?"

"He left the country. Got a lectureship in the States. I get a card from him every Christmas. Where is it he is? The city with the lake ... Chicago. The poor man was never cut out for the rough and tumble of staffroom and boardroom politics. He's much happier now."

"Mr Evans was short-listed for the headship, I believe?"

"Yes, Mr Evans is a different kettle of fish. I couldn't have seen him resigning. Not a man to be pushed around."

"A bit like Dr Buchanan?"

"Oh no, definitely not. Dr Buchanan was a true gentleman. Oh, that sounds bad. I don't mean anything by that. Dr Buchanan belonged to a different age. Mr Evans is more like a businessman. He goes at things straight on."

"And Dr Stevens, was he an internal appointment?"

"No. No. He came from a teacher training college. He had been a head of department."

"And how did he cope?"

"He had no problem. He and the Board saw eye to eye on the changes that were taking place."

"But surely most of the big changes had taken place well before this. The decline in the boarding and the decision to go co-ed?"

"Yes, but there were other changes to do with the in-take and the curriculum."

A loud and deliberate cough could be heard from Mrs Abernethy's office. Mr Ross had arrived and was quite probably recycling his nervousness and embarrassment into a cough of challenging amplification. What a nuisance!

"We must talk again, Mrs Abernethy. I have enjoyed our chat. You have given me a lot of very useful background."

The complicity of Mrs Abernethy's responsive nod made it clear that she was grateful for the inspector's gratitude.

Chapter 3

Ross was indeed nervous. It showed in the evasiveness of his eyes and the continuous vetting which his responses were subjected to before he allowed them to team up with the words that he had waiting for them. He was in his mid-thirties, of vigorous physique; in fact there was something intimidatingly physical in his bearing which contended successfully with his defensive unease. Stuart, who had installed himself behind the headmaster's desk, beckoned him down into the visitor's chair and was mildly surprised to record a reduction in his own defensive tension. After a few polite preliminaries he began:

"I would like you to tell me about the incident with Miss Jordan."

Another cough preceded the reply and a series of minor splutterings punctuated it.

"It was three weeks ago. I had been required to cover Mr Robson's class – it was a history class. Mr Robson had set them some revision work and I let them get on with it. However, after a while I noticed that, although they were quiet enough, they weren't really doing any work. So I decided to show them how to take proper notes and organise them in a form that could be easily remembered. They seemed to respond well to this and I felt it had been a worthwhile exercise. It was a double period. I was only down to cover the first one and Miss Jordan took over from me at the end of my stint. I explained to her what was happening and I left her in charge.

"Half way through the next period I realised that I needed to speak to one of the boys in my English class and I remembered that he had been in the history class I had just come from, so I went back. When I opened the door the room was in darkness,

25

the curtains had been drawn and the class was watching a video – it was a cartoon I believe. *Tom and Jerry* or such like. I couldn't believe what I was seeing and I just stared open-mouthed. I think I said something like '*Unbelievable!*' I asked the boy I wanted to see to come out into the corridor and when I had told him what I wanted to tell him I opened the door for him to go back to class. I was still shocked when I got another view of what was happening, but I didn't say anything. I think another '*Unbelievable*' probably came out. I cannot deny that these '*unbelievables*', although a very restrained response, were probably enough to make the pupils aware of my displeasure at Miss Jordan's antics."

It was clear from the manner of his narration that Ross had gone over this story many times both in his head and to chosen audiences. Despite this the vetting process was still in operation, albeit, one imagined, at reduced intensity.

"I returned to the staffroom and wondered what to do. I saw this as a very serious breach of trust. How could a teacher allow a class to skive like that, ignoring the written instructions of their own subject teacher and rubbishing the efforts of a fellow member of staff! I talked to one or two people about it during break. I thought of going to the head, but I knew he would do nothing, so in the end I decided to let the matter drop.

"However, at the end of lunchtime Miss Jordan came up to me in the staffroom. I was a bit surprised. I assumed she was going to offer some kind of explanation. Not a bit of it! She simply said to me, "*Don't ever speak to me like that in front of a class again.*" I'm pretty sure it was a double 'ever' and she said it in such a soft little voice – it was really weird. Here she was, threatening *me* – and it *was* a threat, believe me. When she had said it she turned and made to go off, leaving me in a presumed state of speechlessness and defeat. In fact I did feel shame coming on – but it was not coming from what I had done: it was from what *she said* I had done. Then I felt horror at my so readily accepting her indignation. That's when I lost it. I simply opened my mouth and yelled at her. I'm not sure what I called her. It didn't really matter. I needed to be verbally violent. I make no apology for that. She had invented this little girly game and expected me to play by its girly rules. No way! She tried to leave the room, but I leaned against the door and told her that she had started this conversation and there was no way she was leaving until she heard what I had to say. It was mainly women in the staffroom at this stage. Some of them, I suspect, had put her up to this, once they had worked up enough feminine indignation over lunch. I suppose I was having a go at them too. None of them said a word. When I had had my fill of my anger I left the room and gave the door a good theatrical slam behind me. Believe me, I was very angry."

"Do you often get that angry, Mr Ross?"

"I do get angry at things quite often, but I usually stifle it. I suppose I'm afraid of the force of it. It takes someone to land the first blow before I can let it loose."

"Are you afraid you might hurt somebody?"

"No, it's not exactly that. I think it's more a question of a fear of ending up with no real control of the situation. While I hold back my anger I can keep on believing that I could take control of the situation if I called on it. But if I let it rip and I didn't manage to change things, then I would feel completely defeated."

"So this time you felt that Miss Jordan had struck the first blow, as you put it?"

"Yes. There was something very threatening about the quiet voice she used. If I had accepted that, I would have been completely overwhelmed anyway. I had nothing to lose by allowing myself to get really angry."

"What happened after the scene in the staffroom?"

"The head sent a message that he wished to see me at the end of lessons. When I went he informed me that Miss Jordan had burst into tears after I left – she thought I was going to physically attack her. Mrs Swanson had driven her home and had made an appointment for her with the doctor."

"How did the head behave towards you?"

"He was very cold and distant. He made me feel that I was a bad smell."

"Did that make you angry?"

"No, by that stage I was a spent force, I was too emotionally drained. During my interview with him I kept trying to imagine I was spectating. It's a technique I sometimes use to get my brain to work rather than my emotions. I can argue my corner if I keep myself emotionally detached."

"I assume you told Mr Kennedy your side of the story?"

"No, not at that point."

"Why not?"

"He showed no interest in hearing my side of things and it would have seemed like grovelling if I had offered an explanation without being asked."

"What did he say to you then?"

"As I said, he treated me like a bad smell. He called me a bully, threatened me with possible dismissal and suggested that Miss Jordan herself would probably be considering a court action."

"And how did you react to that?"

"I told him that that was exactly what I would have expected from him, that he was a total letdown as a headmaster and that I would have things to say to the Board which might not reflect too favourably on him."

"What response did he make to that?"

"He told me to leave his office He said he would get Mrs Abernethy to set up a formal meeting with the necessary witnesses present as the first stage in the disciplinary procedures which he intended to initiate. So I left."

"What exactly did you mean when you said that you would have things to say to the Board?"

"The man is a complete bully. He is afraid of parents of course and finds it easier to side with them against his staff. He avoids contact with the few staff that stand up to him and encourages subservience in the younger teachers, especially the women. Casting me as the dragon fits very well with the image he tries to promote of himself as the mediaeval lord defending his vassals. Fealty will of course be the price to be paid at a later date. If the dispute had been between two of his vassals, then he would have had a real problem, but I'm an easy target, being an outsider to his fiefdom."

"Do you have any realistic hopes of getting the Board to see him in this light?"

"Probably not. But I'll enjoy presenting the case. He has made one or two slip-ups and I'll make the most of them. My friends are always telling me I should've been a barrister – this is my chance to prove them right. As I said to you before, if I can keep my emotions out of it, I can slog it out with the best of them. And to be honest, I've given up on this job and this school and possibly even teaching itself, so I'm free of my demons."

Stuart had listened with shrinking scepticism as Ross's tale had progressed. The candour with which the teacher examined his own doings was impressive and demanded credence. Would a guilty man have referred so openly to his 'demons'? But then Ross was clearly highly intelligent and would be quite capable of laying a false psychological trail. As an English teacher he might also have hidden thespian talents.

"Where were you yesterday around three o'clock?"

"I was doing what all English teachers do on Sunday afternoons, I was marking essays. English is a wonderful subject to teach, Inspector, but pure purgatory when it comes to marking."

"Do you live alone? Can anyone confirm that you were there?"

"I do have a wife, but we have been separated for a couple of years. So I'm afraid I can offer you no proof that I didn't nip out and shoot the bugger."

"Where do you live, Mr Ross?"

"Oh, that would not have been a problem. Since my separation I have been renting a little cottage at the far end of the golf course. I could easily have nipped over to Whinny Way and got back without being seen. In fact it would have been a welcome distraction from the direness of the stuff I was marking."

Ross was now certainly free of the emotion which he claimed tied his tongue. His performance – and Stuart could not escape the feeling that it was a performance – showed increasing self-belief as it progressed. The nervous vetting that had preceded each utterance had melted away, as had the cough which seemingly operated like the choke in a car, only necessary until the engine has had time to warm up.

The question was: what kind of performance was he giving? Was it a performance put on to mislead a policeman or merely the instinctive reaction of a seasoned teacher to a captive audience?

"Do you own a motor bike, Mr Ross?"

"As a matter of fact I do. I sometimes use it to get to school."

"And you would come by Whinny Way?"

"Yes, it is the most direct route."

Stuart was about to bring the interview to an end when a sudden thought struck him.

"When exactly did you and your wife separate?"

"It was two years ago, in July."

"That was just after the murder of Dr Stevens, wasn't it?"

"Yes, but I don't see the relevance."

"Did you ever have a row with Dr Stevens?"

"Nothing beyond what I told your people at the time."

"And what exactly was that, Mr Ross?"

There was a distinct pause – filled by a cough – before Ross replied. The vetting process was clearly back in operation.

"Dr Stevens wanted to replace me as teacher-tutor. He thought that Mrs Vance would do a better job. I was too academic, not interested enough in developing the pastoral skills of the younger teachers and Mrs Vance had done a *course*. No-one can do anything these days without *doing a course*."

"Was there money involved?"

"No. Stevens wanted me to move sideways. He needed someone to take charge of literacy within the school, a so-called literacy co-ordinator. There's another buzz word for you, Inspector. Nothing, apart from courses that is, gets done nowadays – that would be too unsophisticated – everything gets co-ordinated ... It was no big deal. I didn't like the way things were going in teacher-tutoring anyway."

"But you resented Stevens asking you to step down?"

"Of course I did. Wouldn't you? But I'm hardly going to murder the man for that, am I?"

"I didn't suggest that you did, Mr Ross. I'm just trying to find out what the pieces are at this stage. Once I've done that, then I'll have a go at the jigsaw."

When Ross left, Stuart had a few moments to reflect before the arrival of Evans. There was something in the pattern of Ross' fluctuations between uncertainty and confidence that suggested complication. The timing of his separation from his wife might be significant. Stuart was certainly interested in hearing from her on the subject. But now he must think of Evans. His reason for interviewing Evans at all seemed very thin. Evans had certainly been a prime suspect in the previous investigation, but his involvement with the present case appeared to be minimal. But then, these were peculiar cases. The coincidence of the Stevens' murder and the attempt on Kennedy's life pointed to a common motive that in some way involved the school. So it was likely that the crimes had sprung from something outside the normal rag-bag of motives – lust, greed, jealousy, ambition – or of course it might have been any one of these magnified from the miniscule. Without such amplification the school was scarcely a suitable launching pad for any of the deadly sins.

When Evans was ushered in by Mrs Abernethy Stuart was mildly surprised to be confronted with a polished man-about-town. He wore an expensive double-breasted suit, a bright silk tie and a double-cuffed shirt, the starched cuffs appearing discretely from under the sleeves of his jacket. His manner was that of a pressed business executive, prepared to keep up an appearance of patient good manners but, it should be understood, in a spirit of *noblesse oblige*, for clearly he had bigger fish to fry. He immediately snatched the initiative away from Stuart.

"What can I do for you, Inspector ... Stranaghan isn't it?"

Stuart chose to ignore the question form of the address. Confirming his name would have left him a tempo behind his opponent. The image flashed before him of himself being led by none other than himself into this adversarial mentality.

"I am interested in your in-put – that wasn't his kind of word at all! – into the dispute between Mr Kennedy and Mr Ross."

"Understandable. My in-put, as you put it, stemmed merely from my desire to see that the affair be conducted in a professional way. Kennedy was handling it badly and I pointed that out to him. Predictably, he resented my interference and I was obliged to press my point more forcefully than had been my original intention."

"I see. In what way did you consider he was handling things badly?"

"His taking sides before all the facts were established, his failure to have a witness present at the initial interview with Ross, his having this interview at all before Ross had submitted a written account of his version of events. The man hadn't even inquired into the original cause of the dispute!"

"But surely this wasn't really any business of yours. Are you a friend of Mr Ross?"

"Hardly. Ross is a hopeless romantic, like much of the old guard of this establishment. He is reactionary and lacks any kind of vision for the future of education. No, I simply like to see things done properly and if the head insists on surrounding himself with people who are not up to the job of management, then there is a gap for me to fill. But you are quite right. It was unprofessional of me to intervene. I am a professional and I should not offer my services as a charity."

"Many people might see your intervention as a settling of old scores."

"I assure you, Inspector, I have nothing personal against the man. He simply has no understanding of the demands of the post, but he is not to blame for that. It is the Board who are responsible. It was they who appointed him."

"You feel they should have appointed you?"

"It would have been the better option, but it would have been difficult, given the circumstances. The mistake they made was in the previous appointment, the appointment of Dr Stevens. That I did feel strongly about."

"What was so wrong with Dr Stevens?"

"He was certainly a different kettle of fish from Kennedy. Maybe that's why they went for Kennedy; they were caught on the rebound. No, Stevens was everything that Kennedy is not: sloppy, sentimental, touchy-feely. Saw the place as a sanatorium for sad cases, wanted to put the world to rights. Of course, both of them sang from the same hymn sheet. What is it Greenfield calls it? ... *the psalter of sanctified sound bites*. The difference is: Stevens believed all that tosh; Kennedy simply pays lip service to it – he knows what side his bread is buttered on."

"Are you a traditionalist then, Mr Evans?"

"No, I'm a pragmatist."

"But surely that's what you are accusing Mr Kennedy of?"

"No, you are wrong, but I see how you could think that. Kennedy is a lackey, he doesn't try to accommodate prevailing trends, he toadies to them. His only concern is with himself and his own career. I, on the other hand, have always taken a pragmatic view of the long-term interests of the school. Trends cannot be ignored, the gods of educational fashion must be appeased, there is no doubt about that, but when they are done, new gods will come and take their place. Who knows what form they will take. But one thing is certain; the new gods won't smile on those who have given their life blood away to the old ones. Balancing the books, Inspector Stranaghan, that's what counts in the long term. And that applies not just in financial matters, it is vital to balance things out when it comes to education as well.

"I proposed to the Board that we should give up our present premises, or at least the house and some of the land around it. The boarding is on its last legs and without it we wouldn't need all the facilities we have at present. With the money from the sale we could buy the farmland that adjoins the playing fields and build a completely new school. The house and the land are worth a fortune – one of the big hotel chains would snap them up. I know, because I made it my business to draw up a detailed plan of reconstruction for the Board when I was being inter-viewed for the headship. They didn't like the idea. It was too radical for them. Instead they signed up to Stevens' social engi-neering programme."

"What about Kennedy? How did he react to the idea when he came?"

"You must be joking. Any idea that doesn't serve his immediate interests is an unnecessary idea. Kennedy got the job by playing the pastoral card. That was the direction the Board had chosen to take when they appointed Stevens. Kennedy sniffed the direction of the wind then, and his nose tells him the wind has not changed since. The man is a total mediocrity. I wouldn't waste my time on him. And talking of time, Inspector, I have an important meeting coming up in London to-morrow which I need to prepare for. So if there is nothing else, I'll bid you good-day. Of course I am at your service if there is any further background information you may require."

Stuart was on the point of uncritically accepting this arrangement, but he suddenly caught himself on. How had Evans stolen back that tempo? Fortunately he still had to inquire about Evans' whereabouts at the time of the attempt on Kennedy's life.

"No problem there, Inspector. I was returning from Cambridge. There was a pre-scrutiny meeting there on Saturday. I stayed over until Sunday morning and drove back after lunch. I got home about seven o'clock."

"Can anyone verify that, sir?"

"Yes, you can check with the hotel, but that will only confirm my whereabouts until about eleven o'clock. The rest of the day, I'm afraid, I was alone"

"Where did you have lunch? Surely, you remember the name of the hotel or restaurant?"

"No, once again I must disappoint you, Inspector. I found a quiet spot off a side road and ate in the car and listened to Radio 3. I needed a bit of time to myself to mull over a few points that had come up at the meeting on Saturday."

"We'll need details of the hotel. You can leave them with Mrs Abernethy on the way out."

He shouldn't really have said that. Mrs Abernethy was not a police secretary, but what of it? – that lost tempo had to be recovered!

Chapter 4

Hospitals are like the assizes of the afterlife. All those deterged corridors, the advocates of life in their flowing white coats breezing along them in pursuit of some electronic authority, an x-ray, a scan result, or even a more informed opinion, all in the hope that the gods will offer assurance that they continue to take a benevolent view of the lives in the beds. But to-day Stuart was a hospital tourist. Very different from the time when his wife had had surgery to remove a growth on her neck. Then every hospital worker, not just the doctors and nurses, the receptionists, the janitors, even the tea-ladies seemed to share membership of some great judicial process; every last one of them became a potential spokesman for the deities. Every sentence they uttered he had analysed for hidden messages, the choice of words, the intonation, the tone: Was that a note of sympathy? Did it suggest fore-knowledge of a harsh sentence or was it merely the equivalent of a professional smile? The doctors of course had their ears closest to the divine whisperings. It was they who would be the first to receive the verdict. Stuart had wondered if they had all been schooled in the 'nuancing' of pronouncements. By offering no clichés of optimism and no cadences of sympathy they did in fact offer hope, in the form of the *sequitur* that the truth they gave signs of being in possession of did not require any sanitisation. But to-day Stuart was free of all that. Kennedy's fate was a matter of life-and-death only for his wife and family; he, Stuart, could accept the verdict of the gods, whatever it was, without rancour and, above all, without fear. So great was his sense of relief that, try as he might to imagine Mrs Kennedy's pain, he could not. Paradoxically, it was his ability to sympathise in the round that was preventing him from sympathising in the particular.

After Myles had returned to the school he and Stuart had gone to the hospital where Mrs Kennedy was to be found at her husband's bedside. Stuart hated these occasions where the form of things took precedence over the substance. He had a hatred of clichés, but in situations such as these you avoided them at your peril. The right things had to be said and they had to be said in the right way. Any attempts at idiosyncrasy were punishable by disapproving looks from those who '*knew*'. Funeral and wedding line-ups were the worst. Stuart never ceased to marvel at the unselfconsciousness of those who trotted out the conventional formulae. Indeed, their confidence seemed to take sustenance from the ritual, in contrast to himself who always cowered hopeless and tongue-tied before the *commiserati* or the *felicitati*. In this case Myles proved his saviour. Seeing Stuart's discomfiture, he stepped in with a ready supply of the right words. 'Bad business', 'terrible shock' and 'in good hands' all figured prominently. Mrs Kennedy showed no signs of disapproval of either the words or the delivery and Stuart felt the way clear to ask a few gentle questions. She could offer no obvious trigger for the attack on her husband. He had been upset by the two incidents, the unpleasantness involving Ross and subsequently Evans, and the suspension of Mr Devine. She did however mention the existence of a personal computer in which her husband kept notes which he used as a sounding board for ideas and projects. But she did not know the password. It was time for another intervention from Myles; there would be no problem there, the computer people would quickly sort that out. There had been no change reported in Kennedy's condition, but as they were leaving, a *white coat* appeared and Stuart recognised the signs as Mrs Kennedy called on all her antennae for any intimations of a verdict.

"A quick drink before calling it a day?"

Stuart looked hopefully at Myles.

"I don't drink, sir. But I'll join you in an orange juice if you like."

They found a pub which fortuitously was to Stuart's liking. It was, to his mind, like all good pubs, a study in wood and unashamedly old-fashioned – no gaming machines, no mindless musical rantings on puffed-up themes. It was a place for 'good talk'.

"What did you make of Ross and Evans, sir?"

"Both interesting and, I suspect, complicated characters. Ross could be a Jekyll and Hyde; he acts and thinks very rationally but can flip very easily and lose control. He even told me that himself. I found that curious. He knows he is a suspect and yet he tells me things that are bound to arouse my suspicions. On the other hand you could take that as a sign that he has nothing to hide. He's clever enough to anticipate that that's the conclusion I would draw."

"Does he have an alibi?"

"No, he claims he was marking homework. I think we should talk to his wife. They are separated, you know. She might be able to give us something. We should also talk to this Miss Jordan. That's the teacher he had the row with. By the way, did you and Winkworth look into the spat between him and Stevens over the teacher-tutor business?"

"Not really, sir. It didn't seem very important. If people murdered their bosses over things like that, the world would be an empty place."

"Yes, but you were casting your net wider last time. This time we must focus on things that are directly linked to the school."

"What about Evans, sir? What did you make of him?"

"Certainly not what I'd expect of a teacher. He seems more of a business type. He is not Kennedy's number one fan. Tell me – when you looked into this last time, did you discover if he had any financial interest in his plans for the development of the school?"

"No, we didn't find anything of that sort. He knew his stuff and was able to produce a very impressive business plan to the Board, with detailed costings. He had obviously had contacts with developers, but there was nothing to suggest that he had any kind of deal going. It seemed to us that he had gone into the business mainly to impress the Board at his interview."

"I think we should follow up on it. I want you to go through the business plan again first thing in the morning and check out all the contractors quoted in it. If he did kill Stevens and attempt to get rid of Kennedy, he wouldn't have done it out of spite or anger. He's much too calculating for that. But if there was a deal, he might still harbour hopes of bringing it off. There could be millions involved. I'm far from convinced though. It would tie in well with the Stevens' murder, but it's hard to see how getting rid of Kennedy would help his case now. But it's something we can't ignore. Nothing in this business involving the history teacher?"

Funny, if it hadn't been for Mrs Swanson's unintentional pun, he would have thought of him as the R.E. teacher.

"You mean Richard Devine? It was a very trivial incident. He had told a pupil she was stupid, the parents had objected and when Stevens took it up with him, they had a furious row. Devine was abusive to Stevens and stormed out of the study. Stevens, I believe, then called a formal meeting with witnesses present and issued a formal verbal warning to Devine and there the matter rested."

"They're a bolshie lot, these teachers. It'll be interesting to hear what happened this time. But another non-starter, I expect."

By the time Stuart's mini-Merlot had been sipped to a conclusion and Myles' apple-juice prodded, tested and finally rejected, a plan of campaign had been worked out for the following morning. Myles was to work his way through the copy of Evans' business plan, which was still on file, and contact anyone who suggested himself as a possible associate of Evans. Stuart would go and see the sinned-against Miss Jordan before the interview which Myles had set up for him with Devine. The two men should then meet up for lunch at the school and this time they would accept Dr Greenfield's invitation to coffee. Stuart was anxious to get in tune with the staffroom gossip and, if the truth be told, to savour some of the 'talk' which Dr Greenfield's conversation had seemed to promise.

On his way home Stuart collected the files on the Stevens' case and prepared himself for what he thought of as a *lidless* evening. His wife was back in Ireland visiting her aged mother who had had a fall and was recovering in hospital. Curious how he thought of days as having caps or lids on them, events or, more usually, situations occurring towards the end of the day which act as a retention chamber for the day's happenings. A swapping of impressions with his wife usually provided this barrier to the flight of the essences that the day had produced, but to-night he would have to make do with a half-an-hour's television which he would fit in after studying the files. The prospect of an evening devoted exclusively to files left the day shapeless and absurd. It had had a beginning, and if he didn't find an end to cap it with, its middle would bubble over and steam away; it would lose its middleness and become an amorphous lump of the week.

Chapter 5

Shaving is a time for reflection. What is it about shaving that makes it so productive of thought? It was a question that had often presented itself to Stuart's mind as he followed the actions of the razor in the mirror ploughing into the pristine whiteness of the lathered cream. Perhaps he retreated into thought from the sight of a face which never had, but now even less than ever, reflected the centrality of his sense of selfhood. If he saw himself in a crowd he wouldn't give himself a second glance. He had also entertained the rather fanciful notion of some esoteric connection between the reflecting qualities of the mirror and the reflective propensities of the mind. He sensed that there was truth in this, but was wary of trying to articulate it. Better not to force the mind into focus; that defeats the purpose, no, not the purpose, just the nature of this privileged state of beneficent clarity. If Stuart were honest, he would have to concede that his séances with the razor had never yielded any great philosophical insights, but sometimes they had supplied him with a *mot juste* or two, a more felicitous sequencing of a stratagem or a new take on a tired experience. To-day his raised state of consciousness was more akin to the relief you experience when your calf muscles have come out of cramp. Heaped on this was the self-congratulatory sense of merit achieved. Last night the files had loomed before him like a mountain of tedium and he had conquered them. He had fought the good fight and he was now eager to claim his reward. The new day owed him that.

The kitchen offered a solitary breakfast or breakfast in company with the *Today* programme. Stuart felt this morning he could measure up to the *Today* programme. The corn flakes went well; they accompanied the *News* which threw up no more than the usual irritation caused by the BBC's insistence on reporting what politicians were going to say rather than what they had said. The childish and attention-seeking reminders that what of significance had been said had been said 'on this programme' also remained at low blood-pressure levels. However, the toast and coffee did not get off so lightly. A vacuous interview with the Health Secretary in which she ignored the substance of every question put to her, turning it into an opportunity to stress her commitment to 'the well-being of all, especially those who cannot afford . . . ', was followed by an opposition spokesman vilifying the government for the serious under-funding of some obscure project on which 'the future of our children and grandchildren crucially depended'. Saccharin Classic FM or silence? . . . Silence!

The address he had been given for Miss Jordan had meant little to him, but as he drove along the street he was impressed by the dignified opulence of the houses. The front doors had a certain solidity; they smelt of old wood and smacked of old money. The gardens shunned the frivolity of gaudy annuals, even perennials were kept to a minimum; this was an avenue of the shrub. Stuart remembered being taken by his parents along nice avenues like this in Belfast. The owners were seldom in evidence, engaged, he assumed, in worthy, but to him unknown, activities behind those dignified doors. It was one of the grand disillusionments of his adolescence when he discovered that the inhabitants of houses such as these rarely matched them in stature. He was unable to forgive them for this and came to regard them with a contempt they certainly did not deserve. Now he merely wondered why people should want to set themselves up like that. A gracious house demanded a gracious owner and would settle for nothing less. It was much the same as when the uneducated attempt to impress with words and phrases beyond their oral competence. They succeed only in drawing attention to their shortcomings. Poor Miss Jordan was on a hiding to nothing.

When she opened the door her appearance immediately confirmed her unworthiness for the house. The picture of the prim, bespectacled younger sister of a Jane Austen heroine, patiently waiting for her flower to bloom and attract the attention of a handsome suitor with an allowance of £400 a year – her name as well as the house had been in play here – shrivelled to nothing in face of the brash, unkempt young miss in the dressing gown who confronted him. She ushered Stuart into the drawing room and took up a crouching position on the sofa before remembering to offer him the armchair opposite. Surprisingly, the room did live up to the garden and the front door – leather – buttoned sofa, winged armchairs, mahogany tables, bookcase tastefully decorated with hardbacks, just what one would expect in an old gentleman's club or the lounge of an hotel with aspirations. The only challenge to the tastefulness of the ensemble was the excessively large plasma television screen which commanded attention above the marble fireplace. Miss Jordan stubbed out the cigarette she had been intermittently drawing on and nursed her knees in anticipation of becoming the focus of Stuart's attention.

"I've come to ask you a few questions about the unfortunate incident you had with Mr Ross. Would you mind going through it with me?"

He could see that Miss Jordan would not only not mind, she would positively delight in re-telling the tale. Her account, which she delivered in a tone alternating between assured adult and aggrieved adolescent, confirmed the main lines of Ross's version of events. She had taken over the class from Ross. He had passed on the instructions of what they were to do and had informed her of what he himself had done with them. On his departure a couple of the girls had complained to her that they had been working continuously for nearly an hour and asked if they could have some light relief and watch a ten minute video. She had agreed to this and it was while the video was playing that Ross had re-entered the room. When he left, the class started to tease her, saying that if she got into trouble with the head they would back her up. She had clearly felt diminished by this show of condescending familiarity, but the closer she got to pin-pointing this, the more disjointed and ejaculatory her language became. It was at this point that what had started as detached epic narration gave way to almost direct re-enactment. Her anger and hurt feelings were still in serious want of the balm of words.

"What exactly happened when you confronted Mr Ross in the staffroom after the incident?"

"I was so angry. But I managed to keep cool. I simply asked him what gave him the right to embarrass me like that in front of the class. I've just about had enough of these old fuddy-duddies thinking they're god almighty. When I arrived at the school at first, they all pranced around in those ridiculous gowns. But the head soon put a stop to that. He's one of the few men in that school who knows what century we're living in. Most of them seem actually to be proud of being old. Mind you, Ross isn't that old, but he acts as if he is. Anyway, he just went berserk. He started to yell and scream and when I tried to leave the room he pinned me against the door. I thought he was going to punch me in the face."

"Did nobody interfere at this point?"

"I think they were all just as shocked as me. I eventually managed to get away from the door. He ranted on a bit more. You should have heard him – he had lost it completely. I don't know what he actually said, I was totally petrified. Eventually he left. I was shaking like a leaf, I can tell you. Caroline made me a cup of tea and then brought me home in her car. He's a vicious brute, Ross. The pupils are scared stiff of him. And another thing you should know – Caroline bumped into his wife in town one Saturday and she noticed she had a big black eye. I've never seen anyone in a temper like that. People like that shouldn't be let loose; they certainly shouldn't be teaching. I tell you, I'm gong to make sure he loses his job."

"When did you tell Mr Kennedy?"

"Mr Kennedy came here. He was very nice. He told me he wouldn't tolerate that sort of thing in his school and that he would deal with Ross. But he suggested that I should contact my union and see what action they recommended me to take. I was too upset to do anything for a couple of days. Daddy wanted to go and sort Ross out, but mummy wouldn't let him."

"What action are you going to take, Miss Jordan?"

"I have to see the union solicitor next week. The union think that I've a good case for harassment, but it's up to the solicitor to make the final decision. Daddy wants me to see a Q.C., but mummy says that the union lawyers have more experience of this sort of thing."

"Did Mr Kennedy approve of you showing the video?"

Stuart could not resist this inquiry.

"Why shouldn't he? The kids learn more from videos nowadays than they learn from books. Mr Kennedy isn't one of those old fuddy-duddies like Ross and Greenfield; he lives in the twenty-first century. Anyway, it wasn't an issue, Mr Kennedy didn't mention it"

"You don't approve of Dr Greenfield either then?"

"He's about the worst. The man's a total elitist. You should see him with his little band of converts; they think they are God's gift to the world."

"You mean the Thinkers' Club?"

"Yea, they get together every Friday after school and pontificate on what the rest of the world is doing wrong. They're against everything that hasn't been around for at least a couple of centuries. They think that schools shouldn't be teaching I.T. or business studies or life skills or anything like that. If they had their way, we'd all be wasting our time reading Latin poetry or plays written in some other language that no-one understands any more or finding out what some ancient Greek with bad breath thought about women. What really annoys people like Ross and Greenfield of course is that there actually are women on the staff now. They'd like to keep it exclusively male, the old boy network and all that shit."

Miss Jordan was now warming to her grievance and becoming more expansive as her focus broadened. It was with a sense of triumph that she returned to the account of Kennedy's victory over the forces of reaction when he overturned the long-standing tradition of masters wearing academic gowns – *grubby old things* – and then proceeded to replace the Latin grace – *which nobody understood* – with a composition of one of the sixth formers which made reference to the need for modern food production methods to respect the ecological balance – *much more relevant to the needs of the twenty-first century*. By the time Stuart had taken his leave Miss Jordan, now on her third cigarette, had become positively evangelical, interpreting his reticence as a readiness to convert. Stuart left with the vague feeling that he had somehow been bested. The meek Miss Jordan, whom he had imagined he had come to see, had turned into a self-confident crusading Boadicea. The wan smile of her greeting had transfigured itself into a wholesome beam; even her mousy fair hair seemed to have ripened into full Technicolor.

Because of Devine's suspension it had been thought more politic to interview him at home rather than school. The Devine household was considerably less grand than the Jordan pile. The front garden, no more than a patch, had the curious characteristics of the dwarf in that it contained all the features of a 'grown-up' garden – lawn, surrounding flowerbeds, front hedge – but in proportions which accused its size. It was not Devine who answered the door, it was a pretty, but unprettified woman in her late thirties with slightly unkempt black hair through which renegade white announced the weight of experience.

"Inspector Stranaghan, isn't it? My husband is expecting you. He has just popped out for a paper. You've arrived a bit early."

This time there was an offer of coffee, which Stuart readily accepted. He was led into the kitchen and offered a flimsy chair at a small, red, plastic-topped table while Mrs Devine boiled the kettle and poured the water into two mugs.

"I hope you are not going to upset Richard, Inspector. He has been through a lot recently and he is on medication for his nerves. That bastard of a headmaster has it in for Richard. He was just waiting for an excuse to get him and, like a fool, Richard has given him all the excuses he needed."

"What makes you say that, Mrs Devine? Was there anything between them before this incident?"

"No, nothing specific. It's just chalk and cheese. Richard believes in discipline. He thinks there should be firm rules and he insists on the pupils obeying them."

"But surely Mr Kennedy shares that view, Mrs Devine. How else can you run a school?"

"That man has no real interest in the school, Inspector. Anything that gives him hassle with the parents, no matter how important it is for the running of the school, is out. Richard is no yes-man; he does what he thinks is right and if the parents don't like it, too bad. That's why Kennedy can't stand him and would like to see him out."

"You seem very hostile to Mr Kennedy, Mrs Devine. Does your husband feel as strongly as you do?"

He could see Mrs Devine rein herself in. She had seen that her attack on Kennedy was backfiring on her husband. Most people, when they expose strong feelings of anger and hostility to what turns out to be an unsympathetic audience, instantly offer testimonials of their decency and moderation in a desperate attempt to retrieve respectability. With Mrs Devine the effect was reversed; the retreat she felt constrained to make behind a screen of emotional banality had the effect of ennobling her anger.

"You must forgive me, Inspector. My husband has been going through a very bad patch and Mr Kennedy has been largely responsible. A headmaster should be supportive of his staff. You would expect that of a leader, but then Mr Kennedy doesn't really do leadership."

"I believe your husband had also some problems in Dr Stevens' time. Was *he* more supportive?"

"Not really. If anything he was worse. He didn't push things so far as Kennedy, but he completely undermined Richard's confidence. Richard had made a remark to one of his fourth formers. He told her not to be so silly. It's just one of those phrases one comes out with, but her mother reacted to it as if Richard had said her daughter was a stupid bitch. Parents can be overprotective. You expect that, but you don't expect a headmaster to fan the flames. He encouraged her and then made a great play of getting her to withdraw her complaint. He was unbearably pompous towards Richard. He told him that he should show more concern towards the sensibilities of his pupils and asked him to give an undertaking that in future he would not say or do anything that would give offence to his pupils or their parents. Richard couldn't believe what he was hearing. He had expected the head to laugh at the absurdity of the whole thing. The thought that in future he would be at the mercy of pupils and parents for every little remark that he made completely threw him. He became very depressed and had to see the doctor. He put him on a course of medication."

"The depression – was that before or after Dr Stevens was killed?"

"It started before Stevens' death, but it got much worse after it. Richard would spend his weekends in his room. He wouldn't get up until the afternoon and then he would play his jazz with the curtains drawn. It went on for months. But he kept on teaching the whole time. He didn't want anyone to know. Gradually he got better. His confidence grew and he became less apprehensive. He was fine; he seemed to have completely recovered, until this business started it all up again. Now he's worse than ever."

"I need to ask this, Mrs Devine. Where was he on Saturday?"

"He seemed a bit brighter on Saturday. He was a bit distant, but he did get up for breakfast. I had to go to my sister's – she is having a baby and needed someone to look after her other two. Richard said he was going to go for a walk. He often does that when he's not too down."

"How was he when you got home?"

"It was about eight when I got back. Richard was in bed playing his music. I looked in and offered to bring him some supper, but he said he had eaten. He was very tired after his walk and just wanted to sleep. He was sound asleep when I went to bed about eleven."

"And how was he on Sunday?"

"He was very bad. Complained of a headache. But he went for another walk. I offered to go with him, but he said he wouldn't be good company."

"You say he has been seeing the doctor. What did he recommend?"

"He wanted Richard to see a psychiatrist, but Richard would have none of that. Richard is death on psychology. He is always quoting Socrates I think it is: 'Physician, heal thyself.' We've talked a lot about it. He knows he has a problem, but he refuses to allow himself to become anaesthetised, he calls it, to the real problem as he sees it."

"And what does he think is the real problem?"

"The state of the school, the state of society, the woolly-mindedness of people, the lack of leadership. He feels very strongly about these things."

Stuart had finished his coffee and saw from the kitchen clock

49

that it was nearly 11.40. He wanted to have time for a word with Myles before lunch.

"Shouldn't your husband be back by now? He did know I was coming?"

"Yes, he left about twenty minutes before you were due. The paper shop is only about five minutes away. I can't think what has happened to him. Maybe he bumped into someone, but he knew you were coming. To be honest, I'm getting a bit worried."

"I can't wait any longer, Mrs Devine. Here's my mobile number. Phone me the minute he gets back and I'll come and see him this afternoon."

The look on Mrs Devine's face almost tempted him into words of consolation and reassurance. He wanted to tell her that there was nothing to worry about and that there was undoubtedly some perfectly good explanation for her husband's non-appearance. But he thought of the white coats at the hospital and the solidity of their objectivity and he restrained himself. It was of course possible that Devine had just found the prospect of the interview too much and had gone AWOL for no other reason than his obvious mental instability. He would work with that for the time being.

Chapter 6

Myles' face told a story of achievement. It was not smug but his eyes bore a glow of condescension as they took in their surroundings, suggesting communion with a source of satisfaction that transcended what they were seeing. As he got into Stuart's car, the question was: was he going to swirl the moment around in his head a little longer or would he down it?

"I think we may be on to something, sir . . . "

Myles was seemingly not a man for anticipatory preambles.

". . . I read through Evans' business plan. There was one name that kept coming up, Richardson's Development. It's a building firm that specialises in 'executive' housing, just the type of thing that would be ideal for the school grounds. I rang the firm. The boss – a Bob Davidson – wasn't there, but when I told his secretary that it was about the proposed development of St Jude's College, she asked me if I was Mr Kennedy! When I said no, but that I was speaking on his behalf, she asked me why Mr Kennedy had not turned up at the meeting this morning."

"Very interesting. Was this the first meeting between them?"

"No, they've been talking to each other for a couple of months."

"Did you mention Evans?"

"Yes, apparently Evans was there about a month ago. The secretary assumed that he and Kennedy were a team."

"I would doubt that. When can we talk to Davidson?"

"He's in Bristol for the rest of the day. I've made an appointment for first thing to-morrow morning."

Myles was less than all attention as Stuart recounted his morning's adventures. Miss Jordan held no interest for him at all and Stuart felt he detected almost annoyance at the behaviour of

51

Devine, threatening as it did to supplant the Evans-Kennedy line of inquiry as the main thread of the investigation. It was decided that after lunch Myles should have a tête-à-tête with Kennedy's secretary, Mrs Abernethy, while Stuart joined Greenfield's smoking circle. After that Myles should check on the state of health of Ross' wife. The rumour of the black eye needed following up. For his part Stuart declared a post-lunch state of *sans but déterminé*. He remembered picking up this expression in his form three French class and using it to great effect in all his compositions as his French heroes strutted along the boulevards, *gitane à la main*, in search of any adventure within the scope of their author's linguistic competence. It was curious the way his schoolboy memories had been re-activated by the sounds and smells of the corridors.

The smells of the refectory were particularly Proustian. They brought back his schooldays in Belfast. He had not taken lunch in the school canteen. His school had been near an army barracks and had an arrangement with Sands' Soldiers' Home which offered cheap and cheerful meals to pupils willing to race across the busy main road for a place in the queue. The *carte du jour* was always written in chalk on a little blackboard and had all the exoticism of an English menu for a boy who had never made the crossing to Liverpool. Welsh rarebit and Yorkshire pudding had each a ring which mingled well with the confident, elongated English vowels that pervaded the air. He became aware that there was a 'take' on reality going on here. Up to this point in his life it had never occurred to him that the world as he saw it was anything other than the world-as-it-is. It was his first, primitive insight into the power of language not merely to colour in between the hard outlines of reality, but to move those outlines.

The group assembled around the table was similar to the previous day. Mrs Swanson's duties had kept her away, but Dr Greenfield offered the same expansive and inclusive conversation as before. When the two policemen arrived, a bald, middle-aged man, sitting opposite Greenfield, was locked in argument with him. The talk was of the next discussion of the Thinkers' Club which, they were informed, was due to focus on the question of fair taxation. The polite necessities of greeting the strangers loosened only momentarily the bald man's grip on the cables that his mind was sliding along. He was arguing with mounting dismissiveness that it was the needs of the underprivileged that determined the level of taxation and that the concept of fairness would be misplaced if attached directly to taxation itself rather than to the conditions which made it necessary. The force of this argument generated enough heat within him for a full frontal swipe at *the smugness and self-indulgence of our over-pampered society in the face of the destitution and poverty which prevail in the third world and the soulless squalor of contemporary urban life in Europe and America.* Greenfield beamed with delight.

"Robin Hood. Robin Hood in the woods," he squawked, but seeing that he had given offence, he quickly added. "I'm sorry, Fred. I couldn't resist that. I was in Holland once and the landlord of the guest house had only broken English and that was about all he could say to me. But to be serious, what you are in fact saying is that, in the name of the people, the government has a right to take as much as it likes from the better-off in society and that there is no principle to determine the limit, except perhaps to stop short of making them so poor that they would cease to lay the golden eggs that the poor can't survive without?"

"No, I'm not saying that. Of course there has to be a limit, but it should be set on an *ad hoc* basis, and the determining factor should be the balance between the resources of the wealthy and the needs of the poor."

"But if there is no principle at work, who is to make the judgement?"

"The government, of course. We live in a democracy."

"But if the government is not subject to any rules and merely exercises its judgement based on what is perceived as the 'needs' of the underprivileged, then it has *carte blanche* to abuse the minority, for – let's face it – the wealthy will always be a minority. Is it democracy if the rest of us come to your house this evening and decide what should happen to your furniture? You would be allowed your vote of course, but if we as a group decided to give it away to people who in our judgement are more in need of it than you, should the majority decision be respected?"

"But that's not the same thing. You are not part of my family. You have no in-put into my family fortunes and therefore deserve no say over what should happen to them. That's personal. But you and I and all of us are members of society. And politics has to do with society."

"But that's just it. Once I've earned my income and paid my dues to the great social pit, surely what is left is *mine* – my pennies have entered into the realm of what you call the personal. Not according to the government – it might subscribe to the principle of respecting personal property but that doesn't stop it demanding more and more of my 'personal pennies'. I am no longer targeted for earning, I am taxed simply for owning, that is, for *having earned*. If the same principle were applied to criminals, the poor devils would never be able to *pay their debt to society*. But life sentences are not draconian enough to deal with tax payers. When it comes to calling in their pound of flesh, the death penalty is still in force. Indeed, while on the subject of death – when tax-payers die, they cannot make a gift to their relatives, they cannot leave their hard-earned life savings to their children without the politicians insisting on their protection money. And what do the political busybodies claim the right to do with this money? Anything they choose to! Precious little real protection, that! Most of their choices are made in the name of '*mother care*'. It's the great *taxe-partout* card of our time."

54

"Any civilised society looks after its weaker members. Christian charity is the *sine qua non* of moral behaviour. Without it we are all just jungle creatures, moral cannibals."

"Unless I'm mistaken, the Bible puts the emphasis on the act of giving rather than the receiving. The nationalisation of the act of giving through the tax system switches this emphasis around. Modern societies have become breeding grounds for future generations of receivers – and receivers very quickly turn into takers, and then into takers-with-entitlement, the most predatory of the species. As for the giving element, it soon gets puffed away in the air; it has long since been anaesthetised in habit, it's now no more than a mindless acceptance of Robin Hoodism from on-high."

Stuart was enjoying the polemic. He had not been invited to contribute. As he sat listening he remembered standing beside the heaped up coats that served as goalposts, watching the other boys playing football in the street and hoping desperately to get '*picked on*'. He took it as a sign of his increasing maturity that he was quite content to spectate on this occasion. Strange, he mused, how every passive activity is associated with the eye, even those principally concerned with the ear.

Greenfield's Socratic opponent was the Reverend Frederick Foster, head of R.E.. As with all academic arguments it was difficult to distinguish between the clash of ideas and the clash of personalities. Outwardly the two men displayed the utmost courtesy to each other, but blows were landed with scant concern. Stuart knew that he himself had often been open to the charge of aggression towards his opponent, when in fact it was his concern for the idea which was spawning in his mind that was carrying him on. It had often struck him how his wife, who was his main accuser, could be completely ruthless to salesmen and shopkeepers who were 'spinning a yarn'. He on the other hand always found such people too vulnerable to attack their ill-thought-out stratagems, and would cover up with feigned credulity. Not so his wife; she would go straight for the jugular and bring them face to face with the vacuity of what they were saying.

The discussion was broken up by Foster who had to go off to a committee meeting of the S.U.. Greenfield apologised to the visitors for his persistence with the debate in spite of their presence and repeated his invitation of the previous day for them to join him for coffee in the 'alternative staffroom'. Myles made his excuses and headed off in search of Mrs Abernethy while Greenfield led Stuart down a rickety staircase to a windowless basement furnished with about a dozen wooden chairs circling a gas heater. Along all four walls were bookshelves laden with books which Greenfield explained were *rejects from the school library where space was at a premium after the invasion of an army of PCs.* Among the occupants of the chairs Stuart recognised Ross who immediately got up and offered his hand. There were three other men and a woman in the room. Greenfield made playful introductions. The tallest of the men was Henry Watt. Henry taught French and it was rumoured had introduced the French to the game of rugby union from the lofty position of the second-row. From this it was not clear whether he was to be considered a French teacher *de second rang*. James Blair, a canny Scot, had come south with missionary zeal to teach the natives grammatical English; his efforts had been *punctuated* with success. Shaun Connor should have been Irish but had failed miserably. However credit was due him as he had done the next best thing and become a history teacher. The real success of the group was the feminine element, Mrs Elisabeth Black. She had fully succeeded in being Irish. She had refreshing lapses of memory for an Irish native, concentrating instead on her *figures*.

"I take it you are a maths teacher, Mrs Black?"

"Well done, Inspector. I can see you are coping better with Bruce's 'crypticisms' than your predecessor did. I'm sure that bodes well for the case."

Coffee was poured and Stuart invited comments on the two victims. He started with Stevens whom the interval of two years had surely rendered riper for critical comment. There was a consensus view that Stevens was a 'bleeding heart' who 'had swallowed all the post-sixties child-centred cant'. He believed in the intrinsic goodness of man and the diverting wickedness of our competitive capitalist society. He saw education as an essentially political tool that had been wickedly used to preserve the social status quo. He saw it as his mission to reverse this process and he had made a start by admitting more and more disadvantaged children into the school. He dismissed so-called academic standards as a smokescreen for social discrimination. For him the real curriculum was the social interaction that took place in schools between the pupils themselves as well as between the teachers and the pupils. One school subject served as well as the next. He was strongly opposed to the classics and considered Mills and Boon to be as worthy of study as Shakespeare. This brought him into conflict with most of the staff and there were many unholy rows. Quite a few of the teachers either retired or left, and the *downward spiral* began of appointing and promoting people who shared Stevens' views.

"On a personal level, what was Stevens like?"

Shaun Connor was quick to respond to this.

"He gave off an air of decency and open-mindedness which invited compromise and always left you with a feeling that you were being nasty to the poor man. But this decency was a fake. It wasn't that he was deliberately putting on a show; it was the decency that comes with pity. He was so sure of himself and his own decency that he was sorry for you in your lowly state of ignorance and self-interest. When it came down to it, there was no open-mindedness or tolerance; it was just a style that he felt compelled to adopt to give you an insight into what real goodness could be like. The man had pretensions to sainthood!"

"Yes, that's exactly it," said Elisabeth Black. "I remember

feeling totally out-womaned by him. I had given a double detention to a boy for telling me a lie. The boy had appealed to him and he had reduced the punishment to twenty lines. When I complained, he spoke to me very quietly and patiently, explaining that William was undergoing a family crisis – his mother had just been admitted to hospital – and that he as headmaster expected his teachers to take the whole picture into consideration before doling out sanctions. When I pointed out that William's lie was totally self-serving and quite in character for the little rat – I didn't call him that – a smile of compassionate arrogance flashed across his face. I'm sure he was having a 'Forgive her, father, for she knows not what she does' moment."

"You must forgive us, Inspector – although hopefully not à la Stevens," said Greenfield. "We are not exactly the most impartial group when it comes to our esteemed former leader. You are talking to the reactionary set, those unimpressed by the neon-enlightenment of the twenty-first century. There are others who would sing his praises, even now when he is not there to dangle preferment."

"Much too fair-minded, Bruce." This was Ross' first contribution to the discussion. Until now he had contented himself with strenuously subdued smiles of approval. "You are forgetting the resurrection. Stevens may have gone to another place from whence he can no longer anoint his followers, but, don't forget, we have been blessed by another, some would say greater, deity who is there to see that good works do not go unrewarded."

"But I understood that Kennedy was very different from Stevens?"

"That's a fair point. I do the man too much justice. Kennedy has no pretensions to sainthood. He's not so much a theologian of goodness; he's more a clerk-of-works."

This observation was greeted with the mirthful laughter that is usually generated by the convivial warmth of consensus.

Stuart felt almost intimidated enough not to expose his incomprehension.

"I don't quite understand, Mr Ross. Are you saying that Kennedy is just more efficient than Stevens was?"

"He certainly is that, but that's not really what I'm saying."

"What George means..." Shaun Connor interposed, "is that Kennedy has a nose for the prevailing moral winds. In ancient Rome he would have starved the lions to make them hungrier for the Christians, in mediaeval Europe he would have organised double shifts for the Inquisition...."

"It was probably some ancestor of his who invented the guillotine. Think of it, all those heads with not a single social conscience among them!"

Ross took back the baton.

"That's what makes people like him more dangerous than the high priests of morality. You can argue with the people who have formulated or even half-formulated their own ideas. You'll not convince them, but there's always the hope of finding some common ground. With people like Kennedy it's a complete waste of time. People like him are so far removed from the act of creation of ideas that the ideas that they espouse are hardened and fastened; they have none of the soft underbelly of the recently born. They always remind me of a shopkeeper I once encountered. I had gone back with a pair of shoes that had developed a hole shortly after I had bought them. It made absolutely no difference what I said – and I argued my case from every possible angle – I got the same pre-recorded response: 'It's not company policy to offer refunds on sales goods.'"

"I sometimes wonder," said Greenfield, "not so much *how*, more *where* these good people hold their convictions. I love the notion of gullibility. It paints for me a picture of ideas as notion portions slipping smoothly down the gullet of mythical 'gulls' and getting processed into 'gut feelings'. It would be wrong to say that such 'gulls' are convinced they are right – that would imply acknowledgement of the possibility of challenge, however weak. No, 'gulls' are the gourmets of truth; they 'gullify' only the stuff of right-headedness. Their stomachs are too delicate for truth with bits in it."

Stuart was about to push the group into listing their specific grievances against Kennedy, but the bell intervened to produce a dignified, but for all that, obedient exodus. Only Greenfield remained. He had a free period after lunch on Tuesdays which, he informed Stuart, was usually 'wasted' on 'reddening up' his pile of Year 10 marking. To-day, however, would be an exception if the Inspector would join him in 'a second indulgence in caffeine'. Stuart welcomed the one-on-one; he was anxious to hear Greenfield's take on Devine's bust-up with Kennedy.

"A very unhappy soul is Richard. Highly intelligent, but he needs to feel that the world is in tune with his intelligence. That's his problem. I once lent him a translation of a German short story. It's about a journey on a commuter train. The train goes into a tunnel. Everything is normal, people getting on with their everyday activities, reading, doing crosswords, chatting – no mobile phones in those days. After a while the narrator begins to wonder why the train hasn't come out of the tunnel. He also has the feeling that the train is going down a slight gradient, but he dismisses his concern as fanciful since no-one else seems to be exercised by it. However, when, after another five minutes, the train still hasn't come out of the tunnel and the gradient has increased, he tackles the conductor. The conductor assures him that there's nothing to worry about and he again finds comfort in the non-reactions of the other passengers. Another five minutes go by. Still in the tunnel, the gradient now quite steep. This time he presses the conductor, who now admits that he too is concerned and has no idea what's happening. But again, surprisingly, none of the other passengers shows any sign of anxiety. The two men decide it's time to go and have a word with the driver, but when they try to get up to the front of the train, the door of the final carriage is locked. There's nothing for it but to climb out on to the roof. This is extremely difficult as the train is now plunging at a forty-five degree angle. But they finally manage it and climb down into the locomotive. Of course, they find that there is no one driving the train, and the story ends with the train in free fall. It's a black little tale, but I thought it would help Richard come to terms with the great disappointment of his life. I think it had the opposite effect."

"How do you mean?"

"Richard interpreted it quite differently from what the author intended. Dürrenmatt – the story was written by a great favourite of mine, the Swiss author, Friedrich Dürrenmatt – Dürrenmatt was making a metaphysical point; he wanted to show that the world and the human mind both have their own agendas and their points of contact are no more than matters of chance. Richard can't accept this; he believes in the notion of leadership, men who, through the power of their reason and the strength of their will, can bring the world into line. He can't come to terms with the fact that leadership is not a property of modern-day leaders. If anything, it's the reverse that's true – our leaders have become the property of their own leadership role. Leadership is something they have been allocated, not something they take and make. Their constant concern is not with the world and how they can change it for the better, but with the leadership role itself, how they can preserve it and extend it. You might say that we now have headships where we once had heads. As Richard sees it, Dürrenmatt's train didn't have to meet with disaster. The disaster arose because the driver wasn't up to the job, either he abandoned his post or he was too lazy to get up and got someone to clock in for him."

"So neither Stevens nor Kennedy could keep the train on track?"

"Well, they both gave Richard plenty of ammunition for his argument. They both treated him badly, Kennedy more than

Stevens. Stevens had much of the Princess and the Pea about him. The incident was trivial and he should have dismissed it out of hand. But he was a born-again subjectivist and couldn't let the opportunity drop to sermonise. To be fair to Kennedy, he had a more difficult case to deal with. There was actual physical contact and the Law has been smitten by the subjectivist bug. But a better man would have stood up for Richard and taken whatever 'flak' was coming."

"By 'subjectivist' I assume you mean something akin to 'child-centredness'?"

"Yes, if you don't limit it to children. I think of it as a kind of general warning notice: '*Do not Touch! Wet Sensibilities!*' Wetness prevails. Even table-and-chairness is superseded. We don't sit on chairs or eat our dinner off tables that happen to be wet. We sit on the wetness of the chair and eat on the wetness of the table. We see ourselves as having direct dealings with those aspects of the world that affect us, not with a world which is indifferent to us, but which contains elements and properties to which we might react. It's like the biblical illusion that the animals were put on the earth by God to provide food for men."

"But surely it's right that people shouldn't be treated as objects."

"Right doesn't come into it. It's necessary and inevitable. Was Kennedy not treating Richard as an object in so far as he didn't read the situation from Richard's perspective? The question is not *whether* we should do it but *when* we should do it. The moral sentimentalists refuse to face that problem. They go around pretending that people have the inalienable right to be treated as subjects, when it is clear that the human condition requires a constant chopping and changing between doing and being done unto."

"Devine took Steven's and Kennedy's failure to support him very badly then?"

"If you mean by that that he should be considered a prime

suspect, I would say you'd be barking up the wrong tree. The lack of backing he received created a kind of nausea in him which completely paralysed him. He needs the authority that comes from the assurance that reason is in charge for him to be able to function at all, never mind to carry out a murder."

"But maybe he found the courage to kill the demon. If what you say is right, getting rid of Stevens and Kennedy would be like cancelling the void. It would be a kind of double negative."

"Yes, that's true enough, but the onus is still on your line of reasoning to show where he would find the initial strength to break out of his paralytic state."

Stuart was about to cite Devine's failure to show up for their arranged meeting when his mobile went. It was Mrs Devine.

"Inspector Stranaghan, Richard hasn't come back. I went to the shop to see if they could give me some information, but apparently he wasn't there this morning. They hadn't seen him since he collected the paper yesterday. On the way back to the house I bumped into a neighbour and she told me that she had seen him getting into a taxi. You've got to find him, Inspector. I'm really worried he'll do something silly."

"I'll be right over, Mrs Devine. We'll find him. Don't worry."

Greenfield looked concerned, but showed little surprise when Stuart told him what had happened.

"I was afraid something like this would happen," he said. "Richard's world is falling apart. I was sure that at some point he would connive in its collapse."

Stuart collected Myles from his comfortable perch on Mrs Abernethy's desk and the two made their way to Devine's house. There they found Mrs Devine in a state of gritted optimism; the poor woman 'knew' the worst but treated it like a temptation that must be resisted. They got the address of the neighbour who had witnessed Devine entering the taxi and managed to prize from her memory the name of the taxi company. The taxi was easily identified and the driver was able to tell them that he had taken the fare to the station. There a man answering the taxi-driver's description of Devine's manic behaviour was identified as having bought a single ticket to Durham. As the train would already have arrived at Durham there was nothing else to be done than to e-mail a photo to the Durham police and await developments. The only connection Mrs Devine could offer with Durham was that her husband had taken his degree there, but that was twelve years ago, and he had not kept up any contact with anyone who would still be there. Having confirmed that her husband had not taken his medication with him, Stuart and Myles left Mrs Devine in the care of her sister, who lived close by, and returned to the station to compare notes.

Chapter 7

Myles' *tête-à-tête* with Mrs Abernethy had proved quite productive. It had emerged that Kennedy had received several calls from Richardson's Development but had never recorded any meetings with them in his diary schedules, although Mrs Abernethy was sure that such meetings had taken place. She had also disclosed that Kennedy had become very 'pally' with Sir William Aiken, a recent addition to the board of governors, who, as chance would have it, had made his fortune in property development. Sir William had become a frequent visitor and Mrs Abernethy had received a call from his secretary cancelling a lunch appointment with Kennedy of which she had known nothing, since it had not been entered in the diary either. Kennedy had seemed a little put out when she informed him of the cancellation.

"I had to be fairly discreet, sir, but Mrs Abernethy as much as told me that the Board minutes contain no mention of any plans for property development."

"I am getting very curious about what Davidson will have to say for himself to-morrow morning. Any other gossip?"

"Mrs Ross' black eye is common knowledge, or at least the rumour is. But then it came from the same source as we got it from. Miss Jordan is not one to be close-lipped, especially when it comes to anything that would show Ross in a bad light. Mrs Abernethy is not a fan. According to her, Miss Jordan would flirt with anything in trousers. How did she put it? – '*Miss Jordan likes to spray her proprietorial scent around.*' Apparently that extends even to the senior boys. She's a bit of an innocent though. Mrs Abernethy is convinced that there's nothing behind it – just another example of the need for popularity, what Mrs Abernethy describes as '*young teacher syndrome*'."

"Did she have anything to say about Devine?"

"Yes, she is very fond of him, '*a perfect gentleman*' she called him. She's very angry at Kennedy for treating him so badly. It seems that Devine was on the point of tears when he left the study after Kennedy had told him he was suspended. Kennedy seemed to be enjoying the whole thing."

"I take it that Mrs Abernethy is not a fan of Kennedy's either?"

"No, she thinks he's a bully and he has no '*refinement*'. He has no real interest in the pupils, but he '*makes all the right noises*' to people he thinks are important. What else did she say? Oh yes, he's '*a scheming little piece of work*' – I think she was tempted to use something a bit stronger there. That reminds me – Kennedy fails another of Mrs Abernethy's tests. She thinks that the biggest give-away of character is the language people use in private – and Kennedy's isn't good. '*Never trust an educated man who swears in cold blood!*' Mind you, she's not so sure she would describe Kennedy as an educated man."

"What did she think of Stevens?"

"We didn't talk about Stevens, but I remember when I talked to her about him last time, she had nothing but praise for him. Said he was a bit too intense, but that he really believed in what he was doing and had the best interests of the children at heart. She was very upset at the time."

"Did you get around to mentioning Evans?"

"Yes. That's another interesting thing. She suspects Kennedy is scared of Evans. When Evans comes looking for an appointment to see him, Kennedy usually makes up some lame excuse or invents another appointment. Mrs Abernethy is under strict instructions never to give Evans an appointment without consulting Kennedy first."

"Why does she think that is?"

"She puts it down to a personality clash. And obviously, Evans is always on the lookout for reasons to put Kennedy down and show that he's the better man. This business with Ross is a case in point. Evans is not known for championing the underdog – he just couldn't resist having a go at Kennedy over it. There's nothing Kennedy can do about it; Evans is much too senior in the school for him to have any leverage over him. Evans comes and goes as he pleases, he's untouchable and he likes rubbing Kennedy's nose in it. She did say however that things had got worse lately. Earlier Evans had just been cold and dismissive, more recently there seems to have been much more venom in his dealings with Kennedy."

"That could be related to Kennedy's dealings with Richardson's Development. I wonder just how much this Davidson fellow knows about that."

Having set the plan of campaign for the following morning – he to interview Davidson of Richardson's Development and Myles to talk to the black-eyed Mrs Ross before working through Kennedy's computer files with Mrs Abernethy – Stuart headed for another 'cap-less' evening at home without his wife or, to be more psychologically accurate, with his absent wife. He had left instructions that he was to be informed immediately should there be any developments on the Devine front, but he entertained little hope of a diversion from that source.

Back in his kitchen, he heated up a tin of chicken in a wine sauce and micro-waved some flavoured couscous. Wine? Red or white? Yes or no? No! Apple juice from the fridge. Better to keep the head from getting overcast. His nerves were hungry for calm, but at same time repulsive of it. No question of appeasing them with a book or even switching them off in front of the TV; they needed feeding. He persuaded himself that if he first did the *kakuro* in *The Telegraph* he would then be calm enough to fall into the rhythm of the rather slow-moving novel he had started three months ago. This was an old lie, but he jumped at it every time. To add more credibility he put on a C.D. – Rachmaninov's second piano concerto. This had a double beauty for him, the sublimity of the music itself as it toyed with consummation and, on top of that, the memory in which it was now for ever framed for him of the descent towards Lausanne which he and Heather had made some years ago in a golden sunset with the music playing on the car cassette-player. Surely nothing could be better suited to the task of giving his day '*long rest or death, dark death, or dreamful ease*'. The *kakuro* also did its work. The first few squares flattered the ego with a sense of achievement and spurred to more. There followed the inevitable grappling with the squares of intermediate difficulty and by the time the final squares had established a determined recalcitrance to the combinations his flagging brain was throwing up, he found himself ready for surrender and prepared to acknowledge with equanimity the puniness of his intellect. Sleep was now the only truly worthwhile prize.

If dozing off is like a form of drowning, being called back from sleep gives rise to the notion of 'undrowning'. That's how Stuart always perceived being woken up by the telephone – being pulled by his ears, not the fleshy bits, the internal corridors of sound, back into a world that suddenly had a reason for him again. '*The lights begin to twinkle from the rocks.*'

"Sergeant Peterson here, sir. Devine has been picked up in Durham. Sorry, if I woke you, sir, but you asked to be kept informed."

"That's all right, sergeant. Where is he now?"

"He's being kept overnight at the hospital. They've arranged for him to see a psychiatrist in the morning."

"What kind of state is he in?"

"They think he's drunk, sir. Or else he's taken something."

"Have you informed Mrs Devine?"

"No, sir. We thought you might want to do that."

"Okay, leave that with me. Let them know in Durham that I want to interview him as soon as he's in a fit state."

Stuart put down the phone. What time was it? Just after two

thirty. Should he phone or go round? ... he would go round. That felt a better thing to do. Should he shave? That would signal a new day ... He would go unshaven. Cold water on the face, wetted toothbrush on the teeth – enough for a break with sleep.

The roads were wet with rain which had fallen while he slept. Funny how the world only seems to be tired when you are tired, but has the energy to get up to all sorts behind your back once it sees you off. The elongated reflections cast by the wet road made up for the absence of people and populated the night with beacons beckoning away from the here-and-now-ness of the darkness. When it appeared in the headlights, the little cul-de-sac where the Devines lived was almost sepulchral, bathed in the gloomy orange light of its two street lamps. The garden shrubs had taken on the dead texture of artificial flowers and the little lawn looked like an imitation of itself, the sort of thing you used to see in greengrocers' to give the fruit a 'natural' setting. There was a light on in the front bedroom. It occurred to Stuart that, had the house been in darkness, his 'news' was barely heavyweight enough to justify wakening the household, since no action could be taken before morning in any case. He ticked off one hurdle less to be cleared. Instinctively he pressed lightly on the doorbell to keep the noise down. How quaint, he thought, as if the electronic would respond to anything as human as a mechanical movement. The ding was offensively loud; mercifully there was no dong. There was no immediate sign that there had been any victims of the noise and Stuart was faced with the forbidding prospect of launching a second offensive when the hall light went on and the movements of a pink indeterminate figure could be detected through the frosted glass of the front door. The door was opened and there stood a surprisingly bright-eyed Mrs Devine in a pink, padded dressing gown. The brightness had been fuelled by anticipation, but at the sight of Stuart in the place of her husband, disappointment did not have time to register; there was an instant transfer to an expression of panicked enquiry. Stuart was ashamed to fondle the feeling of having momentary possession of the power of the gods. To his credit, he was quick to relinquish it.

"Good news, Mrs Devine. Your husband has been found and he's safe."

He stopped himself from following up with ' ... and well'. When he had given her what few details he had she seemed to be neither relieved nor concerned. 'Absent-minded' was the thought that came to Stuart to describe her reaction. Normally absent-mindedness describes a condition where we are too much concerned with distant enormities to cope efficiently with present trivia. Not so with Mrs Devine; detail got her full attention as she moved trancelike into the kitchen, filled the kettle and prepared the cups. And yet all this she did in the absence of herself in the exact manner of the forgetful professor.

"Too late for coffee, don't you think? Do you take your tea without sugar as well, Inspector Stranaghan?"

Stuart felt caught in the chasm between small talk and 'big' talk. Mrs Devine was right; facts break down the divide. The practicalities of her getting to Durham the following morning, the telephone number and location of the hospital, the time of Stuart's arrival after he had completed the pressing business with Richardson's Development, all filled the looming silence until Stuart felt that 'bigger' talk had a base to establish itself on.

"How have you coped over the past few weeks?"

Mrs Devine was recalled to life. The glazed nondescript-ness of her expression gave way to a darkness that threatened tears.

"It's funny. The worst thing, Inspector Stranaghan, isn't so much the pain and the worry. It's knowing that I'm trapped in a position where I have no choice than to feel these things. It's a strange kind of self-pity. There is a me looking down on the me that is suffering and that me is suffering more than the other one."

This was a condition Stuart recognised immediately, but he had never heard it put in words before. He was enormously pleased to have been offered something which he could genuinely share with this woman.

"I know exactly what you mean. It makes 'Woe is me!' grotesquely appropriate, doesn't it?"

He looked at her, allowing himself the faintest of smiles. It was a dangerous moment; he was seeking and he found in her face the encouragement to go all the way to a full-blown laugh. She followed almost as far.

"It's amazing," he continued. "It works even in the most trivial of circumstances. When my car breaks down, I find myself thinking of myself as a man who has a broken-down car. When I have to go to the dentist's I'm a man who has to go to the dentist's."

They laughed again.

Stuart made his way back home. The rain had stopped and the darkness was showing signs of its imminent banishment. He felt satisfied. He had gone rather than telephoned in response to a vague compulsion to do the right thing, without knowing what the right thing was. Now he was no surer what the right thing was, but, whatever it was, he knew he had done it.

When he got back home he put on the kettle – that always served as a provisional act of purposefulness. His mind was again shunning surrender to the sleep that he knew he needed. No – no tea – kettle off – bed. Back to the *kakuro* – he could surrender to that.

... It was the phone rather than the alarm clock that wakened him – his wife, Heather. Her voice on the telephone always had enough of the unfamiliar to remind him of how he had seen her before the intimacy of their relationship had broken down her otherness. It was a feeling always accompanied by pride – this otherness had surrendered itself to a oneness with him.

"Mother is going downhill fast. The doctors give her a couple of days at the most."

71

"How's your dad?"

"Bearing up. You know my father. He doesn't give much away. He hasn't all his life and he's not going to start now."

"Do you want me to come over?"

"No point. There's nothing you could do and it's best if you hold off until the funeral. You know what it's like. You make a great effort to get to where the grieving is and then you find there's nothing to be done. You only end up twiddling your thumbs in the queue waiting for the cemetery to open, and adding to the flatness of it all. Better to make yourself into one of the things those of us in the queue can look forward to."

Trust Heather, she always has her own take on things. She was coping, that was clear, and that's what mattered. He felt rested now; the day was ready to make a beginning, and the sleep he had grabbed gave him the right to have breakfast.

The day's agenda needed to be re-organised. He wanted Myles with him in Durham and it would be better to have his impressions of Davidson. The research on Kennedy's files could wait. The two of them would interview Davidson and then take the train to Durham, unless they were warned off by the Durham police. Better also to leave Ross' wife for another day. Myles' enthusiastic reaction to the news of his inclusion in the Davidson interview made Stuart aware of the proprietorial feelings that his deputy harboured towards the Richardson's Development line of enquiry, feelings he had carelessly trodden on.

There were two messages waiting on his desk. As expected, uniform had come up with no results in the search for witnesses among the golfers. The second, in the form of an e-mail, was a summons from Superintendent Winkworth. Stuart was suddenly filled with a sense of rudderlessness. He thought immediately of Greenfield's story of the runaway train in the tunnel. Nothing he had been doing had been done with any reference to self-justification. He was not at all sure he would be able to 'talk' a good inquiry thus far; any account would lack an omniscient or even a rationalising narrator. The voice that would tell it would be a very little voice, the voice of him himself, a mere player being jostled in the uncertainty of sequences.

In some strange way, but as always seemed to happen, the tale became coherent in the telling. The Superintendent was impatient when he strayed into detail, but not unappreciative of the underlying reasonableness and pattern of Stuart's response, the very feature that Stuart had feared might be thought to be lacking. He showed greatest interest in the possibility of cracks between the business dealings of Kennedy and Evans. This was an area where he clearly felt on solid ground. Most crimes come down to basic mechanical promptings, money being the most transparent of them. The Superintendent was all for transparency. Devine, on the other hand was an obvious *nutter* and could not be ruled out, but Ross, he felt, was *a very long shot*. It was evident that he remembered both of these men from the previous investigation as one would remember brushes with foreigners speaking an alien tongue.

"What about that weird fellow that Stevens expelled? Have you come across him? No, I suppose you wouldn't have. He's not part of the scene any more and anyway he wouldn't have had anything to do with Kennedy. The German teacher contacted him for us. Glenfield, was that the teacher's name?"

"No, you mean Greenfield, sir."

"Yes, that's it. If the boy hadn't had a cast-iron alibi – he was in Germany – I'd have sworn it was him. Never met a youngster like him. Most boys his age are mad about girls or football or cars – something normal. Not him – he lived in a world of his own and talked about nothing but stuff he had got out of books."

"How come you talked to him if he was in Germany?"

"We didn't at the time. We just checked that he was where he said he was. But he returned from Germany a couple of weeks later and I thought I'd do a follow-up. Shouldn't have bothered. He's an arrogant little bastard! Could hardly understand a word he said. Mind you, he had a real hatred of Stevens and boy, could that boy hate."

Chapter 8

The offices of Richardson's Development enjoyed the anonymity of conformity. Everything about them pointed in the same direction – geometricality, toned in shades and honed in textures. The polished grey marble floors and counters offered no hiding place for vegetable life; the rows of beechwood desks, each housing a black computer monitor, spoke out loudly in denial of their botanical origins; the tasteful plants, placed at esoterically chosen intervals in the open-plan office, served only as sanitised relics of an abandoned barbaric world, little models of a tamed Vercingetorix in a temple to the Roman gods. In the face of such columns of sanitised modernity Stuart always found himself tempted to become a believer; he invariably experienced a temporary loss of faith in '*the groins of the braes that the brook treads through.*'

The *nuns* of the temple exuded politeness in word and smile. They were dressed in an array of trouser and skirt suits of simple navy or black or navy-and-black pinstripe, corresponding, one might assume, to some hierarchical principle as esoteric as the plant arrangement. Stuart was curious to see if the high priest whom they had come to see would further fuel this messianic fantasy for him. Alas not! Davidson was a rough diamond in both speech and demeanour, not the type to personify any kind of idealism or even a glossy version of materialism. In the course of the polite preliminaries he offered little front to his greedy look and his prosaic intonation. The boss of Richardson's Development was so clearly in everything 'for the money' that he tainted even the money. Stuart was spared; Davidson's Gorgon world was exposed for what it was – it was back to the worth of '*wildness and wet*'.

"It has come to our attention that you have been involved in dealings with St. Jude's College."

"You make that sound like a crime, Inspector. What am I supposed to have done?"

"You misunderstand me, Mr Davidson. I just need to know the nature of your business with the college."

"I was contacted a couple of years ago by one of the teachers to provide some plans for the development of the main site. That's all there was to it."

"Did you provide these plans free of charge?"

"There was no fee, if that's what you mean."

"What exactly was there then?"

"Just a normal business arrangement. If the plans were acceptable to the Board of Governors, my company would get the contract."

"Did you agree this with the Board?"

"No, not exactly. I had a gentleman's agreement with Mr Evans."

"But surely Mr Evans was in no position to honour such an agreement. He couldn't speak for the Board. He wasn't even the headmaster of the school."

"Shall we say I backed my judgement? Mr Evans assured me that there would be no problem. The Board would agree to the plan. He had sounded a few members out and the prospects looked good. He would take it from there."

"What went wrong?"

"You'd better ask Mr Evans that. When the old head retired the fools didn't give Evans the job. They appointed that prat Stevens instead. The man was useless – he had no head for business."

"Was there any financial understanding between you and Mr Evans?"

The scowl that this provoked was very unlovely.

"What are you driving at? I resent what you are implying."

"I am not implying anything, Mr Davison. I simply want to

know the exact nature of your understanding with Mr Evans. Did you give any money at any stage to Mr Evans?"

There was a short pause. Davidson had clearly a decision to make.

"Why do you need to know all this, Inspector? I've heard there's been another shooting at the school. What have my dealings with Evans got to do with it? Do you think Evans is mixed up in it?"

"We can't rule out the possibility, Mr Davidson. But you haven't answered my question."

"Look, Inspector. We all have to oil the wheels of business; otherwise everything would grind to a halt. Evans was paid a small retainer, a kind of consultant's fee. It didn't amount to much, a couple of hundred. It's quite normal."

"How many hundred, Mr Davidson?"

"I don't remember. You'd need to check with Accounts."

"And what about Mr Kennedy? Did he have the same arrangement with you?"

Davidson was visibly put out by this and before he could check himself . . .

"How did you know about Kennedy?"

The question punctured the exchange. Davidson had to follow up now with more than a gesture to the truth.

"Mr Kennedy has been persuaded that the development of the school grounds is the way forward for the school. He has shown a great deal of interest in the plans and the two of us are in negotiation over the details."

"With the knowledge of the Board?"

"As far as I am aware, Mr Kennedy was intending to put the detailed plan before the Board at the earliest possible date, but a lot of groundwork needed to be done before that stage was reached."

"Did Mr Kennedy approach you or did you approach Mr Kennedy?"

"I think the initiative came from Mr Kennedy. As you know, Sir William Aiken, one of our directors, has been recently appointed to the Board and it was through him that the plan was revived."

"Has Mr Kennedy been in receipt of any 'retainers'?"

"Definitely not. Mr Kennedy wouldn't hear of it."

"Does that mean it was offered?"

"Not by me. You'd need to ask Sir William."

"Why then did you say that Mr Kennedy wouldn't hear of it?"

"Because I know Mr Kennedy well enough to know that he is an honest man."

"Are you saying then that Mr Evans isn't?"

Davidson was in disarray. He was putting up a miserable performance. It was clear to Stuart that something was inhibiting him from committing to more convincing, full-blooded lies, but it was probably no more than the proximity of his Machiavellian doings to a real-life murder.

"Listen to me, Mr Davidson. I have more to do than concern myself with the underhand dealings of development companies. Nor am I interested in schoolmasters who take backhanders. My only concern is getting a clear picture of what was going on, so that I can find the murderer of Dr Stevens and the would-be killer of Mr Kennedy. If you obstruct me in that, Mr Davidson, I'll pass on my suspicions to the fraud office and they will come down on you hard. If, on the other hand, I'm satisfied with what you tell me, I can afford to be a little less conscientious. Now, let's start again. How much did you pay Evans?"

"Ten thousand into an account in the Isle of Man."

"And what was his cut if he could pull it off?"

"Seven and half percent of the net profit."

"Amounting to roughly what?"

"We reckoned we would clear ten million."

"That works out at about £750,000. Was the same deal open to Kennedy?"

"No, Kennedy refused to take anything on account. He didn't want there to be anything that would compromise him."

"Did Evans know about the deal with Kennedy?"

"Evans is no fool. Of course he knew. It was Evans who put Kennedy on to it, but Kennedy took over and approached us directly. It was his idea to get Sir William on to the Board. He said that would strengthen his hand."

"But how did he manage that?"

"Easy. There was a seat going. Sir William is on the board of a couple of other companies. He persuaded one of them to set up a bursary for St Jude's and in gratitude he was offered the seat."

"But surely Evans could have blown the whole thing sky high?"

"That's why he was on a sweetener. If things went well he stood to make a few bob."

"Was he satisfied with that?"

"No, far from it. He stormed into my office about three weeks ago and demanded a bigger cut. I told him to take it up with Kennedy. The company had allocated a certain sum and it was between them how it should be divided."

"How did Evans propose to get the Board onside after Stevens was appointed head? Surely Stevens would have been opposed to the scheme."

"He was always a bit coy when we asked him that. He just said that Stevens would be brought into line."

"Thank you, Mr Davison. You have been most co-operative. I would like you to come to the station as soon as possible and make a statement. From what you have told me the conduct of your company has been within the law. So you have nothing to worry about."

"But what about Sir William? Does he have to know about my statement?"

"Only if we need to use it in evidence. And that depends on who we arrest."

Myles had made no interventions in the interview, but his applauding facial language had made the encounter seem like a home match to Stuart. When they sat down in the café across the road from the plush office block, his face showed the sense of achievement which, for some reason, sports fans feel justified in sharing at the success of their team. Stuart was very happy to share the success with him – better the admiration of a team-mate than the adulation of a fan. This was the first time in this investigation that he had felt his own weight. As he drank his latté Myles continued to radiate co-achievement.

"I can't wait to hear what Evans has to say when we confront him. Shall we bring him in immediately, sir?"

"No, not yet. Let's get the details of that bank account first and see if it has any other tales to tell. You deal with that. You can also get on with Kennedy's computer files. Now that we know what we are looking for, I think that would be more useful than you coming up to Durham with me."

"You're still going to Durham, sir? Surely Evans must be our man. He's tied to both murders now and we've a better motive than we could ever have hoped for. £750,000 is good enough reason to kill your granny."

"Slow down, Myles. First, we've only one murder victim as yet and second, we're a bit short on anything other than motive. We've got to keep our minds open to other possibilities."

Myles seemed less than convinced, but was very happy to be left in charge of the main line of inquiry while his boss did the skivvy work on the periphery. The news from the Durham police was that Devine was ready to be interviewed and Stuart was found a train which was leaving shortly after midday. He had just enough time to dash home and pack an overnight bag before taking a taxi to the station.

The three-hour journey was uneventful. He had too much of an impression of being between things to appreciate the particularity of what he was seeing through the window. That was disappointing. He always looked forward to a train journey. Railway tracks cut through the uncharted and leave it uncharted, quite unlike roads which chart everything that they cut through. Every farmhouse, field or lane curtsies to the road, the same road that links up the points of origin and destination of the traveller. The motorist is condemned never to get off the map, as wherever he goes, the map keeps on being made. Not so the railway passenger. The countryside pays as little attention to the tracks as a family to a child who has come to tea; it simply gets on shamelessly with its own doings and leaves the intruder to make of them what he will.

A police car met him at Durham station and took him straight to the hospital. On the way he was given an update by a rather gruff Yorkshire sergeant. Devine had been spotted in the grounds of his old college. When he saw the patrol car he took off into the grounds of the botanical gardens which adjoined the college. One of the constables went in pursuit and brought him to the ground with a rugby tackle. Devine had fallen badly and needed hospital attention. He was also heavily intoxicated and was verbally abusive to the officers who arrested him. It wasn't a psychiatrist who had seen him this morning; it was just the general medical registrar, who had declared him fit for questioning. The hospital wanted to keep an eye on him though and were waiting for the results of some tests, but they expected to be able to discharge him later in the evening. Mrs Devine had arrived earlier, but they had only let her see him briefly. She was waiting in the relatives' room.

The little room where Devine was being treated was bathed in hospital light. It offered no nooks and crannies to shade, and denied not only the prospect of privacy but the very notion of it. Stuart decided immediately that this was no place to question anyone, let alone a complex introvert like Devine. He advanced towards the bed with a self-conscious smile which he was trying hard to invigorate with warmth – actors could do it, why not he?

"My name's Stranaghan. I'm a police inspector. We were to have a talk yesterday morning but you obviously had better things to do, Mr Devine."

He was going to make a joke about teachers and policemen and captive audiences, but the unresponsive, far-away look in Devine's face told him he was groping in the wrong area for tone.

"I believe you are to be discharged from here in a couple of hours. You and I need to have that talk, so, as soon as you are finished here, a police car will bring you to the station and we'll talk there."

To Stuart's surprise this produced a response, a flicker of a grateful smile which seemed to emerge from the far end of a tunnel of fear. Perhaps it was the often remarked-on unpolicemanlike quality of his Ulster tones that had done the trick. The voice that followed the smile out of the tunnel shocked Stuart; it was the very sound of confidence and lucidity. Stuart had never heard Devine speak, but given the circumstances, he had projected on to him a voice somewhere in the higher tenor regions, certainly not the rich bass that the cowering figure now produced.

"I have been very foolish, Inspector. I want to put the record straight. I look forward to our meeting."

Mrs Devine had been informed of Stuart's arrival and was waiting for him in the corridor when he came out. The intimacy which had suggested itself between them the previous night had taken root.

"Can I have a word with you in private, Inspector Stranaghan?"

She pointed towards the relatives' room and Stuart followed her lead. When they were in the room, she closed the door behind him and took a step towards him.

"I have been thinking about this all night and on the way up here in the train and I've decided that the best thing to do is to

82

tell you the truth. The thing is, my father was in the Royal Engineers during the war and he brought back a few trophies, including a German army pistol. Richard, being an historian, is fascinated by the war and he and my father used to talk endlessly about it. When my father died he left the pistol to Richard."

"Do you know the model?"

"Yes, it's a Walther P38, the type used to kill Stevens. Richard was in a panic about it. I told him there was nothing to worry about; the police would be able to tell that it wasn't the one used in the murder. But he couldn't find it. We ransacked the house and the garage. So we decided in the end that the best thing to do was to keep quiet about it."

"What has changed? Why are you telling me about it now?"

"I didn't trust Winkworth. I'm sure he was honest enough, that's not what I mean. He wasn't a man for subtleties. For people like him two and two are always two and two; they don't deal in fractions. I told Richard I was going to tell you. It's time he confronted his demons; we can't go on the way we were. We are putting ourselves in your hands, Inspector."

Stuart suddenly saw himself wearing the white coat and allowing himself to be seduced by the lure of giving comfort. He had to resist that.

"Margaret, I'm very flattered by your confidence in me, but you must know that I can't simply take Richard's word for it that the gun had gone missing. The fact that he owned the gun in the first place and then chose to keep that a secret from the police is pretty damning stuff, and when you add to that his rows with both men and his running away yesterday, not to mention the general pattern of his behaviour, it doesn't look good."

Mrs Devine bowed her head in acknowledgement of the truth of what Stuart had said and then looked up and fixed him with a gaze that was both gentle and strong.

"You talk to Richard, Inspector, and you'll know that he hasn't done anything wrong. I know you'll know."

Chapter 9

The station canteen struck Stuart immediately as the natural habitat of the modern HP sauce bottle. He had always had a soft spot for the old, traditional bottle. With its black-and-white photo of the Houses of Parliament and its incongruously French text – he remembered how gratified he had felt as a boy translating it for his parents – he looked on it as, almost literally, a pillar of the fifties. As the sixties progressed, however, it went the way of its more vulgar cousin, the tomato ketchup jar. Now it is just a plain brown sauce in a nasty brown plastic container. Popular culture, it would seem, had sometime acquired self-confidence and no longer deigned to reach up and rub shoulders with its betters.

He chose not to share these mental bubblings with Sergeant Thorpe who had been kind enough to ensure that he had company over dinner. Football was the putt that eventually sank as they struggled to find a common slot for their conversation. The sergeant was a keen Leeds Utd fan and was delighted that Stuart could name most of the team of the Revie era. The talk flowed from Thorpe. To this enthusiasm for the subject Stuart responded with some tales of his own, his first international, Northern Ireland versus England at Windsor Park, the dribbling skills of Best, the cliché-shunning words of Danny Blanchflower. Sergeant Thorpe could listen as well as talk, but Stuart's often trotted-out remark about the incompatibility of English football managers and English adverbs was a step too far; it went totally unsmiled-at.

After a quick wash and a half-hour stroll in the old quarter of the town Stuart felt sufficiently clear of the fatigue of his journey and his over-indulgence in football talk to concentrate on the interview with Devine. He was not one to plan interviews meticulously in advance. He had found over the years that he was good at responding spontaneously to what was said. He needed of course to have a general angle of approach, but if he was too sure of where he wanted the interview to go, he was less likely to pick up on the language and internal coherence of his target. The question in this case was whether Devine was to be a target or an interviewee. Interviewees were given space; targets he denied room for manoeuvre. From what he had seen of Devine, despite the weight of evidence against him, little purpose would be served by treating him as a target.

Devine was sitting upright in the chair as Stuart entered Interview Room 3. The timorous look was gone, replaced by a fixed expression of nervous concentration which seemed prepared to make only the most necessary concessions to the demands of the immediate present. These did include Stuart's arrival, which he acknowledged not inimically, but without a smile. Stuart was again taken somewhat aback by the authority of the voice that came from him.

"My wife has told me that I can trust you, Inspector Stranaghan."

Most people, when they make such an observation, pause either to receive assurance or to underline the patronising nature of the remark. Devine did not pause.

"I have behaved very badly. Margaret is beside herself with worry and I have become a nervous wreck. I should have told the truth right from the beginning."

"And what is the truth, Mr Devine?"

"That I owned the gun that killed Stevens."

"How can you be sure of that?"

"Stevens was killed with a Walther P38 pistol. I have a Walther P38 pistol. What could be clearer? I know there were a lot of them around after the war, but not that many after all these years for it to be a reasonable coincidence."

"When you say you 'have' this gun, do you mean the gun is still in your possession?"

"That's the problem. I lost the gun. Sounds pathetic, doesn't it?"

He hesitated for a moment and then seemed to concede to a thought that was distracting him.

"It sounds a bit like an excuse you'd get from a first former. *Lame* is the word. Just like one I once got from a boy when he came back late after lunch. I asked him why he was late and he told me he had been down paddling in the river and a frog had stolen his socks."

There was a shadow of a smile on Devine's face as he told this, which broadened when he picked up Stuart's whole-hearted beam.

"When did you first notice that the gun was missing?"

"As soon as I heard of Stevens' murder I checked in the drawer of my bureau and it was gone. There was a spare magazine and it was gone too."

"What did you do?"

"I told Margaret and she advised me to say nothing. Nobody knew about the gun. I hadn't mentioned it to anyone at school. I had had this terrible row with Stevens and it would have looked very bad if the police knew I had the gun."

"Are you absolutely sure you didn't mention the gun to anyone?"

That look of decision-making pressure, which Stuart had become so adroit at recognising, flitted across Devine's face. The two men knew that it had appeared and each knew that the other knew.

"Well, there was one person who knew. I told him years ago, but I'm sure he has forgotten."

"And who was that, Mr Devine?"

"Dr Greenfield. We often talk about the war – he's a German teacher, you know. I remember mentioning it to him. But I don't want to get him into any trouble. I'm sure if he had remembered he would have told the police."

"Quite so. Tell me, where you were at the time of Dr Stevens' death."

"I had been very upset by the fuss Stevens made about me calling one of my pupils silly. I couldn't believe that someone in his position could get things that wrong."

"But surely you can't go around calling pupils stupid?"

"That's the point. I didn't call her stupid; I simply said, 'Don't be so silly, Jenny'. That's a very different thing. I would expect someone who is trusted to hold down the position of headmaster in a school such as ours to be able to distinguish between an unpardonable insult and an intellectual gee-up. It shook my faith in the whole system."

"What did Dr Stevens actually say to you?"

"He delivered a lecture on the need to empathise with immature minds that could be very sensitive to remarks such as I had made and might easily '*define themselves unnecessarily restrictively*' as a result. Those were his actual words – can you believe it? He said that assault was assault in the eyes of the law even though it had a very wide range and that the same applied to verbal assault. He was condescending enough to assure me that he did not consider me a nasty person, but I should have the maturity to acknowledge that I was in the wrong and try to put right the damage I had done."

"I take it you didn't react well to that?"

"You could say that. I told him that I shouldn't have to listen to drivel like that from anyone, let alone him. If he could not operate within the full range of registers of the English language he should be looking for another job. He remained very calm and told me in the most withering of little voices that it was the pupil's, not his, ability to sort out the registers of English that was at issue. I then asked him if it was not our job to teach the pupils such things and not to pander to the effects of their ignorance. The word 'ignorance' was a red rag to a bull. I was now accused of calling the pupils ignorant as well as stupid. I'm not a violent man, Inspector, so I decided to take it out on the door."

"But that wasn't the end of the matter, was it?"

"No, Stevens didn't take kindly to my slamming the door. A couple of days later I received a letter by recorded delivery requiring my attendance at a formal interview. I was entitled to have a union official or some other person whom I could nominate to attend with me. I took Greenfield. He wasn't allowed to say anything, but he could take notes and, if necessary, act as a witness to what was said.

"Nothing of any great moment happened. Stevens asked me to give an undertaking that in future I would not say or do anything that would give offence to any of my pupils or their parents. I asked him to change the wording to 'could *reasonably* be considered offensive', but he refused, saying that the children and their parents were the best judges of what was offensive. Anything which they found offensive was by definition offensive. He would not take my point that this made them victim, judge and jury and therefore delivered not just me, but any teacher into their hands. I offered to apologise to him over my bad manners in slamming the door, but I made this conditional on him accepting that I had been provoked by his distortion of my use of the word 'ignorance'. Again he refused, saying that 'ignorance' was an offensive word, which illustrated perfectly the point he was trying to make. The interview ended in a stand-off and he issued me with an official verbal warning."

"Can we get back now to the question I asked you earlier, Mr Devine. Where were you at the time of the murder?"

"As I said, I was very upset by this business and when I get into that state I need something to prise me out of it. Music can do it for me, but it doesn't always work. Reading never works; I need to be at least half over it before reading has any effect. This particular time music wasn't doing the trick, so I went off to the museum."

"The museum?"

"Yes, Inspector. The museum has a fine art gallery. There are about a dozen paintings there which I call my foul weather friends. They seem to have the power *to restore my soul.* I'm careful not to call on them except in an emergency, because every time you use them you put another layer between you and the wonder of them."

Stuart knew what he meant. He remembered re-visiting places from his childhood. The first couple of times it was like being transported back in time, but after that all they evoked was memories of having the memories.

"There's one picture in particular. It's a snow scene and you can almost hear the silence of the snow when you look at it. I dread the day when that picture doesn't do that for me anymore."

"So, you went to the art gallery. Did anyone see you when you were there?"

"But I was asked these questions last time, Inspector. I told your sergeant last time that I hadn't talked to anyone."

"Okay. Tell me now about your row with Mr Kennedy."

Devine drew a deep breath and unslumped himself into a more upright position in his chair before continuing.

"During the memorial service a couple of the girls were giggling when the names of the dead were being read out. I caught the eye of one of them and signed for them to stop, but this had no effect. They knew I couldn't do much without disrupting the ceremony and I don't teach either of them. They thought they would get away quickly when the service was over, but I anticipated that and managed to get hold of one of them in the corridor. I grabbed her by the arm so that she couldn't run off, and I read the riot act to her. That was all. No .... I issued her and her friend with a detention; they were to write an essay on how they would have reacted if they had lost loved ones and silly little girls had shown the same lack of respect that they had just shown."

"You will use that word 'silly'."

"No, that wasn't the problem this time. They simply denied they had misbehaved and refused to do the detention. They said I was picking on them and got their parents to complain to Kennedy. Mrs Bergère, the school nurse, was called and a large red mark was discovered on the girl's arm where she said I had gripped her and deliberately hurt her. One other member of staff, Jane Stannage, was able to back me up; she had spotted them giggling and was intending to speak to them about it afterwards. So that part of their story was exposed as a lie. The red mark she manufactured was actually on the wrong arm, so I know that was made up too."

"You told this to Kennedy no doubt?"

"Yes, but it was my word against hers. Kennedy could have got to the bottom of the affair if he had really wanted to, but the easy way out was to suspend me. The girl's parents are quite influential people and this way Kennedy shows he's serious and it won't be up to him to make the final decision about me. No stress, no responsibility – that's the kind of leadership we get nowadays."

"What kind of tone did Kennedy adopt when you talked to him?"

"Businesslike. The complete opposite of Stevens. In a way that was worse. It's as if my actions were outside some kind of moral radar. At least with Stevens you felt you were on the losing side of a moral debate. With Kennedy the morals have been all done and dusted and it is only a matter of clearing up the practicalities. Stevens was a moral prig, Kennedy acts like a moral storm trooper who never questions orders."

"You must have been very angry?"

"I'm not sure that's what I would call it. Anger needs a focus and Kennedy didn't provide one."

"I don't understand what you mean."

"If you compare it with fear and anxiety. You are afraid of things that pose a direct threat – wild animals, lethal weapons, getting the sack in your job. Anxiety on the other hand is when you are afraid that there might be a reason to be afraid. Anxiety is part of the human condition; we are never free of it. Anger works much the same way. The problem is we don't have a word for it in its second degree phase, when we are angry that there is something to be angry about. I was angry that Kennedy reminded me that the state of affairs in this school, in present-day education in general and, probably, in the political assumptions that abound in modern day society, are things to be got angry about."

"But surely Kennedy was the focus of all that anger?"

"No, only symbolically. I don't believe in voodoo, Inspector. Killing the doll does nothing to change the reality. No, it reduces me to a state of powerlessness and despair. I feel as if I am treading water. The job is too big for me and I simply give up on even the smaller things that I could put right."

"Why did you come to Durham?"

"I suppose you could say I was in search of time past, Inspector. When I was a student in Durham I thought the world was a wonderful place, full of promise. I was trying to remind myself of that. Even the paintings didn't help this time. And Durham didn't work either, so I downed a bottle of vodka to deaden the disappointment."

"You didn't think of the worry you were causing your wife or how it looked to us when you ran away?"

"Yes, but I wasn't running my life at that stage. I was merely spectating. Spectator-me is not married to my wife and you certainly can't lock him up."

Stuart had the policeman's professional reluctance to accept language as a guide to truth. Criminals interview in all sorts of literary styles; from the words-spared, truth-shared minimalists through the dear-reader-intimates right up to the psycho-babblers, they can all convince if they ply their art well. Devine would have had to be ranked among the psycho-babblers, but all that he said smacked of a truth that had not been casually brushed against, but thoroughly lived-in. Greenfield had put his finger on it when he had posed the question how Devine would generate enough impetus for an action such as murder. Hopefully, the revelation that he owned the murder weapon would release him from the anxiety that had been preying on him, but this anger in the second degree of which he had spoken was a condition that he would probably take with him to his grave.

"I want you to make a list of all the people who came to your house between the last time you saw the gun and the time you realised it was missing. Obviously, if you remember mentioning its existence to anyone other than Greenfield, I want to know that too. Now, I would advise you to find a nice hotel and treat your wife to a first-class meal. I'll be in touch when you get back home to-morrow."

This was a good note to end the interview, especially when he saw the look of surprised relief in Devine's face, but Stuart felt, even at the risk of sounding silly, that he somehow owed it to this man to step down from the phoney position of objectivity that had been conferred on him by his policeman's role.

"I think all thinking people are subject to the condition you've described, Mr Devine. I've a name for it. I call it *ratio abscondita*. Every time I show signs of suffering from it my wife tells me to go and watch the traffic flowing smoothly at a busy road junction. I find it helps a bit."

It did sound silly, but it was the best he could manage.

Chapter 10

It was too late to make the journey home and expenses could stretch to a comfortable hotel. Normally with Heather he preferred B&Bs, but when he was on his own they could be rather cheerless and so he opted for a hotel with a cheery bar where he could read his *Telegraph* in an atmosphere of peaceful distraction. He was about to start on the letters page, always his first port of call, when it occurred to him that he had switched off his mobile some hours ago to save the battery and had forgotten to check for messages. There were two, one from Myles and the other from Heather. Heather's he opened first.

"Mum has died. It was quite peaceful in the end. Ring me when you get this."

Stuart was instantly saddened. Sadness usually creeps up on you, but this time he felt it almost attack him. It wasn't grief; it was just sadness in its most militant form. Old Betty had not been his friend over the years; they had tolerated each other for Heather's sake, but gradually the toleration had developed into a mild, unselfconscious mutuality. He clumsily '*digitalised*' Heather's number – that was not the word, but it was what he felt one ought to do to things digital. She answered immediately, as if in waiting.

"Hello, Stuart. You got my message. It happened just after three o'clock. She never really recovered consciousness."

"When's the funeral? Friday or Saturday I suppose?"

"No, the only slot we could get at the crematorium was early on Thursday."

"The children will hardly be able to make it. Have you contacted them?"

Stuart and Heather had two children. Their daughter Megan

was doing a year at the University of Toulouse as part of her degree course at Oxford in French History and Civilisation. Gareth, their son, was in America working in the New York office of a London firm of solicitors.

"I got Gareth. He can't get away. Megan is like you; she never has her mobile on, but I've left a text message for her. I don't expect her to make the effort. It's a long way to come for a funeral."

"I'll come over to-morrow about tea time. I'll check what flights are available."

When he rang off it occurred to him that the conversation had proceeded without any break in factuality. His wife's mother was dead and there, he had not offered a single word of comfort to her. Strangely, he found himself pleased at this. The intimacy of understatement is a much more precious thing than the crude, full frontal nudity so beloved by emotional voyeurs.

Myles' message did not need a response. It stated simply that Kennedy was showing signs of recovery and that the doctors were fairly confident that he was close to regaining consciousness.

Unlike the journey up to Durham, the return journey was its own thing. The pressing of the present was more than offset by the memories that came trickling back of Heather's mother and the early years of his courtship and marriage. Escaping into memory is an unjustly maligned affair; it suggests a cowardly seeking of asylum from the present, when it is in fact an attempt to re-connect with the here and now. When the present is experienced in its pure form it shares its main feature with the past; both come free of the future-orientated anxieties that beset the workaday present like a crowd of parasites that grow and grow until they have deposed their host and feed off their own dung. The present needs to de-louse itself from its future fiends and what could be more natural than to turn to its natural ally for support? The morning sunlight that bathed the fields was the same morning sunlight that he had experienced as a six-year-old travelling with his Aunt Jean and his cousin Hannah on the train to Dublin; the light he was seeing was its own thing, not something that would give way to the glare of the afternoon or the glow of the evening. All our yesterdays are to-days without the distraction of to-morrows. When he got off the train, Stuart had the anchorage of a man who had re-discovered the ancestry of his *nowness* and re-established it as something more substantial than the lightweight harbinger of *nextness*.

Myles greeted him with a smile that was growing distinct features of familiarity. The perfunctory inquiries after Stuart's enjoyment of the journey and his appreciation of the cathedral city did not extend to the runaway Mr Devine. It was clear that Myles had news of his own which he did not want to be digressed from.

"I've investigated Evans' Isle of Man accounts and they make interesting reading. I found the payment from Richardson's Development, but there's more. The account has been open for about ten years and the first payment was made by a company called Language Services. They made a payment of £10,000 in 1996 and this was followed every year by a payment of £6,000. There was no payment made last year."

"Perhaps he does some kind of consultancy work for them?"

"Hardly, sir. Remember, he's a physics teacher. No, Language Services are the company that rent the school premises in the summer to run summer schools for foreigners. I checked with the bursar and he tells me that the school receives an annual payment of £20,000 from them. He felt they could make more out of the deal than this and approached Kennedy, since the contract came up for renewal last year. Apparently Kennedy was very keen on the idea at first, but later changed his mind and told the bursar that they should stick to the existing arrangement. He had consulted other heads, it seems, and they had regaled him with all sorts of stories of abuse of their premises by outside agencies. He thought it better to stay with the devil they knew."

"Evans really was having his fiefdom pillaged. It gets interestinger and interestinger."

"I've also been through Kennedy's files. Nothing much of interest – notes on the Devine and Ross cases, nothing we didn't know about. However, Mrs Abernethy informs me that he has a special personal file which needs a password to access. Now that might make more interesting reading."

"We must get to those before he regains consciousness. Otherwise we'll have no excuse. Get our computer people on to it."

"I've already contacted them, sir, and they're on their way."

"I don't suppose you've had time to see Mrs Ross?"

"Sorry, sir. Been quite busy as you see."

"You've done well, Myles."

Stuart then brought Myles up to date with what had happened in Durham. It was remarkable how he always felt awkward moving away from a topic that involved an expression of gratitude from him. He never knew the right moment to change the subject after he had been given a present. When he had finished his story, Myles looked unimpressed. He had taken what he saw as the digression from the Evans' line in good part and asked good-naturedly but almost panderingly:

"Shall we divide the work? You check out Mrs Devine and I'll deal with Dr Greenfield?"

It had never occurred to Stuart that Mrs Devine needed to be checked out. He had no real doubts that Dr Greenfield was anything other than a trusted confidante, but obviously checks would have to be made. But Mrs Devine? Myles was right of course. She was one of the three people who they knew were aware of the existence of the pistol and where it was kept. She was a loyal wife and must have harboured deep feelings of hatred towards these two men who had caused her husband's breakdown. But two things did not make any sense. Why would she use the pistol the second time, knowing how much damage that would do to her husband's state of mind? And secondly, why would she tell Stuart about the weapon? Myles had no answer to either of these questions and was content to rest on his half-hearted insistence that her alibi must be further investigated. But having got that little island sortie diplomatically out of the way, he returned to the mainland of the investigation.

"There must be some way Evans knew about the pistol. Did you ask Devine any questions about Evans?"

"No. I think we'll get more out of Devine once the pressure is off him for a while. Let's leave Evans until we dig a bit deeper into Kennedy's personal files. You check out Mrs Devine and when you've done that we'll meet up and pay Mrs Ross a visit. In the meanwhile I'll have word with the esteemed Dr Greenfield. That gentleman owes us an explanation, don't you think?"

This was not a decision that met with Myles' wholehearted approval, but he 'walked' from the crease like a gentleman batsman of the fifties.

After a quick word with the Superintendent to inform him of his proposed absence and to update him on the latest developments, Stuart booked a six o'clock flight to Belfast and made his way to St Jude's. It was nearly lunchtime and he would be able to talk to Greenfield without formally having to get him out of class.

The lunchtime scenario was now becoming familiar to Stuart. Greenfield seemed to act as a kind of impromptu master of ceremonies, introducing some topic of general interest and inviting comment and reaction from those adjacent to him. Whether by chance or by design, the Reverend Frederick Foster was again playing the role of sophist to Greenfield's Socrates.

"You can't seriously be suggesting, Bruce, that punishment achieves anything? It is completely negative and goes against the Christian teaching of forgiveness. It dehumanises the recipient and diminishes the state that administers it. Surely we of all people should be stressing the need for rehabilitation and re-education."

"You sound so civilised, Freddie, and you are inviting me to put my head in the noose. No, sorry, bad metaphor. That would make me a victim rather than a culprit of justice, and that wouldn't do at all, would it? You are very fond of the word 'forgiveness'. Did you know that it is the Germanic form of the Latin 'per-donare', our English word 'pardon'? It means 'giving completely'? That's a fairly close synonym for 'abandoning'. The morality of abandon or the abandonment of morality? That's exactly it, that's what we as a society are in the process of doing, abandoning our world to the craven licence of 'non-judgemen-talism'. How often do you hear the weasel words: '*Who are we to judge? That's God's prerogative; it's not for man to reason …* ' – need I insert the 'why'? Does it ever strike you that if we cannot judge the criminals, then we cannot judge those who judge the criminals either? Funny, how the forgiving liberal establishment suddenly becomes dramatically less forgiving when it comes to '*fascist conservative reactions*' to crime. It is the act of self-assertion in the '*fascist*' condemnation that liberalism finds intolerable. Willingness to forgive is no more than a white flag in a moral combat zone. Actually, it's a whiter-than-white flag; it says, if I don't condemn you, you've no right to condemn me. It's not an act of moral generosity at all; it's just well-marketed enlightened self-interest. The utilitarianism of forgiveness – could there be a more fitting ethic for our money-grubbing culture?"

Greenfield's response ended in the playful note Stuart had come to expect from him, but also detectable was an underlying tone of suppressed anger which the playfulness only partially disguised. This surprised Stuart. In fact he found himself a little shocked. He had no right to be. The impression he had formed of Greenfield as a sort of intellectual court jester who 'entertained' ideas because of their inherently entertaining value, was based on far too little evidence. Perhaps it was a projection of his own attitude. In any case, the revelation warranted a re-assessment of Greenfield's part in the proceedings and added a second question mark to the question he was about to ask him.

When lunch was over – the stricken reverend didn't finish his pudding without getting in a few darts of his own on the dangers of the unreceptive nature of the ideological cocoon – Stuart asked Greenfield to forgo his normal coffee circle and give him a private word. Greenfield showed no surprise at this and led Stuart through a series of corridors strewn with abandoned schoolbags, a Pompeii-like scene caused in this case by the electrics of the lunchtime bell, to a small office at the back of the resources room. There he produced a kettle along with two cups and proceeded to brew coffee for the two of them.

"You want to know why I did not tell you about the Walther?"

"Yes, I think you owe me an explanation. What's more, you owe Kennedy an explanation."

"I owe Kennedy nothing. But I'm sorry I didn't feel able to tell you the truth."

"You assumed I would jump to conclusions about Devine?"

"No, I assumed your predecessor would do that. And having kept the truth from him, it was difficult, as you might guess, to break the silence. However, I phoned Margaret yesterday morning and advised her to tell you about the gun. I left it to her to decide."

"You realise that your failure to tell the police about the gun is itself a criminal offence? What's more, it makes you a suspect."

"Of course I realise that, Inspector. You must do your worst. Do you wish to charge me with obstruction or some like offence? If I had thought for a moment that it was poor Richard who had killed Stevens I would have reported the gun right away."

"What made you so sure that he hadn't?"

"Well, one cast-iron reason would have been if I had committed the murder myself, of course. I had access to the murder weapon, I had the opportunity and I also had the motive. Are you not tempted, Inspector?"

"What do you mean, you had the motive?"

"Come now, Inspector. Everything that that fool Stevens stood for is anathema to me. Education, if it is anything, is a process of self-transcendence. We come face to face with the opaque and then slowly begin to see the reason in it. It is a humbling process; you ache with your own inadequacy and when you do finally succeed in getting your head round something that had previously eluded you, you feel you have been admitted into an inner circle of the enlightened. But that doesn't puff you up with your own importance, for you know you are only a house member. The feeling never leaves you that you only got in by chance and that at any time you will be found out and exposed as the fool you are. The reward is to see connections that you have never seen before. This in turn gives rite of passage to the best company and deepest friendships to which man can aspire. Nothing binds men better than sharing the scraps of patterns that have been so hard gained. It is a monkish thing."

"Stevens did not share your view?"

"*Tu rigoles, mon vieux.* Stevens was a missionary. He wanted to spread the good news to the cerebrally under-developed. In willing such a thing he was of course in danger of committing the unpardonable sin of endorsing the principle of interventionism and thereby opening the door to what all self-respecting, enlightened post-missionary post-modernists call cultural imperialism. But even these priests of non-judgementalism have their blind spots; they draw a line in the sands of tolerance at activities such as cannibalism and human sacrifice. Not so the dear doctor. According to him, anything that was relevant to the lives of our little charges constituted a worthy area of study. Relevance – that was his touchstone. The love lives of pop stars, the careers of footballers, the rap lyrics of drug addicts, the history of soap operas, these were all judged worthy of their time and energies. Because these activities now happen in schools they must be judged to be 'educational'. Poppycock! They are no more 'educational' than human sacrifice and cannibalism would have been Christian, if they had been happening in a church."

"But the 'monkish' thing you mentioned can surely never be the basis for mass education. Surely you must set your sights a bit lower than that."

"That's a fair point. Academic education has always been and always will be the pursuit of a small minority. The notion that vast swathes of people can be educated to university level is tenable only if we reduce the notion of education to the nonsense that Stevens and his ilk will have us do. For the majority of children, there is training, and there is nothing at all wrong with training. Since it involves discipline, training has a strong educational element. But it has a wider motivational appeal than the purely academic because it produces the job skills that are needed in society – medics, engineers, lawyers at the top end, down the scale plumbers, secretaries, motor mechanics. At the higher end you need a good rounded education as a base for the training, at lower levels all that's needed is a good grounding in the three Rs. Yet more and more of to-day's children are not getting even that. What they get instead is this let's-pretend-its-education-educationalism. I would like to see a society of people who are good at their jobs and take a pride in their skills. I would also like to see an education system that would give everyone the opportunity to come into contact with and be uplifted by some of the best minds that the human race has produced. This is why I became a teacher in the first place – not to baby-mind activities best left at the nursery."

That note of suppressed anger was back in Greenfield's voice. The man was always fluent, but this was the fluency of a barrister or a political analyst. What had started off as a confessional tease was gradually acquiring a seriousness, a seriousness which certainly mocked, but Stuart wondered if what it was mocking was the notion that the mockery was not to be taken seriously.

"Did you object to Dr Stevens opening up the school to more children of limited means?"

"Not in the least! I wouldn't have taught in the school if there had been no opportunities for pupils of deprived backgrounds. What I objected to was his lack of discrimination. He did not make his decisions on educational grounds; he made them as part of a political creed. Education was for him, as it has been for many of his generation, the great engine of political change. People like him call it the democratization of society. I call it *Vermassenmenschlichung*. It sounds like a German word, but actually I made it up myself. There is a German word *Massenmensch* – it refers to the typical human product of our modern consumer society. The *Massenmensch is* bereft of the most basic skills, he scorns intellectual activity unless it leads directly to material gain for himself or his family, he is convinced that everything is getting better every day – this comes from his Panglossian faith in modern science and technology; he gets his opinions like he buys his clothes; both must pass the same test, they must be in line with the latest trends and, of course, he brooks no dissent, since all that comes into his head has the weight of received wisdom behind it. The Stevenses of the educational world merely dish out designer labels to glitzify this crassness, when what they should be doing is devoting themselves to its eradication. And – before you say it – it's not a class thing. That's another great liberal myth. All the classes are the victims of it, albeit in different ways. Take language for example. The vulgarly inarticulate are intuitively aware that they are the victims of their language limitations, but the middle classes who speak with posh accents and received vowels are just as likely to be led by the nose by a language over which they have no control: the difference is, they don't know it. I don't care what social class our pupils come from. The only criterion of any relevance is their ability and willingness to take the opportunities we offer them. There has always had to be a certain trade-off. The wealthier pupils have always helped subsidize the poorer ones, but the influx of all those funds gave us a wonderful opportunity to help even more able children from poorer backgrounds. Stevens wasted that opportunity. The children he has brought into the school are gaining nothing that they would not have had in any ordinary sink comprehensive, except of course the snob value of having attended St Judes."

Greenfield was in spirit no longer addressing Stuart. He was arguing a case before the gods, with Stuart cast only as the messenger. Prometheus, Stuart imagined, could not have defended his stealing of the fire with greater humanitarian intensity. A question suddenly popped up in Stuart's mind. It came out uncensored and unpolished.

"Do you think that anyone – and I include you in this – could feel strongly enough about this business to kill Stevens over it?"

The question was brutal; it showed no respect for the internal coherence of what Greenfield had been attempting to articulate. It was a question no messenger had the right to ask. Greenfield seemed to need time to come down from where he was, but when he had, he showed no resentment, either feigned or real. He simply looked thoughtfully at Stuart and replied in almost a whisper: "Yes, I do." The thoughtful and deliberate way in which he seemed to draw the answer out from within suggested that it was a question that he had posed and answered a dozen times, but that he was making one final check before allowing it out into the public gaze. After an equally long pause he continued:

"When you start to consider what motivates people to do all sorts of terrible things to their fellow men you realise that the equations seldom balance even for the perpetrators. This struck me many years ago. In the village where I lived a builder started to build an estate of about a hundred houses; he had only outline planning permission and he broke every rule in the book. The planners were weak and let him away with murder, well not literally. He ended up destroying the character of the entire village. There was no mystery as to why he did it. Money, I once heard someone say, is the WD40 of the human engine. Some time later I was talking to someone who knew the builder and she told me that he spent his Saturday evenings playing snooker in his big house for wagers of £100 a time. It was then that I realized that we all get our sums wrong when it comes to motivation."

"But what connection could Stevens' murder have with the attempt on Kennedy's life? From all that I hear the two men were chalk and cheese. Kennedy was no missionary."

Again there was a pause. In contrast to its earlier fluency Greenfield's mind now seemed to be working a passage through raw material.

"To continue the metaphor, if we think of Stevens as an early missionary, Kennedy is part of the second colonial wave, the merchant. Trade consolidates what the pioneers have opened up. The Kennedys are just as pernicious as the Stevenses. They put the follies of the Stevenses out of the reach of criticism by building over them and conventionalising them. They are ideological innocents, but they must take their share of the guilt."

In response to Stuart's failure to register any facial approval he continued,

"The law distinguishes between murder and manslaughter, does it not? It is a very narrow vision of man that restricts man's responsibility to those acts which are committed in the full light of consciousness. The *reductio ad absurdum* of such a position would be the notion that the only thing that matters in human conduct is the presence or absence of a good will. We seem to be getting there. In the past Government ministers would resign when serious mistakes were made in their department. Now they just shed a tear or two, expose their 'humanity' to the public gaze and assure us all that they couldn't possibly have willed the gaffe. These are the same politicians who every now and again feel they must 'apologise' for things that happened generations ago, long before they were born. The concept of responsibility has been reduced to a vague feeling of regret that something has happened; it has been so successful in distancing itself from guilt that it has now become a means of self-glorification. 'Look at my soul, look what a *Mensch* I am!' We need a new word for what has happened. When you fuse sentimentality and morality what do you get? I think I'll run that as a competition in the Thinkers' Club."

"Okay, you've succeeded in persuading me that someone could have killed, or tried to kill, both men for the reasons you have given; now persuade me that that someone wasn't you."

Greenfield looked disappointed by the question. The smile that came to his lips was more like a glaze that established a barrier between the two men.

"There are two ways I could answer that question, Inspector. I needn't trouble you with the second. At the time of Stevens' murder I was conducting a 'field trip' with my *Thinkers*. We went up to London to see a German film. It was called *Das Versprechen*; it was an allegory on the break-up and re-unification of Germany. I didn't retain the tickets, but I can give you the names of the four pupils I took with me if you like. Last Sunday I spent most of the day on my computer. I am writing a paper on conventional English approaches to German grammar. I needed to check a few cross-references with a friend who lectures at Cambridge. He phoned me back a couple of times. His name is Reinhold Dornbach. There's his number. You can check with him."

"It's only a formality, you realise, but I'll have him contacted. Your phone records will give us the precise times of the calls. As to the trip with the *Thinkers*, I'm pretty sure I read that in the files. But you said there were two answers to the question. What about the second one?"

"Oh, it's much more convincing, but a court wouldn't find it so. I have spent my whole professional life, Inspector, developing and encouraging a critical approach to what passes for conventional wisdom in all sorts of areas – politics, religion, literature, even language. I've huffed and I've puffed, but never in my life have I actually done anything. If the truth be told, I haven't even produced a really first-class piece of scholarship. When I told you earlier that Richard couldn't be your man because he would never be able to find the *élan* to act so decisively, I was speaking from the heart. Richard and I are very different in many ways from one another, but one thing we do share is this metaphysical paralysis. I don't know if you remember the old Monty Python sketch where the Greek philosophers were playing football against the German philosophers? The first half never really got started; the Germans couldn't decide on the rules of the game, the authority of the referee or the reality of the physicality of the ball. When half-time came they were still deep in thought. The same happened in the second half when it was the Greeks' turn to kick off. Then, just as full-time approached, Archimedes seemed to light up with a thought and dribbled the ball past all the stationary opponents and scored. It was a brilliant sketch. What spoiled it a little for me was the choice of the scorer. It should have been Nietzsche or Kierkegaard; they are the founding fathers of existentialism. You see, there I go again. I am wrong. They were right to pick Archimedes; everyone knows him as the man who jumped out of his bath and ran naked down the street; most people have never heard of Nietzsche or Kierkegaard. You see, even as a critic of the sketch I stand condemned as a 'passivist' ... I've just had a thought. Can you imagine an update on the sketch, showing the script-writers failing to make the original sketch because they can't make up their minds as to who is to run with the ball?"

The two men laughed heartily. When the moment was over Greenfield looked at his watch and then at Stuart, there was a pause for assessment, then he said,

"I'm sorry, I have a class now, but we can talk again, Inspector."

In words it was a statement, but judging from the eye contact initiated by Greenfield it was a request for Stuart to indicate if he was satisfied with where they were at with it. Stuart replied in kind.

"I've enjoyed our chat, Dr Greenfield. I'm no nearer the end than I was at the beginning, but at least the route seems a little clearer now."

The meeting had been declared informal.

Chapter 11

As there was still nearly an hour left before he was due to meet up with Myles, Stuart decided to take a walk round the school and see what was to be picked up. Almost without thinking he headed straight for the playing fields. In the distance he could hear the high-pitched enthusiasm of youthful voices being periodically pierced and silenced by the even shriller whistle of a referee. Memories were evoked of schooldays gone-by, curiously not of his own schooldays, for in these surroundings his personal memories were merely in the way, covering over a more authentic past, a past to his past, which he had gleaned from the pages of boys' own stories, emitting pre-war public school heroes who batted with broken arms or other such incapacitated limbs for the honour of the House or scored the winning try in the mud against the odds for the glory of the school, tales that had enthralled him, a working-class boy from the back streets of Belfast. His own experiences subsequently on the rugby field had been but pale shadows of these folk-images. It was not just the glory and success of achievement that had fallen short, that wasn't it at all – it was his failure to emulate the naïve decency and courage of the heroes, that's what took the salt out of the post-dream reality. Yet every time he smelt the mud and wet of the earth and the sap of the grass, his hopes never failed to re-awaken.

At the side of the pitch there was a group of three older boys showing occasional interest in the muddy endeavours of the competing terriers. One of them had the flag of authority of a touch-judge, but he held it in such a manner as to suggest anarchist leanings. Stuart greeted the three with as casual a nod as he could muster. He had a horror of those adults who get it all wrong when they *engage with* the younger generation. When serving his time as a *younger-generationist* himself, he had often squirmed at misguided attempts at *mateyness* from the other side of the age barrier and had resolved as an adult never to make a display of generously disowning his accumulation of years. Better to stand by the fifty odd that he had accrued, and treat with those with less acumen from there. There is nothing more condescending than a conscientious effort to avoid condescension.

The three showed little interest in Stuart's arrival and continued their desultory exchanges, impenetrable to an outsider through the layers of references to school life and in the relative absence of grammar. Stuart wondered if his presence had caused these allusions to multiply. He also seriously doubted that such anorexic syntax was capable of sustaining communication beyond the short burst. Any hopes he had entertained of getting into informal conversation now seemed just silly, so he identified himself, hoping that his position would carry more weight with them than his persona. The effect was instantaneous. The vagrant that had been refused charity at the back door suddenly became the honoured guest to whom every courtesy was due, not least Sunday-best grammar and syntax. After entry had been effected Stuart continued tentatively.

"Are any of you in Dr Greenfield's Thinkers' Club?"

"Gordon is," said the anarchist flag-holder, pointing to his bespectacled companion. "I used to belong, but I found it all a bit tedious."

"What kind of things do they get up to?"

Flag-holder again took the lead.

"They talk a lot. Sometimes it's okay when they talk about politics and things, but when old Greeners ... sorry sir, Dr Greenfield ... when he gets on one of his hobbyhorses it can get a bit heavy."

This was too much for the bespectacled member. An intervention was called for.

"No sir, that's not right. Jimmy there is just a bit thick. He can't follow what Dr Greenfield is on about. Dr Greenfield's a great teacher. He gets you to understand things you've never even thought about before."

"Like what?" This was from Jimmy, the flag-holder. Stuart was in definite danger of becoming an honorary spectator.

"Like that German story he told us about the Russian Revolution. The one where the young guy kills the politician even though he thinks he's great. The point was he didn't do it because he fancied doing it, he just thought it was the right thing to do. I always thought that anything you thought was right would seem right to you. This seemed wrong to him and yet he decided to do it because he somehow *knew* it was right."

"I remember that story." This was the first contribution from the third member of the group, who up till now had been showing more interest in what was happening on the rugby field. "Greeners told us that when he was covering for *If-If*."

"Who on earth is *If-If*?"

Stuart was happy to take the bait.

"*If-If* is the Reverend Foster, sir. His first name is Fred which gives us F-F and he is always asking hypothetical questions – 'What if . . . ?'"

There was a robust strain of pride in the delivery of this answer.

"This was during an RE class, you say?"

"Yes, Dr Greenfield was making the point that morality has nothing to do with sentiment, it's a matter of Reason."

Stuart was more than a little taken aback by this sudden rise in register and coherence. Clearly the nick-nomenclature had served its purpose as a form of password into the conversation and was now to be dispensed with. Flag-holder and companion were clearly just as impressed with the sentence and felt the need for a potted presentation of its composer.

"This is Goodall, sir. He's the school genius. Gets all the prizes on Speech Day. Mind you, his head's bigger than his brain – it's a bit swollen."

"You don't go to the Thinkers' Club?"

"No, sir. I had a metaphysical disagreement with one of the members a couple of years ago and I never went back."

"The disagreement was to do with metaphysics, really?"

"Strictly speaking, no, sir. It was a basic question of ethics. I only used the word metaphysical to underline the fundamental nature of our disagreement."

"Which was ...?"

"This guy Snoddy maintained that morality is just a series of conventions which reflect the economic realities of a given society. I disagreed. I said that the notions of what is right and just only undergo minor changes in response to wider social change, but essentially they remain the same."

"Do you mean Robert Snoddy, the boy who left the school just before Dr Stevens' death?"

"He was expelled, you mean. Yes, that's him."

"Surely, that's what the Thinkers' Club is all about – disagreeing with other people's opinions? Why did you leave it over that?"

"Snoddy became quite vicious. He was in the Upper Sixth at the time and I was only a Fourth Former. Every time I went after we had our 'heated argument' he kept having a go at me. He said people like me made him sick, getting on their high horse and thinking they are so whiter than white when it comes to morality. He kept calling me 'a little rich boy' who had no idea what real life was like."

"Was Dr Greenfield aware of any of this?"

"Snoddy got most of his ideas from Dr Greenfield. And Dr Greenfield thought the sun shone out of Snoddy's backside. It was a mutual admiration society, that's why I left."

In the course of this exchange the play on the field had moved down towards the far twenty-two. This had obliged flag-holder to sidle along the touchline and his friend Gordon, possibly alarmed by the syntactical purity of what he was hearing, had followed. This provided Stuart with the privacy for an indiscreet question.

"Do you know why exactly Snoddy got expelled?"

"It was all very hush-hush, sir. There was a rumour going around that Snoddy was into drugs, but I never believed that. Snoddy was too much of a control freak for that. I can't imagine him letting himself get hooked on anything. He always liked to be in control. Whatever it was, it must have been pretty serious, for *See-No-Evil* – that's what we called Dr Stevens, sir – the man didn't have a clue; he had a forgiveness thing. If you made a clean breast of it, he always let you off."

Just then the honey pot was punted back up the field and the swarm, clad as it happened in jerseys of yellow-and-black hoops, followed in hot pursuit. It suddenly dawned on Stuart that both sides were wearing the same bee-like strip. How the referee was coping was anyone's guess. It gave new meaning to the proposition that in sport participation is all. He had not realized before that this glorification of the existential above all else could be extended even to the rules. "*Power to the 'is'. Down with the 'ism'.*" He did not share this thought with the cerebrally endowed Goodall. It was time to catch up with Myles. So he bade his new-found friends farewell and made his way back to the main school.

On their way to Mrs Ross' house Myles told Stuart that the hospital had rung to say that Mr Kennedy had regained consciousness, but was in a confused state and that there would be no question of interviewing him until the swelling on the brain had come down. Mrs Devine's alibi had, as expected, proved solid. He had spoken to her sister on the telephone and she had confirmed that Mrs Devine had been with her at the

112

time of the shooting. When his turn came, Stuart reduced his account of his interview with Greenfield to the basic facts, which, he became uncomfortably aware, were minimal. Greenfield had supplied him with the phone number of his academic friend from Cambridge and Stuart now passed this on for Myles to check. The speculation on the potential horse-power of an ideological motive he chose not to mention to Myles. He did, however, casually bring up the encounter on the rugby field and the curious business of the expulsion of Robert Snoddy. The mention of Snoddy had an instant effect on Myles' driving; it now seemed to require all his concentration.

"Surely you must have looked into this last time. Were there drugs involved?"

A change of lane was required as the car in front was turning off to the right. Myles applied himself to this manoeuvre with the focus of a learner driver. Only after the vehicle in front had not been bumped into and permission to move into the inside lane had been sought, granted and taken up, did Myles find a slot for a reply to Stuart's question.

"No, there were no drugs."

Stuart waited for him to continue, but the road was seemingly unrelenting in its demand for his sergeant's attention. Stuart looked. It was almost totally free of traffic.

"If there were no drugs, why was Snoddy given the sack?"

There was another pause. Then there was a frantic checking in the rear mirror, the two side-mirrors and the driver's side window. Myles was making a driving decision. But this time you felt that the driving decision was in some way in answer to Stuart's question. He brought the car to a halt at the side of the road, put on the hand-brake, switched off the ignition and turned to his boss.

"Sir, I have a confession to make. I didn't tell you, and I didn't tell Superintendent Winkworth, the real reason why Snoddy got expelled. He got expelled because one of the female teachers accused him of sexual harassment. She claimed he touched her when they were having a tutorial after school one day."

Stuart stared at his sergeant in total incomprehension.

"But why on earth would you keep information like that to yourself? That makes no sense; it's just crazy."

"Dr Greenfield asked me to, sir. No-one else in the school knew about it except Dr Stevens, the woman herself of course, and Dr Greenfield. The teacher – she was called Gillian Sloane – didn't want things to go any further once he had been expelled, and Dr Greenfield said that the boy had suffered enough and if it got out in the newspapers his whole future would be affected. Snoddy was in Germany at the time of the murder and I made a point of checking very thoroughly on his father, so it wasn't really relevant to the case."

"Yes, but that wasn't your decision to make. It was up to Superintendent Winkworth to decide what to do, not you."

"I know that, sir, but Dr Greenfield volunteered the information to me. If he hadn't told me we'd never have known. Everyone, including the boy and his father, had agreed to go along with the story about the drugs. Dr Greenfield thought that Superintendent Winkworth would not have handled the situation well and he put his trust in me, sir. It was foolish of me, I know. When I hadn't told the Superintendent about it, it was hard for me to tell you. You can see that, sir?"

Myles was pleading for his career. If Stuart told the Superintendent, Myles would be finished. But then there was his own career to think about. If he kept quiet about this and it later came out, then he would be in even more trouble than Myles. *His own career* – that had the sound of something real and substantial, something that had a beginning, middle and end to it. Long ago, when he was in his thirties he had believed in the reality of a career; he could almost see where he stood in it and what direction he was facing in. He had never been ambitious in the meanest sense of the word; he was quite happy to bob along like a fisherman's float, more up and down than along, assured that the tide was taking him to better places. But every now and again he would become aware of someone scurrying past him as if they were being reeled in to the shore by the knowing gods to answer some higher purpose. It was at such moments that he felt the need to 'move forward' so as not to be overtaken by men whose qualities gave no clue as to why they had been chosen. As a student in the seventies he had read Sartre's miserable study in existential nausea; he had 'intellectually interiorised' – that was the jargon of the day – the notion of absurdity and the urgency of its denial by men in desperate search for life-patterns, but it was only in his later years, when confronted by the fiction of his career, that the penny had finally dropped down into the pit of his stomach. At Myles' age it was still reasonable to have faith. He would not tell on him. No harm had been done and, more important, a good will had been at work.

"I'll get Dr Greenfield to break this news to me and I'll take the credit in my report for a good piece of detective work. But don't put me in this position again."

Myles' face was a register of confusion, but the waters parted and a smile of appreciation appeared. The resultant struggle for ascendancy between gratitude and embarrassment was resolved by a very subdued 'Thank you, sir' and the mechanical operations that required his attention to re-start the car and get it back into the stream of traffic.

Mrs Ross answered the door at the first ring and beckoned them in. She was a strikingly beautiful woman, long black hair, dark brown eyes and a youthful skin which was just brown enough to offer both a contrast and a complement to her captivating features. The living room was more of a lounge than a drawing room – too many soft furnishings, cushions, posed photographs in 'tasteful' frames and a carpet with too long a pile. They sank down below the level of their knees into the pale blue sofa that was offered. They were thus forced to peer over their knees at their hostess who had perched herself on a 'captain's chair' padded in a darker, toning blue leather.

"I'll come straight to the point, Mrs Ross. I hope you don't mind my directness, but it has been reported to us that recently you showed signs of having been assaulted. You must understand that we are investigating two very serious crimes at the school and that anything unusual or suspicious which comes to our attention must be investigated. Can you tell us please how you came to have the injuries?"

Mrs Ross swivelled a little on her chair before replying. When she finally spoke, it was with the charm of a distinctly Spanish accent.

"I don't want you to get the wrong impression, Inspector, but my husband and I sometimes have rows and it sometimes gets a little out of hand."

Myles jumped in. In the presence of beauty, it seemed, he was less prepared to take a back seat.

"Are you saying your husband physically assaults you, Mrs Ross?"

"I know it sounds bad, but it's as much my fault as his. When I get angry I throw things. My husband's a very clever man, he's very good with words and I get frustrated and throw things at him. That's when he becomes ... physical."

"What do you have these rows about, Mrs Ross?" Myles continued.

"Oh, all sorts of things. I'm afraid I've been a great disappointment to my husband. He's a very clever man and has ideas about everything. He talks sometimes to me about things that he reads about, but I don't understand. I try, but I never seem to say the right thing. I've tried very hard. When we met at first my English was very weak. I went to classes when I came to England and two years ago I got a GCSE in English literature."

"But you don't have rows about things like that, do you?"

116

Myles was determined.

"Sometimes, but mostly it's about little things that I have done wrong. He doesn't want to go out with our friends. I buy too much at the shops. I buy wrong things."

"Is that why you are separated?"

"We had a big row last summer. It was about our credit card. He said I spend too much money."

"Do you?"

"Yes, I suppose he was right. I wanted to go and see my mother in Barcelona and I booked a flight. It cost a couple of hundred pounds. He said I could have got it much cheaper if I had booked it earlier on the internet. He said that I never think about such things and that I was very stupid. I threw a plate at him and he got very angry and punched me in the face. He left after that and said he had enough of me."

"How badly were you hurt?"

"Not bad. I went to the doctor and he gave me an anti ... anti ... I can't remember the word. It was to bring down the swelling ... anti-inflammatory."

"What do you do for a living, Mrs Ross?"

"I have no job. When I met George I was a waitress in a bar in Barcelona. He was doing a course at the university. When I was serving I tripped and spilled coffee over him. He was very charming. We got married after six weeks – it was a big wedding, all my family was there, my uncle Juan came all the way from Argentina – and I came to live in England."

Stuart felt that Myles' questioning needed a re-focus.

"Can you tell me, Mrs Ross, how things were between you at the time when Dr Stevens was killed?"

"George did not like Dr Stevens. He was very angry when his job was given to Julia."

"You mean Julie Vance?"

"Yes, I forget. I always call her Julia. Julia is my friend. She came to see me when I was ill and she presented me to her friends."

"When were you ill?"

"After a couple of years in England. I became pregnant, but the baby did not live. I became very depressed and did not go out. George did not know what to do with me."

"Can you remember where you were and where George was at the exact time when Dr Stevens was murdered?"

"You think George is the killer? No, that is not possible. George would not do that."

"How do you know? He is violent with you, is he not, Mrs Ross?"

"No, that is different. That is the passion. George is not angry with me, he is disappointed. I am not what he wants me to be. With Dr Stevens he was angry, but his anger does not feed his passion. It is he who feeds his anger."

"Were you with him when Dr Stevens was killed?"

"No, I was with my mother in Barcelona. He called me the day after to tell me what had happened."

"How did he sound?"

"He was upset. He told me to stay another week in Barcelona."

"That was a bit odd, don't you think? Why would he want you to stay on in Barcelona?"

"He said that everything was unpleasant here, the police would ask many questions and I would be happier if I wasn't there."

Stuart felt that that was as far as they could go, but as they were leaving Myles had a final question.

"How are things between you and your husband now, Mrs Ross?"

"George does not live with me now. He comes to me when he is lonely, but he says it is better that he does not live here. I wash his clothes and give him food that I have cooked. He pays all the bills. I have no money of my own."

"Are you happy with this arrangement?"

"No, I am very sad. If he does not come back I will go back to Barcelona. He says that he will come back when things get better, but I do not believe him. He says that only to stop me going back to Barcelona. I don't know what I will do."

As they made their way back to the car the two men maintained a silence that was somehow reverent, the kind of silence that descends on an audience leaving the cinema after a heart-tugging film. In the end it was broken by Myles.

"What makes a woman like that tie herself to the likes of Ross? She is a beautiful woman, she could have any man she wanted and yet she clings to a man who insults her and beats her."

"The pat answer to that is *chemistry*, Myles, but I've always found pat answers particularly irritating. They always make me think of my old German teacher. Every time I asked her to explain some point of grammar I didn't understand, she would think for a moment and then come out with the same old thing – it was all a question of *Sprachgefühl*. I don't know why she bothered to think at all. Of course she might well have been right, but it didn't help me in the slightest."

"I was thinking more of '*Opposites attract*'."

"Yes, now that, I think, is closer to the mark. Most beautiful women are happy to be just that, beautiful. And they spend most of their waking hours reasserting it to themselves. They flirt and tease and generally revel in their own attractiveness. But did you notice? There's nothing flirtatious about Mrs Ross. She seems amazingly unaware of her own beauty. Did you notice too how often she referred to her husband's intelligence? Intellect, I think, is her form of beauty. She is pulled towards it and wants to embrace it, but she can't. Ross on the other hand has found in her the beauty of his life, but that's not enough, he wants it all; he wants the fusion of beauty and intellect and he is frustrated with her because, as he sees it, she has promised so much and has let him down. He can't let go of her completely of course, because when all's said and done she is half of what he wants."

119

"Can we rule him out of the investigation, do you think?"

"I would be inclined to, but there was one thing that I think we should be clear on before we do that – this business with Julie Vance. I think we've established that Ross's aggression is tied up with his relationship with his wife and we have no reason to suppose that he would be violent in other situations. But Julie Vance may provide us with some kind of connection. She was at the centre of his row with Stevens and she is also his wife's friend – the two threads may have somehow got tangled up with each other."

"We'd need to question her then. We'd have time to do that now, sir."

There would not be time for this before Stuart left for Belfast and it was awkward putting Myles off going on his own. If there was any mileage in this at all, it was likely that it would require very delicate handling and Myles, although promising, was still no more than a houseman. He also knew how keen Myles was to interview Evans, but that was now the major line of the investigation and required the presence of the senior man. The gun was an important key and urgently needed investigation. Hopefully, Devine had had time by now to get his head together and provide an interesting list of people who might have taken it. That was a line for Myles to pursue while he was away.

Chapter 12

Going back home was always a bruising experience for Stuart. The first encounter with the guttural vowels and the aggressive consonants of the Belfast voice left him with a sense of what-you-hear-is-what-you-get, the feeling that these are people who, a bit like the *Centre Pompidou*, are devoid of internal workings. He looked at the faces that went with the voices and imagined he knew everything about them. Belfast itself was the same. He had only noticed this after he had been to London. There he was still able to wander the streets and feel he was in a place which in some way belonged to an elite group of faceless city fathers with experiences and thoughts and feelings 'well beyond his ken'. It was the same feeling he used to have as a child in his home town, an impression that the city had a core dimension that was tantalisingly just beyond the reach of the kinds of people he knew. That feeling was now irretrievably gone. Now when he came home, Belfast seemed to him like a huge public property, something in the sole ownership of its population, a familiar network of streets and buildings that held nothing in reserve outside the coinage of the artless faces and voices of the most humdrum of its citizens. He remembered an old saying of his Uncle Davy: 'Better to be lord of the back entry than nobody in the main street'. But Stuart still hankered after the reassurance of the somethingness of the main street.

Heather was waiting at Aldergrove Airport. The sight of her reinforced the impression that her voice on the telephone had suggested, of a self-contained separateness. It came almost as a surprise to him when she threw her arms round him and hugged him warmly, almost passionately. But then she seemed to revert to self-containment. She spoke in sentences designed for the purpose of factual communication, syntactically insulated against any hint of pathos.

"We are staying with cousin Roy. There isn't enough room for us all at mum and dad's, so I volunteered to move out when Roy offered to put some of us up. I thought you'd be happy to keep away from Ruth."

"Where is the funeral?"

"It's at the crematorium tomorrow at 11.30. Connor is going to say a few words and I'm going to read a poem. Ruth insisted on a reading from the Bible and she wanted a hymn as well. Dad said she could have the reading, but he wouldn't hear of a hymn. He doesn't feel up to saying anything himself, but he has written a small piece and he has asked me to see if you would read it for him."

"Have you seen it?"

"No, he hasn't quite finished it yet. He'll give it to you tomorrow."

"What about the children?"

"Megan is arriving in the morning. She's due in at 10.00. I thought you could pick her up. As I expected, Gareth couldn't get away."

As they drove in the dark towards the lights of the city Stuart felt an increasing need for touch contact with this independent other half. It struck him, not for the first time, that when they were separated like this they were the best company in the world for each other. Despite this there was a natural urge to break down this separateness and escape the isolation which it preserved. Ironically however, the greatest depths of isolation invariably came whenever, having achieved this undisturbed oneness, they tried to cling on to it. There was something, quite literally, doubly unpleasant about isolation shared. What he was feeling now however was *un moment privilégié* in the dialectic, a rejuvenation of tension between oneness and twoness and a heightened awareness of the value of each.

Cousin Roy and his wife Bertha welcomed them on their arrival and offered them the intimacy of a cup of tea '*in their hand*'. The initial reaction of horror at the broad Belfast sounds was gradually being replaced, as happened every time, by a mild sense of irritation bordering on acceptance. It was as if the ear had finished its protest and the mind was at liberty to judge the substance of what was being said. Roy was a thoroughly decent man. He had worked hard and had provided well for his family. His home was a credit to his commitment to providing and to Bertha's dedication to maintaining. But Stuart had always found him difficult to talk to. He was one of those people who filled Stuart with the panic that there was nothing left to be said, that words were an unnecessary distraction from . . . and that was the problem. If he could fill in the gap, he would have something to talk to them about. As it was, car talk and holiday talk marked time before real conversation could be conjured. But it always turned out to be time spent *waiting for Godot*. Tonight was an exception. The funeral provided ample purposefulness to their conversation. Roy for once had a viewpoint to express on matters non-practical. He shared in Ruth's disappointment at the absence of a hymn and felt that Aunt Betty deserved better at her funeral service. Heather's reply that her mother had been a convinced atheist all her life, amazingly carried little weight. She was a good woman, God had obviously touched her life and she deserved a proper Christian burial. It was her deeds that mattered, not her mistaken views on religion. A hymn would have done no harm. Stuart resisted the temptation to challenge this well worn Ulster presumption.

Respect for the occasion was not the only reason why he said nothing. He had long ago lost his crusading zeal for atheism. During his time in England he had seen all too clearly the subversive effect of easy non-belief, how it melts away confidence in the whole sphere of the non-tangible. All very well for the clever intellectuals he himself had once sought to emulate, to pooh-pooh the simple notions of the masses. But what had they offered to counter the dying of the light as it got snuffed out in the long shadow of crass materialism? Why was it that the philosophically agile – always on the lookout for sophistication – could never come up with anything sophisticated to say in justification of the city fathers of ancient Athens for defending their citizenry against the subversive Socrates?

The following morning the delicious tension of separateness had given way to an intimacy that was still not so comfortable as to be unaware of itself. Breakfast, although taken on the hoof, was not totally lacking in the rituals of '*familiality*'. It was Bertha's car that Heather had driven to the airport the night before and it was in it that Stuart now set off to collect his daughter. He looked forward to seeing her. Megan was an *âme généreuse* who brought youthful optimism to almost everything that crossed her path. He wondered if she would have a cure for the funeral. The question reminded him of how, when he was a boy, he had a looked up to two or three special adults, who, he felt, could enrich the most mundane reality by their mere presence. There was one in particular, an angler friend of his father's, who had the magic knack of giving people and places a history or simply a story, which lifted them out of the stark isolation in which he, Stuart, had had them confined. It was like seeing a true artist's drawing of something that you yourself had spent hours failing to capture. Megan's magic worked in a different way, but it had the same life-giving effect.

He caught sight of her as she came out of the terminal building. His timing for once had been perfect. Her smile of recognition switched on her whole face. She bounced over to the car and got in. The clumsy business of car-bound continental greeting was thankfully reduced to a minimum; she simply found Stuart's cheek in the course of her smooth dive into the passenger seat.

"Are you practising for your own funeral, dad? It's not like you not to be late."

They talked about 'granny' and then about Oxford. She was full of her special project, *The Persecution of the French Huguenots with special reference to the Establishment of the Linen Industry in Ulster*.

"Granny would have been interested in it. Did you know that at the siege of La Rochelle where the Huguenots were being starved out by Richelieu's forces, they were about to surrender and were stopped only by the young men who insisted in going on fighting? It's just like the Apprentice Boys and the siege of Derry. The only thing is, when I went to La Rochelle, the guide showed us the table which one of the young men had stuck a dagger into to emphasise his point. He showed us the hole made by the dagger, but then pointed out that tables of that design were not around until at least a hundred years after the siege."

She bubbled on in this vein through the journey and through the coffee stop they made on their way to the crematorium, impatient with the slowness which words were imposing on her efforts to communicate. Oxford academic gave way in turn to Oxford sporting and Oxford social. A hockey Blue was a distinct possibility depending on the responsiveness of the captain's Achilles' tendon to rest and her own efforts to fit in the extra training to compete for a place on the team. Boys were mentioned mainly collectively. If however they were found worthy of individual mention, their surnames were supplanted by references to their most salient skills, knowledge or, failing both, places of birth – a kind of re-enactment of the '*surnaming*' process. Stuart felt himself lightened in this vacuum-bubble of vitality.

They drove through the city and reached the crematorium with about fifteen minutes to spare. There was a little coffee shop where the next shift of mourners could congregate while awaiting their half-hour slot. Heather's father, Archie, was the main focus of the sympathisers. As always, it amazed Stuart how free others seemed of embarrassment when uttering the normal banalities. It was only when his own parents had died that he came to appreciate that these did offer comfort. But any thought that that realisation would dispel his sense of his own hamfistedness had to be abandoned at the very next funeral he attended.

The service – it was not to be a service, but thinking of it anything else was a bit like thinking of football linesmen as assistant referees – began with an extract from a recording of a Chopin Etude. Ruth then read that well-known passage from Corinthians 1. She read it well, but it was in some new, updated version which sounded to Stuart like a long-wave broadcast with protracted bouts of crackly interference punctuated with short intervals of relieving clarity. He particularly loathed the jettisoning of the grand old word 'charity' in favour of 'love'. In his mind he could hear the *terribly-positive-about-life* intonation of some Church spokesperson calling up the dreaded *'fit for the twenty-first century'* line in justification.

He had had a few minutes to have a quick read over the little piece that Heather's dad had asked him to read. It was easy to decipher as it was written in the hand of an era that still respected the need for a norm. It briefly traced the main outlines of the story of their life together, their meeting at university, marriage, children and the shared journey through middle life to old age. It ended with the reflection that their togetherness had never been a cowering in the face of their aloneness; it had embraced their aloneness and given it its due.

Heather's younger brother, Connor came next to the podium to give a more detailed account of his mother's life. Betty had been the last of six children *'born and bred'* in the Shankill Road district of Belfast. This was a Protestant working-class area where political awareness did not stretch normally beyond militant resistance to Irish republicanism. Betty's father had been a master-moulder in the Belfast shipyard. He was not an educated man, but had read extensively and earned a reputation as someone who could write compelling letters of application or complaint to those in authority. Politically, he was a committed trade-unionist and socialist. Betty had inherited these qualities and attitudes from him. She won a scholarship to grammar school and then to university, a considerable achievement for a working-class girl of her generation. The only professions psychologically open to people of her background were teaching, medicine and the ministry; she chose to be a teacher. She combined this with an active interest in local politics. She worked hard for the Northern Ireland Labour Party and eventually won a seat on the Belfast city council where she served for many years.

Her main interest had been in education and she had taken great pride in the success of the Ulster schools in bringing so many children of similar background to her own through to university and the professions in the sixties and seventies. She believed fervently in the meritocratic principle, but her faith in the Labour Party was shattered when it introduced comprehensive education in England and later tried to impose it in Ulster. She saw this as a kind of inverted snobbery rather than the pursuance of a high ideal. Education had transformed her life, not just economically and socially, but spiritually and intellectually. She wanted as many youngsters as possible to have the same experience, but there had to be a meeting of the waters; the aptitude and ambition of the children should not be ignored. She wanted education to improve the entire person, but she increasingly saw it being reduced to a product of the consumer age, something adapted to the needs of *the customer* rather than as something informing the needs of the *spiritually underprivileged*. 'Spiritually underprivileged' was her expression; it was how she always described the state of present-day society as it fell further and further into the morass of capitalist consumerism.

In the end she became very disillusioned with what she saw as the betrayal of socialism by the *patronising behaviourists* – her words – who accepted the spiritual poverty of the people and settled for an alleviation of economic inequality. The struggle to improve material well-being she considered as a battle more or less won and of decreasing relevance in an age of economic prosperity. Indeed, she felt that modern socialists' fixation with it had added to the problems of the decent working class by fanning the flames of material greed and lending it respectability. For her the true socialist battle in modern western society was to create equal opportunity for all to lift themselves out of the terrible affliction of spiritual poverty. It was a source of particular sadness to her that the grammar school system in Ulster, which she held so dear, had come under so much threat; but she was philosophical and said that in any case it was already in the process of being destroyed from within by the small-mindedness of the ambitious self-promoters who saw compliance with the orthodoxy of mainland education policy as a way of advancing their own careers. She used to smile and say: *'The Lord will not forgive them for knowing not what they do'.* She liked the irony of that.

It was now Heather's turn. She reminded the mourners of her mother's great love for poetry and asked them to open the little order-of-service programme which had been supplied. It contained a poem which her mother had written and which, she thought, provided an insight into her mother's feelings towards the struggle which Connor had just described. She then read it in the hope, as she put it, of capturing the spirit of defiance which had taken her mother so far, but also the quiet sadness which she felt in her ultimate defeat. The poem was entitled *'Capitalist Picnic on Socialist Grounds'*.

> Crisp-white like chalk sticks crunched,
> With cracks on their varnish like on virgin ice,
> Springy, scent-sweating, taut, resilient,
> Cigarettes, paper bags, oranges,
> … awaiting.

'Take Your Litter Home'
Defiantly withstanding
The oncoming crowd with living to pursue,
Bearing itself bravely
To jag its meaning
Through.

Nicked, butted or burned out to ash,
Crumpled like shattered windscreens melted,
Frigid, frosted, wound down, ghostless,
– strewn.

A notice reclaiming –
Unsticking, unappealing,
Curled scroll-like above bespattered sods
On a bushwhacked totem
To yesterday's
Gods.

The proceedings ended with one of Connor's children playing
The Londonderry Air on the flute, too much of a clash, Stuart
thought, with the naked unsentimentality of Betty's poem.
Against that, it gave appropriate expression to her love of the
flute. She didn't play herself, but she enjoyed telling stories about
her father and her brothers preparing for the flute band world
championships held in Belfast every November. Stuart himself
remembered going to football matches as a boy and hearing the
band, often a flute band, at half-time. The stirring Sousa
marches he had heard then were his first step towards what
musical enlightenment he had managed to achieve.

They filed out of the chapel into a little reception area lined
with groups of wreaths, each set out as above a grave. This is
where Stuart remembered the dreaded line-up took place when
you queued up to offer your condolences to the chief mourners.
To his relief no line was formed; instead an unceremonious

intermingling took place. The little chapel had been full, with all the pews occupied and the side aisles three deep, just like in the old cinemas when a new film came to town. Outside, a pleasant morning beckoned, offering dappled sunlight under the copse of maples and beech trees in the garden which the austere reception area gave onto. Stuart was happy to lead the natural gravitation out towards the light.

Many of the faces were in varying degrees familiar to him, but they carried names which were mostly blurred or misted over in his memory. Even the ones with names that suggested themselves did not inspire enough confidence for him to try them out. He struggled to spare the faces that approached him the anonymity which, with his unresponsive memory, he threatened to inflict, when suddenly he caught sight of a profile that came with its name attached; it was Gareth, his son! But surely Gareth was in New York? The instinctive horror of facing his complete failure to register what had been going on, of having missed what everyone else had picked up on, kicked in ahead of the glow of pleasure at seeing his son. As he came up and hugged his father, Gareth wore an aren't-I-confusing-you grin which intensified and expanded into a now-I'll-put-you–out-of-your-misery smile. He did however pause to wait for the anticipated 'What are you doing here?' before offering medicinal support in the form of an explanation.

"I'm doing a bit of *mitching*, dad. The New York office sent me to advise some clients in Chicago. When mum phoned I didn't think I could get away. I knew if I asked they'd refuse. They're workaholics, the Americans. No self-respecting attorney would even think of asking for time off in the middle of an important consultation to attend his granny's funeral. So I just packed a bag and came."

"But won't you get into trouble?" It was instinctive for Stuart to try to chaperone Gareth's career.

"Only if I'm caught. The New York people think I'm in

Chicago and the Chicago people think I'm consulting with New York. I should be back before anyone is any the wiser. Granny was a bit of a special person. I owe her a lot and I certainly owed it to her to come to her funeral."

The wake was held in a nearby hotel. It was a sober affair, it being rather early in the day for widespread recourse to alcohol. Besides, funerals of long lives tend to produce a glow of quiet satisfaction in the mourners rather than the studied ignoring of the void that comes with lives cut short. Stuart could not monopolise his 'Yankee boy' and he strongly resented the imperative to mingle in gatherings, leading, as it inevitably did, to the repetition *ad infinitum* of the same biographical updates. Catching his brother-in-law Connor's eye, he moved over to the small group that had formed in front of the French windows, engaged in a conversation that in its intensity suggested something more than the exchange of factual particulars. As Stuart moved over to the group Connor was in full flow.

"Gloss and floss! That's why we can't get into the Home Counties. You look at the kind of books that are being produced for English schools and you'll see lots of high definition photography, wonderful graphics, the best quality paper, trendy captions – need I go on? What you'll not find is clear syntax, well reasoned explanations, logical sequencing. They're more like teenage magazines than school books."

The talk was obviously picking up the thread of Connor's oration at the crematorium. Connor had followed his mother into teaching, but after a few years had moved into educational publishing, forming a small company which relied on local teachers to provide low-cost textbooks for the home market in both parts of Ireland. The company had later expanded and set up production units in Africa and India.

"But isn't it just a question of moving with the times? Modern teenagers are used to the gloss and floss as you call it, just like they're used to central heating," ventured the bravest of the souls in the group. Emboldened by the revelation of the possibility of resistance, a second joined in on the rhythm of dissent.

"That's just what the early church did. The early Christians knew they had to accommodate themselves to the pagan practices of the time. They built their churches in places that were already considered holy and used all sorts of pagan symbols in their worship. In fact I think that's why we have Christmas when we do. It really ought to be 1st January, if you think about it."

""You're missing the point, John. You're talking about style as if it were nothing more than decoration. Style and substance are joined at the hip; you can't change one without changing the other. What these people are doing with their fancy gimmicks is undermining the whole business of education. They're turning it into a breakfast television show. Fill the screen with beautiful people, keep things on the move, don't let the eye get bored, lots of chat but not too much serious stuff, we don't want to overtax our viewers. Sorry, change that – we don't want to tax our viewers. The main thing seems to be to give the pupils the impression that they've understood things, whether they've understood them or not. This builds up their self-confidence, we're told. And that's apparently what matters. What it actually does of course is create a culture of arrogance. Anything that cannot be grasped instantly and without effort is dismissed as boring and not worth understanding. It's a grotesque distortion of the humanist ideal – 'Man is the measure of all things'. It's more like 'Baby is the measure of all things'."

"Your mother will never be dead while you're alive, Connor," said the only woman in the group. "Your speech at the crematorium was right on the button. No-one believed in education more than your mother did and no-one was ever more disillusioned. She told me not long before she died that socialism wasn't worth a spit once it turned its back on education.

Another thing she said that struck me. 'True education,' she said, 'treats patients, what passes for education nowadays deals with customers.' For her, modern education had sold out and become another tentacle of capitalist consumerism."

Connor smiled. He obviously heard the voice of his mother in the words.

"It's sad, isn't it, that we can sell our textbooks to the children of the third world, but they are rejected on behalf of the underprivileged of this country as too demanding and too unrelated to the culture they are coming from? That tells us a thing or two about where they are going, wouldn't you say?"

The dissident voices were constrained to silence. Connor's case might be challenged, but not the feelings of the woman to whom they had all come to pay their respects. The subject needed changing. Stuart, whose entry into the group had been merely eyed in acknowledgement, was now seized upon.

"You and Betty used to have some humdingers of arguments, Stuart. Do you all remember? They'd last for hours. And she loved every minute. She really missed you, you know, Stuart, when you and Heather went to England."

Stuart recognized the official version of relations between them. He and his mother-in-law had certainly enjoyed their ideological battles, but there had been collateral damage. When Stuart had decided to join the police he had insisted on moving to England. Betty was appalled at that; she wanted him to join the RUC and help in the fight against terrorism. But Stuart had seen too many RUC officers being used as a political convenience. They were the front line in the confrontation with the paramilitaries that threatened ordinary civilized living. Ordinary people looked to them to preserve their everyday safety – and that included, when it came to the crunch, many who were ideologically opposed to the very existence of the force. But every time a situation threatened awkward political fallout, individual officers were thrown to the wolves. Stuart would not be used in this way. Betty got very angry with him and even accused him of cowardice. This caused a major family rift, for Heather was present when it was said. Gradually familial relations were patched together again, but bygones are never just bygones and Stuart and Betty never got back enough confidence in the other's opinion of them to expose their minds to the other's scrutiny. Betty had no doubt been upset at the prospect of losing her daughter to *across-the-water*, perhaps even of losing him. This had certainly played a part in the vehemence with which she had opposed his decision.

"I missed her too. She was good fun. I remember her telling me once that governments who form *policy* without asking '*y*' are bound to end up with a *police* state. We argued about that of course."

Not everyone got the play on words but there was general approval that some kind of swipe had been taken at '*right-wingism*'.

The wake lasted for a couple of hours. When it broke up, the inner circle of the family went with Heather's father Archie to a restaurant in the university area and had an early dinner. There was family business to be done; Archie was showing the first signs of dementia and arrangements had to be made for him. It was agreed that Heather would stay on for another week or so and she and Connor and Ruth would sound out the nursing homes. There is a period in the life of a gathering that seems to demand communal conversation. This of course requires a main focus, and on this occasion it was on Gareth. No-one was very sure how, apart from relieving clients of their money, a lawyer performed 'financial services', the branch of law Gareth special-ized in. New York came under scrutiny and provoked a few anecdotes about heat and taxis and the vandalism of vowels. Megan entertained everyone with the latest variations on the theme of how the French *sensibilitiés* had come to be *offensées* by the barbarism of the *monde Anglo-Saxon* at its most Anglo, or was it at its most Saxon? Gareth added that there were things that the Europeans knew they didn't know about America, but there were also things they didn't know that they didn't know and that was the source of their arrogance. This led to speculation on the nature of the relationship between the two continents. Gareth thought it was as between a grown-up son and his aged parents; the parents can't get used either to the fact that the son has grown up or to the fact that they have lost their spark. Connor saw an analogy here with Ireland and England, but Gareth flatly refused to accept that Ireland had grown up. Heather came in to referee, suggesting that they both had a point; Connor was talking education and Gareth was talking national identity.

This conviviality extended through the starters, but the main course demanded focused application of knives and forks and so lent itself more to private exchanges to the left or the right. It was Ruth who began the exodus. She and her husband Richard had not taken part in the exchanges, whether out of disinclination or disapproval was not clear. Stuart in any case welcomed the transition. He had been careful to position himself between his two children; he wanted to confront his niggling concern over Gareth's truancy.

"It really isn't a problem, dad. You worry too much. I'm getting the first plane to London in the morning. That'll allow me to take the 8.40 am flight to Chicago. The flight to Chicago takes about eight hours, but I'll gain six hours, which means I'll be in Chicago by about 11.00 am local time. A taxi from O'Hare and I'll be in the office in good time for my lunchtime meeting. No-one will have any idea I was out of the country."

It all sounded so straightforward. Stuart knew he had a blank when it came to modern travel. He had grown up with the long, tedious journeys to France when he was a student. The Liverpool boat leaving Belfast at 8.00 pm, ten hours hard sit, arrive Liverpool just after dawn, train to London, day hanging about waiting for student boat train, Channel-crossing at midnight, finally – the *coup de grâce* – twelve hours on the train to the south of France. You arrive exhausted, with your French buried in your subconscious, resisting all your attempts to prise it out. *Que le monde a changé!* He was re-assured. He could take his son's career off his worry list.

They left the restaurant towards seven and headed back to the parental, now reduced to the paternal, home. Stuart wondered how much its magnetism would now be reduced. He suddenly got an insight into something he had learned at school and which he could never quite see, the notion that gravity can distort everything, even light, which crosses its path. The parental home is like that; it sucks all the streets around it into a kind of whirlpool in its orbit and even shapes the orientation of places well beyond its direct draw. His own parents' house, still standing but occupied now by strangers, retained even yet, some years after their death, much of the pull of former years and he could not walk down adjacent streets without getting the feeling that he was not where he was, but nearly where he should be. Farewells, both formal and felt, were made before Heather and he got into the car and drove to the airport. A quick hug, one which whispered rather than declaimed that each would be missed, was exchanged at the car boot and Stuart betook himself and his little bag to the checkout, conscious that he might be registering in Heather's mind an image of the forlornness that he felt. The whiskey he ordered on the plane did nothing to alleviate the erosive feeling he had of being in the process of leaving rather than arriving.

Chapter 13

"I spoke to Kennedy yesterday."

Stuart had barely had time to exchange even the facial expressions of greeting. Myles obviously considered his news important enough to interrupt the normal schedule of civilities. Stuart liked the normal schedule of civilities and refused to lob him the anticipated question to have him smash back the answer. Myles would have to generate his own pace.

"He didn't see his attacker, but he did remember spotting a motor bike leaning against a tree at the side of the lane just before he was shot. He couldn't tell me anything about the bike. He only caught a glimpse of it and anyway he wouldn't know one motor bike from the next. They're not his kind of thing."

"You didn't mention the business of Richardson's Development, I hope?"

"No, sir. The doctors only allowed me a few minutes. He's still very weak. It'll be a day or two before he's up to a proper interrogation. I couldn't read anything from his body language either. It was hard to say whether he was wary of me or not."

"You did ask him, I suppose, if he knew of anyone who might want him dead?"

"Yes, I didn't think that would do any harm. He said what I thought he'd say – a headmaster treads on many toes, but hardly enough to get himself murdered."

Stuart felt vaguely cheated by Myles' boyish enthusiasm. There wasn't anything new or revealing here, certainly no reason to interrupt normal programming. His usual sense of having shown inadequate appreciation did not surface when he changed the subject.

"What about Devine's list? Anything there?"

Myles was oblivious to the dismissive implication of the *'there'* in Stuart's question. He was not to be put off his zestful reporting.

"He remembered mentioning the pistol in the common room once when a story hit the headlines about a Nazi war criminal who had been discovered in France. He wasn't sure just when that was, but I later checked on the internet and it was about six months before Stevens was killed. He couldn't remember everyone who was in the common room at the time, but he did say that Ross and Evans were certainly there. He also suggested that Greenfield might have mentioned the pistol to the Thinkers' Club. I checked with Greenfield and he confirmed that he had. That would have been about the same time, for again it was the arrest of the war criminal that had sparked the discussion."

"And what about visitors to the house?"

"Greenfield obviously, several times. Ross once or twice. Evans did call in once, but it was only to collect an entry form for an exam which needed to be sent urgently to the exams' office. There was a meeting of the Thinkers' Club held in the house. Devine couldn't remember exactly which pupils were there, but Greenfield gave me a list of all who attended."

"Did it include the redoubtable Snoddy?"

"Yes, it would have been just a week or two before he was expelled."

"You know, I've been thinking about our friend Snoddy. When I was back in Ireland, my son made a surprise visit home for the funeral. As far as his bosses were concerned he was in Chicago and he said that no one would be any the wiser when he got back. It occurred to me that maybe we have been taking too much for granted about our friend's absence in Germany. What checks did you make that he was where he said he he said he was? Can we be sure he didn't sneak back home and kill Stevens?"

"We checked with Interpol. They sent someone to the farm where he was working and interviewed him and the farm manager. There was no doubt he was working there."

"What about the actual time of the murder?"

"I'd need to check, but I think he said he was ill that particular weekend."

Myles went to his desk and produced a very neatly handwritten file which he consulted with an unhurried confidence.

"Yes, here it is. He was lodged in a big barn house – he was the only casual worker and hence the only resident at the time. His meals were supplied by a cook employed by the estate. She had no direct contact with him, she merely left his meals for him in the dining area and collected the dishes later, but she was able to confirm that he had eaten all the food she had left. He reported for work as usual on the Monday morning. It looks pretty convincing, doesn't it?"

"Yes, except that he wasn't actually seen by anyone. I think we'll take a closer look at Mr Snoddy, but first I'm going to let you loose on Evans. He's still our best bet."

Myles's face, which had been bright throughout this exchange, now passed from winter sunshine to summer radiance. The mood was taken up by the pellucid haziness of the autumn morning as they made their way to St Jude's. A few lines of Goethe, which Stuart had been required to learn for his A level German, emerged from the scrap heap of the long-forgotten:

> *Wie herrlich leuchtet mir die Natur,*
> *Wie glänzt die Sonne,*
> *Wie lacht die Flur . . .*

The recollection of the lines took him a little by surprise. Memories pulled him in – of the German lessons in the little store room, of Mrs Skingles with her treasured *Sprachgefühl*, of the girls in his

139

class, Sally and Laura – he had gone out with Sally, but Laura had a boy friend with a sports car. That the past is on constant stand-by in the present was not a revelation to him, but the vital immediacy that envelopes it never failed to bewitch. When they arrived at the school grounds he felt a strong disinclination to get out and deal with the demands of the here-and-now; he would much sooner have lingered longer in the weightlessness of this limbo between the now and the lost-and-gone.

They were shown into what was growing into Mrs Swanson's office by the motherly Mrs Abernethy. There were definite signs of owner-occupation, the little family photo on the desk, the fig plant by the window, but most of all the welcoming hospitality in Mrs Swanson's voice.

"I've heard the good news, gentlemen. Isn't it wonderful? The doctors say that Michael should make a full recovery."

Stuart's unworthy gremlins of scepticism took another look at the fig plant and the family photo before he could order them back up to their dark attic.

"Yes. Myles here has been to see him. I was away in Ireland, but I hope to get to the hospital some time to-day. I see you've settled in."

"Yes. Needs must. I've managed to find someone to take over my classes. It's not really possible to run a school and teach at the same time. The paper work is, as they say at all the best interviews, 'challenging.'"

"I can imagine. My brother-in-law always says that if teachers stopped ticking boxes and started boxing ears education would be in a healthier state."

Mrs Swanson's face instantly told him that he had said the wrong thing, but just as instantly it re-adjusted and resumed its normal expression of benevolent tolerance.

"What can we do for you to-day, Inspector?"

"We would like to interview Mr Evans. There are a couple of points we'd like to clear up with him."

140

Mrs Swanson consulted the computer screen on her desk after a few clearly knowledgeable digital movements.

"I'm afraid he's teaching at the moment, Inspector. Could it wait until break?"

Stuart had the distinct impression that he was sailing towards the shallower waters of Mrs Swanson's good manners. He was certainly in that area where sincerity becomes suspect and doubt casts ripples over the bright smiles.

"I'm sorry, but I must insist. DS Myles and I have a very busy day ahead of us and we can't hang around waiting for Mr Evans."

He had never been good at navigating in the shallows of politeness; he was always quick to run aground. Mrs Swanson smoke-screened her umbrage in efficiency.

"It will take me a moment or two to arrange cover for Mr Evans, Inspector. Mrs Abernethy will show you to B13 where you can conduct your interview. If we can be of help in any other way, please let me know."

It was with a sense of banishment that Stuart awaited Evans' arrival. Myles seemed unaffected. Stuart was not sure if his insensitivity was a function of his nature or simply of the man-with-an-agenda mode in which he was currently running. The efficiency mode which Mrs Swanson had adopted proved itself more than the first refuge of the offended, when, after less than the briefest of exchanges between the sergeant and the inspector, Evans appeared at the door. He was dressed as before in an obviously expensive, navy pin-striped suit with the cuffs of his shirt showing the prerequisite half-inch of plain white – all the appearance of a man deigning to be in charge of the school. Generous restraint in the face of provocation from obtrusive bunglers was, it seemed, to be the pose of the day. The minion Myles was studiously ignored.

"I suppose you have your reasons for interrupting my class, Inspector. The little blighters quickly lose the thread, you know."

"I'm afraid we do, Mr Evans. We would like you to tell us about your dealings with a company known as Richardson's Development."

Evans visibly flinched. For a brief moment the unpolished version of the man bared itself from behind the man-above-school persona which graced St Jude's. The voice however quickly rescued the persona. It was a voice that gave every word its due and in return seemed to pass on the charge to the listener.

"Richardson's Development is a company which I consulted when preparing my report for the Board on the possible reconstruction of the school. If you have read my report, Inspector Stranaghan, as no doubt you have, you will have seen reference to it."

"We did read the report, Mr Evans, but we could find no reference to payments made to you by the company. Would that be because you didn't want to burden the Board with unnecessary detail?"

Myles the Minion had leapt with obvious relish from his anonymity. There was a momentary re-appearance of the unpolished Evans, the Evans that had gone to bed or eaten his greens when his mother had told him to. The voice speeded up to cover up, but the words, now being given less than their due, lost something of their former imperious authority.

"That's business, Inspector." – *Myles remained unaddressed* – "I would have thought that you would have enough experience of the world to realise that that's the sort of thing that goes on all the time." Then, a more stately speed restored, he added, "Enlightened self-interest is the lubricant of public affairs. You should know that, Inspector Stranaghan."

"The question is: should the Board know it?" *Myles had taken over.*

The question finally won recognition for the speaker. Evans turned towards Myles and addressed him for the first time.

"Worms come best in unopened cans, Sergeant. I think

you'll find that the Board will be more than happy to let sleeping worms lie, if you will excuse me the mixed metaphor." Evans' confidence was now feeding freely off his words. But Myles was not to be outdone.

"Was Mr Kennedy one of the worms?" Stuart would dearly have liked to have added 'a worm that turned', but his sergeant was doing fine.

"What exactly do you mean by that, Sergeant?" Evans' words had again forsaken spin for pace.

"Mr Kennedy became aware of your little deal with Richardson's and decided to get in on the act. You didn't like that and so you decided to get rid of him, just as you had got rid of Dr Stevens when he wouldn't play ball."

Evans looked at Myles with an expression that to the credulous observer bespoke outraged bewilderment, but which the sceptic might just as reasonably interpret as unearthed guilt. There was a long pause before an answer came, and it came at first very hesitantly with each word spaced in its own little cameo. One had the impression that this attention was now less a reflection of the pride of the wordsmith than an awakened awareness of the necessity for wary treading.

"Mr Kennedy and I have had serious disagreements over our roles in this matter. He took the view that I should play a smaller part in promoting the development. I considered that unacceptable, given that I had been the prime mover in the affair. It's the kind of dispute that arises every day in the world of business. To suggest that I tried to kill the man is utterly absurd. First of all, I was nowhere near the scene of the crime and secondly, what would I have had to gain from his death? I am not an emotional person and I am not given to acts of unreason. As to Stevens, we went through all that last time. Stevens was a social worker, one of those people who pontificate about how best to spend the money other people have made. The Board would eventually have come round to seeing that and would have been ready to take on some of my ideas. Given that I was not appointed myself, I couldn't have wished for anyone more suitable than Stevens. They were not going to appoint me after what had happened between me and Stevens, so why, I ask you, would it have been in my interests to try to kill the man who replaced him?"

The answer had covered too much ground and Myles struggled to select the best thread to pick up on. Stuart intervened.

"You say you're not an emotional man, Mr Evans. Would you not count anger among the emotions that visit themselves upon you?"

"Anger is something which I try to avoid, Inspector. It is a relic of an era when physicality played the major part in survival."

"Trying to avoid it is not the same as being free of it. We have evidence of you being in a temper on more than one occasion, Mr Evans, quite a violent temper at that, from what we have been told."

"I do not lose my temper, Inspector, I use my temper. Kennedy is a coward at heart. If I can put enough fear in him, he will take the line of least resistance and bring me on board. That particular tactic loses its effectiveness somewhat, don't you think, if I give my anger full rein and kill him."

"And what about Mr Davidson? Why did you burst into his office and give such a convincing performance of an angry man?"

"You are very slow, Inspector. It would not be in my interests to 'lift the lid' on the Richardson's deal. Davidson knows that. But if I can persuade him that I am likely to act in an irrational manner, then I pose a real threat. The problem with a world governed by the principle of rationality is that everyone becomes predictable. One pawn is the same as another, the only difference between them – and it is the vital difference – being their position on the board. My position in the present game is not a strong one, so I stopped being a pawn. There you have it, Inspector."

It was Myles' turn to rescue Stuart.

"What can you tell us about Language Services, Mr Evans?"

"That's a company that hires the school premises every summer to run language courses for foreigners. I am sure you have already found out that they paid me a small fee to look after their interests."

"Do you think it's quite ethical for you to be taking a fee from a company when you should be representing the interests of your employer?"

"If there had been a conflict of interest, you would have had a point, but there was no such conflict, and if the company choses to offer me a modest consideration it would have been rather silly of me to turn it down, don't you think? As I'm sure you are aware, schoolmasters are not overpaid."

"Are you sure there was no conflict of interest? The Bursar seemed to think that the school could have done better elsewhere."

"That's something you should to take up with our esteemed headmaster. I washed my hands of the whole business last year."

"You mean Kennedy got into the act and left you out in the cold as he did with the Richardson's business? Kennedy is a real thorn in your flesh, isn't he, Mr Evans?"

"Do I have to go through this all over again, gentlemen? I have already explained my strategy in regard to Kennedy. What applied to Richardson's also applies to the language people. Now, if you've nothing else to ask me, I propose to return to my class and thread some strands of reasoning through very little minds."

It was time for Stuart to step back in.

"You do realise, Mr Evans, that the Board is likely to become aware of your activities and is not likely to react very favourably?"

"By '*your*' I assume you mean '*my and Mr Kennedy's*', Inspector? I look forward to a bitter-sweet experience. Good day, gentlemen."

"Just one question before you return to your call from the wild, Mr Evans – do you possess a motor cycle?"

That would have been too perfect an exit for Stuart to grant to Evans.

"What a quaint old word, Inspector. Your next question, – let me guess – is going to be: 'Am I the proud owner of a scarf and goggles?' As a matter of fact I do, that is to say I plead guilty to ownership of the motor cycle, alas not of the scarf and goggles. I do in fact own a bike. It's a Harley."

"Have you ever used it on Whinny Walk?"

"No, Inspector. You don't buy a Harley-Davidson to drive it along lanes like Whinny Walk. It's for the open road when you need to fly and get cleansed of the tiresome small-mindedness that you are forced to put up with in places like this. But I don't suppose you'd understand that, Inspector."

"Perhaps I do, but then there's another way of getting free of small-mindedness, isn't there, Mr Evans? – get rid of the small minds."

"Your own mind seems to go round in ever decreasing circles, Inspector. If it's not careful, it will end up swallowing itself down its own plughole. I'm sorry, but I really must insist on returning to the small minds back in my classroom. Their parents have after all paid for their implants."

This exit was not to be sabotaged. Evans strode out of the little cupboard-room as out of a restricted mind-set. Stuart was left with the uncomfortable image of Myles and himself having being abandoned to the mercies of the looming plughole.

"What do you think should be our next step, sir?"

"We need to get Kennedy's angle on Evans. Then maybe something will turn up. At the moment I can't see how we can press Evans any further unless we come up with something new. His answers were clever and, I have to say, fairly persuasive. I'm not at all convinced he's our man."

Myles' disappointment was spread like a paralysis over his face. "But surely he must have done it, sir. Who else has a motive like his? Apart from Evans, all we have come up with is petty squabbles, the kind of things that happen every day in workplaces all over the country. It's all very trivial stuff. But Evans..., if he had pulled off the deal with Richardson's, he stood to make a fortune. Stevens got in the way. So Stevens had to be got out of the way. Then Kennedy came along and tried to take over his operations and squeeze him out. He says he's not emotional, but surely that works two ways. He's certainly not a man to let any feelings of decency or conscience hold him back if he thought that someone needed to be dealt with. He might even see it as punishment. And he is such a superior type that I wouldn't mind betting he thinks he has every right to punish anyone that gets in his way."

Stuart was impressed by the smoothness of Myles' reasoning but yet he felt it was somehow not engaging the gears. As was usual with Stuart when his instincts dominated, he started to soliloquise. He had but the vaguest of notions where his words were going; there was only the unclear hope that at some point, without getting prior permission from the brain, feeling would engage with them. If and when this happened, the brain would get to take over again – a bit like the turbo in a car.

"What you say makes sense only if you assume that Evans operates at a moral level. It's ironic, but it boils down to the fact that it's only if he has some sense of morality that he is likely to have committed the crime. If, on the other hand, as I suspect, he is completely devoid of moral awareness, his actions will be dictated by either passion or rational calculation. The two crimes were well thought out – they were clearly not the result of a sudden explosion anger or frustration. Anyone – even the coldest of fish – can be swept along by emotional irrationality, but given the time scale required for the planning of the two crimes, I wouldn't give Evans' emotions a cat in hell's chance of carrying the day over his highly developed enlightened self-interestedness. Personally, I found the explanation he offered for his shows of anger very convincing. Of course he was exaggerating – I'm sure he felt the anger and the frustration very keenly – but they were not in charge of him, they had been press-ganged along with everything else by 'Evans' Promotions'. And 'Evans' Promotions' did not stand to gain anything by the death of either man. No, I am inclined to think that we're going nowhere with this. Don't worry though, Myles; I'm not closing my mind to it. Let's wait and see what Kennedy has to say for himself."

Chapter 14

Myles went back to the station and Stuart waited the few minutes until the morning break to have a word with Greenfield. He needed of course to be 'told' about the circumstances surrounding the expulsion of Snoddy, but he had other questions he wanted to ask Greenfield. The whole Snoddy business had received far too little attention from the first investigation. This was understandable given that Snoddy was out of the country, but if for any reason that proved an unreliable 'given', he would have to be re-considered for prime suspect status. There was also of course the second difficulty of relating him to the attempt on Kennedy's life. He had left school before Kennedy's arrival on the scene and there was nothing to suggest that the two had had any contact with each other. Nevertheless, Stuart's instinct told him that there was too much darkness in this area and it was time to seek some light.

Stuart managed to catch Greenfield just as the bell was ringing and the haemorrhage of bodies from the classrooms began. Coffee did not need to be abandoned; Greenfield had a free period immediately after break and they could go to the *alternative* staffroom which was not used at break-time.

"I want you to tell me about Robert Snoddy's expulsion," Stuart began. "I understand you were less than frank with my predecessor on that score."

"I saw no reason to drag the nasty business out into the public demesne. Robert is a young man; he has his whole future in front of him. What purpose would it have served if he had been publicly accused of sexual assault? In any case, that Sloane woman was a lying bitch. I don't believe for a moment Robert did anything improper."

"But that wasn't your judgement to make, Dr Greenfield. It was up to Superintendent Winkworth to decide what was to be done with the information. Do you realise the position you have put my sergeant in? He could lose his job if it became known that he had withheld information from his superior officer."

"I realise that, Inspector Stranaghan, but I don't think there's much danger of it coming to light. I certainly have no intention of telling on him, do you?"

"Okay, Dr Greenfield, but this is the second time you've failed to provide me with information that was clearly relevant to the case. I have no wish to throw my weight about, but I must warn you that that I will not tolerate this a third time."

"I assure you, Inspector, I have no more dark secrets to hide from you. Please accept my sincere apologies and my assurance that I have every confidence in your good sense and judgement. I feel assured that any confidences I might have made would be safe in your keeping. *Pax nobiscum.* What do you say?"

Greenfield offered his hand and Stuart clasped it. He wondered at his own lack of doubt in the sincerity of this man who had twice been ungenerous in his dealings with him. It did cross his mind however to ask himself whether wonder at this lack of doubt did not itself constitute doubt, and then he realised that the man's presence was the decisive factor: it demanded belief.

"You say you think Miss Sloane was lying. What makes you think that?"

"Two reasons. One: Robert told me he didn't lay a finger on her. Two: she has all the vindictiveness of the weak. Have you noticed, Inspector, how the miserable of this earth always demand the righting of their wrongs on a scale that would do honour to the gods. It's the reverse of the principle of *noblesse oblige*. How about *faiblesse exige*? It should be emblazoned over the portals of all the DHSS temples to our wonderful state-funded dependency culture."

"How did Robert explain the incident then?"

"He told me that she had been insulting towards his father and that he had got angry with her and had been verbally abusive. She had become hysterical and he had tried to restrain her when she started throwing things at him. This accounted for the bruises on her arms which she later produced as evidence of his attempt to rape her."

"When had all this happened?"

"It was at her flat. She had asked him there to discuss a literary essay he had written. She was one of his English teachers."

"And how did Dr Stevens react to the allegations?"

"Poor old Stevens. He didn't know what to do, poor man. He was programmed to sniff out victimhood and embalm it in oils of political correctitude. But what was he to do in this instance? It was like in ancient tragedy with the clash of good with good, only here it was victimhood clashing with victimhood. On the one side you had the damsel in distress, wronged by a youth of doubtful character, on the other the boy from the deprived working-class making good despite the stultifying pressures of American-inspired capitalism. How could he do his knight-in-shining-armour-thing while at the same time remaining true to his oath of allegiance as a Guardian reader? I think he made a pretty good fist of it, actually. He managed to locate his *via media*. Tragedy is an alien concept to true liberals, you see, Inspector; they always believe that a table can be found to sit around and 'thrash out' a solution – you'll forgive the implied violence of the metaphor. Stevens did just that. He supported the damsel Sloane by expelling Robert and he supported the pawn of capitalist exploitation by trivialising the charge and imposing a non-punishment – Robert was due to leave school in a few weeks in any case. He turned the whole affair into a triumph for the liberal thesis that original sin belongs in the primeval garden and should not be served up at the dinner-party table."

"But surely he did handle the situation well. I can't see why you are being so critical of him."

"Why I am being critical of him, Inspector, – and you being a policeman, I would have thought you would have spotted this – is that he made no effort whatsoever to establish the truth of the matter. He uncritically took Sloane's word for it that Robert had attempted to rape her. It never seemed to occur to him that she could be lying and that Robert was telling the truth. And the reason for that, Inspector, is that his primary concern was ideological. What for him needed redressing was not an injustice, but an imbalance in the situation which threatened to propel him into a response which would offend his sense of his own liberalism. In a sense he did not truly believe Sloane's account of what had happened. Don't misunderstand me – he did not disbelieve it, but it was not a reality for him, it was merely an inconvenient piece of information that could not be ignored, something which needed to be 'processed' without upsetting his sanity as a right-thinking man. You as an Ulsterman should be very familiar with the notion. How often have we all heard the mantra being trotted out, 'Nothing must be allowed to upset the 'peace process.''? What we are dealing with here – and I suspect it wasn't very different in Ulster – is the 'peace-of-mind process.'"

What Greenfield was saying had a resonance of familiarity for Stuart. He had indeed frequently been disgusted by the doings of 'reasonableness' in Irish politics and its insouciance of truth. It always came over to him as fear in pursuit of respectability.

"And Snoddy was happy to go along with this? I haven't met him yet, but from what I've heard about him, I would have imagined he would have dug his heels in."

"That's exactly what he did do at first. He came to me once Stevens had put the plan to him, and raged and raged. I sympathized with him, but pointed out the practicalities of the situation. Stevens was never going to challenge his number one victim, and if it came to a court case, Robert would be the loser whether he won the case or not. I gave a great performance as the wise counsellor, but I didn't really believe in what I was telling him, I was just saying the things that my image of a wise old man would have said. If I had been in his shoes, I hope I would have taken the bitch on, but I hadn't the courage to take the responsibility of advising him to do it. I kept thinking of Miss Jean Brodie. In a way I was just as bad as Stevens. Anyway, he resisted all attempts from me and his father – his father tried as hard as I did – to calm him down, and then all of a sudden and for no apparent reason he changed his mind and agreed to Stevens' proposal. I arranged a job for him with one of my contacts in the Black Forest and he left about a week later."

"How did he seem after the change of mind?"

"He was very calm ... no, that's not the word ... he was intent. I must say, his reaction puzzled me. I took it as a sign that he was summoning up a great strength of will to accept something that he found totally outrageous. He had one A level exam to complete before he left for Germany. Stevens would not have him in the school, but he arranged for him to take the exam at Belvoir College."

"Did you have much contact with him while he was in Germany?"

"We corresponded by letter. And before you ask, Inspector, I'm not prepared to let you see his letters unless you force my hand and produce a warrant. He did, however, send me a short story he had written which he was intending to enter in a competition for young unpublished writers. The story in fact won second prize. I have a copy which I can let you have, if you like. I think you'll find it interesting. Apart from its literary merit, it will give you an insight into his *take* on reality."

Greenfield dug in a drawer of an old battered desk that supported piles of papers and coffee-ringed notebooks, and handed Stuart a small volume with a white glossy cover.

"What happened to Miss Sloane?"

"The dear Miss Sloane departed the school almost immediately aftewards. It was just a few weeks before the end of term. I must confess I took no interest in the fate of that particular lady. But no doubt the school has a record of where she took her talents to, should you wish to make contact with her."

"You accused Stevens of not even considering the possibility of Snoddy's innocence. Aren't you just as guilty of the same charge as far as Miss Sloane is concerned?"

"Not quite, Inspector. I made it my business to make some inquiries and I discovered that the damsel made something of a habit of being in distress. She was an undergraduate at Bristol where I have an old friend in the English department. He informed me that there had been a very similar incident involving Miss Sloane and one of their PhD students. The accusation was less serious – she only accused him of pinching her bottom and harassing her with a series of improper suggestions – but in the present climate of so-called political correctness it was nearly enough to have him sent down. Fortunately, my friend and a couple of his colleagues persuaded her to withdraw the charge and there the matter rested. You see what I mean, Inspector – Stevens could have found this out, if he had taken the trouble to make a few inquiries."

"If you knew this, why did you not tell Stevens and clear the whole matter up?"

"I only found out after Robert had been expelled and it was too late to make any difference. But I did tell Stevens. He was unimpressed. He said it proved nothing; there was no reason why Miss Sloane shouldn't have been a victim of sexual assault more than once. Logically, he was right of course, but it shifted the balance of probabilities in Robert's favour. Stevens didn't do probabilities, at least not after he had come up with what he considered a beautiful response, even though it might have been a response to the wrong problem.

"Have you noticed, Inspector, how easily people confuse methods and purposes? Politics has become an arena for purpose promotion. Politicians are judged for their good intentions, not for the methods they have come up with to achieve these worthy aims. Political astuteness nowadays consists in reading the signs of a politician's sincerity: can we trust a man who has an affair with his secretary? – did you notice something in the way he smiles or in the tone of his voice that makes you wary? Any sign of negativity is death on a political career, except of course if directed against paedophiles or racists, because good intentions are positive things that show the hand of an *âme généreuse*. It never ceases to amaze me how our politicians can get away with the crassest incompetence in the running of the country, but one minor infringement against the law of good intentions and they're out."

Stuart's nod of recognition was all the encouragement Greenfield needed to continue.

"Methods are like bastard sons in former ages; they are set up well in life but are never acknowledged for what they are. They are their own thing and are to be judged accordingly. If there is anything of beauty perceived in a method – and fashion is the arbiter in such matters – it is hailed not only as a good method, but more often than not it acquires the sole rights to methodhood. There is a kind of franchise in these things. Any criticism of its efficacy is considered at best irrelevant, at worst indicative of a broken down *Weltanschauung*. We poor souls in the world of education suffer more than most from this cult of method-sanctification. Sorry ... I'm getting carried away. To get back to your question, Inspector, Stevens was inclined to regard reality as a nasty inconvenience that it was best to ignore. It posed too much of a threat to his good intentions and too strong a challenge to his lovely methods."

When he finally left Greenfield to his pile of papers, Stuart headed straight to Mrs Abernethy's office. He found her in her usual good spirits at the keyboard of her computer which she always seemed to be feeding as one would a pet dog on its hind legs.

"I need some information on a Miss Sloane who taught here a couple of years ago. What can your magic computer tell me about her?"

"Oh, I remember her well, Inspector Stranaghan. She left to take some time out. She said she was going to see the world. It was just after Dr Stevens' accident ... no, not accident, you know what I mean. I'm afraid we would only have her details from two years ago. We wouldn't have anything more recent."

"That'll be fine, Mrs Abernethy. Actually I'm just as interested to know what the lady behind the computer can tell me about her. Did you have much contact with her?"

"I'm afraid not, Inspector. To be honest, I didn't take to her very well. She was ... vulgar. Oh, she spoke well, she dressed very fashionably and she knew about books and the like, but there was something rough and crude about her. It's hard to put your finger on. She came into the office once and asked to see Dr Stevens. I told her very civilly that Dr Stevens was busy and that unless it was an emergency, she wouldn't be able to see him until the next morning. Well, I wouldn't say she flew into a rage, but there was a sudden change in her whole demeanour, especially her voice. It was as if her mask had fallen; she spoke to me in a bullying kind of way and there was a real coarseness in her voice. It was a momentary thing. She caught herself on very quickly and tried to smooth things over before she left, but I remember thinking to myself, 'You've shown yourself up in your true colours to-day, my girl.'"

As they were talking, Myles appeared at the office door. He was due to collect Stuart, but his face betokened a development. Mrs Abernethy handed Stuart the print-out of Miss Sloane's details and the two men left. As they walked along the corridor, which, now in the absence of pupils, exuded an air of hallowed calm familiar to the sites of ancient battles, Myles could hold back his news no longer.

"The computer people have got back to us. They have found an e-mail on Kennedy's computer. It had been deleted, but they were able to retrieve it. It's very peculiar. It says, '*There is no innocence in ignorance. By their actions shall they be judged. Suffer shall the "children" that come unto me.*' It sounds like a threat. What do you make of it, sir?"

"Were they able to get any details about who sent it?"

"They are able to say that it was sent from an internet café and, of course, the e-mail address of the sender comes with the e-mail, but that doesn't tell us much. E-mail addresses are easily got and there's no check on the identity of the people who apply for them."

Stuart handed Myles the print-out that Mrs Abernethy had given him.

"I want you to find Miss Sloane and get back to me as soon as you have."

"What are you going to do, sir?"

"I'll stay on here. I can have that chat we meant to have with Julie Vance about Ross; and I'd like another word with Dr Greenfield. I want to know what he thinks of our little biblical pastiche. And when you're at the station, phone the hospital and see if Kennedy is fit to be interviewed this afternoon. It'll be interesting to hear what he has to say about it, but I've a strong suspicion he's not going to be able to shed much light on this particular subject."

Chapter 15

Getting Miss Vance out of class required an embarrassing application to the stung Mrs Swanson. Mrs Abernethy was surprised at so early a return, but showed him in with knowing sympathy.

"I'm sorry to trouble you, Mrs Swanson, but I must impose once again on your good nature. I need to speak to Miss Vance."

Scowling was not in Mrs Swanson's repertoire of negative signals, but her irritation did not go unrecorded. She gave one of those smiles that make a good start but then freeze on the instant withdrawal of warmth.

"As you made clear last time, Inspector, *the Law* is there for us all to obey. I will cover for Miss Vance myself and you can use my office for your interview. I trust it will not take long."

The smile intensified in stretch but diminished even further in glow as she picked up the file she had been perusing and left the room.

Miss Vance was most un-Miss-Vance-like. Stuart had imagined a plain Jane with national health spectacles and a straight skirt of rough tweed bulging in the wrong places. What he saw was a shapely woman in her mid thirties with eyes that gave an instant promise of intelligence and vitality. Stuart responded to the promise and signed for her to sit down on one of the easy chairs that filled the corner of the study in front of the large picture window.

"Mrs Ross tells me you have been a great support to her, Miss Vance. I'd like you to tell me what you know about her relationship with her husband. I can assure you that Mrs Ross has been perfectly frank with me and there is no question of you betraying a confidence."

"Isabella is a wonderful woman. She has a loving nature and

is totally devoted to her husband. She has done everything in her power to make the marriage work, but there is no pleasing George."

"Why is that, do you think?"

"I don't know. You'd need to ask him, but I think he is just one of life's malcontents. Whatever he has is not enough. I think he loves Isabella – you've seen what a beautiful woman she is – but he wants her to be perfect. She is not a stupid woman by any means, but she is not his intellectual equal. He doesn't seem to be able to accept that."

"We know he has been violent with her, but we suspect she is trying to play that down. Has he beaten her badly, do you know?"

"Oh yes. Once I had to take her to casualty. She had badly bruised ribs. They kept her in overnight. When it happens he has a period of self-recrimination which can last for two or three months, but then some little incident sparks it off again. To be fair to him, he has realised that things have got out of hand and that's why he has moved out. I think he is genuinely afraid of what he might do to her."

"How did he react to you when you took over from him as teacher-tutor?"

"He wasn't pleased, as you can imagine, but he was a perfect gentleman. We had a chat and he told me that he bore me no ill-will and that he would do anything he could to help me until I had found my feet."

"Why did Dr Stevens make the change?"

"He felt that George was too academic. He was more interested in the subject matter of teaching and not enough in the psychology of pupil-teacher interaction. I have some background in psychology and so he thought that I was better placed to help the young teachers."

"Did Mr Ross ever confide in you as to his feelings towards Dr Stevens?"

"No, not directly. Except that he always referred to Dr

159

Stevens as the Old Hen. I think he saw Dr Stevens' decision as more than personal. For him it was a move away from the traditional approach to education into a new area which I think he felt threatened by. Some of the younger staff regarded him as a fuddy-duddy, part of the Greenfield clique. But that wasn't fair; in fact it's not fair to any of them. Some of these so-called fuddy-duddies, including George and Greenfield, are excellent teachers. And what we should be trying to do is to combine the focus they bring to their subjects with the new pupil-centred approach. I think some of the younger teachers are a bit in awe of the level of scholarship of the fuddy-duddies and are all too keen to emphasise any weaknesses they can detect."

"Were you present when the blow-up occurred between Mr Ross and Miss Jordan?"

"Yes, I was, and I'm not likely to forget it. I was chatting to Jean Potter, one of the maths teachers, at the time and suddenly I heard this booming voice. George was absolutely furious. I don't think I've ever seen anyone so angry. Mabel was scared stiff – you could see it as she backed away from him. And when she got to the door he leaned against it and prevented her from leaving. I can't remember exactly what he said, but I do remember him saying that she was a silly girl and a disgrace to the profession. His body language was very threatening, but I never thought for a moment that he was going to strike her. That's why nobody intervened, I suppose. To be honest, Mabel *is* a silly girl and a lot of us were secretly quite pleased that she was getting her come-uppance. There are a couple of the young teachers on the staff who seem to think that their proximity in age to the pupils gives them some kind of special knowledge that is denied to the older teachers. It's a funny kind of professional reversal. In most professions experience is revered, but increasingly not in teaching. I once heard Greenfield say that if the medical profession followed the same lines, consultant posts would only be given to doctors with serious illnesses."

"What makes you say you were sure he wasn't going to attack Miss Jordan physically?"

"For all that he has been violent towards his wife, I don't think he is a violent man. I know that sounds Irish – oh, I'm sorry, Inspector. No offence meant. What I mean is that he doesn't care enough about the Mabel Jordans or, indeed, the Dr Stevenses of this world to summon up the violence within him. Isabella is his great passion and only she can unleash these tides of raw emotion. What was it Oscar Wilde said?"

"'Each man kills the thing he loves' I believe it was."

"Yes, that's it. George is a romantic and romantics fly too close to the sun. I think you'll need to look elsewhere for your murderer, Inspector Stranaghan."

Stuart thanked Miss Vance for her clarity and frankness and apologised for any inconvenience her temporary removal from her flock had caused. He was anxious to get to Dr Greenfield's classroom to show him the e-mail message, so they left the study together. As they walked down the corridor, conversation became surprisingly self-conscious and elusive. He asked her what class she had been taking and she replied that it was a Year 12 and obligingly kept the struggle against silence going with a self-driving complaint about the burden of GCSE coursework. This lasted, with a few assists from Stuart, until they reached her room and the conventional formalities of departure took over.

Chapter 16

Greenfield's classroom was like a Pharaoh's tomb. In contrast to the walls of many of the other rooms which were plastered with pupils' work, Greenfield's walls were draped in treasures. In pride of place the great Johann Wolfgang von Goethe looked down with proud benevolence from within a heavy, ornately gilded frame. An ancient-looking scroll, also framed, imparted some indecipherable wisdom in what looked like Old or Middle High German. High up towards the ceiling along the back of the room there was a line of about eight parchments each depicting a heraldic scene or coat of arms. And in a corner Stuart's eye caught a montage of postcard-sized pictures of German authors and philosophers – he recognised only Kafka and Nietzsche. The central top section of the whiteboard at the front of the room was covered by a banner with a text written in English but in a Germanic font. While Greenfield was giving the class of seven sixth formers something to occupy them 'gainfully', Stuart deciphered the script.

Language study trains the mind, the taste and the character and reveals the very anatomy of thought.

He could't resist an inquiry when Greenfield had finished.

"Oh, that's a piece of wisdom I picked up at a conference some years ago. I was at a lecture given by some preposterous professor of education. The good gentleman was at pains to pour scorn on the 'quaint irrelevance' of modern language teaching before the dawning of the great day of 'transactional utility', by which is meant, in case you have remained

162

'unexposed' to the jargon, Inspector, the ability of the enlightened learner to go abroad and perform the remarkable task of asking *à l'indigène* for a *Weizenbier* in Germany or a *rioja* on the *Costa*. He used this quote to illustrate the warped thinking that prevailed in the bad old days when it was considered rather more important to rescue pupils from the stultifying grip of word-dominated thinking. It was high time for the modernisers to get to work. They started with Latin and Ancient Greek, which were summarily consigned to the scrap heap. Let's face it; they didn't have much to recommend them as status symbols abroad. They were dead languages and now it was time to give them an indecent burial and 'move on'. So 'move on' we did and where do we find ourselves now? ... Why, tour-guiding around the vocabulary of relevancies such as shopping and travelling and footballing. What else?"

He paused, but it was only to take breath.

"Well actually, there is a 'what-else' – something the missionaries of modernity show no interest in un-blinding themselves to. You must have noticed the wonderfully 'modern' way in which our tabloids are spreading their tentacles, and how *un-reluctantly* the broadsheets, not to mention the BBC, are playing catch-up and *self-tabloidifying*. Young minds are the most at risk from the beguiling power of words; they, more than any other group, need help to survive their onslaught. Yet, rather than develop an insight into the mysteries and intricacies of their magic, the cognoscenti choose instead to fiddle around with what they grandiosely refer to as modern-day survival vocabulary. If they were prepared to get out of their consumer-led obsession with the trivial, they might just get round to forming a grown-up notion of what is modern ... I keep this banner at the top of my board, Inspector, as a daily reminder of why it can still be a noble thing to be a modern language teacher."

As always with the good doctor, it was hard not to sign up

for the digressions, but Stuart did manage to pull away and placed the sheet of paper that Myles had given him on the desk.

"I've a little puzzle here that I'd like your opinion on."

Stuart produced the message. He resisted Greenfield's inquiry as to the source; he wanted to see if Greenfield himself would make the link with Kennedy or perhaps even feign ignorance of it.

"Does it suggest anything to you?"

Greenfield read it aloud, but in a voice for himself.

"*There is no innocence in ignorance. By their actions shall they be judged. Suffer shall the 'children' that come unto me.*"

He paused, read it again, and then after a second pause he spoke, his words coming in a way that suggested they were teleprinting from his mind.

"A clear parody of Christian *caritas*, I would say, Inspector. Intimations of Nietzsche ... Ancient tragedy ... Let me make a copy of it, Inspector. I would like time to think about it, before I give you an answer. Come to my house this evening. We can share a *Weizenbier* and I'll tell you what I think."

While he waited for Myles to pick him up, Stuart had time to take a leisurely walk in the grounds. The sun was struggling with the humidity in the air, producing a gentle brightness that seemed to descend rather than penetrate. As he wandered aimlessly, savouring the vague sense of liberation which the light was dispensing, he focused his gaze on the grass just ahead of him. He felt like a helicopter pilot flying low over a rainforest as he took in the little clusters of clover that had survived the groundsman's chemical treatments, the bare patches that signaled battle scars from recent encounters, and then a white line. He stopped, looked up and saw that he was crossing the eighteen-yard-line of a football field. A whole topography suddenly imposed itself on his awareness; he was whisked away from the lumps and the weeds and grass, from the particular to the generality, from the here-and-now to the then-and-there. It was like in a wallpaper sample book; you could flick from page to page and see the same pattern in different shades. This pitch was interchangeable with any that his memory could recall, pitches that had played host to games he had seen as a boy with his grandfather watching his team, Cliftonville, do battle against the greater forces of the Irish league; or the grey pitches of black-and-white television where the great Real Madrid of the early sixties played to the background accompaniment of the voice of Kenneth Wolstenholme. When he turned round and faced in the opposite direction, the eighteen-yard-area lost the urgency of the penalty box; it softened into the zone of immunity where goalkeepers were free to bounce the ball as they conjured the rhythm for a long kick up-field. It was an experience that offered communion, a kind of antidote to existential isolation.

He found a bench at the side of the pitch and sat down. It was an occasion when he would have enjoyed a long, thoughtful smoke on his pipe, but he had been forced to give it up when constant sore throats had raised the spectre of a life-threat. Old habits, especially old bad habits, die hard and his hand moved instinctively to the pocket where for years the pipe had waited on constant stand-by. It encountered instead the folded-up copy of Snoddy's short story which Greenfield had given him earlier. He opened it and began to read.

It was a fanciful story about football of all things. It was set in a political future when it had been decreed that football must comply with the tenets of 'a people's democracy' and embrace the concept of 'equalisation'. Rich clubs could afford much more talented players than their poorer rivals. It was therefore necessary that this advantage be offset by the imposition of a handicap system. Each match was preceded by a hearing at which the clubs were required to argue their case before a panel of judges whose job it was to decide how to convert the score in the physical game into an official result. The skill of the manager consisted in creating a squad of players which balanced those who performed well on the pitch with those with enough 'warts of victimhood' to impress the panel. All sorts of disadvantage ranging from the social and psychological to the openly physical were exploited. The hero of the story was a young lawyer signed by a leading club as part of their legal team to argue their case before the panel. He was very excited at being selected to play for the legal team of the club that he had supported from childhood and he did a good job in his first few *matches*. However, the 'dreaded forces of equalisation' had become aware that the skills of the teams of lawyers were now also beginning to have a significant influence on outcomes. Naturally, the wealthier clubs were in a position to afford the best lawyers. So if parity was to be maintained, a handicap system needed to be introduced for the lawyer teams as well. This resulted in the young hero-lawyer losing his job, since he had neither a social impediment nor a psychological disability to his name and he was burdened with qualifications that were excessively impressive. There was however a glimmer of hope for his career. The story ended with him applying for a position on the team of lawyers now being constituted to plead the case for the vulnerability of the lawyers on the first team.

The piece was quite well written; there were moments of insight into the buzz of collegiate solidarity experienced by the hero on his signing for the club, but there was less comedy than would be expected in such a satirical portrayal of ideological correctness. The dominant mood was one of impotent frustration; the author had identified too much with his hero, and this had the effect of obstructing the free flow of the dark humour. It was nonetheless a remarkable piece of writing for a sixth-former. This boy saw the world from a distinctly oblique angle. The question in Stuart's mind, as he folded the pages and put them back in his pocket, was just how oblique this angle might be; was it sufficiently askew to find a way through normal human sensibilities and plot the murder of two men who, to all appearances, seemed to have confined their activities within the conventional limits of acceptability?

Myles was waiting in the car park. He had found an address for Miss Sloane. She had not gone on her proposed world tour. She had got a teaching post in 'a school for young ladies' in the West Country, but had left after the first year to start a new career in advertising. She was now based in London with a PR firm called *Mercurial Messaging*. As chance would have it, she was on a few days leave at the moment to look after her invalid mother who lived only a mile or so away from St. Jude's. He had phoned her and arranged for them to go and see her at 3.30, giving them time to fit in a visit to the hospital after lunch.

"You have left only one decision for me to make, Myles, but it is the vital one: where to have lunch?"

Myles' face had tightened to register challenge before it relaxed into a smile of comprehension.

"As you say, sir, that's a decision that calls for rank."

They found a pub with a beer garden and a menu that offered pies that, the landlord assured them, had not done time in the freezer. Stuart chose the chicken and mushroom to accompany his merlot, but Myles resisted all Stuart's sirenical solicitations and insisted instead on a plain salad with an equally sensible sparkling water. Stuart had been undecided whether he should show Snoddy's story to his sergeant – the younger man's critical awareness in matters literary was unlikely to prove insightful. But he was just a little peeved at Myles' abstemiousness; it had left him filling the role of the Hogarthian rake. He was now of a mind to hit back and expose his sergeant's cultural shortcomings – *Unzulänglichkeiten* was the word that suddenly popped into his mind. It was an A level German word he had long forgotten that he knew; it had come with Greenfield, hadn't it? Decision made, he handed Myles the folded pages and asked him to have a read through them while he went off to the loo. 'Challenge' made a return to the Myles' face.

Stuart took his time. He wanted to give the candidate every opportunity to prepare for the *viva voce* that was to follow. In the bar area the T.V. screen was radiating its stock command-to-attention. It went largely ignored by the bulk of the clientele, refreshingly determined to assert their agnosticism, but a few poor souls, one or two with not even a mobile phone to talk to, the rest disengaged from conversations that were clearly too thin to repel the penetrating rays of the screen, were caught in an admission of their social *Unzulänglichkeiten*. On his way back from the toilet he noticed an empty table with a dog-eared newspaper on it. He picked it up and brought it back out with him into the light. Myles was still working his way through his challenge. The waiter had brought the drinks. Stuart sipped his merlot and leafed through the paper. It was a tabloid of the kind he used to read at the barber's before Heather had undertaken to cut his hair for him and save him the long wait. He hadn't read a paper like this since that time, some five years ago. He was immediately struck not by its similarity, but by its utter sameness to what he had read at the barber's. He heard his inner voice reading it in exactly the same unbeautiful accent and at exactly the same assertive pitch as the excitable voice he heard in the ads for it on the telly. Everything, from the politics to the sport, was reported in a spirit of no-nonsense, bottom-line awareness, and bottom-line awareness consisted of the smugly cunning realisation that all men are at all times motivated by undying craving for 'a good time'. The images of this 'good time' abounded in the pages of the paper, from page-three-girls who had 'spilled over' to other pages – the 'naughty humour' of the style was evidently catching – to pictures of so-called rock stars 'revealing all', that is, making mock confession of instances of over-indulgence, ostensibly in order to re-assert the eternal values, but in reality only to titillate the aspirations of the readers with glimpses of a hedonistic life-style as yet beyond the reach of their grasping hands and gaping mouths. Stuart had often been invited to wonder what Christ would make of the modern church; it now occurred to him that Freud would be equally sickened at the sight of the free play now being accorded the forces that his voice had been recruited to summon from the infernal regions.

As he made his way through the paper Stuart became aware that Myles had got to the end of the story.

"Well, what do you make of it, Myles?" (Stuart was only slightly ashamed of himself.)

"To be honest, sir, it seems a bit silly to me. I don't think there's the slightest chance of anyone taking that attitude to football. The public loves winners; that's why they pay through the nose to see the big teams and the big names. You should see the crowds we get when we play Manchester United or Arsenal in a pre-season friendly. It's only a training session for the big teams and they turn out mostly their reserves, but as long as they carry the tag, no matter how ordinary they are, the crowds come flocking. I know it's not meant to be taken literally, but what's the point of making up a story that is so inappropriate? The other thing I thought was really silly was the ending. If the team of lawyers was going to be vetted for handicaps, then the second team would need to be vetted too, and so on, there would be no end to it."

"But that's the point, don't you see Myles? Our obsession with absolute fairness flies in the face of reality; fairness is something you can dab around here and there, but once you think you can apply it to the whole world, you get to be like one of those housewives who see all forms of organic life – including their husband and children – as a threat to the house that they've been slaving to make a dirt-free zone. As far as the football is concerned, it's precisely because football is about the last place that this kind of thing is likely to happen that it's the focus of the story. It draws our attention to what is happening in other fields where we have been sleepwalking into it."

169

"Where do you think it's happening, then?"

"Isn't it part of the whole political correctness thing? In our job, for example, aren't there double standards at work? Don't the courts try to 'fiddle the figures'? All sorts of social and psychological deprivations are taken into consideration in judging a criminal's guilt. It used to be we needed to establish only two things, the fact that he did it and the fact that he did it with intent. Nowadays these are just two in a queue alongside all the other factors that must be taken into consideration – the offender's home background, his standard of education, his level of intelligence. What gets the put-everything-right lobby really excited though, is if they can ferret out any failure of the authorities to respond to any signs of the criminal's *vulnerability* before he was *driven* to do what he did. Yet just try to suggest that any of these factors should be used to assess competence in other areas, say for example to see if the offender was capable of voting meaningfully at a general election or acting on a jury, and then stand back and see what happens ... You'd need to stand well back for there would be such a tornado of moral outrage that you'd be blown off your feet."

"But surely that's only fair. Some people do have handicaps in life, it's only right that they should be taken into consideration, isn't it?"

"Yes, but where does it end? That's the question that's being asked here. Once we accept that some people are not wholly responsible for their actions and deserve to benefit from some kind of handicapping system, how do we decide on the degree of handicap and what areas of life do we allow it to operate in? These are difficult questions, but the really big question is: what happens to the notion of merit? I don't think you can call any of these silly questions. Perhaps the fools are those of us who don't even think to ask them. 'What's the harm in doing good?' That's the only moral question most people can muster these days; it's so smug it doesn't even recognize itself as a tautological absurdity."

Stuart seemed to have reached a position he didn't know he held, but having reached it, he could see no reason for not holding it. The arrival of the cavalier pie and Myles' roundhead salad provided a suitable hiatus for the introduction of a lighter topic of conversation, but Myles, it seemed, wanted to persist in the deep waters.

"I don't know if you know about it, sir, but I recently was to blame for one of the fellows at the station losing his job." He hesitated before continuing. "There had been a complaint made against him by a young thug. We had arrested him for breaking into an elderly couple's house, but we couldn't charge him for lack of evidence. He claimed that Josh – that's the name of the officer – had grabbed him by the throat when he arrested him and threatened to smash his face in unless he confessed. I had to testify before the tribunal and I told them exactly what had happened; Josh had manhandled him, nothing serious mind, and he did threaten to give him a good hiding. He was bluffing of course, we both knew that. But that made no difference; he was dismissed from the service and the young bastard got compensation for 'his pain and suffering' . . . Do you think I did the right thing, sir? The lads at the station think I'm a right bastard. They've given me a pretty hard time since."

Stuart was aware of a change in Myles' voice. There was more age and more of the dust of experience in it. It was clear that he would set store by Stuart's answer.

"You played it by the book, Myles, and we all need to support the *book*, otherwise we would all be floundering around making our own judgments and those judgments could get very messy. They'd get mixed up in all sorts of things, self-interest, personal prejudice, ignorance, inexperience. The *book* has the wisdom of experience in it, it may not be perfect, but it gets it right more often than any of us using our own judgment would. What you did took a lot of character. Most people would have lied to save their colleague, but the trouble with lies is that they infect trust and without trust society can't function."

As he spoke, it was not clear to Stuart whether he really believed what he was saying. It was one of those situations which seemed to recur with him when he could not decide whether he had caught himself believing a half-truth or half believing a truth, and this always set him to wondering if there was in fact any real difference. For some reason it was suddenly clear to him on this occasion that there was. This was a truth that demanded some allegiance, but then there were other truths, in conflict with this one, which demanded allegiance too. If Myles had lied for his colleagues, Stuart could just as easily have found himself stressing the need for trust and loyalty within the group and he would have been just as right.

Myles' appetite for assurance was not satisfied.

"But I didn't play it by the book when I kept that business about Snoddy to myself and didn't report it to Inspector Winkworth, did I? I told myself I had done the right thing, but it bothered me a lot. It would be nice to tell myself that I took a brave decision to save a young man's career, but, to be honest, I think I just let myself get talked into it by Dr Greenfield. It wasn't brave, it was a weak thing to do and I shouldn't have done it. And what about you, sir? – you aren't sticking by the book by not reporting me, are you?"

"When I was at university, Myles, we studied a play by a famous French philosopher. It told the story of Orestes. He was the son of Agamemnon, the king of Mycenae. When he returns from his travels he discovers that his father has been killed by his mother Clytemnestra and her lover. Justice demands that he avenge his father's murder and this means killing his mother, but it is a terrible thing to kill your own mother. He eventually brings himself to do it and when he does, he is pursued by the Furies – they were the ancient spirits of vengeance that tortured the guilty by unleashing their conscience on them. The only place he can get away from them is in the temple of Apollo. Apollo was the god of wisdom and reason – his approval endorsed the killing as an act of justice – but he didn't have any jurisdiction over the Furies – as soon as Orestes leaves the temple he is set upon again. The whole point of the play is to show that we all have to come to terms with the fact that doing something that is right in itself gives no immunity from the guilt of having done wrong while doing the right. I don't think you quite make it as an Orestes, Myles, but you understand what I'm getting at? You make your judgements in good faith and then you live with them."

"Are you saying there is no right and wrong then?"

"No, I'm saying there are lots of rights and wrongs. That's what the Greeks believed, they had lots of gods and even Zeus, the king of the gods, couldn't control them. He had to resort to politicking between them. When I was a kid I was taught at Sunday school that there was only one God and that no man could serve two masters. We were made to feel so superior to those heathens who believed in more than one god. It was a bit like the bandwagon we all get on nowadays against those who reject Darwinism or think the earth is flat. Experience has taught me to be more humble."

Stuart was now beginning to seem wiser to himself than he really felt. It was as if he had been granted a temporary mastery of the rational art over the world of experience, but he knew that this 'mastery' was an illusion – in different circumstances and in different company it would melt away and the alien forces of existential contingency, which have driven greater men than him to desperation and superstition, would punish him for his presumption. Myles on the other hand seemed, if not satisfied, at least diverted, by the inspector's philosophising. It had spared him prolonged exposure to a double discredit, his disloyalty to his colleague and his submissiveness to Greenfield. And for that he was grateful to his boss.

Chapter 17

Lunch done, the two men made their way to the *Mater Infirmorum*. They found Kennedy in a different ward, sitting up in bed reading a magazine with glossy pictures of cars on the cover. Stuart had not really noted his physical appearance on the previous visit; it was far from clear at the time whether the crime victim was still deserving of full living human status. Seeing him now returned to life in all its triviality stirred incredulity at the absurd arrogance of a will bent on putting an end to something so small and rabbit-like. Kennedy cut a very unimposing figure; he was myopic, he was bald and he was fat. All the usual means of misrepresenting his appearance were denied him as he sat there sweating lightly in pyjamas that were not up to the strain put on them by the fleshy exuberance of his midriffs. The situation hardly constituted a stately *levee*. Kennedy was keenly aware of his disadvantage.

Stuart introduced himself and made a casual enquiry as to the invalid's state of recovery. Whether out of naivety or as a delaying tactic, the enquiry was set upon and worried to death by a long and detailed answer. It took a concerted muscular effort on the rudder from Stuart to steer the conversation back into fishing waters.

"We would like you to tell us about your dealings with Richardson's Development. We understand you have been in negotiations with them over the possible sale of the school-house."

A look of dismay came over Kennedy's face. He reached for the glass of barley water on the tall cabinet beside the bed. Myles saved him the final strains of the stretch. After a deliberate and prolonged sip of the reviving liquid he seemed more composed.

174

"You think Richardson's Development has something to do with me being shot?"

"Possibly. But tell us first, what exactly is your involvement?"

Another sip to aid composure ... or, as Stuart cynically suspected, composition.

"After a short time in post it occurred to me that the school would benefit greatly from a re-evaluation of its underlying financial structure, particularly in relation to its main asset, the schoolhouse and adjoining grounds. These are prime land for residential development and it would be easy for us to re-locate to the far end of the sports grounds. They are more extensive than is strictly necessary; the farm and the riding stables are a total anachronism and could easily be dispensed with. So I looked around for a company that could provide the necessary professional expertise to help me draw up a coherent plan to bring before the Board. That company was Richardson's Development."

"Are you suggesting that this whole thing was your idea, Mr Kennedy?"

Kennedy searched Stuart's face for clues before deciding on his answer.

"No, I would not claim original ownership of the idea. It was like most good ideas, Inspector; it was more in need of execution than of birth."

He gave a subdued chuckle in modest self-admiration.

"But perhaps the midwife fancied a turn in the firing squad. Did you think of that, Mr Kennedy?"

The grin which had followed the chuckle fossilised.

"You think it was Evans who shot me? Of course, I never thought ... It never occurred to me he would go that far. Of course, it must have been him. Do you have any evidence?"

"You admit then that you stole the idea from Evans and cut him out of the deal with Richardson's?"

"I admit nothing of the kind. Evans' original idea needed

major adjustments to make it viable. It was me who made those adjustments. As far as Richardson's is concerned, it made more sense to go to them since they had already done most of the spade work on the project. As I'm sure you know, Richardson's had already paid Evans for his services, such as they were. I owe Evans nothing, Inspector."

"That's hardly the point, is it, sir?" Myles intervened. "What matters is how Mr Evans viewed the situation. And I hardly think he saw it the way you've just described."

"You're absolutely right, Sergeant. When are you going to arrest him?"

Before Myles had to avoid answering, Stuart produced the piece of paper on which he had written the e-mail message from Kennedy's computer. He handed it to Kennedy.

"What did you make of this when you received it?"

Kennedy clearly recognised it immediately.

"Oh that. When you're a schoolmaster, particularly a head-master, you have to learn to live with rubbish like that. One of the boys I think – it didn't sound like the kind of thing a girl would write – must have got hold of my e-mail address and sent it to me. I changed my e-mail address the day after I received it."

"But what did you make of it? What do you think it was trying to say to you?"

"I didn't think about it. It was vaguely menacing. I assumed it had something to do with the business with Devine. I'm sure you know all about that?"

"Yes, but what made you associate it with the Mr Devine?"

"Around the same time I got a letter telling me that I was treating him very badly and that I shouldn't have suspended him, I should be supporting him. It was terribly offensive. It said that people like me shouldn't be appointed headmaster, that I was part of 'a sickly wave of mediocrity' that was threatening to wash education clean of virtue ... no, it wasn't virtue, it was a word like virtue, it was Latin."

"Could it have been 'Virtus'?"

"Yes, that's it. I asked Pargeter about it. He's our classicist. That's right ... I remember now. He told me it wasn't the same as virtue. It referred to the so-called manly virtues – duty, honour, courage, that sort of thing. He got quite excited about it, I remember. Treated me to a whole lecture on the subject. I'd trouble getting away from him. They're such bores, these so-called academics."

"I take it the letter was anonymous?"

"No ... not exactly. It was signed 'The Old Thinkers' – clearly some of Greenfield's mob."

"Did you show it to Greenfield?"

"You must be joking. Greenfield hates my guts. Do you think I'm going to go running to him when I get a bit of hate mail? I wouldn't give him the pleasure."

Myles again intervened.

"Do you not think you were a bit unfair to Mr Devine? He was after all standing up for the school rules. Do you not think he deserved your backing?"

Kennedy gave him a look of pristine incredulity.

"There was nothing I could do, Sergeant. Devine is a grown man; he knows the rules. I didn't write the rules. But they clearly state that there should be no use of physical force except in the most exceptional circumstances. He broke these rules, so he has to take the consequences. Surely that's exactly what the Greenfield mob was on about."

Myles was clearly unhappy with this reply, but was cowed by its formulation. Stuart was on hand to help.

"What Mr Kennedy is saying, Sergeant, is that it's tough being a man in a woman's world."

Kennedy's welcome for the reinforcement bandaged clumsily over the scar of incomprehension.

The outside air was like water to thirst. The line '*a poor thing, but mine own'* was a frequent visitor to Stuart's head, inevitably provoking him to search his memory to unearth its origin. But it always came to him when he was in no position to check it out; and when he was in a position to check, he always forgot. Poor old St Judes! What had poor old education done to deserve headmasters like that? Having drunk their fill of the air, inspector and sergeant got into the car and drove to their meeting with the maligned and maligning Miss Sloane. The doorbell was answered by a middle-aged woman with hair greying discreetly and eyes with just a hint of nostalgia-appeal. Both Stuart and Myles metaphorically blinked before it was explained to them in tones which complemented the hair and the eyes that this was the mother and not the offended herself.

"I am pleased to see that you have made a swift recovery, Mrs Sloane. Your daughter's ministrations have been highly effective I see."

Facial signs of puzzlement were ruthlessly dealt with at the foetal stage and legitimacy instantly restored.

"Yes indeed, Inspector. My daughter is very attentive to her old mother. I would be lost without her."

At this point the daughter appeared. She had the good looks of the mother, but there was less assurance in her voice and less promise in her eyes. As if conscious of this, she tended to focus on any object that could be loosely seen as an illustration of what she was saying rather than look directly at her collocutors. The conservatory, the wicker chairs and the kitchen to which her mother dispatched herself to make the coffee were all easy escape routes, as were all references to St Jude's, which apparently was located just over Myles' right shoulder. Any direct mention of Snoddy – she herself avoided the name – caused her to look to the floor.

"He was writing an essay on Shakespearean tragedy and I offered to go through a few points with him after school. We had the tutorial here. It was more convivial. I just hate being in school when the pupils have gone – it's so lifeless. I poured him a glass of wine and we worked through his draft. There was only one copy, so we had to sit together on the sofa. At some point he asked for a second glass of wine. I wasn't keen to give him any more, but I didn't want to cause offence, so I did."

"Did you have a second glass as well, Miss Sloane?"

"Well, yes. As a matter of fact I did. It would have been rude not to."

"I'm sorry. No criticism intended. I only wanted to get a clear picture of what happened. Please go on."

"We went on discussing the essay. There was one bit we couldn't agree on and he got rather animated – he tends to get animated. He got up and poured himself another glass. I remember, he knocked it back in one gulp and then emptied the rest of the bottle into his glass. This seemed to calm him down and he came back and sat down beside me."

"Is this when he attacked you?"

"No, that happened a bit later. His mood seemed to change entirely – it was the wine, I suppose. He became relaxed and ... comfortable. If you knew him, Inspector, you would realize how unusual that was. He's normally as prickly as a porcupine. First, his voice changed ... softer, more muted, almost tender. Then I became aware that he was sitting much closer and I could feel his leg brushing against mine. I didn't want to acknowledge to him what was happening, so I made an excuse to get away and fetch a book from my room. But he followed me and when we were in the room he grabbed me and flung us both on the bed. I was really scared. I didn't know whether to scream or try to reason with him. I tried reason, I told him as calmly as I could that I wanted him to stop and to go home and that I wouldn't tell anyone what had happened. But he paid no attention and started trying to undress me. By this time I was petrified. He had torn off my pants and was grappling with the belt of his trousers and then I just threw up all over both of us. I will

179

always remember the look on his face; it's the nearest anyone should ever get to looking evil in the eye. He called me a bitch and left."

"Where was your mother when this was happening?"

"She was out with friends and didn't get back until after midnight."

"Did you tell her what had happened when she got back?"

"No, I closed myself in my room. I needed time to decide what to do."

"When did you tell your mother?"

"She told me the next morning, Inspector." – Coffee and biscuits and Mrs Sloane had emerged from the kitchen – "I advised her to go and see Dr Stevens and tell him everything."

"Did you tell Dr Stevens everything you have just told us, Miss Sloane?"

There was a moment of consultation, seemingly with the memory, before she replied.

"Not exactly, Inspector. I didn't go into details. I just told him that Robert had tried to rape me."

"Why didn't you tell him the whole story?"

"I suppose I was embarrassed, Inspector. It's not easy for a girl to talk to an older man about such things, especially her headmaster. But I showed him the bruises on my arm, where Robert had grabbed me."

"But surely Dr Stevens pressed you for details. He was after all going to expel a pupil on the strength of what you were telling him."

"Dr Stevens was a gentleman, Inspector. No doubt he wanted to spare me further embarrassment. The details didn't really matter. Robert's behaviour was completely out of order – he simply had to go. What would have been the point of putting me through the ordeal of spelling everything out?"

"If Snoddy's parents had challenged the expulsion you would have had no choice, Miss Sloane."

"But they didn't, did they, Inspector?"

Stuart caught himself on. This was becoming a silly line of questioning. He was seeking to pressurise rather than obtain information. He needed to halt the rhythm of the exchange. He would have liked to ask her about the incident with the PhD student, but any reference to that at this stage would have the effect of a regiment crossing a bridge in step, so he switched attention to what she had been doing since the incident.

"What made you leave St Jude's?"

His tone was still wrong; it was the voice of an apology that retains its claim on innocence. She responded in kind.

"I would have thought that was perfectly obvious, Inspector. I needed to make a complete break. I tried for a while to behave as if nothing had happened, but I found it all too painful."

"But you didn't settle down at your next school?"

He tried hard to defuse the hectoring edge in his voice; he stopped himself short of an accusatory 'did you?' and even clumsily infused a few droplets of tonal empathy. The clumsiness clearly escaped Miss Sloane, as did the infusion.

"Perhaps if something like that happened to you, Mr Stranaghan, you might begin to understand what a lasting effect it has. But then nothing like that is going to happen to you, is it? If you must know, I found it very hard to settle and decided in the end to get out of teaching altogether."

Myles came to his rescue.

"How have you found the change, Miss Sloane? Has it helped you put the incident with Snoddy behind you?"

The empathy in this inquiry, unlike Stuart's attempts, was obviously perceived as a thing for itself. Miss Sloane turned to Myles and replied with an intimacy which took its warmth from the coldness to which it was consigning Stuart.

"It has been a real tonic, Sergeant. Working with adults allows you much more anonymity than working with children. You're not constantly under scrutiny and the centre of attention of thirty pairs of little eyes, all looking to see what they can do to put you off your stride."

"But surely there were many admiring eyes as well? You can't tell me that you didn't have lots of admirers, Miss Sloane. Do you not miss having that kind of attention?"

Myles' sincerity came under urgent scrutiny, but his face must have shown up guileless since Miss Sloane continued as if the conditions of their intimacy had not been breached.

"But that's the whole point, Sergeant. I don't want that kind of attention. I left teaching to get away from it. I'd much rather be ignored than become the object of the kind of attention that might lead to a repeat of ... "

It was clear that she could not bring herself to use the well-worn euphemistic and baulked equally at the no-nonsense. Stuart felt that an old-fashioned, stiff-upper-lip 'Quite' was the required means of rescue, but, having retired hurt from the exchange, he left it to Myles to find a more modern equivalent. Myles didn't, he simply ignored the need and went on with his questioning.

"Have you had any contact with Snoddy since the incident?"

Another moment of consultation, seemingly with the memory, caused the suspicion of a delay before the answer came.

"No, Sergeant. I haven't."

Ego bandaged up, Stuart returned to the crease.

"I'm sorry, Miss Sloane, but you don't seem altogether sure of that?"

Miss Sloane ignored the provenance of the question and continued to address Myles.

"Well, you asked me if I had any contact with him. I didn't, but he made contact with me. I received a very abusive letter from him a few weeks after the ... incident."

"Do you have that letter?"

"No, I burned it. I felt unclean even touching it."

"What did he say in the letter?"

"I don't remember exactly. I only remember the tone. It was scary."

"Did he threaten you?"

"No, he just called me a lot of names."

"Did you tell anyone about it?"

"No, I just wanted to put it out of my head."

"Is that when you decided to leave St Jude's?"

"Yes. I thought if I got away from St Jude's he would stop bothering me."

"What surprises me, Miss Sloane, is why he felt so angry towards you. After all, you had not pressed charges against him and you had even agreed to keep the whole thing quiet. Surely, if anything, he should have been grateful to you."

Miss Sloane turned away from Myles whom she had continued to address throughout the exchange and directed a look towards Stuart that was fuelled with contempt.

"You're the detective, Detective. If you want answers, you should at least know who you should be asking the questions to. That's not a question for me, that's a question for Snoddy."

Pear-shaped! Stuart had read somewhere that the expression was coined by RAF pilots when they saw planes crashing down nose-first. But as he and Myles left the Sloane household it suggested more the outline of Obelix, the clumsy menhir-toting companion of Asterix – the proverbial bull in the china shop. Myles reinforced the self-image. He was not sure what he had wanted to get out of the interview, but whatever it was, he had certainly not got it. He had managed to antagonize someone he should have treated as the victim of a crime, and to what purpose? The scepticism he had brought to it had been fed to him by Greenfield. His mind should have been more open and he should have drawn Gillian Sloane out rather than send her into a defensive shell. There was one thing she was right about; Snoddy was the person he should have been interviewing. He left Myles to set up the interview for the following morning and make the travel arrangements to Oxford and the two men parted company. He needed a good walk to re-focus his mind and to shake off the gnawing feeling of self-dissatisfaction that threatened to irk him for the rest of the day.

The trouble with walking as therapy is that it can only help once the recovery has begun. The intake of images and sounds and smells is the best antidote to the haunting chimera of dissatisfaction when it is at its work, festering and causing vacuity within. But the process can't kick off until the healing powers of the world are granted a fair hearing, and authorization for that is in the gift of the very spectres that are inimical to them in the first place. In his pipe-smoking days Stuart had become aware of the same phenomenon. The pipe-smoker is the archetypal figure of calm and self-control. Whenever he needed to escape the niggling sense of having done the wrong thing, or what is often worse, of having failed to do the right thing, he would light his pipe and wait for composure to descend. But it rarely did. He had gradually come to see that a prior furtive infiltration of calm – a kind of Trojan horse – was always needed before a mass immigration could be unleashed.

He had driven to the tow-path of the river which was the spine of the city. He parked his car at the old disused bridge which now acted as a car park for dog-walkers and joggers and started to walk upstream. He was aware that the water was sparkling and that the sun was playing light games with the faintly misty air, but he simply recorded the fact like the camera, that great buffer that holds out the possibility of a deferred experience and removes the responsibility for on-the-spot appreciation. The niggle of his botched performance still rang through him like radio interference and demanded a rhythm of thought that could be heard above it. Experience told him that he needed to get his mind into mechanical mode. He would plonk one thought after another and hope that something would emerge from between the 'plonkings'.

Why had he been so keen to discredit Gillian Sloane? Was it merely on Greenfield's say-so? Was he falling under this man's spell just as Myles had done in the earlier investigation? He wasn't sure ... perhaps. There was another reason. If Miss Sloane was fibbing about the attempt on her virtue, then that was all the more reason why Snoddy would be very angry about the whole affair. He would feel extremely aggrieved, and from what he had heard from the boy at the rugby match, he did not seem the type to take things lying down. But then why vent his anger on Stevens? Surely Miss Sloane would have been the focus? Stevens would have himself been the victim of deception, if deception there had been. It would not have been reasonable for Snoddy to take it out on Stevens and leave Miss Sloane to her own conscience. It would also have required intricate planning for Snoddy to have slipped away from his billet in Germany, done the murder and returned undetected in the course of a weekend. And what about the gun? At what point would he have stolen it from Richard Devine? Before he knew he needed it? Or was that part of that frenetic weekend? Or did he fit it in before he left for Germany? All three of these possibilities needed dragging by the hair, as the French would say, to sit on the same bench as plausibility. But the biggest obstacle of all to fitting Snoddy into the murderer's shoes was Kennedy. As far as anyone could see, Snoddy had no connection whatsoever with the man. Then perhaps, they were all jumping to conclusions. Could it be that despite all appearances there was no link between the two crimes? There surely had to be. There could be absolutely no way round the gun, unless of course Stevens' murderer had left it in the bushes, it had not been found by the dozens of policemen who had combed the area, but was later picked up by chance by someone who had the bright idea of killing Kennedy with it to throw the police off the scent. Drowning men and straws!

The way forward? Clearly, he needed to talk to Kennedy again. The Richardson's affair was still open-ended, although he no longer pinned any fleshy hopes on it as the key to the mystery, and then perhaps – who knows – some link with Snoddy might emerge. And there was that message on Kennedy's computer that needed explaining. And the gorgeous Miss Sloane ... He had a friend at the Met. He would get him to go round to *Mercurial Messaging* and see if there was anything to be dug up on that front. That would at least provide him with some useful background when he went to interview Snoddy to-morrow. It wasn't much of a plan of campaign, but it was better than a blank page. He had not made any real progress – nothing had emerged from between the cracks as yet, but he had plodded his way through the gloom to a new Micawberish confidence. During his musings the river gradually had been coming back into focus and was now beginning to make demands on his attention. And when he heard a blackbird in a near-by bush giving off to all and sundry, he knew he had been summoned back to the land of living things. It is strange how these first bars of the overtures that beckon back towards life always inspire shame in the breast that has harboured emptiness. Emerging from the pit of nothingness the prodigal is made aware of the futility of his greedy lunge for all-ness when every thing around him has been crying out for attention to its singularity.

Chapter 18

Mercurey, that's what he would bring to Greenfield's. He still had a bottle in his garage, the last of the half-crate he had bought when he had visited the village with his wife some eight years ago. When, last summer, they had finished the fifth bottle, his friend Claude had told him to drink the last one soon, but he had a natural leaning towards affective thrift and had not been able to bring himself to forsake the interest of anticipation for the cash of experience. But to-night he could offload some of the responsibility for appreciating the wine on to Greenfield. It goes unrecorded, the debt we all owe to the *bons viveurs* of this world for the way they energise all the ions of value that the rest of us stash away in the deferral box under the stairs.

"Come in, come in." Such were the welcoming tones that greeted the Inspector on the Greenfield doorstep. "I hope you haven't eaten. My housekeeper, Mrs Lehman, had to go out – she goes to bridge on Tuesday evenings – but she has left an excellent goulash in the pot with instructions as to how it can be successfully transferred to the palate."

The *Mercurey* was met with clearly genuine approval and opened immediately to have its brief, but enriching encounter with the air. Stuart was shown into a curiosity shop of a sitting room in which what wall space that had not been taken up with bookshelves was stickered with water colours and the occasional oil. In one corner slouched a large pock-marked oak writing desk beside which lurked an incongruous *meuble* in light mock-wood, supporting a computer and a retinue of accessories. Greenfield directed himself towards the other corner to an old bureau from which the necks of whiskey and gin bottles strained upwards for attention.

"You'll have an aperitif, Inspector?"

Stuart resisted the impressive CVs of the malts on offer and settled for a modest *pastis,* which Greenfield handed to him with the air of a man thwarted in his ambitions. The two men sat down in facing armchairs in front of a large stone fireplace in which spluttered the beginnings of a blaze. Greenfield embedded himself snugly behind his whisky glass which he held in both hands and raised almost ritually to his lips. The conversation sniffed around various topics, a bit like a dog exploring lamp posts. But in the end Greenfield dismissed the nose and engaged the teeth.

"Are you a believer, Inspector?"

"A believer in what?"

"Oh, I would have thought that coming from where you do, the question would be clear enough."

"You mean, 'Am I a staunch Prod or a devout Catholic?' Strange isn't it, the way nobody ever expects Catholics to be staunch or Protestants to be devout? No, I'm neither. But I was brought up to *god-fear.* I even used to win prizes at Sunday school. We had to learn huge chunks of the Bible and entire psalms off by heart. It did wonders for the memory and was a great induction into what words can do."

"But you no longer believe?"

"No, I remember as a child how the notion of God as pure spirit was presented to us as a really sophisticated idea. We were made to feel pride in getting our heads round something that whole civilizations hadn't been able to grasp. Then, as time went on, I started thinking that it would be even more sophisticated to lose not just the body of God, but the consciousness as well. As you can imagine, that did not go down well when I suggested it to other *god-fearers.* For most people it's tantamount to denying God's very existence, so I just call myself an atheist now."

"And what about the Christian Ethic? Don't you subscribe to Christian morality?"

"I could never get to grips with the notion of Christ dying for the sins of the world. No one has ever been able to explain that in a way that made any sense at all to me. But if you mean the simple notion of doing unto others as you would have them do unto you, yes, I suppose I do, more or less. But then surely every civilized person does?"

"Perhaps, but personally, I would always run a mile from notions as vague as that. Where you get wool you get sheep. Sheep are attracted to woolly ideas. And this one is a gift – I almost said manna from Heaven – for a society as self-indulgent as ours. How could the weak, self-obsessed amalgam of individuals that passes for modern society possibly refuse such an immunity sticker? The lower the notion you form of your duties and obligations towards yourself and others, the greater your tolerance must be for the greed and selfishness of those others. With this kind of tolerance you get a free subscription to moral pretentiousness. It comes free because it arises out of your very lack of moral striving. No wonder it sells so well; there is a huge market for it. It's a moral alchemist's dream – moral gold produced out of the ugly, two-a-penny pebbles of universal egomania.

"If, on the other hand, you set yourself some standards of behaviour and consider yourself worthy of censure, should you fail to live up to those standards, then you acquire not only the right, but the duty, to censure others for *their* failures: 'Let him who is free from sin cast the first stone' is a recipe for moral paralysis. It is precisely those who know themselves not to be free from sin who should be casting the stones, provided of course they are prepared to accept that stones might also be thrown at them."

Stuart beamed in admiration of a thing well said, but nevertheless felt that it behoved him to offer even unconvincing resistance.

"You make Christianity sound like a mutual society for the morally handicapped."

"Well, if the cap fits . . ."

"But surely it's not Christianity that's at fault here; it is the use it's now being put to. The Victorians for example had a much more robust Christian view of the world. They believed in sin and punishment; they also believed in some kind of divine justice which linked sin with failure and virtue with success, and as back-up they had Heaven and Hell available to them to mop up any anomalies that Life might allow through."

"Yes, you have a point there. We keep coming back to Marx. Do you remember what he said? The cultures of all societies are shaped by the prevailing economic necessities. The Victorians were entrepreneurs, explorers, conquerors . . . people at the forefront of industrial and economic expansion. The virtues they needed to instil were the virtues of hard work, rigorous self-discipline, intellectual striving and self-improvement. Failure brought a sense of guilt and self-loathing; there was no pride just simply in being a member of the human race. *'Human rights'* hadn't been invented. God-fearing people certainly had obligations to those less fortunate than them-selves, but only to the extent of giving them a helping hand when they were down on their luck. Charity was all about providing *opportunity*. If *opportunity* was spurned, obligation was at an end. It's a very different story nowadays of course with our now beloved *human rights* – now obligation is a life-sentence. We're told we owe this or that to our fellow humans. Why? – simply because they are our fellow humans. What they actually do is of no consequence; whatever they do, they *'deserve'* our charity.' He paused for a moment, and then added with a glint in his eye: "'*Deserve*' – now there you have a prime example of a verb abrogating its responsibilites as a *'doing-word'*.""

Stuart smiled in appreciation of the little *jeu de mots.* His companion was clearly in his element scuba-diving under the clichés of conventional thinking. It generated a sense of adventure and complicity. Greenfield was now in full flow.

"It's funny, isn't it, the way we have come to recognise this in relation to third world charities? It has become conventional wisdom that giving hand-outs only adds to the poverty in the long run. Why has that little piece of wisdom not percolated through when it comes to our own underclass? What we give to them materially, we take from them spiritually. You'll have another glass, Inspector?"

Stuart hesitated. He had come in his car, not knowing what to expect from the evening but – what the hell – he could get a taxi home and collect the car in the morning. This promised to be an evening with a real lid on it. As he refilled the glasses, Greenfield continued undeflected.

"The reason of course is that we think of our own underclass as canon-fodder – not in the sense that we need them to fight our wars – that belonged to the age of empire – or to feed our factories – that was during the early period of industrialisation. No, what we now need is for them to be consumers, they must spend and spend and spend and keep the wheels of capitalism turning. How can they spend if they are allowed to stay poor? As Marx said, the loftiest moral notions are but a thin disguise for mechanisms which promote the economic ambitions of the society that espouses them.

"It's not really hypocrisy; it's too deeply embedded for that. In fact, if you took this illusion of good-doing away, there would be nothing left in terms of ethical drive. Can you imagine a colonial England or an Imperial Rome that did not set courage and honour as its highest virtues, or the industrial eighteenth century without its respect for thrift, hard work and financial independence? Yet where are these virtues today? The encouragement of physical courage among young boys is condemned as militarism. Honour as a concept – that went out with the flood. Thrift – now there's a real moral antique. *Buy now, pay later*, that's where we're at. Financial independence ... what's the point? If you save and try to make something of yourself, you get lined up with the Sheriff of Nottingham's men and are fair game for fleecing through our sacred wealth-redistribution cycle which we call the tax system."

"I'm not sure what you're saying here. You sound as if you are disapproving of our modern world view and yet are you not saying that it's inevitable? If that's the case, then what's the point of either approving or disapproving? Surely there isn't any?"

"*Touché*, Inspector! You've hit the nail right on the head. Those of us who have eyes to see are condemned like 'the moving finger' or should we say 'the roving gaze', simply to record and, having gazed, move on. Ours is not to interfere, nor even, if truth be told, to chastise."

"If you took your Marxism seriously, you'd have to change the whole economic system in order to bring about a major change in the moral climate. And good old capitalism with all its scars and warts seems as if it might be around for some time yet. It has seen off communism in the Soviet Union and even China is beginning to show signs of weakening."

"True, but Marx, I believe, will have the last laugh. Economically and materially, the capitalist thirst for 'growth' is unsustainable. Apart from anything else, the planet will not be able to take it. Imagine the whole planet indulging itself the way we in the West do now. I can quite imagine the whole charity culture being turned on its head – campaigns to *reduce* wealth, *poverty* creation programmes, a religious revival even, only with one major difference, ... the replacement of the traditional all-powerful but caring deity by a vulnerable but vengeful Nature. You would be brought back into the fold, Inspector. There, you would get your god minus the consciousness. But in the meantime we must live with the nonsense of the sentimentality that now passes for moral concern."

The conversation flowed as Greenfield poured himself a

third whiskey, Stuart having declined all exhortations to complicity. As Greenfield expanded, he drew on references to his personal life. He was a less than confirmed bachelor, having failed to find his 'ideal of the *eternally feminine* in the instances of womanhood that had crossed his path'. Teaching had filled the need for influence on his fellow souls, but he admitted to only partial success in replenishing his resources after the constant drain of imparting what he had distilled.

"I often feel," he said, "like the man in the middle. When I read the great writers of the past I am constrained to silence. I only get into a kind of dialogue when I relay their thoughts to my pupils, but then the silence merely transfers from me to them. I talk and they listen. Occasionally however the cycle of silence is broken. That's when I get an outstanding pupil in my class. Then the loose ends join up and the whole learning-teaching experience becomes a dynamic progression."

Stuart was at that moment acutely aware of his own ineffectiveness.

"I suppose Snoddy was one of those special pupils?"

"Snoddy was the very best I've ever had. His mind is razor sharp and I mean sharp like a razor. It is unforgiving of what it considers irrelevances. Most academic minds take their greatest pleasure in unearthing, indeed sometimes inventing, detailed subtleties and weaving complex patterns around them. The crowning glory of their cleverness is to be able to declare a course of action naïve or an argument oversimplified. I sometimes despair of my fellow academics; they write papers and when you've read them you ask yourself why they bothered. When it comes to politics or moral questions you wonder if they are really using their intellect to find answers or are they merely in the business of justifying what they instinctively felt before they started out and, in the process, showing how clever and sophisticated they can be.

"Snoddy is better than that. He has no interest in joining in

193

on this pantomime. He wants to use his mind to discover courses of action to follow rather than courses of action to reject. In our personal lives when we are considering radical change we act on what we think offers the best chances of a positive outcome; in the academic world they reject anything that doesn't give a promise of the perfect outcome. It's not that academics aren't prepared to accept all sorts of preposterous theories and innovations. If these can be shown to be in line with political or moral or, most important of all, emotional orthodoxy, any kind of counter-intuitive nonsense is an acceptable gamble and a welcome way of proving their intellectual virility.

"In education, for example, the political orthodoxy is pro-democratic and anti-elitist. Think of all the nonsense that has been tried within the parameters of pro-democratic egalitarianism and consider the nature of the arguments against a commonsense approach to academic selection; they all come down basically to the insight that some pupils might suffer the so-called trauma of rejection – an unthinkable offence against the present emotional consensus. What also weighs heavily is that this 'flaw', magnified of course out of all proportion by the efforts of those anxious to sport their *caring hearts*, shows up early in the educational process – no need therefore for us to explore further along the line of consequences. We can conveniently ignore the longer term effects of our decision.

"Or again, think of the non-going debate about crime and punishment. The liberal credo is now firmly established – we all now '*know*' that the possibility of a single mistake is enough to make capital punishment totally unacceptable to any civilised society. But somehow our liberal sensibilities seem supremely unengaged with the plight of those who die as a result of our humanitarian decisions to demonstrate compassion towards convicted murderers, in many cases by releasing them early.

"Reason clearly demands that we proceed on the basis of

which approach offers the greater good or, conversely, the lesser evil. There will of course be disagreements when it comes down to judgements of particulars, but ideas are not to be rejected on the basis that they fail to offer the perfect solution. We come back again to the grown-up view of the world, Inspector. In the real world the gods fight it out; there is no one god who can resolve everything and heal all wounds. The Ancients knew this, but we deluded Moderns persist in our search for undiluted Good. What was it Samuel Butler said? '*A virtue to be serviceable must, like gold, be alloyed with some commoner but more durable metal.*' But what a pride we take in our purity, even if it is only an ornament. As a form of idealism it's in perfect keeping with the spirit of the consumer society – something to savour the mere possession of."

The two men had moved to the table, the *Mercurey* had been poured and Mrs Lehman's goulash served. Stuart was enjoying his role as a less than outstanding pupil, despite the naggings of his pride that he should make his mark.

"Let's get back to the little problem I set you earlier this afternoon, Dr Greenfield. "*There is no innocence in ignorance. By their actions shall they be judged. Suffer shall the 'children' that come unto me.*' Have you managed to come up with anything?"

Greenfield gripped his wine glass firmly by the stem but kept it held at arm's length in the manner of a chess player uncertain as to where to place the piece. It was as if he had to decide before speaking where his speech would take him, a difficulty which, one suspected, did not present itself very often to him. Finally he spoke, but there was a marked change in his tone.

"As I said to you earlier, Inspector, I see Nietzsche written all over this. The attack on Christianity is obvious; Christ said, '*Suffer the children to come unto me*', a declaration of compassion and love showing a reverence for innocence and purity. Here the statement is completely perverted; it has been turned into a demonic threat to innocence and purity. The reference to children suggests an educational context, although the use of the inverted commas would suggest that the word 'children' is not to be taken literally.

"What is not clear is the 'me' in it. Is the 'me' the origin of the threat, or merely the medium, like a plague victim who passes on the disease in spite of himself? This second possibility would tie in well with the first part of the message. What I think is being said here is that the absence of ill-will is in itself no defence against the charge of wrong-doing. We normally assess culpability on the basis of intent. Murder, for instance, is not murder unless there is the intent to commit it or at least to inflict serious injury that might result in death. But there is an alternative moral view. According to it, we must all bear the responsibility for the effects of what we do, whether we intended them or not. In certain fields this is widely accepted. A politician or a general who makes a serious error of judgment is expected to fall on his sword, as it were. But that is limited to the field of professional competence. In the moral sphere there is of course the crime of manslaughter; it invokes the principle of culpability in cases of severe negligence or downright folly that result in the death of a third party.

"The degree to which this principle can be extended into other areas of life is a matter of judgement. As it is, we seem to be willing to apply it to cases involving self-indulgence and professional incompetence, but it is unusual to see it applied to evil resulting from good intentions. The only area where that has operated in modern times, I think, was in cases of euthanasia and we have been moving away even from that in recent years; juries now simply ignore the law and refuse to convict if they are satisfied that the accused has acted in what could reasonably be considered the victim's best interests. I think that's what is behind the phrase 'by their *actions* shall they be judged', i.e. not their *intentions*.

"But you didn't tell me where you got this ominous message, Inspector?"

When Stuart told him that it had been found among Kennedy's e-mails, there was a visible reaction from his companion, but not one that the inspector could easily pin down. It had all the hallmarks of surprise, but it might have been feigned. The problem with surprise, or indeed delight, in its simulated form is that it is not necessarily totally phony, it might be no more than a polite intensification of the genuine article so as not to disappoint the expectations of the news-bearer.

"Do you find it odd then that Kennedy should receive such a message?"

Greenfield poured the remainder of the *Mercurey* into his glass and sipped distractedly, looking all the time into an area somewhere behind Stuart's right ear. It always irritated the inspector when people did this; it was as if they had sight of something that was denied to him, unless of course he chose to look round and the very consideration of such an absurdity intensified the feeling. The only thing to do was to wait for the pronouncement from the Oracle. Finally Greenfield spoke, but in tones that bore no trace of lofty Oracular impartiality; his words came with a hesitant intimacy which offered a share in its sense of exploration and uncertainty.

"Kennedy is a very simple man, Inspector. I mean that in the sense that he is totally lacking in doubt about his own identity or about where he wants to go in life. In Freudian terms you might say he is lacking a superego. There is no one in the inner watch-tower checking up on his ego as it goes about its business in pursuit of its goals. The goals are cast in stone – or maybe gold – and the only problem for him is how to get to them. The sole constraint on his '*beaverings*' is imposed by a process of social risk assessment; he does what he thinks he can get away with and remain acceptable to the kind of society that his ambitions are planted in."

"But what you are describing there, Dr Greenfield, is the way of the world, surely? Is this not the way most people behave and, I suspect, have always behaved?"

"Yes, you're probably right in that, but don't we have the right to expect a little more from a headmaster? He is after all a man charged with the responsibility of planning the shaping of attitudes and mindsets that will inform whole lives. He is not a moral civilian; it is his duty to man the watch-tower."

"Are you suggesting then that he might have been attacked not for something he did, but for something he failed to do?"

"I think 'something' is perhaps an understatement, Inspector. Morally speaking, one could argue that he was not even operative. 'Everything' might therefore be a better choice of words."

"And as a result of that the little 'children' that came unto him have suffered."

"Yes, but the statement is deliberately ambiguous. I go back to the inverted commas, Inspector. Perhaps – and I am merely speculating here – perhaps Kennedy is himself one of the 'little children'. His innocence is his lack of conscience and hence his freedom from any sense of guilt. '*He knows not what he does.*' These words are at the core of the Christian rationale for forgiveness. But here they are being challenged. Ignorance is being rejected as a defence against guilt. Innocence is the state of doing no harm – that, don't forget, is what the word literally means. Kennedy seemingly is deemed to be the cause of the suffering of those in his charge and hence the legitimate target of this mysterious avenging angel. Sorry, that is a most inappropriate phrase."

"And the avenging angel – who could it be? Is Robert Snoddy a possible candidate?"

Greenfield's head gave an involuntary jerk as if he had been abruptly woken up from an easeful flow of consciousness. His eyes took sudden interest in his wine glass, now nearly empty of the burgundy which had long since replaced the *Mercurey*. It came almost as a surprise that the glass did not form the focus of his communication when he finally allowed words to pass his lips.

"I'll leave that one for you to decide, Inspector. You've more experience of killers than I do."

An ephemeral smile crossed his face as he added, "I've a very old *Margaux* that I've been saving for a special occasion. Shall we sacrifice it to the evening?"

Chapter 19

It is a curious thing how fear of indiscretion is the first feeling that defines itself after a night of Bacchic indulgence. But on this occasion, as he shaved, Stuart was savouring the sense of virtue and innocence that comes with the feeling of being free of it. The wine had not had its wicked way with his tongue. It was Greenfield who had taken the stage and indulged in wine and words. How, Stuart wondered, did *he* feel this morning? But had his companion in fact been indiscreet? His philosophical meanderings had certainly pointed the finger at his former pupil, but he had stopped short and refused to confirm the conclusion which his insightful analysis of the message seemed clearly to demand. Perhaps he had been so preoccupied with the colourful by-ways he had taken that he hadn't cared to look to where they were leading him. But then again he might have been already very familiar with the destination and have decided that the flat-footed plods needed some directions. What had not come out, despite Stuart's best endeavours, was the nature of the personal relationship between teacher and former pupil. Academic admiration, a sense of pride of influence, an excitement at the prospect of what youthful energy might achieve after such a start as Greenfield had given, all these were clearly in evidence in the tones in which the protégé was spoken of. But when it came down to the simple question if Greenfield actually liked his gift to the world, the answer was far from clear. The more the inspector thought of it, the more the absence of warmth and affection in the master's voice was borne home to him. Greenfield was certainly not one to succumb to the sentimental lure of the trail that leads us along, on the back of the pride we take in our acceptance by those we admire, up to the credit we claim for our chimeric insight into the rich vein of decency and humanity that others, seemingly, have lacked the perspicacity to divine. But there were other routes he might have gone down; he might have acknowledged even the ugliest forms of youthful egoism and set them against the boy's individual take on the world, offered not by way of excuse, but merely to provoke an uncomfortable confrontation between the general and its nemesis, a smokescreen that the Anglo-Saxon mind often throws up to avoid Teutonic obedience to rationalist bullying. But there was little or nothing of the personally individual in Greenfield's references to Snoddy, no little anecdotes that cherished a heart, even a flawed heart; everything was focused on the brain, a brain which soared through the airs of rationality and had no need of the endorsement of the intimate. But a doubt lingered: did the words reveal more of the wordsmith than of the truth?

Myles arrived and the two men set off for Oxford, Myles driving, through the streets which were taking their first gasp of relief after the morning pounding by the city's commuters. Stuart remembered the excited anticipation he had known as a child at the prospect of getting out of town into 'the countryside'. But 'the countryside', with its obligatory sunny meadows, red Ferguson tractors and hearty, ruddy-faced farmers speaking in tone-patterns that seemed to emulate the rustic environment, was lost now somewhere beneath the surface of things, replaced by the baldly rural, a less than significant variant on the urban. Stuart was of a mood to sympathise with himself for his loss, but he was pulled out of the languor by the gleam of morning enthusiasm in Myles' eyes. It injected a needed sense of beginnings.

"Tell me, what exactly did you do last time to check on Snoddy's whereabouts?"

"We checked all the German airlines, we contacted the German police and they checked with the farm where Snoddy was staying – as far as the people at the farm could tell, Snoddy had not left the farm that weekend. Remember, he had been ill and had spent the whole weekend in his quarters, which were in one of the out-buildings."

"What about food? What were the eating arrangements?"

"He was always left to fend for himself at the weekend. That particular weekend he had asked them to leave him some bread and cheese since he wasn't well enough to go out and shop for himself."

"And no one checked on him even though he was ill?"

"No. It was a very large estate owned by a German prince and run by an estate manager, not at all personal. For them Snoddy was just a farm hand, and not a very useful one at that, from what they told the German police."

"Did you make any checks at Snoddy's home?"

"We checked on the father. We thought he might have been implicated, but as I told you, he was involved in a darts match at the time of the murder. I don't see where you are going here, sir. Snoddy's alibi seems pretty secure to me and what motive could he possibly have for trying to kill Kennedy? – he didn't have any contact with the man."

"We'll know better then we've talked to Mr Snoddy."

This was the best Stuart could offer. Myles was right; everything that restricted itself to the factual pointed to Snoddy's innocence; on the other hand many things in the high nebulosity of the polemics of the previous evening had pointed in the direction of his guilt. But he could hardly explain to Myles that their mission to Oxford was to bring the clouds down to earth.

They reached Oxford as part of a large herd of vehicles inching inwards from the outskirts. Their decelerated entry into the city seemed to Stuart like the penultimate phase of a bungee jump; he almost expected to be spat back out. Myles had the address of Snoddy's digs which they had no trouble in locating, only to find from one of the student occupants that he had an early lecture, but could probably be found immediately after in a small café just round the corner from the college. They parked in a multi-storey and rediscovered their feet, the sense of vitality renewing itself as the anesthetic of motoring wore off. The welcome thought of coffee colluded with the aroma as they entered the café, deserted apart from a couple of middle-aged women in a corner swapping expertise on bargain shopping and an elderly academic reading *The Guardian,* critical eye at rest. Stuart observed while Myles ordered the coffee and scones.

The lecture was not due to finish until eleven, so they had a quarter of an hour to wait before a group of youthful faces and self-consciously noisy voices imposed themselves on the little café. Stuart was relying on Myles to identify Snoddy, but when they entered his sergeant had gone off to the loo. There were seven in the group, two girls and the rest youths vociferously new-fangled with their adulthood. They sat down at a big table close to the window in the manner of an occupying army – the girls were dispatched to deal with the order. Stuart had a good view of the faces. The tallest of the group was also the loudest. The topic under discussion – less under discussion, more bubbling on top of the waves of the talk – was Goethe's notion of an intellectual élite. Tall boy was dominant in his rejection of it as a symptom of the bourgeois oppression of the lower classes. A second voice forced itself through to make a case for paternalism, *provided it had a liberal base and was not driven by capitalist greed.* This caused a great show of anger from two of the remaining participants, who sneered at the absurdity of the thought that the middle classes could act out of any motives other than the capitalistically imperialist. Myles had returned to the table by this time and was anxious to point Snoddy out to his boss, but Stuart signed to him to sit back and listen. He had little doubt as to which was Snoddy, but wanted to hear more before confirming his suspicion. When the indignant outburst had spent itself, everyone seemed to look for a lead from the fifth member of the group, who up till now had said nothing. Stuart found it hard to know how he knew, but he was in no doubt that the silence that this figure had been zealously guarding held more sway with the group than the over-articulate utterances so ostentatiously paraded by the others. When silence met silence, this became crystal clear. There could be no question about it: this was Snoddy.

He was not tall, indeed he was the smallest young man in the group, but his shoulders were broad, and with his shaven head he exuded the threat of someone you wouldn't want to meet on a dark night. This image was reinforced by a persistent look of dismissal that radiated from his eyes and a mouth that was larger than should have been put on a face such as his. Yet despite all this, he did not have the look of the archetypal mindless thug. There was something in his comportment that suggested a high intelligence. Stuart was reminded of the invariable failures of make-up artists to make film actors look like apes.

After a moment of reflection Snoddy responded to the silence of the others. His accent was localized and his syntax interspersed with vulgarities, but neither had much import beside the quality of the voice which carried them. It was not the voice of a young man; it was a voice that resonated beyond its source and gave a stamp of authority to what it conveyed. Anyone who had been taken in by the thuggish exterior would have felt very foolish once they heard the voice.

"Goethe offers us the only hope we've got, and it's a pretty thin one. What you're talking about, Mike, is balls. Since when did the bourgeoisie ever produce an intellectual élite? What's been driving the world since time began is the f-ing *Zeitgeist*, but that's the biggest laugh of all – the great, so-called *Mind of the Time* is pure mindlessness. The middle classes are good at pandering to it and getting into its good books. What we have to do is get in there and change it, so that it starts doing the things we want it to. God is out of his mind, so we can get in!"

The shadow of a smile passed over his face and he consummated his little *tournure* with a brief sip of the coffee which the girls had brought back from the self-service counter. He then climbed back on to his pedestal of silence. As the others began to digest what the oracle had confided to them, Snoddy surveyed the room, more, one suspected, as a distancing exercise than as a search for visual intake. In the course of their optical wanderings, however, his eyes encountered the figure of Myles. A look of recognition was succeeded almost instantaneously by a broad smile which radiated pleasure. He got to his feet and, cup in hand, made his way through the obstructing tables and chairs to where the two policemen sat. As he approached, he extended his hand, obliging Myles to stand up to receive him.

"Sergeant ... Myles, isn't it? Have you come here to see me? I'm greatly honoured. And this is ...?"

"This is Inspector Stranaghan. He's in charge of our present investigation."

"Delighted to meet you, Inspector Stranaghan. I hope you cope better than your predecessor with the vagaries of life outside the brain-crèche. But why has the investigation been reopened? Has there been what you guys sinisterly call – a development? Do tell – I'm dying with curiosity."

Myles was clearly needled but Stuart broke in before a tone could be set.

"You haven't heard then about the attempt on Mr Kennedy's life?"

"I may have done. To be honest, what happens in that establishment now is of no interest to me. They can all blow each other's brains out as far as I'm concerned. There are very few good brains there anyway."

Myles was not to be broken in on.

"Can you tell us where you were around 4 o'clock last Saturday?

"What my sergeant means is: we want to eliminate you from our enquiries and to do that we need a brief statement from you.

This isn't the best of places to deal with such matters. Would you mind accompanying us to the station? – as we guys sinisterly say."

The smile of pleasure returned to Snoddy's face.

"I would be delighted to help you with your inquiries, Inspector – provided of course I am allowed a reasonable quota of clichés and you and your sergeant don't keep them all to yourselves."

"We promise to share them out, but if you feel you are being short-changed, you can demand to see your 'brief'. Listen, we're in no great hurry here. How about another coffee before we have to go and do the boring paperwork?"

"Your inspector is very different from his predecessor, Sergeant Myles. I'm surprised he was passed anatomically eligible for the force."

Myles looked at Snoddy in the manner of a cornered animal. He wanted to vent his anger by challenging his tormentor to explain what he meant, but knew it would be *his* weakness that would come out. Snoddy was clearly disappointed when no challenge came.

Myles was dispatched for the coffee.

"You seem to have formed a poor opinion of Inspector Winkworth – he's now *Superintendent* Winkworth by the way."

"Why does that not surprise me? I've looked into this and I've discovered that the sure way of climbing the greasy pole is to *prove* that you've broken through the mediocrity barrier, while at the same time giving all the required signals that you won't do or think anything that anyone, who wasn't a total mediocrity, would do or think. And the only really convincing way to carry this off is to *be* the nobody you say you aren't. The man's mind was like a sixties council estate; there was little of any quality in it and what was there was set out in straight lines. It was he who inspired the idea of *Plod's Law*."

"Which states . . . ?"

206

"All them what do bad things that the likes of us honourable Plods can understand, are criminals what us honourable Plods can catch and rehabilitate. Conversely, all them what do bad things that us honourable Plods can't understand are better not caught anyway, for it would only be playing into the hands of them nutters, allowing them to mess up all the decent truths that us decent folk know about decent skulduggery."

"And where do you set the parameters of *Plod's* ken?"

"Oh, he's most at home in matters material – thieving, blackmail, fraud – no problems there whatsoever. Sexual passion and thwarted ambition, he can do those too. Political activism – now he's getting a bit uncomfortable. His instinct is to wriggle back to more familiar territory. Terrorism of the left, that's easy – he has been instructed to put it down to economic deprivation, but Islamic terrorism, now that's genuinely tricky. The manual hasn't been written yet. So he is on his own with nothing more helpful than *guidelines.* To get what passes for his mind round it, he has to come up with a whole warren of racial provocations and for good measure he throws in a bit of brain-washing – *much must be forgiven for they know not what they do, and all that crap.* Mind you, in coming up with these excuses, he must make sure not to tread on any of his '*racial no-goes*' or he'll be in real trouble. These *racial no-goes* are worth keeping though – they come into their own when it comes to violence from the right. This is the one area where the Church of the Righteous allows divorce between badness and economic '*I-want-ism*'. The general notion of the Devil is of course a great social no-no – Old Testament rubbish and all that – but we have a New Testament version of *the Bad News.* Hitler! He came and dwelt among us and we were sore afraid. Since his death he has taken on the sins of the world and caused all good burghers to live in fear of a second coming. He *was* about as evil a bastard as you can get, there's no doubt about that, but why the focus on him? Why hasn't Stalin for example or Pol Pot achieved the same cult status? I suppose it's down to our background in monotheism; it rules out any propensity we might have had for '*polydiabolism*'. But what they don't get, these good burghers, is that they are allowing Hitler to continue to spread his evil by drawing all the resistance to it to himself – taking on the sins of the world – and letting the other forms of it have a free run. Sorry – I've strayed away from Standard *Plodism*. We are now on to *The Gatecrasher's Guide to the Dinner Party*."

"Did you come across many 'Plods' at St. Jude's? Surely my poor old boss wasn't the first to inspire you?"

"I wouldn't have used the name – his feet were too small and his accent was certainly much too clipped – but I suppose you could have described the dear departed Dr Stevens as a kind of Plod guru – a man worth his weight in words at any dinner party. Even those taking their first self-conscious steps in innocence he could talk up into a fury of goodness. Nothing was so bad that it could not be explained as a response to the impersonal forces of world capitalism. '*Forgive them, for they know not what they do*' – that was his motto – he even applied it to the capitalists themselves. According to him, we are all victims of ideological oppression – although just how he and his ilk came to be free of it enough to alert the rest of us to the danger, he never got round to explaining. There should have been a preservation order on the old bugger – he certainly shouldn't have been allowed to take his secret to the grave with him. Whoever killed him has deprived us all of the answer to one of the great philosophical conundrums – if we are all morally conditioned, what's the bloody point of any of us trying to come up with moral judgements? If moral determinism rules, all is permitted. So we're all wasting our moral energies: – them what make moral judgements, and equally, them what make moral judgements about them what make moral judgements. Unless of course we allow for a special category of human being outside the loop – say, all them what get to get to the dinner party, or, more accurately, them what get invited *back* to the dinner party. But surely that would make the dear departed doctor and his ilk something that dare not speak its name – *fascist liberals?* There, I've gone and said it. Are you truly shocked, Inspector Stranaghan, that I speak so ill of the dead?"

"No, I can understand your bitterness. It was he after all who expelled you from the school. You must have felt very angry about that."

"Not with him. He was too pathetic. You might say I was angry with the forces behind him. You want irony, you've got irony. I could forgive him, for *he knew not what he did.*"

"But I thought you didn't go along with his behaviourist assumptions."

"No, I don't, not exactly. I don't deny that people are driven by the force of the received opinions that come at them like piped music from all directions, but that doesn't exonerate them from the act of taking them into their heads. Having bad opinions doesn't necessarily make you a bad person, but it does make you a plague-carrier and plague-carriers can't be allowed to come and go as they please, can they, Inspector?"

"You are saying then, unless I have misunderstood you, that *there is no innocence in ignorance.*"

"Bravo, Inspector Stranaghan. I couldn't have put it better myself. You have grasped my meaning."

Myles had returned with the coffees and was listening attentively to the exchange. The expression of exasperation, which provided a facial commentary on what he was hearing, changed to one of sudden revelation at the mention of the snippet from the e-mail message. As if to celebrate his return to comprehension, he re-entered the fray.

"Did you think Mr Kennedy was ignorant too?"

Snoddy gave Myles a contemptuous look before replying through Stuart, who seemingly had been honoured with the job of interpreter.

"I had no personal dealings with the gentleman, but from

what I have heard on the grapevine, he was more of a *Plod* than a guru. I heard he is prepared to confer '*Judification*' on all, whether rich or poor, willing or unwilling. He doesn't seem to care what puny minds or efforts the new generation of *Judeans* bring to their studies. They are all his little children and they are welcome on his knee. You will excuse me if I shed a little tear in the presence of such high-mindedness. Don't make me laugh. Stevens at least believed all this guff. Kennedy simply works it."

"You sound remarkably like Dr Greenfield, Mr Snoddy."

"I've a lot to be grateful to old Greenfield for. He taught me a lot, but don't ever confuse me with him, Inspector Stranaghan. We don't see eye to eye on the relationship between word and deed. I don't suppose you have read *Faust*, Inspector Stranaghan?"

"As a matter of fact I have, Mr Snoddy. I read Part One when I was preparing for my scholarship way back in the mists of time."

"My God!" he said, re-admitting Myles to the conversation, "Your inspector really is a complete misfit. How did he ever get through the police medical? Did his brain not show up on the scans?"

Myles took his re-inclusion reluctantly under his notice.

"You remember at the beginning of the play," Snoddy continued, immediately re-cancelling Myles' membership of the group, "when the old sod is doing his head in to find an alternative to '*In the beginning was the Word*'? He's not happy with *the Word* as a translation of the Greek *Logos*. He tries *the Thought*, then *the Power*, but in the end he settles for *the Deed*. That's where Dr Greenfield and I go our separate ways, Inspector Stranaghan. He's a *Thought* man; I'm a f—ing bastard."

"You identify with Faust, do you? What kind of pact have *you* been making with the devil then?"

The expression of playful superiority drained from Snoddy's face. It now took on a look that seemed to call a halt to play and address the doings of adults.

210

"If you mean by that – have I walked out of the Garden of namby-pamby innocence? – then I suppose you might say I've fallen in with bad company. Whether you would call it Mephisthelean is a matter of interpretation. I don't do things merely as an exercise in power, although I put my hands up to enjoying the buzz you get from that. And I don't do what I do, thinking my actions are no more or no less than what I think they are. What I do is open to everyone's take on it. That makes the things that I do good, bad and indifferent, all at the same time. I might savour the good in them, but I don't expect a sainthood in the moral honours list. You can't expect gratitude from God for filling in for him; it just shows the old bastard up."

"So you play God, do you, Mr Snoddy?"

"No, Inspector Stranaghan, like I said, I sometimes fill in for him. I do what the self-righteous bastard should be doing. If, on the other hand, I wanted to mimic him, I'd join the good old C of E and preach the vanity of deeds. It would probably involve a series of workshops on innocence-cultivation or purity-arranging. Or is that the W.I.?"

"Could you give us any examples of these job-sharing arrangements you have with the Almighty?"

Snoddy paused for a moment in what seemed mock reflection.

"I could do, but I won't, Inspector Stranaghan. The Law is a sanctuary of the saints and I wouldn't like to cause any offence; there are certain things you don't talk about in front of the saints. They are such sensitive souls, you see."

A broad grin flooded his face; there was now more grown-up, less adolescence in his disdain.

Myles had sat through the whole exchange in an obvious state of resentful anger. He had taken the tone in which Stuart had conducted the interview as a "keep-out" sign to those, the likes of himself, who had not been formally inducted into this world of pretentious hot air. Finally, he could bear it no longer.

He drank down what was left of his coffee, stood up and announced it was time for them to go to the station and take the statement. Stuart was surprised, but not unimpressed, by this act of self-respecting assertion. Snoddy, on the other hand, leaned back in his chair, stretched ostentatiously and yawned like someone determined to prolong an already long lie-in.

"I've just remembered, Inspector Stranaghan. I have a tutorial at noon. It's not a big deal, but Dr Maitland takes it very badly when I don't turn up. He's a bit of an old woman – reminds me actually of the dear departed Dr Stevens. He's returning my latest contribution to literary criticism today and I'm quite curious to find out how he has reacted to my contention that modern French poetry is a load of bollocks. He outrages so easily, the poor man. Could I drop in at the station and do my thing around two?"

Chapter 20

They had a couple of hours to kill, enough time for a good walk along the river. Myles was one of those people who seem to remain oblivious to natural surroundings. When their attention is drawn to something outside the loop of their preoccupations – a bird singing, or a cow or some other animal inviting an anthropomorphic interpretation of what it's up to – they acknowledge reception of the impression, but leave you with the feeling that, even as they speak, the imprint is being washed away in the sand. The day was dull, almost overcast. The hint of rain in the air added to the sensation that they were on a formal visit from the indoors. Stuart had much to ponder and would have liked to give himself to it without the enthusiastic prodding of his sergeant whose earlier scepticism over Snoddy's guilt had now clearly fermented into devout belief.

"He's our man, sir. There can be no doubt. He practically confessed. Bragging on about '*filling in for God*', but he wouldn't tell us what exactly he meant. If he had, he would have had to tell us that he murdered Stevens and tried to murder Kennedy. What else could he mean?"

"Yes, but there's a lot that doesn't make any sense. If he were guilty, surely the last thing he would do would be to cast himself in the role of some kind of avenging angel. Did you notice how he kept using phrases from the e-mail? He talked about '*the little children*'. He made a very deliberate reference to the quote from the Bible, '*Lord, forgive them for they know not what they do*'. When I fed him the phrase '*there is no innocence in ignorance*', he made a point of saying that he couldn't have said it better himself. He was telling us that he was the author of the e-mail. But why would he do that?"

"It's his arrogance, sir. It's obvious. He thinks he's a master-mind; he wants to show how clever he is and how stupid we are. He's confident that, even with all the clues he feeds us, we'll not be able to charge him."

"There's no doubt he likes his mind games. But surely he can't have behaved the same way when you interviewed him last time?"

"He was just as nasty, sir, but he was much less forthcoming. I would have said, more defensive. He gave Inspector Winkworth a very hard time. He kept referring to books and characters from books, just like he did with you to-day, sir. But the inspector didn't know what he was talking about, and I could tell he didn't like it, and I can't say I blame him – Snoddy's a nasty piece of work. But as I said, the fact that he was in Germany at the time of the murder ruled him out as a suspect. So, thankfully, we didn't have to have any more dealings with him."

"I imagine that was a double relief to you after you had kept shtumm about the rape business with Gillian Sloane."

"To be honest, sir, that's when I really began to regret what I'd done. Dr Greenfield had painted a completely different picture of Snoddy to me – I imagined a decent, young, working-class lad trying to better himself in the world and being held back by some haughty bitch who thought she would put him back in his place. But I never for a moment thought he had anything to do with the murder."

"As far as the evidence is concerned, Myles, nothing has changed. We can't put Snoddy in the country, let alone in the area, at the time of Stevens' murder, we have nothing to link him with the murder weapon – not that we have a murder weapon, strictly speaking – and as far as we can tell, he hadn't had any dealings at all with the second victim. All we have is a kind of *literary* confession, based on words and phrases which he chose to use or endorse, not the kind of thing to impress the CPS. But *nil desperandum*, this afternoon might be the bringer of better bounty."

After a rejuvenating lunch in a pub by the river, Stuart and Myles made their way to the station where an interview room was made available to them. It was twenty past two before Snoddy appeared. No apology was offered for his lateness. He made the most minimalist of greetings and, without being invited to do so, sat down in a chair facing the table and leaned back, arms behind his head, in a pose of challenge to all-comers. Stuart allowed Myles to take the lead. Myles explained that they wanted to go through his account of where he had been at the time of the Stevens' murder and also at the time of the attempt on Kennedy's life. They then needed him to make and sign an updated statement. Snoddy paid as much attention to him as a boxer to the referee before a fight.

"You said in your last statement that you were in Germany, working on a farm in the Black Forest at the time of the murder of Dr Stevens. On the day in question you were ill and were confined to bed. Is that true?"

"It is not only true, Sergeant Myles, it is clear evidence that you have definite reading ability. At a guess I would say that that would put your reading age at at least twelve."

"What I find curious, Mr Snoddy, is that after two days in bed you were able to get up at six o'clock on the Monday morning and do a full day's work, farm work at that. That was some recovery."

"I'm afraid, Sergeant Myles, I can't account for the behaviour of the microbes and viruses that were behind my illness. Maybe you should try and get a statement from them. But you're quite right to suspect them. They're bad enough to make people ill – perhaps they're bad enough even to kill!"

"Did you at any time leave Germany during your stay there?"

"I think I understand your question, Sergeant Myles, in spite of your pathetic efforts to formulate it. Yes, I did leave Germany on one occasion. I went to see a friend in Strasbourg; it's just over the border, you know."

"When was that precisely?"

"That would have been the weekend before I was ill."

"And the name of this friend?"

"Monique Morin. She's a French girl that I met the previous summer when I was on a course at the university. I can give you her address if you like."

"Yes, we will certainly want to speak to her. Now, let's go back to the business with Miss Sloane. In your previous statement you said that you were expelled because some cannabis had been found in your possession. Do you stand by that statement?"

Snoddy gave a little nod, not to Myles, more to himself, as if confirming a detail in an audit. His reply bore the joy of antici-pated surprise.

"As a matter of fact I don't, Sergeant Myles. What I told you about my expulsion was a complete load of tripe. It was a little fairy tale devised by the good Doctor Stevens to make the world a better place, where good is done unto evil and evil gets hidden under it. There were no drugs. Little Miss Crumpet didn't take kindly to it when I didn't take gratefully to her invitation to give her ... – oh, I don't want to shock you, Sergeant Myles – her invitation to sex. So she made up a story that I had raped her. But I take it you know all this already?"

"Could you tell us exactly what went on?"

"We were supposed to be discussing Shakespeare's sonnets. It was her idea. I wasn't keen. She never had anything interesting to say about anything. Anyway, I went along and it soon became obvious that she was coming on to me. I pretended at first not to catch on, but when she put her hand on my leg, I had to react. I told her I wasn't interested and then she got offensive. She started insulting me and my family. She had heard that my father had been to jail and she latched on to that. I ended up slapping her across the face."

"Gillian Sloane is an extremely attractive woman. She could

have her pick of men. You expect us to believe first of all that she threw herself at you. And then you expect us to believe that you turned her down. Come off it, Mr Snoddy."

"I wouldn't expect you to understand, Sergeant Myles, but to me she is not in the least attractive. She is a cow – a set of reproductive organs. Sex with a woman like that is just fornication. It exposes nature's big idea in all its boring repetitiveness. Have you never looked at the birds building their nests and feeding their young? Do you never ask how they have been fooled into doing it? Well, mindless bitches like Gillian Sloane have that effect on me. I'm damned if I'm going to let nature use me like that."

"So you don't like sex? Or is it just women you don't like?"

"You really should learn to listen, Sergeant Myles. But then what's the point of listening when you don't have the brain to take in what you hear? If you ask your inspector very nicely, he might explain to you later what I've just said. Next question!"

"You must have been very angry with her when she came up with the allegation of rape?"

"*Anger* would cover it, I think. Of course I was bloody angry. What would you f—ing expect?"

"But you did nothing? You didn't try to get *revenge?*"

"Revenge. I notice you didn't say *justice.* Justice is only for the meek and mild, revenge is for the bold. If you're not prepared to be patronised by the great and the good and accept what they think is good for you, then you lose all claim to justice. They want to embalm you in victim-preservative, so that they can feel good about how sympathetic they feel towards you. Lift a finger to assert yourself and get justice for yourself and they turn on you and call it vengeance. It's *Uncle Tom's Cabin* all over again."

"Okay, let's call it justice. Did you try to get justice?"

"Do you mean 'Did I do anything to little Miss Crumpet'? You should ask her. But I'm sure you have already. Did she claim that I *punished* her?"

"No, but then maybe it was Dr Stevens that you took your anger out on. You felt he let you down, didn't you?"

"You could say that. The old fart was a kind of crooked cop, only in reverse. Instead of planting evidence to convict, he planted evidence to exculpate. He wanted everyone to be innocent in the most innocent of all possible worlds. That way, he could bask in the glow of his own goodness at appreciating goodness in everyone he encountered. He was a self-satisfied git! What really gets me is the way these people expect the people they patronise to live with the shit they refuse to deal with."

Stuart decided it was time for him to come in.

"Let's get back to what happened between you and Miss Sloane. You said she became abusive towards your family and your father in particular. Your father did nine months in prison about four years back for grievous bodily harm, I believe. He attacked one of your neighbours and broke his jaw. The neighbour was only a juvenile. What was all that about?"

"That's another one of those wonderful magic words, *juvenile*. It belongs to the world of '*all things bright and beautiful – the Lord God made them all*'. Douglas Mercer was a thug; he bullied everyone in the neighbourhood and made life a misery for the entire street. He'd come home late at night with his boozy mates and they'd play their music and keep everyone awake till all hours. If anyone complained they would get a brick through their window or their car would be scraped. They once set fire to a cat. It was old Mrs Tweed's. She saw them and reported them to the police. They got off with a caution and a couple of days later she had weed killer sprayed on her garden – next to the cat, that was her pride and joy. This went on for the best part of a year. The police were called out practically every week. Very often they just didn't show up and when they did, they did nothing. One evening my father was coming home from work. There was a group of about four of them drinking in front of the post office at the corner of the street. As he passed, one of them threw a can of beer over him. My father's not a big man, but he's very strong. He kicked the bastard in the goolies and went after Mercer and gave him the hiding of his life. The neighbours had to drag him off him; he would have killed him. The others all ran. This time of course the police did show up. Mercer was taken to hospital and my father was charged with causing grievous bodily harm.

"At the trial it was amazing how the truth got distorted. It was like a hall of mirrors at the fair ground. Suddenly Mercer and his mates all became victims of broken homes and lack of parental guidance; they had been failed by their schools and driven by their lack of economic prospects to a life which '*incarcerated them in a downward spiral of hopelessness*' – I remember that phrase particularly. They were '*young people*' who had a right to expect more from society than society had given them. Their behaviour was misguided certainly, but little more than youthful exuberance; it was certainly not deserving of the thuggish reaction of this mature man who should have known better. Nothing could excuse the viciousness of his attack on them. The jury of course was not allowed to hear what they had done to the cat – that would have been prejudicial to the case. If the jury system is such a wonderful system, how come they can't be trusted with all the facts? Anyway, I doubt if it would have made any difference. According to the mad logic that seemed to rule in the courtroom, the worse their behaviour got, the more it served to show how *vulnerable* – now there's another great word – how *vulnerable* they were to the forces of alienation. It's a wonder they weren't given bloody medals for the great bravery they had displayed in battling against the social pressures they were under and confining themselves to such a low level of crime."

Stuart and Myles listened with increasing attention as Snoddy's tone deepened. It was still spiced with cynicism and argumentativeness, but it had now taken on the gravity of remembered pain. He spoke more slowly and gave the impression of someone perfecting a text that had been gone over many times in his own head. Myles was untouched.

"But you're doing exactly the same thing, aren't you? You're making your father out to be an innocent party here. You said yourself, he had to be pulled off Mercer. He behaved like a vicious brute."

Snoddy's attention which had turned inward, rootling under the stones of the past, suddenly vented itself venomously on the sergeant.

"People like you make me sick. You want everyone to play your stupid goodness-and-badness games. Why the hell should we? Goodness is never allowed to win – it would stop being goodness then, wouldn't it? Better to keep it in its wrapping paper. Save it for a rainy day. It's like all that bloody nonsense about heaven, or like my granny's front room where no one was ever allowed, except the vicar when he called once every two or three years. Can't you see that my father was outraged? He wasn't just angry, it wasn't the beer that did it, it was the injustice of it all, and the acceptance of that injustice on his behalf by others who had no right to speak for him. Mercer was a piece of scum, but the authorities decreed that people like us, like me and my father and my mother, should put up with crap like him. They call it 'living in the community', that's their name for it. It's a great word – so much nicer than sending the scum – sorry, the disadvantaged – packing them off to the colonies, as they did in the bad old days. So much more caring now, isn't it? In Luther's day the rich got years off their purgatory with a few backhanders to dear old mother church – there was no need for them to worry their pretty little consciences about the nasty things they were up to. Now the approach is different, but not all that different. The respectable middle classes concentrate on having nice thoughts about goodness and keep telling themselves about how good it is to turn the other cheek, but it's always other people's backsides that get whipped, not theirs. They make bloody sure of that. The only badness that these people take seriously is goodness that's gone off. And goodness always goes off when you take it out of the freezer."

"Did Dr Stevens ever treat you the same way that the court treated your father?"

"No, you see I was one of his star victims, especially after my father had been to prison. There was a definite increase in both the quality and the quantity of head-patting that went on when I had the status of being a convict's son. Mind you, being the son of an *ex*-con keeps you pretty high up the sympathy tree. One of the sixth formers, a bastard called Frazer, had a go at me about my father and ended up spitting in my face. I was only in fourth form at the time and he was a lot bigger than me, but I managed to get a good grip of his windpipe and held on until he went blue. I was sent to the head's study. Stevens told me that I shouldn't have done what I did, but that he would take a lenient view, given the problems I was having at home. He gave me lines. He clearly thought I ought to be grateful to him – he could have expelled me – but I wasn't. When I asked him what he thought I should have done, he said I should have reported it to my house-master and he would have dealt with Frazer. I pointed out that that would have been more of a punishment for me than for Frazer – you can imagine how that would have gone down in the dorm. But Stevens insisted that the right thing was the right thing and I should have been prepared to take the flak. He got as close to angry as I ever saw him when I told him that was crap – he was expecting me to accept punishment for being the victim of a crime. I told him I had no ambition to be bloody Jesus Christ."

"So you resented Stevens for that – for being kind to you?"

"You simply don't get it, do you, Sergeant Myles? Stevens was a narcissistic creep who couldn't see past his own image. I had less respect for him than for the likes of old Scottie. Scottie would give you a thump round the ear if you did something wrong, but any time you thought he'd been unfair to you he'd listen to what you had to say and give you a straight answer. And he was interested if ever you came up with an idea that he hadn't thought of himself. But they're getting rid of teachers like that – they don't fit the profile, the straitjacket more like."

"Let's talk about Kennedy. You said you heard on the grapevine that Kennedy was intending to change the scholarship system and let in pupils from poor backgrounds irrespective of their academic abilities. Do you have a problem with that?"

"You are beginning to catch on, Inspector Stranaghan. Pity your sergeant isn't. Of course I've an f—ing problem with that. What the Kennedys of this world are doing is putting the varnishing coat on the sickly sweet shit that the Stevenses have already laid down. It seals in the smell and makes the shit scratchproof. When idiots like Kennedy, who have never had a thought in their heads except how to put things on top of other things, give this seal of approval to the crap that the Stevenses have been spouting, that establishes market confidence and the punters rush to buy into it. No one will be able to smell the stench for a generation."

"I didn't realise you took such an interest in current happenings in the *alma mater*, Mr Snoddy. This grapevine – how does it get to you?"

"Dr Greenfield keeps me up to date and I've kept in touch with one or two others on the staff."

"Who, for example?"

"There's George Ross – we e-mail each other from time to time. And then there's Rick Devine. He's writing a book and he likes to try some of his ideas out on me."

"Were you aware that both these men were having difficulties at school?"

"Yes, of course I was. Kennedy has been a right bastard to both of them. Suspending poor old Rick was completely out of

order. But what else could you expect from a *STASI* plod? Rick
doesn't see it that way, though. He believes in the office and the
authority of the office, but between them Kennedy and Stevens
have done a demolition job on his sense of upness and
downness. The man has completely lost it. It's his own fault
really – no one should ever pin their hopes on order hitting it off
with reason."

"Did you know that Devine owned a Walther P38?"

"Yes, he showed it to me once."

"You didn't think to mention that when you were questioned by Superintendent Winkworth?"

"Why should I? I didn't like Stevens, I do like old Rick. If
Rick killed Stevens, good luck to him. Mind you, if he did, he'd
be a better man than I take him for."

"That's a very strange thing to say. Do you mean to say that
you approve of the murder of Dr Stevens?"

"I can see you're shocked, Sergeant Myles. It's not nice, is it?
You're obviously a purist; you follow the recipe: '*Hear no evil. See
no evil. Do no evil*'. But think for a minute. If we get rid of the
negatives in the first two and open our ears and our eyes to the
evil that goes on in the world, does it not follow that the third
negative has to go as well?"

"And what Dr Stevens was doing was evil, was it?"

"It's not the word I would use, but certainly what he was
doing and what he stood for was a threat to the whole substance
of human intercourse. Call that evil if you like."

"That's complete rubbish. In what way could Dr Stevens
possibly be seen as a threat to '*the substance of human intercourse*' as you call it?"

"When dealing with other people it's usually a good idea to
treat them as if they were there. It's a distinctly bad idea to act as
if they were shadows that merely reflect the goings-on of forces
in some '*realer*' world. And that's exactly what our brave new
breed of '*-ologists*' do. In their ivory labs – which of course are off

limits to reality as you or I would understand it – they play their little games, turning up and turning down different frequencies of cosmic radiation – parental in-put, neighbourhood contamination, cultural noise – all this in an attempt to form a picture of what being human would really mean if all these influences were removed. And what do they find? They find a void! But think about it; what else could they find? ... People are what they are-in-the-world and if you take away what they are-in-the-world, they are nothing. These guys with their '-*ology*' degrees mean very well of course; all they want to do is mop up all the nasty things that people get up to and brush them out of the sphere of blame. But they can't stop it there. If people aren't responsible for the nasty things they think and feel and do, then what allows them to take credit for the good things they think and feel and do? It's funny, we always see Frankenstein as a fascist loony; it never occurs to the good burghers of the liberal left that *they* are the modern Frankensteins; it's they who are in the process of diminishing what it means to be a human being. They're well on their way to turning the whole of society into a huge nursery, with them and their good intentions tucking us all in of a morning and wishing us all day-time beddie-byes."

"So you see people like Dr Stevens and Mr Kennedy as the enemy, do you?"

"Well done, Sergeant Myles. You've eventually caught on. You'll go far. Maybe even as far as superintendent, like your last boss."

"Where were you then at the time of Kennedy's shooting?"

"And when exactly would that have been, Sergeant Myles? If you are going to set a testing question you have to supply the necessary information. Or was that the test? Did you want to know if I already had that information? Shame on you, Sergeant Myles! Always pitch the exam at the level of the student."

"Okay. Where were you around 3 o'clock on Sunday a week ago?"

"Easy. You do ask terribly easy questions, Sergeant Myles. I went for a long walk along the river."

"Were you alone?"

"I'm never alone, Sergeant Myles. I have always a whole box of thoughts to keep me company. If you mean, was I sharing them with anybody at the time, no I wasn't. Three would have been a crowd."

"Did you meet anyone in the course of your walk?"

"Not to my knowledge. But people might have met me. You'd need to ask them."

"Where did you go when you got back?"

"Now there's your first interesting question – at what stage was I back? Was I back when I returned to the flat or was I back when I got to '*The Pig and Poke*'? I think I'll opt for '*The Pig and Poke*'. About 8 o'clock."

"Can anyone confirm that?"

"Try Paul Cooper, Marion Müller, Dirk Lendenmann and Françoise Vaillard. I think I made some kind of impression on their retina and, I am immodest enough to say, on their cerebra, when I got there."

"We will check, Mr Snoddy. Be sure to give us their contact details when you make your statement."

"Tell me," said Stuart, "Would you happen to be the proud owner of a motor bike?"

"I'm impressed, Inspector Stranaghan. Was it the ruddy hue to my complexion – clear evidence of frequent exposure to wind – or something bicyclic in my speech patterns that gave me away?"

"Are you sure you weren't using the bike on that particular Sunday?"

"I have a clear recollection of looking down and seeing my feet under me. They were – and I can swear to this – definitely completely un-wheel-like, Inspector Stranaghan."

"Our forensic people will need to examine the bike. Where is it at present?"

"It's in a little lock-up which I share with a few other students. Your forensic people can be my guests; they can even take it for a spin, if they wish – provided they put some petrol in it."

"Thank you Mr Snoddy. Sergeant Myles will take your statement now and you can give him the details of the people you mentioned and – of course – the keys to the lock-up."

Stuart got up and left his unfortunate sergeant to his unenviable task. There was always the chance that the loss of an audience might deprive Snoddy of the spur to scorn. In any case over a coffee in the station canteen Stuart would resist the patrician guilt of getting minions to do what you don't want to do yourself. He had thought of phoning Heather. He hadn't heard from her for a couple of days and her presence was seriously beginning to be missed. Was that the same, he thought, as her absence beginning to be felt? He extricated his ancient mobile from his briefcase. He had a horror of mobiles; it wasn't the technology itself, just the sense of battery time ebbing away when nobody rang, and nobody ever did ring since he kept it switched off most of the time. To his surprise there was a message when he opened it up. It was from the desk sergeant back at *Somerton Road*. He had had an urgent call from Margaret Devine, who was anxious that Stuart should ring her immediately. She had stressed the urgency but had refused to say what it was about. Stuart rang the number she had left, but he got no reply. As he usually did, he responded to the let-down by refusing the cheery invitation of the answering machine to leave a message. There were follow-ups to be done in Oxford, checks on Snoddy's account of his movements and, of course, the forensics on the bike, but he could leave Myles to sort that out. He would take the train back and leave his sergeant the car.

Chapter 21

He tried Margaret's number again as he sat looking through the train window with that cosy sense of '*aboveness*' that often accompanies the still contemplation of the continuous dislocation of streets and gardens and homes. This time Margaret's real voice, not the puppet voice of the answering machine, responded. Over the phone it struck him more forcibly than before; she had the voice of a woman in her prime, youthful enough to suggest fetching vulnerability and mature enough to offer motherly sanctuary.

"Thank you for getting back to me so promptly, Inspector. I'm at my wits end. I need to talk to you urgently."

"I'm on my way back from Oxford, but I'll come round as soon as I get back – in about an hour?"

"No, I'd rather we met somewhere else. I'd prefer to talk to you in private. There's a pub on George Street. It's called *The Red Lion*. We can meet there."

Stuart's curiosity was aroused, but he knew too that he wanted to meet Margaret for other, more personal reasons as well. He realised that she had forged, or rather he had allotted her, a slot in his awareness – it was certainly more his doing than hers. He remembered how, when he was very young, his grandfather had made a bagatelle for him out of wood and nails and how, when he played, the little ball-bearing had certain slots and nail traps that it tended to end up in, whereas others simply never came into play. It was like that with the people he encountered – and in his job he met a lot of people; one or two seemed almost instantly to acquire that power of attraction and make him feel that he was 'coming home' when their presence beckoned. Greenfield was another. Two in the same investigation – that was a first for him. He realised now why he had not waited to tie up the loose ends at Oxford; he had not wanted to *share* her with Myles. The thought did not gratify his image of himself.

He took a taxi from the station to the *Red Lion*. He was a little early and had time to order a glass of merlot and take in the atmosphere. The landlord had many of the characteristics of the archetypal proprietor, friendly, in-charge, and slightly corpulent, but he fell short in one important respect; his voice was too high-pitched. Not only did this rule him out for top marks, it failed him totally – his other qualifications had raised expectations much too high; in consequence, they had too far to fall. Margaret's voice on the other hand, it had the opposite effect. It possessed that numinous quality that points beyond the limits of the here-and-now and raises it above any situation in which it is called upon. He thought of her as an inverted Eliza Doolittle and of himself in the role of a Henry Higgins restoring her life to a level of calm and control in keeping with the texture of the voice. He was quite lost in this sequence of thoughts and imaginings when the voice was suddenly fired with noise coming from 'out-there'. He looked up and there was Margaret standing in front of him. He felt an immediate stab of shame – like an incompetent artist having his painting exposed for the first time to public view. How dare he take the things of reality and reshape them as playthings in his own little inner world!

"It was very good of you to come, Inspector Stranaghan. I didn't know what to do. I'm at my wits' end."

She looked even more out of kilter with her voice than usual. Her hair clearly had had to fend for itself but had managed quite well and stumbled on some kind of ad hoc order. She was wearing a cream coat – Stuart had no idea how the effect was produced, but it was one of those coats which manage to emphasise the 'petite-ness' of feminine arms and shoulders and arouse the masculine instinct to protect. Recovering from his shameful sense of exposure, he offered to get her a drink. She would take nothing stronger than an apple juice. He went to the bar, ordered the apple juice and another merlot for himself and returned to the table to find his companion staring distractedly into the embers in the large fireplace.

"What has happened, Mrs Devine? Is it your husband?"

"Yes." There was a pause before she committed herself to what she had obviously rehearsed. "Richard is a good man, Inspector. You couldn't get a more trusting friend, but that's the trouble. He has been too trusting. He always thinks the best of people, and then they let him down. For such a clever man he can be such a fool."

"Who has let him down this time?"

"It's that little shit, Snoddy. I told Richard time and again not to have anything to do with him, but he wouldn't listen. He insisted that there was good in the boy. He said that we mustn't confuse breaking the rules with badness. Snoddy had an original mind and could see that many things need changing that the rest of us have just come to accept. He was angry certainly, but who wouldn't be if you had the clarity of vision at his young age to realise that the world is being run by a pack of lily-livered idiots."

"What has Snoddy done to him?"

"He got Richard to lie for him. That business about the gun – Richard told you that the gun had gone missing. Well, it turns out that that wasn't strictly true. He lent the gun to Snoddy!"

"But why did he lie? I thought he was concerned that we would suspect him."

"So did I, Inspector. I had no idea he had lent Snoddy the gun. But he told me the whole truth this morning. Apparently, Snoddy asked to borrow the gun and Richard was silly enough to let him have it."

"What about the bullets. Did he let him have them as well?"

"No. He insists that there were no bullets in the gun when he gave it to Snoddy."

"And when exactly did Snoddy ask for the gun?"

"It was just before he set off for Germany. He said he would like to take it with him and do some research on it when he was over there. He thought he might be able to trace its owner and find out something of its history."

"But surely Richard asked for it back when Snoddy returned from Germany?"

"Of course he did. But Snoddy came up with this most elaborate story of how he had given it to a dealer who had promised he would try to trace it and how the dealer had decamped when he went back to retrieve it. Richard actually believed him. You see what I mean?"

"But surely he must have been suspicious?"

"No. He said Snoddy was in exactly the same position he would have been if the gun had stayed in his possession. There are lots of Walthers in circulation and it was quite possible that it was not the same gun. Anyway, Snoddy was in Germany and couldn't have killed Stevens."

"So that's why he got so upset about the attempt on Kennedy's life. Snoddy didn't have as strong an alibi and the doubts started to creep in. So why then didn't he tell me the truth at that stage? I don't understand that."

"You're wrong, Inspector. He still believed in Snoddy. It was just that the whole business had flared up again."

"So why the change of heart now? What made him tell you the truth this morning?"

"It was the phone call he got from Snoddy yesterday afternoon. Previously Snoddy had been very grateful to Richard for keeping quiet about the gun. He had even offered to spare Richard the burden of it all and had told him to go to the police if the pressure ever became too much. This time, however, Snoddy's tone was totally different. He was almost threatening. He said that Richard might be seen as an accessory if he went to the police now and that it would be in his own interests to keep quiet. Richard was very upset. He went on the bottle again. I didn't know what was wrong, but this morning I finally got the truth out of him."

"Does Richard know you are telling me all this?"

"Yes. He agreed to that. He is still recovering from the alcohol and we thought you should be told as soon as possible. Are you going to arrest Snoddy?"

"No, I'm afraid not. There's a lot to be done before we get to that point. I'll need to talk to Richard myself and I'll need a new statement from him."

"What will happen to Richard? Will he be arrested?"

"No, but this time it's vital that he tells the whole truth and holds nothing back."

"You have been very good to us, Inspector Stranaghan. I can't say how grateful we both are."

Stuart thought to have noticed a slight force on the word 'both', but rejected it as wishful thinking – he had never been any good at reading women's signals, he tended to over-read them or to miss them entirely. There were many other questions he would have liked to ask Margaret, none of them to do with the case. He would really have liked to be allowed to know what occupied her mind when it was free from the this-and-that that imposed itself on her. But the aura of her damaged husband snaked around her, forming an impenetrable barrier to an affair even of this innocence. He could not begin to imagine any acceptable way of diverting the focus they shared away from the immediate concerns she had as a wife. He was reminded of his clumsy handling of the bereaved at funerals.

When Mrs Devine left, focus unassailed, he debated whether to get a Chinese carry-out and finish the evening in front of a dispiriting television or to go back to the station and do some homework. The canteen should still be open to provide something eatable and perhaps a little bit more stimulus for the soul than what was likely to be on offer on the box. He opted for the canteen, but when he got there he found that the smells of fried food did not do enough to add interest to the pristine vacuity of the empty rows of plastic tables. Apart from a few isolated diners reading a tabloid or staring into space, the place was deserted and decidedly cemeterial; it gave all the signals that it was time for humans to leave it to its nightly penance of plasticity. He ate quickly and drank down the metallic-tasting coffee, anxious to escape and open up contact with the computer on his desk.

He typed in the name 'Raymond Snoddy'. The photo revealed a striking family resemblance with the son. Snoddy senior had been charged with causing grievous bodily harm. His victim, a Douglas Mercer, had received a broken nose, three broken ribs and a minor fracture of the skull. Snoddy was found guilty and sentenced to eighteen months.

He then tried 'Douglas Mercer'. The incident with the cat was the most serious of a number of so-called minor offences which he had committed since the age of twelve. There were few details available, but the magistrates had expressed shock at the cruelty of the act and had ordered probationers' reports on the five boys. In the light of these reports which stressed the broken family backgrounds – alcoholic or absent fathers, feckless or simply overwhelmed mothers, poor educational attainment, slum housing, all the depressing ugliness of the vomit of modern society – it was decided to place them all on one year's probation. Stuart noted the names of the prosecuting officers in both cases and checked at the desk to find that both were still employed at the station and that one of them, the constable who had dealt with the cat incident, was in fact in the building.

"One of the nastiest little bastards I've ever had to deal with. He was the ringleader and you could see he took real pleasure in what he did. If it had been down to me, I'd have given old man Snoddy a ruddy medal. It was a piece of bloody nonsense sending him to jail for standing up to scum like Mercer. I'd just love to see how some of those toffee-nosed old farts behind the Bench would react if they had to put up with the likes of Mercer day in and day out. I tell you – we've lost the plot. Anyway, there must be some kind of justice in the world. Mind you it certainly doesn't come from the Bench."

"How do you mean?"

"Mercer has ended up in a wheelchair. Didn't you know? He had a serious motorbike accident."

"When was that?"

"A couple of weeks after the trial. He was doing his usual thing – well over the speed limit, showing off how big a man he was – but the brakes failed and he went off the road. He was a lucky bastard, mind you – ended up in some bushes, they lessened the impact. Otherwise he'd have been a dead bastard. Pity he isn't. But at least we've got him off our hands; it's the NHS that's stuck with him now."

"Did 'traffic' investigate?"

"Yes, but they didn't come up with anything. The brake fluid level on the bike was very low. That's what caused the brakes to fail, but as to why it was so low, that's anyone's guess. Anyway, for once we weren't stuck with *being professional* – whatever that means – and being forced to look a gift horse in the mouth."

"Tell me about the trial."

"The magistrate did allow that Snoddy had been provoked, but he said his reaction had been totally disproportionate, especially since his victim had been a minor. I'll always remember what he said when he was sentencing. He said that people like Snoddy had to be made to realise that *the law was a matter for the law* – those were the words he used, can you believe it? . . . the pompous git!"

"How did Snoddy react when he was sent down?"

"He took it on the chin. But his son . . . now he was a different kettle of fish. Spitting blood he was . . . called the magistrate for all the f—ing bastards."

"Who was the magistrate?"

"I can't remember. But it'll be on file."

Stuart felt he now had done enough to placate the gods of the day and went back to his *capless, lidless* home and slept the sleep of the justified.

Chapter 22

The next morning Stuart made an early call on His Worship Mr Jonathan Harte. Mr Harte was a man of slight build. His hair was his most striking feature. It was theatrically long with waves of grey, which, Stuart was mean-minded enough to suspect, had been strategically placed at the temples to honour the cliché of a head distinguished for its wisdom. Holywood would certainly have insisted on a pipe in his mouth. It was a glorious morning and the magistrate and his wife were finishing breakfast on the little patio at the back of the house. Stuart accepted the coffee that was offered to him by Mrs Harte before she retreated into the house. He did not fully explain his presence other than to say that he was interested in details of the Snoddy trial. (He did so against stiff competition for attention from a very insistent blackbird.) He expected to have to prod the Harte memory on the subject, but no such prodding was necessary. Mr Harte launched into a vivid and detailed account with almost indecent haste; Stuart was barely allowed to complete the syntactical necessities of his question.

The account followed the contours of what he had already heard the previous evening, the extra detail acting only as colouring. Snoddy had barely defended himself. He had shown no remorse for what he had done and in fact had indicated that he would do exactly the same thing again, should similar circumstances arise. He complained that decent people were not allowed to get on with their lives without being molested by vermin such as Mercer. The prosecutor poured scorn on Snoddy's claim to be on the side of decent people. How, he asked the jury, could anyone who inflicted such wounds on a boy lay claim to decency? Snoddy's true character betrayed itself when he used the word *vermin* – and he used this word a lot. Did that not show an arrogant, fascist contempt for his fellow humans, the kind of contempt that the Nazis had shown to the Jews? Snoddy had tried to play judge and jury; he had decided what treatment should be meted out to a boy whose family circumstances cried out for compassion, not punishment. Snoddy just told him he was talking shit. The jury did not take kindly to that – they found him guilty and he felt totally justified in giving him the heavy sentence he so clearly deserved.

"You felt he deserved the maximum sentence, did you, sir? Did you not agree that he had been severely provoked?"

"He most certainly had been, Inspector, but you've been misinformed; I didn't give him the maximum sentence. I was severe on him certainly. But don't you see? – It was precisely because he had so much public sympathy that he had to be seen to be punished. He took the law into his own hands. That was a more serious offence than the actual injuries he inflicted on that young man. We can't allow the authority of the law to be challenged by this kind of vigilantism. If I had let him off lightly it would have been a signal that in some way the law was sympathetic to what he had done. Look what has happened as a result of the leniency shown in euthanasia cases. *De jure* rulings have now been almost totally eclipsed."

"But wasn't that just a little unfair to Snoddy?"

"Perhaps, but you must never forget one of the basic precepts of the law – '*il faut encourager les autres*'. It is sometimes necessary to take the wider view. You must surely realise that, Inspector. Snoddy not only broke the law, he threatened its very basis."

"I believe the younger Snoddy reacted badly to the sentence you gave his father."

"Yes, he threatened me. At the time I didn't give his threats much credence. In my position you get used to that sort of thing. If I were to take all the threats and insults I get seriously, I'd been in a mental institution. But in the weeks following the trial a number of unpleasant incidents occurred. I'm in little doubt that young Snoddy was behind them."

"What sort of incidents?"

"My car was quite badly vandalised – the tyres were slashed and the paintwork was badly scratched. And then a week or so later weed-killer was sprayed on that large flowerbed over there. It contained some of the dahlias I was thinking of entering in the county flower show. One of our cats died of the poison."

"Did you contact the police?"

"Yes, I did. They looked into the matter. They spoke to young Snoddy, but they couldn't link him directly to the incidents. Nothing happened for a while after that, but then we were subjected to a prolonged period of harassment. Every evening a motorbike would race up and down the street and a couple of youths would position themselves on the other side of our garden hedge and play very loud pop music. No matter where you went in the house you couldn't escape it. My wife had to see the doctor for her nerves. She got that she couldn't bring herself to stay in the house and in the end she moved out to her mother's. It was several months before she had the confidence to come back. Even now she is on edge at the slightest sound of a motor bike, however distant. She's still on tranquillisers. I'd have to admit that it got to me too. I dreaded coming home in the evening. I thought of putting the house on the market, but I realised that that wouldn't work. They'd find out where we'd moved to and the whole thing would start up again. The police couldn't do a thing. The boys made sure to keep within the law. They kept within the speed limit on the bike and they stopped playing the music at eleven o'clock."

"How many boys were involved in this?"

"I'd say there must have been about a dozen at least. Never more than two or three at a time, a couple playing the music and of course one on the bike. They came in different combinations, as if they were working a rota."

"Did Robert Snoddy ever show up?"

237

"Oh yes. He was a regular. He used to leer at me if ever I got close enough. It was clearly part of his plan that I should know that he was behind it. He enjoyed watching me suffer."

"And how long did this go on for?"

"Oh, it stopped when the nights got shorter. But then when the clocks changed in the spring it started up again, although only on an occasional basis. Mind you, it had the same effect as it would have had, had it been every night. Your evenings were ruined anyway, for you spent them in a state of anticipation of them coming and you could never be sure they wouldn't until the evening was over. Once or twice after you went to bed and you thought you could breathe easily, the horrible violence of that motorbike noise would start up. The worst of it was the feeling of impotence. You willed it to stop, but then you remembered that unforgiving leer. You tried to grit your teeth and see it through, but you couldn't do that for you had no idea how long it was going to last. An eternity of noise seemed to stretch before you. I really got to hate Master Snoddy. He knows just how to twist the dagger."

"And there have been no further recurrences in the last couple of years?"

"Thankfully no. About two years ago I got an e-mail. It simply said – and the words are still engraved on my memory – '*Law, Law, why hast thou forsaken me?*' There was nothing further after that."

Chapter 23

Rather than return directly to the station Stuart decided to pay a call on Mr Snoddy Senior. The contrast of the drab surrounding streets with the leafiness from which he had come hit forcefully home. There were no high rise blocks, just little battery buildings, presumably designed to house little battery people. But then sixties and seventies designers didn't see the world that way. They saw the straight as the answer to the crooked, the clean and modern as the antidote to the dirty-old, and pre-cast concrete and glass as more resistant to time than the organic frailty of rotting wood and decaying brick. They had evidently ignored Shakespeare's warning of the futility of resistance to *Time's scythe*. Perhaps that was why they showed so little concern for *the breed to brave him*. The *breed* to be brooded in these batteries was likely to have something much less messy than blood in the veins and something about as spiritual as plastic in the soul.

Even at this early hour there was a group of youths standing at the corner outside the kebab take-away where Stuart had found a space to park his car. Funny how youths always *congregate*, yet somehow never succeed in forming congregations. No Messiah, Stuart supposed. The group seemed less threatening close up than at a distance, but close up your ears were assaulted by a pattern of speech straining to underline world-weariness, a superior been-there-done-that-ness. They paid him no heed.

He had no difficulty locating the house – number 47. The front door stood out from all the rest. The council must at some stage have received a job lot of green paint, for every house had been attacked with it. Not so, number 47 however. On it four large panels had been grained, each with a stippled design

239

within a mock frame producing a three-dimensional effect. The high varnish added dignity and gave promise of a proprietor, not merely an occupant. The door was opened after a couple of rings by a thick-set, grey-haired man wearing rather incongruous light suede slippers and holding a newspaper in one hand and a pair of what were presumably reading glasses in the other. There was something forbidding in his appearance; one could not tell whether he was showing simple curiosity as to the identity of the caller or a reflex hostility to a stranger at his door. The question remained unresolved when Stuart introduced himself, and when he was admitted to the house, he remained unsure whether curiosity had won the day or if he was being invited into the lion's den.

"I've come to ask you about your conviction for causing grievous bodily harm, Mr Snoddy."

Snoddy senior made no response. Turning his back on the inspector, he went over to the table at the window and deposited the newspaper and glasses. The thought occurred to Stuart that this freeing of the hands might be preliminary to an assault on him. However when he turned round, Snoddy's face showed no willingness for fight; it was the face of a man familiar with defeat.

"Take a seat, Inspector. I'll make us both a cup of tea."

Without waiting for a response Snoddy shuffled into the little kitchen and Stuart was left to his own devices. The room he found himself in had a Dickensian feel to it. On the walls were a couple of old prints – a lithograph depicting the Charge of the Light Brigade and a rather faded print of Constable's *Stratford Mill*. There were three small shelves of books to the right of the sad electric fire with its imitation wood surround which cheapened the room. Stuart got up and looked along the titles. There was a predominance of nineteenth-century novels, Anthony Trollope in all shapes and sizes of paperback, some George Eliot and what looked like the complete plays of George

Bernard Shaw. Among the non-fiction there were several introductions to philosophy and, much wrinkled at the edges, an old blue Pelican edition of *The Uses of Literacy*. Stuart remembered it well from his student days – or rather he remembered about it well – a study in the decline and falling of grass roots culture. The details were long forgotten – all that came back to mind was the supplanting of the homely *People's Friend* in the nation's affections by the vacuous charms of the modern women's glossies. He was renewing his acquaintance with the text when Snoddy shuffled back with two mugs of tea in his hands.

"I see you're a reader, Mr Snoddy."

"Here's your tea, Inspector. I can get you sugar if you want. Yes, I read a bit."

"No sugar for me, thank you. I see you have a lot of Trollope and Shaw."

"Oh, it's a long time since I read the books on those shelves. I get my books out of the library these days. The way things are going though, it'll soon be that there won't be any books to borrow, just downloads and pod casts and all that junk. What do you want to know about me thumping that little bastard?"

"I understand he and his mates were terrorising the neighbourhood. You must have been very angry when the judge gave you such a stiff sentence?"

Snoddy's eyes gave a flicker of aggression, but the flicker faded immediately, suggesting either a mere memory of a response or a response to a memory.

"No, by that stage I was past it. The whole set-up is just a bloody waste of time. It used to be ordinary decent people were encouraged to get on with it. Not any more. You're expected to put up with the likes of Mercer. The police don't do anything. I don't really blame them either. Some of them are just as pissed off about it as we are – they have to do what their lords and masters tell them to. It's all a bloody stupid game. Nobody asked us if we wanted to play, but the big boys need pieces to push around the board. That's us."

"By the big boys I suppose you mean people like the judge who sentenced you?"

"And the politicians and the press and the people that run what they call 'the public services'. I hate that word. They see the public as things that need servicing, just like cars."

"Did you know that after your trial the judge was subjected to a campaign of intimidation orchestrated by your son?"

"Yes I did, Inspector. And good on him. He didn't break the law. But I didn't ask him to do it, if that's what you're driving at."

"When you say that he didn't do anything illegal, that's not quite accurate, is it? Mr Harte had his car vandalised and one of his cats poisoned."

"There was no proof that my son was responsible for that. But if he did do it you won't find me shedding too many tears. It's about time the Judge Hartes got a taste of the medicine that they and their kind are making the rest of us swallow."

"And what about Mercer? I suppose you approve of him being put in a wheelchair for the rest of his life?"

"I couldn't give a shit about Mercer, Inspector. I suppose you're shocked. I know we're supposed to forgive and forget when something like that happens. Not me. Mercer was the lowest of the low and I am glad that life is going to be one hell of a pain for him. I wouldn't wish that on many people, but I do wish it on him."

"Someone wished it on him enough to tamper with his motorbike. Could that have been your son, Mr Snoddy?"

"I have no idea, Inspector. Your lot tried to pin it on him, but they couldn't. I'll tell you one thing though. If it was him, I'd be bloody proud."

"Proud that your son has become a criminal and has put someone in a wheelchair for the rest of his life? You're happy that your son should turn into a monster? Surely not, Mr Snoddy."

"There was a time when I would have been disgusted, Inspector. But not any more. If them that matter refuse to do their job and protect us from the vermin like Mercer, then what's the alternative? – We've got to do it ourselves. Sitting down and taking the shit that those vermin throw at us, just because the law almighty won't let us do anything, that would be like going to the gas chambers without putting up a fight. Given the choice ordinary decent people are being given these days, only a bloody moron or a mummy's boy with a big yellow streak would do the big-wigs' bidding."

"Tell me about Robert being expelled from school. How did you feel about that?"

"That was the saddest moment of my life, Inspector. I'd always believed in education and I had been brought up to have respect for people who had to do with education. I'd have loved to have had a good education myself. When I was a boy, I always thought it was a wonderful thing the way people like doctors and teachers could take an ordinary muddled piece of life and give it shape and meaning and have power over it. My father encouraged me to work at my books, but when it came to the crunch, he wasn't prepared to put his money where his mouth was. I had to leave school when I came sixteen, and go out and bring in some cash. I was determined that Robert would get the chance I didn't get. And he had done so well. He won all the prizes that were going and even got accepted to Oxford University. When that lying bitch made up that shit about him, I thought his chances were blown and he'd lose that place at Oxford. I don't say this lightly, Inspector, and I suppose you're the last person I should be saying this to, but I really think I could have strangled her with my own bare hands."

"So you must have been very grateful to Dr Stevens when he took the line he did?"

243

"I was and I wasn't. Of course I was glad Robert's career was saved. That was the thing that mattered most to me. But I'd expected more from a man of education like Dr Stevens. What's the point of all this education if you can't tell right from wrong? He should've taken her on and shown her up for the lying bitch she is. But he wasn't interested in the truth; he just wanted to smooth things over. It wasn't even that he didn't believe Robert; what really got me was he didn't care whether Robert had done it or not. If Robert had done it, he'd have deserved everything he got. I'm his father and I wouldn't have let him off if I'd thought for a minute he was guilty. Stevens didn't even like Robert. That was as clear as the eyes in your head. Yea, he said all the right things and went through all the right – what do they call it? – body-language – that's the word – but I could tell he hadn't a clue what makes Robert tick and he didn't really want to know. So what made him so keen on saving Robert's career? I'll tell you. It was all too good an opportunity to pass up to show how much he cared about this vulgar kid from the back streets. It wasn't Robert's career he was saving, he was just collecting material for one of those books of his. I went along with Stevens' shitty compromise, but I tell you, Inspector, it left a very bad taste in my mouth."

"So you don't think he had Robert's best interests at heart?"

"The man was living in one of those, what do you call them? ... those big glass domes they build to test how eco-systems work. The last thing he wanted was for nasty common messy bits to get in and muck it all up. People like Stevens don't give a damn about other people – and definitely not about people like Robert or me – they're all wrapped up in their own precious little eco-domes. I shouldn't have backed down and let him walk the way he did all over any faith I ever had in justice, or education for that matter, but I just didn't have the bottle for it. I have to admit, I let the buggers get me down."

"But your son hasn't, has he?"

Throughout the exchange Snoddy had become increasingly animated, but suddenly a weight seemed to descend on him and the energy drained from his face. He gave no reply. Stuart saw there was nothing more to be got from the interview.

Chapter 24

When he got to the station he found Myles in a state of excitement. The results had come through on Snoddy's motorbike; the mud deposits found on the tyres were similar to the soil in the woods around Whinny Way; it was not conclusive, but the soil in that area contained an uncommonly high amount of lime and there were few places even in the surrounding countryside where similar levels were to be found. To make matters better, the track marks found at the scene were consistent with the tyres on Snoddy's bike, although, unfortunately, this was less significant as they were quite a common make. The desk sergeant came with a message for Stuart that Superintendent Winkworth wished to see him. The message carried the same penetrating coldness for him as always, but this time he was spared the customary empty feeling in his stomach. Quite the contrary, he found himself welcoming the opportunity to demonstrate achievement and gain approval. But why in heavens' name, he thought, did he still crave approval? He quickly brought Myles up to date on the Devine confession and set him to work to find out if Snoddy had used an airport across the border in France, Strasbourg or Mulhouse, to get back to England, and then he went off to the confessional.

Winkworth listened with increasing discomfiture as Stuart built up the case against Snoddy. Stuart had associated the failure of the previous investigation to home in on Snoddy not with Winkworth himself, but with Myles' failure to report the true reason for the expulsion. He, of course, cut his sergeant's folly out of his account. This left the superintendent with nothing between him and what was beginning to emerge as a gross sin of omission. As this gradually dawned on Stuart, he tried to add a sympathetic edge to his voice, but he failed miserably. Winkworth seemed to pick up on this attempt and spurned it, in fact almost spat at it. He had no outlet for his resentment, but he could at least disguise his hurt. At least this is what Stuart concluded as his superior's voice became more and more clipped and his sentences more and more mechanically logical. So much for Stuart's anticipated pat on the back! It was decided that for the moment there was no need for a visit to Strasbourg to talk to Mademoiselle Morin. If Myles' investigation into the flights turned something up, there would probably be enough evidence to arrest Snoddy. In the meantime they would take things slowly.

"I'm afraid he has gone into school, Stuart. I didn't think he was in a fit state, but he insisted he was all right. He's suspended as you know, but he wanted to prepare some notes and pass them on to his A level class. He checked with Mrs Swanson and she had no objection provided he had no direct contact with the children. It makes him sound like a leper, doesn't it? People can be such prigs – sententious bitch!"

Stuart had never really seen the point of the vocative case – Why, as Churchill once observed, have a special case to address tables and the like? – but on this occasion the use of his Christian name muffled the informational aliment in the message.

"That's unfortunate, Margaret. I had intended to come round and get his statement this morning. As it is, I'll need to speak to him at school."

The '*unfortunate*', Stuart had to admit to himself, as he put down the phone, was the missed opportunity to see Margaret Devine. What was going on there? He felt the same kind of exhilaration that he had felt when he talked to girls when he was six or seven. Was it that innocent? Was there a test? Yes, it was innocent – he felt no guilt whatsoever towards Heather. But why had he not rung her? She could no doubt be doing with some

247

support from him; this was a difficult time for her. Then again, she had not rung him either. Was a gap developing? He would ring his wife this evening.

Myles had set the wheels turning, but as yet had not received any results from his inquiries from Strasbourg and Mulhouse. If they left immediately they could get to St Jude's just before morning break. It is curious how first impressions of a place gradually get worn away and familiarity is free to install a sense of certainty that a true picture has at last been forged. Equally curious is the way that certainty can be momentarily undermined, although never destroyed, when the memory flashes back to initial impressions. Stuart now remembered the sense of institutional formality that had imposed itself on him the first time he and Myles had driven up the path towards the main school building; the memory was a warning to him to be wary of the easy casualness which he had slipped into with the people he had come to have dealings with. But the juxtaposition dealt a blow to both versions of his perception of the place; there was equal disappointment that there seemed to be no human titans within the walls to match this architectural magnificence.

Mrs Swanson was decidedly less '*titanic*' than before. If previously she had seemed newfangled with her elevation to acting head, she now seemed to be simply '*fangled*'. Stuart resolved to look up the word at the earliest opportunity – he was dubious though that it had anything to do with '*tangled*' and '*fraught*'. The voice had the same calm assurance, but the eyes were no longer under the same spell; they darted about like mice in a room. Mr Devine would be in the staff study room which was just next to the Common Room. But they would have time for coffee first. The bell was just about to go for morning break.

On seeing the two detectives entering the Common Room with Mrs Swanson, Dr Greenfield left the small group he was apparently not quite lost in discussion with and greeted them heartily.

248

"*Quoi de neuf, mon cher ami?*"

Stuart always found such questions disconcerting; he never knew whether to acknowledge them as greetings or to make a gesture towards an honest answer. His response almost invariably resulted in a mild attack of tongue-tied confusion, followed by a wave of disgust at his poor performance. This time Myles rescued him with a very cheerful, but decidedly too informatory:

"We think we might be getting there."

Greenfield's face immediately flared up in an illumination of confused signals, but, not without a clear sign of effort, order was almost instantly restored and normal output resumed.

"And where might *there* be, Sergeant Myles?"

This being clearly a question, not a greeting, Stuart now felt up to the task of rescuing his sergeant.

"'*There*', my dear doctor, is where we might start digging, but then, as you know, rainbows are such volatile things."

"Ah, but not beyond the powers of a Wizard of Oz, such as yourself, I'm sure. Have you come to see me, Inspector? I'm not free until lunchtime, but I could be persuaded to visit a hostelry for lunch – alcohol-free of course, Mrs Swanson. I've a couple of frees immediately after and St Jude's and Mrs Swanson I'm sure could manage without me until battle lines have to be drawn with the Lower Fourth – I'm sorry, Mrs Swanson, Year 9 is it?"

"As a matter of fact it wasn't you I've come to see, Dr Greenfield, but I think I could manage lunch. Say one o'clock . . . at the *Green Fox*. That's the handiest to here, isn't it?"

Richard Devine had not joined the rest of the staff for morning break. This was apparently his first visit to the school since his suspension and Stuart assumed that he wished to avoid the embarrassment of handshakes and well-wishes. In actual fact, Mrs Swanson had made it a condition of his coming to school that in the interests of protocol he keep a low profile and avoid contact as much as possible even with his colleagues.

When break was over and the staff were filtering out of the Common Room, Mrs Swanson pointed the two detectives in the direction of the leper, while she herself went off in the opposite direction in pursuit of a couple of Year 12 girls who, she informed them, were staging an all too visual demonstration against Nature for its failure to provide womankind with a sufficiently alluring range of hair colour. She offered no more than a tight-lipped smile to Myles' quip that at least their *streaking* had not involved the removal of their uniforms.

There was a little private office off the main staff study area, used mainly by Year Heads when they needed to interview parents. Devine was waiting for them there. He looked 'rough at the edges'; he had not shaved and his clothes gave the impression of having been foisted on him. He looked the way Stuart always felt when circumstances compelled him to put on the previous day's sweaty socks. The man was a complete mess. Stuart wondered what his wife was still seeing in him. Whatever it was, he felt a strong impulse to snuff out what was left of it. Pity is an emotion that is difficult to rekindle without it descending into something more akin to contempt.

"I hear you have been less than honest with us, Mr Devine. I must warn you that you have tried our patience and unless you tell us the whole truth this time you could be facing charges of obstructing the police."

Devine's face showed no register of what had been said. His mind was focused solely on what *he* was going to say.

"I have not told you the whole truth, Inspector. I deeply regret that. I thought I was doing the right thing, but I see now that I was wrong. I lent the pistol to Robert Snoddy. I thought that it would look very bad for him if I told you and I thought I knew he was innocent, so I said nothing. Once I had made that decision I couldn't go back on it. It might have looked as if Robert and I were in it together, but I swear to you, Inspector, I had nothing to do with either shooting."

"Let's be clear this time. When exactly did you lend the Walther to Snoddy?"

"It was just after he had been expelled. Bruce – that is Dr Greenfield – had got him the job in Germany and he came along and asked if he could borrow the pistol – he said he might be able to discover something of its provenance while he was in Germany."

"But you told us last time that no one apart from Dr Greenfield knew about it."

"I didn't want you to know that Robert knew. As a matter of fact I've used the gun occasionally in my history lessons. It's important to add flesh to the bone. Not recently though. We don't do the Nazi period any more for A level, but I did once show it to Robert. He's very interested in the effects of Nazi thinking on post war politics. He has a special thing about that."

"What did you do when you discovered that Stevens had been killed? Did you get in touch with Snoddy?"

"I didn't know what to do. I went to Bruce and asked his advice. He told me that he would phone his old friend in Germany and get Robert to phone him immediately. It was a couple of days before Robert rang back. Bruce told me he still had the gun and would bring it back when he returned, which was to be in about three weeks time. He advised me to say nothing about it."

"What reason did he give?"

"He said that if the police found the murderer in the meantime a lot of pain would have been caused for no purpose. And if they didn't come up with anything I could always say that I was afraid they would suspect me and forensics would show that it wasn't the murder weapon."

"But in either case he was against you involving Snoddy? Were you happy to take all the blame yourself in order to protect Snoddy? Surely you had no obligation to lie to the police just to protect Snoddy? Why was Dr Greenfield so keen to keep Snoddy out of it? If I'd been you, I'd have been very suspicious about the advice I was being given."

"Dr Greenfield has been like a father to me, Inspector. When first Stevens, then Kennedy let me down, Bruce was like a rock. Without him I would have been in complete despair. The man's a saint, Inspector. He was trying to help Robert just as he had helped me. I was never going to say no to him."

"But did it not occur to you that Snoddy had a better alibi than you and that by protecting him you were making your own involvement look even more suspicious? If Greenfield had had your interests and Snoddy's interests equally at heart, he should have been more concerned with yours than with his in this particular scenario. What, do you think, made him put Snoddy before you?"

"I was Robert's teacher too, Inspector. I had just as much reason to help him as Bruce had."

"Okay. Tell me exactly what Snoddy said when he got back from Germany."

"He came to see me immediately he got back and said the most terrible thing had happened. He had made inquiries about the Walther and had got nowhere. Then one day he met this chap in a pub who told him that he knew someone who would be able to help him, but he would obviously need to see the gun. Robert brought it along the next day and that was the end of that; he never saw the fellow or the Walther again. He had been too embarrassed to tell me over the phone, but when he heard what had happened to Stevens he was terrified that he would come under suspicion with such a weak story. He really looked quite frightened – it wasn't at all like him. I agreed to say nothing to the police."

"But you changed your mind yesterday. Why was that? Why are you telling us the whole truth now? I assume this time it is the whole truth?"

"Up until yesterday Robert had been very appreciative of

what I had done. He had been a great support to me over that business with Stevens when I was accused of calling the girl stupid – and then again more recently when Kennedy suspended me. He phoned me a couple of times and even wrote me a long letter of support. It convinced me I had done the right thing by him, in spite of all the sleepless nights. But when he rang me yesterday he was completely different. He said I shouldn't have any silly ideas about telling the police about lending him the Walther; there was no proof that I had, he'd deny it and it would just be my word against his. And given the circumstances, the rows I had had with both men and keeping quiet all this time about the pistol, I'd be the one the police would suspect. He was so vicious in the way he talked and I just couldn't understand why he was saying these things to me, all completely out of the blue. I hadn't threatened to tell anything to the police, absolutely nothing had changed since we last spoke – why this complete *volte-face?* Then it dawned on me that it might have been him after all – he might be the murderer. I had never suspected him for a moment and I didn't feel at all guilty keeping quiet about the Walther. But after what he said to me on the phone ... "

"One thing I have real difficulty understanding, Mr Devine, is why you made up that cock-and-bull story about losing the gun. Why bring it up at all if you weren't going to tell us the truth?"

"It had been preying on my mind for some time – if truth be told, from the very beginning. I kept trying to remember who knew about the gun. I might have mentioned it casually in the Common Room ... I just couldn't remember. I had to live with the possibility that someone might have picked up on it at the time and then suddenly remember. In fact George had a quiet word in my ear and advised me to admit to owning it. It was he who suggested the story that I told you."

"George? Do you mean George Ross?"

"Yes. George remembered me mentioning the gun a couple

of years before Stevens was murdered. There was a small group in the Common Room at the time. One or two of them had left the school before the Stevens' business and poor old Charlie had passed away. But Peter Watt and Jimmy Blair were there at the time. They must simply have forgotten. In any case they didn't show any signs of remembering. But you never know – the memory can play strange tricks and I couldn't take the chance."

"Let's get this straight. You're telling me that Ross knew about this all along? Does anybody tell the truth in this school? When exactly did Ross offer you this advice? Was it during the Stevens' investigation?"

"Yes. But I just simply couldn't do anything then. I felt totally paralysed. And then nothing happened. I thought I'd got away with it. Then, when Kennedy was attacked, it all came back, like a nightmare – and in the middle of my spat with the man. I knew I simply had to do something. But it took a few bottles of Vodka and that silly attempt to bury my head in the sand in Durham before I could bring myself to speak to you. I hate telling lies, Inspector. It has nothing to do with being good, it's just such a terrible burden."

"And what about your wife? Did she know all along what was going on, or were you able to bear the burden of telling lies to her?"

"Margaret knew nothing. When things started to go wrong I realised that at the time – as luck would have it – I hadn't said anything to her about Robert borrowing the Walther. So there was no need to lie to her, it was just a question of going on saying nothing. She knew I had an old World War II pistol, but the name meant nothing to her and she didn't make any connection with the weapon that killed Stevens."

"Yes, but you involved her in that story about the gun going missing."

"I had no choice. Once I decided to lie to you, I had to lie to her. The last thing I wanted was for her to be involved in the lie.

Margaret is the best wife a man could have. She deserves better than me, I know that, but I try – believe me, Inspector – I try."

Devine was either the world's greatest actor or he was a man again close to breakdown. Stuart had little doubt that he was witnessing the genuine relief that comes with confession. He had seen it many times in his career, but always from men – women had a relation to truth that had mysteries he had never been able to fathom.

"Do you still have the letter that Snoddy sent you?"

"Yes. I have it at home. I always keep letters. It's funny. I have this feeling that when I come to the end of my life, if I read through all the things I have written or have been written to me, I'll somehow be able to make sense, or at least see some pattern in the way I have lived."

"I would be very keen to read that letter. My sergeant here will go home with you after you have made your statement and retrieve it."

Sending Myles would be an act of penitence. He could have managed to fit in a trip to the Devine residence himself before his lunch appointment with Greenfield, but a sense, not of guilt – he had done nothing to feel guilty of – more a realisation of having overindulged made him now savour the feeling of abstinence. Margaret Devine was a lovely woman, but she belonged in his head along with the Platonic image of 'lovely woman'. *Making the Word flesh* – in a sense that's what he had been doing. But that sounded less innocent than it was; the game he had been playing was really no more than the obverse of nostalgia, which enchants the mind when mere physicality becomes transfused with the saintly ghost of remembrances.

Chapter 25

It was a few minutes after 1 o'clock when Stuart arrived at the *Green Fox*. He had not yet had time to register his response to the news that Greenfield had lied to him again. He knew that anger and indignation would be appropriate, but he knew equally that the precise words and tones and facial expressions that emerged from the opening few bars of their encounter would play a much greater role in shaping his emotional reaction than the indubitable fact that he had been lied to by a man he had come to think highly of. It had often occurred to him that most of his feelings towards other people, especially the negative ones, were not hand-crafted by him at all; they were off-the-shelf as it were, waiting for circumstances to suggest that he buy them. Indeed, he had often had the feeling of having been duped, after he had used them beyond the point of being able to return them to the shop. Greenfield was sitting by the window, the *Daily Telegraph* spread out like a kite at the end of his outstretched arms and a bottle of claret lurking with an innocent air on the other side on the table before him.

"I thought alcohol was to be off the menu, *Herr Professor*."

Greenfield dismantled the paper and with it the barrier to the claret and his companion. His face bore all the signs of undiluted goodwill.

"What I say to the Mrs Swansons of this world, Inspector, is under special licence. It's something akin to poetic licence, but it's more extensive; it includes the content as well as the form. Mrs Swanson didn't believe my pledge of abstinence for a moment, but she was very happy that I offered her the opportunity to believe."

"You're not a great believer in truth then?"

"Ah, you're offering me the opportunity to cliché my way through a soliloquy on the nature of truth. Offer rejected! – but I might venture a few thoughts on the problem of belief."

"Yes, I would welcome your thoughts on the phenomenon of a credulous police inspector who falls upon a band of pedagogues all of whom seem to claim special exemption from veracity, and one in particular who gives every impression of being a seeker-after-truth but is in fact a maestro of mendacity."

Greenfield's face came to a halt in a no-man's-land between joviality and one knew not what. The 'what' was never revealed; joviality was resumed without even a blink of acknowledgement that the service had been interrupted.

"Tell me, Inspector, if I were to guess what you are referring to, would that persuade you that that was the only lie between us?"

When Stuart paused he did not wait for an answer.

"It's about the Walther, isn't it?"

Stuart nodded.

"Well, I would say it's about friendship. How could you expect me to tell you that a dear friend of mine has lied to you? The truth was his to tell. You don't expect me to rob Peter to pay Paul?"

There! It was decided! Anger was off the agenda. Stuart allowed his companion to pour him a modest glass of the claret, lunch was ordered and the two men got back to where friendship begins. It was not long before Stuart felt he could push for some more answers about Snoddy.

"Did you ever meet Snoddy's father?"

"Yes, I did. I attended his trial. Robert was very upset and he asked me to go. It was during the half-term break, so I was able to. Men like Robert's father are what make any decent society work. What happened to him was a disgrace, but it's not unusual. Our world is full of idiots in positions of authority. The endorsement they get from having been given their positions makes them think that they know best. If ever they are challenged into self-doubt the only test they ever make on what is best is how well it lends itself to expression in the language they use. It was ever thus of course, but I can't help feeling that things have got worse in this great age of communication. We are brilliantly inventive at devising ways of talking to others, but we haven't learned yet that it's in our talk to ourselves that the greatest dangers lie. People should not be let loose with words, Stuart. Think of the mayhem they caused when they were allowed to churn religion up into a cloud of lethal gas; during most of the twentieth century ideologies became their *airfix* monster of choice; nowadays it's just off-cuts of thought – a political correctness here, an *aren't-I-the-right-kind-of-person* attitude there – it's amazing just how much damage can be done when words get out of control. It used to be that we sent children to school to learn how to remove the poison from this great chalice of words, but now we just churn out different designs of the mug. Our increasing failure to teach our children how to cope with language has unleashed tens of thousands of *sorcerer's apprentices* into our administrative systems, not least into the higher echelons of education itself."

"People like Stevens and Kennedy you mean? You think they both let the school down? They are on a par with the judge who punished Snoddy senior?"

"Exactly so. They are the drones that move us closer and closer to the *brave new world* of word domination. We don't need newspeak – ordinary-speak is dangerous enough if we don't get on top of it. Ask any farmer – he'll tell you, a cow can kill you just as easily as a lion."

"And young Snoddy would share these views?"

Greenfield took a sip of claret and smiled. Stuart could not tell whether it was a smile of anticipation or if it had a tinge of sadness at a point regretfully passed.

"Are you bowling your Chinaman or your googly, Stuart?

You want me to tell you that I think Robert killed Stevens and shot Kennedy?"

"Did you know about his campaign against Judge Harte?"

"Yes, he discussed it with me. It was after he had vandalised the car and poisoned the cat. I told him to stop and advised him to stay within the law and organise a few of his friends to make life quite unpleasant for His Worship and his family."

"So you approved of what he did?"

"Yes, I did – apart that is from killing the cat. I'm fond of cats. Yes, people like Harte – and for that matter Stevens and Kennedy – only feel pressure coming from one direction. It's all very impersonal for them – they are only obeying the dictates of *professional correctness*. Well, maybe it's about time that a personal element was introduced and then, maybe, just maybe, they might start to act and think like fully rounded human beings."

"But surely then, given what you knew, you must have been aware that Snoddy was the most likely killer of Stevens? And yet you said nothing? In fact you went further; you persuaded my sergeant to keep quiet about something that would have pointed the investigation in the right direction."

Greenfield's smile returned, this time fronting a more distant soul.

"Another case of robbing Peter to pay Paul. And to be honest, Stuart, it wasn't such a problem. I liked the last Peter a lot less than I like the present one. And what's more, I'm not at all sure that Paul is totally off course for a better world. When I was a boy, my father used to take me to see cowboys and Indians at the local cinema. The conventional wisdom was that *Geronimo* was a stupid hothead who was leading his people astray, while *Cochise* was the wise one, advocating an accommodation with the white man. Even as a child, I could never accept that avoiding violence and war was wise, when the alternative on offer was a miserable existence eked out on a reservation. I see

259

no reason to betray those who put up a stand against the reservations we are putting people into to-day."

"Even when that involves murder?"

"Even then."

"But you are not seriously suggesting that Stevens and Kennedy were bad men who deserved to die?"

"When soldiers are fighting a war, do they try to ascertain whether the enemy they are trying to kill are good men? Would it make any difference if they were? The only criterion that carries any weight is the degree of threat they pose."

"So you see Snoddy as fighting a war?"

"I didn't say that, Stuart. All I am saying is that if he were, I would not betray him. I don't know if he is or not."

"But you clearly suspect that he is. Otherwise, why try to protect him?"

"I think you'll find that he has very little need of my protection. He is quite capable of looking after himself. As a friend though, I would warn you against arresting him. You would be making a very big mistake."

"I'll arrest him if he's guilty. How can that be a mistake?"

"You'll arrest him if you think you can prove he's guilty, Stuart. That's not the same thing. There, I've gone and broken my golden rule. I *have* robbed Peter to pay Paul. But don't expect me to pick Peter clean, even for you, my dear Paul."

Greenfield had returned to the tone of affable nonchalance that normally wove through his wit, but he refused to be drawn further on the question of Robert Snoddy. The conversation turned, as was usual with Dr Greenfield, to matters more general and Stuart left the *Green Fox* marvelling at how feebly and faintly anger and indignation had pleaded their case. Greenfield's warning to him not to arrest Snoddy had not come over as sinister at the time of its delivery, but as it cooled down away from the embers of the exchange, it was hardening in his mind into something resembling a threat. And with it the question began to form as to whether Greenfield was no more than its messenger – was he in fact its agent? But what started to gnaw at him most was the weakness that he had shown, and not for the first time, in allowing himself to be charmed out of reason.

Myles had taken Devine's statement and had returned with Snoddy's letter which he handed to Stuart, still in a state of self-recrimination and bemusement, as he entered the office. Not yet having decided what his exchange with Greenfield had amounted to, Stuart was not of a mind to pick over it with his sergeant and was more than happy to avoid the reflection of his unflattering picture of himself by soaking his concentration in Snoddy's epistle. And epistle it was.

Dear Richard,

I've just heard that you have been suspended by the pin-head Kennedy. I understand you had the audacity to have physical contact of a censorious kind with a fledgling female. For those with a limited treasury of English vocabulary 'to mouth', there is only one pigeon-hole available, you should know that; it's clear-cut case of 'Assault', in the same way as any physical contact of an approving nature would have been magnetically pulled towards the gravity of 'Sexual Harassment'. If you had merely spoken harshly to the girl, you wouldn't have fared much better; she'd have had layers of sensitivity suddenly bestowed upon her. The slightest raising of the voice, and that redoubtable browbeater 'Threatening Behaviour' is called from the shadows. A gentle word in her ear, provided of course you didn't get too close to the orifice, would probably have been the safest course of action, because effectively – or is it ineffectively? – it would have been a course of inaction. And inaction, didn't you know, is what is expected of those in authority, except of course when required to deal with others in authority or 'in loco imperatoris', who were silly enough to think that it's their job to act. In such cases the usual dose of tut-tuttings recommended for those in authority is really not quite good enough. This is an opportunity not to be missed, the chance to exercise authority over those in authority. It's the only time authorities get to be really in authority, and by God do they enjoy it! They find themselves in the unique position of being able to exercise authority and keep their consciences clear of all the stains of action; they are assured of benediction from the great white angels in the sky, for by exercising authority over those in authority, they are in effect _exorcising_ authority. And only good can come on their heads for that!

You are going to tell me that Kennedy doesn't know all this. You are going to say he is an ignoramus whose only concern is to contrive a career and build up a bank balance. You'd be wrong. He knows all he needs to know. Your name doesn't have to be Marconi to use a radio. It did a century or so ago, but not any more; nowadays any Tom, Dick or Kennedy can operate even the most sophisticated systems of latitudinarianism. It's just like IT skills; there's no point in applying for any position of authority nowadays until you can demonstrate possession of the necessary latitudinarian competences – side-stepping, ducking, euphemising, buck-passing, buck-passing denial, intention-valeting, all of these of course leading to the ultimate goal – immunity from the prosecution of criticism. A few years ago there was a drama series on TV with a judge as the hero. I couldn't believe it. The concept of heroic authority! I had to see how the BBC could live with such an ideological oxymoron. It didn't of course. The good judge was the hero, but what made him the hero was that he was constantly railing against the authority of those in authority over him. It's little wonder that pin-heads such as Kennedy pick up the vibes and mimic the behaviour.

But all may not yet be lost. You can't have failed to notice *the pride with which our present-day Knights of the Liberal Licence challenge and slay the dragon of nasty fundamentalist Christianity. They keep bringing the poor thing back to life so that they can valiantly slay it again and again. God, are they proud of themselves and the courage they show in refusing to bend the knee to the nasty and outmoded devils of theistic authoritarianism. Have you noticed though that, when it comes to Islam, it suddenly becomes 'inappropriate' to slay the dragon; the talk is of sensitivity, respect for other cultures, religious tolerance? Some tut-tuttings, yes, but no contemptuous intolerance for intolerance. And why not? Might it just have something to do with the fact that the bold knights are not all that keen to mix it with dragons that just might do a little bit of burning of the non-metaphorical kind?*

Keep the spirits up. You told me once you had Welsh ancestors. Maybe you should trust to the dragon.

Ex actionibus veritas
Robert

"What do you make of it, sir? What's that bit at the end?"

Stuart had had time to read the letter through a couple of times before Myles interrupted him.

"It's Latin, Myles. It means *truth comes out of action*."

"I don't understand that. How can truth come out of action? Surely truth has to do with how things stand; it's a kind of mirror, not something like a bicycle."

"Some philosophers think that we make things true rather than just see whether they are true or not. Our sense of what's true and false, and not only true and false – right and wrong, beautiful and ugly – arises out of the shape we give to our lives and that we make up our lives as we go along. So, ultimately, what we do determines the nature of what we think is true."

"But you're only talking about opinions here."

"Yes, but these opinions are so deeply held that we don't

263

recognise them as such. And when there is a social consensus on what is true, there is nothing to flag it up as an opinion. And when language gets in on the act, then that hermetically seals it in a big envelope marked 'Not to be challenged!' Karl Marx went even further. He said that all the notions a society has about good and bad and right and wrong can be explained by the way it earns its living and how successful it is at it. So if you want to make any major change to the social consciousness you can't just get up on a soap box and argue your case, you have to take some action that will change the base that the truth is built on."

"So that's what Snoddy is doing, do you think? But what does he want to change?"

"I think I can see what he wants to change, but what I can't understand is how he thinks what he is doing can have any effect. If nobody knows what he's up to, how can they be affected by it? It makes no sense."

The thinnest of layers of protective film had had time to set over what Stuart could only describe to himself as his emotional sell-out to Greenfield and he now felt up to sharing it – but only the purely factual aspects of it – with his sergeant. There was the vague hope that it would get reconfigured in the re-visitation. However just as he was moving towards this act of catharsis the phone rang. It was for Myles. Stuart was disinclined to put up with the irritation of the fill-in-the-gaps exercise which listening to other people on the phone always insists on, so he signed to Myles to join him in the canteen when he had finished his call.

The coffee tasted as bad as ever; far too much metallic dominance, but there was relish to be had in the doughnut he had bought; it tipped the balance back towards the organic. He picked up a copy of the *Sun* that someone had left on the seat and flicked aimlessly through it. The aimlessness of his flicking was matched by the attraction of the articles. He remembered Snoddy Senior's little library and the tatty copy of *The Uses of Literacy*. Someone really ought to write an update. Perhaps somebody had. If the pages of this newspaper reflected what was happening in the nation's psyche, then we truly were a nation of nasty children. The emotional reactions on offer were pitched at full volume and they had only two settings, toadying admiration or sycophantic anger. In either case sycophancy ruled. Anger filled most of the lead articles. It mattered little whether the venom was being directed at the thug who mugged an old lady and stole her pension or the football manager who had bought unwisely and failed to 'magic' a winning formula, the decibels of fervour deafened like the unrelenting rhythms that the young enthuse to when they go '*clubbing*' ... *Suffer shall the children* ... The words startled Stuart as they forced themselves on his consciousness.

Myles had the distinct air of a man bearing gifts as he pulled back the chair opposite Stuart and sat down. But just as the giving of bad news needs preliminaries, so, it appeared, did good news.

"You know I have been in touch with the various airlines that fly out of Strasbourg and Mulhouse? Well, it turned out that there are quite a number of them and I spent hours yesterday making contacts who could speak English. Well, one of them has just got back to me; he had the records of all the passengers who flew in and out of Strasbourg during the period we are interested in – I gave him a three-week period by the way, just in case it threw up something we didn't expect. Well it did! A certain Robert Fabian Snoddy travelled from Strasbourg to London on the 21.15 flight on Friday the 15th and returned on the 22.25 on Sunday the 17th. We've got him, sir! I'd like to see him get out of this one."

Stuart felt the obligation to live up to Myles' anticipation of his reaction. He was pleased certainly, but not elated. 'Pleased' would hardly cut it, so he simulated 'elated' – badly, and, seemingly, unnecessarily, for Myles was not yet done.

"I thought I might throw a couple of other names into the

265

hat, sir. So I got him to feed in the names of Devine and Ross and Greenfield, and you know what? On Saturday 23rd the 08.40 flight to Strasbourg was taken by none other than our friend Dr Greenfield! Now, there's a turn up for the book. It looks as if the good doctor is in on it too."

Elation was definitely required of him now, but all he could manage was a sickening sense of his own weakness. Why had he never seriously suspected Greenfield? Why had he allowed this man to impose his rules of engagement on him? He didn't really want to know the answer; he suspected he knew it already. Greenfield offered the stimulus of a world of interconnecting thoughts and impressions, a world much richer than the policeman's dreary daily orb of warmed-up fast-food consciousness. He couldn't really blame himself for accepting the gift and for being grateful for it. Anyway, the fact that he had gone to Strasbourg didn't mean that he was involved in the murder. There were many possible explanations. He was sure Greenfield would come up with something he could believe in. But was that not the problem? Did he believe Greenfield because he wanted to believe in him? Back to doubt and self-recrimination.

"I think we have enough to arrest Snoddy now. If we leave right away we can get to Oxford about tea time."

"And what about Greenfield, sir? Should we bring him in as well?"

Stuart had forgotten. Myles had as much reason to feel betrayed and to feel the self-loathing that this kind of betrayal brings with it just as keenly as he did. In Myles' case it seemed to have solidified into something more ready to assert itself and seek relief in its self-assertion.

"First things first, Myles. We'll arrest Snoddy and find out what he has to say. Dr Greenfield will be for another day."

Chapter 26

The journey to Oxford was a flat affair. Myles, who was driving, invited conversation, but Stuart was reluctant to venture out of himself. His thoughts were confused and he saw little prospect of giving them shape by exposing them to the cheery gaze of his sergeant. The sky had darkened and intermittently produced rain and the threat of rain, while the traffic threw up a constant shower of dirty spray. The windscreen wipers screeched a kind of disapproval at the dirt and spread it, as if it were part of their protest, in streaky whorls across the windscreen, until the washers were called in or the sky showed mercy. Stuart felt himself drawn out and caught up in the workings of the lubrication system of some great traffic engine. He tried to resist – better the warm confusion within than this horrible grating *'mechanicality'* without.

This time they had no difficulty in locating their man. Snoddy was at his digs. They were let in by a long-haired youth in T-shirt, jeans and trainers, all worn, as it seemed to Stuart, in the manner of an *I'm-a-cool-person* badge. Snoddy, who was similarly dressed, was at the kitchen table tucking into an opened tin of baked beans. The image of Popeye sinking his can of spinach in preparation for some mighty feat was irresistible.

"Inspector Stranaghan! And Sergeant Myles! What a surprise! I trust you have not come to chase the scholars from the temple of learning, so that the high priests can get on with their real business of bringing in the shekels."

It was Myles who responded.

"We would like you to accompany us to the station."

"Ah, so you *are* here to rid the college of that troublesome priest. I am flattered that I come so high on the list of thorns.

Was it the way I challenged the reverence we are supposed to owe to the *Nouveau Roman*? No, I've got it! Someone must have overheard me saying nasty things about that pretentious prig – sorry, that great man – James the Almighty Joyce?"

"If you don't come with us, we will have no choice but to arrest you."

"Now, that just shows how standards have fallen. In the old days the detective sergeant would have invited me to get my hat and coat. I know – I've seen it in the old B movies. Policemen were expected to stab competently at the rules of good manners. Standard grammar and received pronunciation were of course also *de rigueur* in those days. Even from the lower ranks, sergeant!"

"Are you coming or do you want to be arrested?"

"*J'arrive, mon vieux. Il n'est pas besoin de m'arrêter.*"

Stuart tried to hold back a smile but failed. He hoped Myles hadn't notice. But even worse, Snoddy had.

They drove the mile or so to the station. Snoddy gave a continuous commentary from the back seat on the various figures they passed, supplying them with voices, invariably self-absorbed and self-pitying, to register their opposition to the weather and all it stood for in their blighted lives. His observations were directed ostensibly towards Myles, but Stuart was clearly the intended registrar of his wit. If he was anxious about the impending interview, he did not show it. On the contrary, he had the air of a free spirit at play, enjoying the prospect of even greater treats to come.

They had phoned ahead and an interview room was made available to them when they arrived. Myles started the recorder and made the standard introduction.

"Did you ever think of a career on the stage, sergeant? I think you would be perfect as the narrator in Anouilh's *Antigone*."

Myles committed the briefest of pauses before 'ignoring' the remark.

"Ah, I can see you are not familiar with the play, Sergeant

Myles. It's a bit more of a challenge than *The Mousetrap* or *An Inspector Calls*, which I suppose form part of your training in the force – sorry; it's *the service* these days, isn't it? It's a funny kind of play, *Antigone* – not comedy, you understand. All the actors are sitting or lying about the stage at the beginning. They're dressed in their period costumes – ancient Greek, you know – and this guy wearing modern clothes comes on stage and introduces us to these comatose thespians and talks us through the roles they are going to play, what gods they are going to live for, or – it's a tragedy after all – what gods they are going to die for. You sounded just like that narrator, sergeant. It was something in your voice that made me think of him, or again, maybe it was just your suit."

It was with some reluctance that Stuart decided to take charge. In the course of his career he had developed the habit of allowing suspects, even witnesses sometimes, to follow whatever beacons guided them through the maze of memories and demi-thoughts and dramatised feelings that made up their engagement with the world. It was often a path through confusion into confusion, but sometimes the trail would lead to a treasure of coherence.

"I think we should get down to business now, Mr Snoddy. You told us you were in Germany at the time of the murder of Dr Stevens. Is that correct?"

"On both counts, Inspector. What I told you and that I told you."

"Can you then please explain to us how it is that you were on the 21.15 flight from Strasbourg to London on Friday the 15th and on the 22.25 return flight on the 17th?"

Snoddy smiled, although not in bitter acceptance, more, it seemed to Stuart, in approval of what had been said. In any case the smile was abandoned before he replied.

"You're mistaken, Inspector. How could I have taken those flights when I didn't take them?"

269

"But you did take them. We have the documentary evidence to prove that you did."

"By that you mean my name on the passenger list. Anyone could have used my name."

"You don't seriously expect us to believe that. Everyone has to give proof of identity before they're allowed to board, so not just anyone could have used your name. You were on that flight. If you continue to deny it I'll have no alternative but to formally arrest you."

"An inspector has to do what an inspector has to do, Inspector."

"Okay. If that's the way you want it. Robert Snoddy, I am arresting you on suspicion of the murder of Dr Gerald Stevens. You do not have to say anything. But it may harm your defence if you do not mention when questioned something which you later rely on in court. Anything you do say may be given in evidence. Do you understand?"

"Yes, I watch *The Bill*, so I know how it goes. I'm getting really excited. What's next, Inspector?"

"Tell me exactly what you were doing on the weekend of the 15th to the 17th July 2005."

"But we've been through all that. I've a low boredom threshold. I'm not going over it again. So this is where I get to say 'No comment'. I've always wanted to say that. If you asked me lots of questions I could try it out in Cockney, Geordie, Scouse – I could even have a go at Belfast. But then again that would hardly be fair. I think maybe I should save us all a lot of time, Inspector – I refuse to answer any more of your questions until I've been given access to a lawyer. You see, I know my rights. *The Bill* is a very educational programme. Every law faculty in the land should have it on its syllabus. Think of all the PhDs that could be done on it."

"You have a lawyer then?"

"Well, I could call a friend – the TV keeps coming up,

doesn't it? He's a PhD law student. Don't worry, Inspector, he's fully qualified. I tell you what – if you give me pen and paper I'll write a statement, but I'll not show it to you until Dave has approved it. How about that?"

The writing materials were supplied and Snoddy was left to write his statement in the interview room while Stuart and Myles, strangely redundant after the lawyer had been contacted, went for a ritual coffee in the canteen. The mood was one of anti-climax. Myles tried to keep up a bluster of enthusiasm, but he was performing like a car with kangaroo petrol. Stuart felt a strange disappointment. At first he could not feel his way back to its roots, but it gradually came home to him that he had expected more of his adversary. All that show of wit and intellect and then nothing more than a simple denial that he had returned to England? He must surely realise that by flatly denying what could be so easily proven he was adding to the impact his clandestine trip would have on a jury? Then again, maybe despite all the sophistication, or more likely, in keeping with it, Robert Snoddy was just a common-or-garden teenager, guilty of the folly of all adolescents in thinking that cleverness can fill the boots of experience.

When the lawyer, a Mr David Montgomery, finally arrived he spent a good half hour with his client before the detectives were summoned to read the statement that had been produced and approved. Stuart expected a retraction of his denial of the visit to England and some kind of ingenious explanation of the facts. He was disappointed. The 'statement' stated little.

'I, Robert Fabian Snoddy, do hereby deny involvement in the murder of Dr Gerald Stevens. At the time of the murder I was employed on an estate in Germany. The pistol used in the murder was of the same make as a gun which had been entrusted to me by Mr Richard Devine, but at the time of the murder that pistol was no longer in my possession. It had been stolen from me by a

German person unknown. As regards motive, I do admit to having grounds for wishing to see the victim become just that – a victim. He was a man who had dealt in victimhood. He was a spiritual passivist, yet he was smug enough to exempt his own judgement from the imperative to exempt from judgement. Quis custodiet custodes? Who gets to be the psychiatrist in the loony bin? Maybe Dr Gerald Stevens died as a punishment for his arrogance – the arrogance of the forgive-them-for-they-know-not-what-they-do brigade? Perhaps someone did not want to be forgiven.'

Stuart read the statement and then re-read it, conscious throughout that expectancy was being directed at him. He passed it over to Myles and, ignoring Snoddy's interrogatory gaze, addressed himself to the lawyer.

"What kind of a statement is this? Are you happy for your client to make such a statement? What he takes with one hand, he gives with the other. He denies involvement in the murder, but then goes on to offer up a motive which I'm sure a jury will be very happy to accept."

"I am satisfied, Inspector, that the statement reflects what my client wishes to communicate. The motive element is his way of helping you with your inquiries. He wishes to encourage you to look in waters that are outside the normal navigation charts of Her Majesty's police service. It was in this spirit of cooperation that the statement was made."

Snoddy was grinning like a Cheshire cat.

"What I was trying to say, Inspector Stranaghan, is that in my view you shouldn't be looking for someone with a grudge; you should be looking for someone with a cause for gratitude! To be more precise, someone with attitude to his gratitude!"

Stuart ignored the jeer.

"But that someone is you, isn't it?"

"You remind me of myself, Inspector Stranaghan. But before you get excited, it was me as a ten-year-old that I'm talking about. When I was in primary school we had a student who tried to give the class its first lesson in algebra. He kept talking in letters. I got more and more frustrated. I wanted to know what the letters meant in figures. I thought he was just being awkward when he wouldn't tell me what x was. But, of course, he couldn't, could he? The value of x depends on what equation it's in. All I am saying, Inspector, is that x is the murderer; it's your job to solve the equation."

"Perhaps I should ask Dr Greenfield. He was the one who helped you organise your little campaign against Mr Harte, wasn't he?"

"Don't you think I could manage such a little thing all by myself then? I'm disappointed you have such a low opinion of my abilities, Inspector Stranaghan."

"And he came to visit you when you were in Germany, didn't he? That was just a few days after the murder. Why did he come? What business did you two have?"

Snoddy was about to answer, but the lawyer stopped him.

"Mr Snoddy has made his statement. He has nothing more to say to you at this stage. If you wish to know why Dr Greenfield made his trip to Germany, you should address yourself to him."

"I certainly will. But I must warn you that unless I get some answers from your client I will be charging him with the murder of Dr Stevens. I will go and see Dr Greenfield now and your client has until I get back to decide if he wishes to talk to me."

273

Chapter 27

Stuart found himself put out by the thought of confronting Greenfield. It was something that he clearly had to do, but he knew that he was irrationally predisposed to believe in the man's good will and he hated the thought that his credence was at the mercy of a man who had underfed him the truth two or three times already. He remembered what someone – it was Greenfield himself, wasn't it? – had said about Richard Devine, that he needed to believe that god was in his heaven and that made all right with the world; the tragedy of Devine's experience had been that the people in authority fell so short of the wisdom and integrity he craved that he was left floundering with no existential compass. Authority wasn't what Stuart craved – he had worked under such an assortment of spiritual and intellectual inadequates that he had developed a skin thick enough to protect him against the need to believe that there was a direction to be lost in the first place. What he had felt, with an increasing sense of disappointment, was his disconnectedness with his fellow beings. He had trained himself to curb his expectations and see the souls he encountered as souvenirs that a tourist might bring back from holiday – things peripheral to the business of the present, but nonetheless giving anchorage to the precariousness of being-in-the-world. Every now and then however he would be tempted out of his agnosticism and start to believe in other worlds out there supporting life forms similar to his own. Invariably though he would be forced to confront the dispiriting realisation that things were not as they seemed. The worlds that had promised so much invariably revealed themselves as barren of spirit, mere desert landscapes made up to appear as something lush and rich, but supporting nothing more restoring to the soul than the equivalent of insect life. The thought that really haunted him however was that the sand of this desert had also entered his soul, desiccating it and turning him too into one of these juiceless, bloodless creatures. In the early years of their marriage Heather had helped relieve this sense of cosmic isolation, but as the years passed the two of them had lost their borders to each other and, for him at least, their relationship had become a kind of *isolement à deux*, more self-assured and self-affirming certainly, but just as pressingly under siege from the surrounding void.

It was very late, past eleven o'clock, when he got to Greenfield's house. He had left Myles to arrange Snoddy's transport back from Oxford. In fact, he had used that as an excuse to see Greenfield alone; his sergeant's presence would have acted as an echo to his embarrassment and, if truth be told, it would have cut him off from his last chance to indulge his faith in the man. As he stood at the front door the sound of a Mozart flute concerto came through the glass like the third impression of a carbon copy – every note was audible, but the muffled music lacked the resonance to work the charismatic magic that is sparked when texture and pattern come together. When Greenfield opened the door however – at the third or fourth ring – the full sound poured out with the light and engulfed Stuart in an irresistible wave of reassurance that all might yet be right with the world. Greenfield almost instantly discarded the look of a man interrupted, and ushered Stuart into the study, the fountain head of the sound. He switched the music off and when Stuart refused his offer of a glass of old malt he poured himself an indecently large one before settling into one of the armchairs. During this time nothing was said by either man, but the silence between them had the same natural feel as the quiet that acknowledges bereavement. Stuart welcomed it; it made for a shorter distance to where he must bring the talk when it ensued. It was Greenfield however who was first to speak.

275

"You have come to reproach me, Stuart, perhaps even to arrest me?"

Stuart was grateful. Greenfield was making it easier for him.

"I have discovered that you went to Strasbourg a few days after the Stevens murder. I need to know why and, equally important, I need to know why you chose not to tell me about it."

"I don't suppose you would believe me if I said I am very fond of Strasbourg. I still think of it as the city of the young Goethe, rather than the home of that monstrosity of a European parliament. No, you're quite right: I went to Strasbourg to visit Robert."

"And why did you feel the need to visit Snoddy at that particular moment, in the middle of all the commotion here over Stevens' murder? Don't tell me you were just making sure he was settling in well."

"I could tell you that and that I had booked the trip before Stevens was murdered, but I'm sure you have the means of checking the booking times and they would show that I booked the trip just the day before I left. No, I went to see Robert because I had my suspicions that he was responsible for Stevens' death."

"And what were these suspicions based on?"

"They were based on conversations I had had with him when Stevens expelled him."

"Tell me about them."

"I'm not sure that I can, Stuart. I know the law doesn't recognise it, but I feel that the confidences made by a pupil to his teacher are just as privileged as those between patient and doctor or what is said in the confessional. I have never understood how it takes all that silly superstitious mumbo-jumbo for the law to show respect."

"I suppose then you are going to claim the same immunity over what was said when you talked to him in Germany?"

"I'm afraid so. In any case anything I reported him as having said would come under the heading 'Hearsay', wouldn't it? In which case I am not withholding evidence, am I?"

"It's a very complicated business. I'm not sure that you're right. I'd need to check with our legal people. But there's one question you should have no difficulty with: why did you not tell us about your visit?"

"Well, think about it, my dear friend. If I am not prepared to tell you what was said between us either before or during my visit, what possible purpose would have been served by my telling you that I had these conversations? And if I am not going to refer to the basis of my suspicions, why should the mere, unsupported fact that I had suspicions be of any interest whatsoever to the police?"

"Okay. But if you had suspicions, why on earth did you encourage Myles to withhold evidence that might have pointed us in Snoddy's direction?"

"That was a mistake. I acted out of a mentor's instinct to protect. And, of course, once I had done what I did, there was no going back. Poor Myles – he's a very decent lad – his career would have been finished. I trust by the way, that whatever comes out in the end we can still keep this between ourselves?"

Stuart felt his attack begin to crumble, but shame had some fight left in it; it still resisted the temptation to believe.

"Bruce, I would dearly love to believe you, but you must be aware of my position. As things stand, it's quite possible I have grounds for arresting you for obstructing justice. That would be a matter for the CPS. Believe me; I really don't want to go down that road. But you've got to help me here. Give me something that you can square with your conscience that will show that you are cooperating with this inquiry. I really need that from you."

As soon as the words were out, he wanted to bite them back. He had got the tone all wrong. Greenfield fortunately did not seem to pick up on it. He gave no sign of having been accorded the driving seat, and as he considered what Stuart had said, it was clear that he was working in a spirit of compliance; there was no trace of the condescension that Stuart had invited.

"I think there may be something I can tell you that may be of use to you, Stuart. When Robert went to Germany he had a motorbike, not the same as the one he has now, a small Yamaha, I think it was. There was no question of him taking it with him, so he lent it to one of his friends, a chap called Andrew Whitfield. If I were you, I'd have a word with Whitfield. I'll put it this way. It wouldn't surprise me if he didn't have something interesting to say about the whereabouts of the bike on the day of the murder."

The image of a dog, head bowed, tail between its legs, scampering for the door, flashed and then lingered as Stuart laboured through the necessary civilities before finding himself back on the street. Greenfield could not give an address for Whitfield, but he lived in the next street to Snoddy and would be easy to find. . Enough, though, for to-day. It was late … No, he would phone Heather. He had just enough energy left for that. She had left a couple of messages on the answer phone – nothing of any importance – and he had not got round to replying to them. But now phoning was somehow pressing to be done. *Telephonendum est Heatherae.* The old Latin gerundive had always appealed to Stuart; it ignored the '*who*' and spoke to the need for pure activity in a way that English could never manage. Besides, it was always a most useful *let out* for the detective who hasn't got his man.

They caught Snoddy senior just as he was leaving the house to get his morning paper. When he was told that his son was 'helping them with their inquiries' he showed no obvious reaction. The picture presented itself to Stuart of a man dragging himself across a glacier, hammering his ice pick into the ice as far ahead of him as he could reach and then pulling himself towards it – a cycle complete in itself and unapologetic for its lack of ambition. You could imagine that when he was younger he had been duped into trying to stand up and walk proudly on the ice; now he had learned his lesson and was settling for salvaging what dignity he could while crawling on his stomach. He knew young Andy well – a good lad, not as bright as Robert, doing a degree in something or other. He and Robert had been friends since they were kids, but he didn't get a place at St Jude's and had to go to the local dump. He'd have made a good plumber or electrician, but his parents wanted the best for him and he went to university. Last time he had talked to him, Andy was sick of the whole business – a complete waste of time, he said. All this came out unsolicited from the elder Snoddy, and in a flow that contrasted sharply with the reticence he had shown at the news of his son's arrest. When the flow dried up, he gave them the address and left them, making his way to the newsagent's and reverting to a sadness that brought back the image of a life dragging itself out.

Andrew Whitfield was, as Snoddy's father had said, a pleasant young man with a winning smile and a straightforwardness that offered the promise of a good will. He showed no surprise at the appearance of the two detectives on his doorstep and had no hesitation in answering their questions. He remembered the day of the murder well. The murder itself had stamped it on his memory. 'Bobby' had called just before lunchtime and had told him he needed the bike for the day, but would bring it back late that night and leave it in the lock-up garage where it was kept. Andrew had given him the keys of the garage which were to be pushed through the letter box if, as Bobby expected, he got back too late to find anyone up.

"Did he say where he was intending to go?"

"No, and I didn't ask him. It would have made it sound as if I needed a reason to let him have his own bike. But he did ask me not to tell anybody that he was back. Nobody knew and he wanted to keep it that way."

"Was anyone else here when he called?"

"No, he didn't actually call at the house; he called on the

phone. I met him at the garage and gave him the key."

"So nobody apart from you saw him or spoke to him?"

"My mother answered the phone, but she didn't recognise his voice. I know that for she asked me afterwards who had rung."

"And did you tell her?"

"No, as I said, Bobby didn't want anyone to know."

"But were you not suspicious when you heard about the murder? Surely you must have wondered if 'Bobby' had something to do with it."

There was a momentary abandonment of openness in the reply, which was hesitant and unaccompanied for the first time by an obvious desire to please.

"Bobby is my friend. I didn't know this headmaster man. Even if Bobby had something to do with his killing, why should I take his side against Bobby? I trust Bobby and I trust his judgement. If it was the wrong thing to do, then I trust he didn't do it. And if it was the right thing to do, then why should I shop him?"

"But you are 'shopping' him now, aren't you?"

"No, Bobby told me to keep stumm, but if the police were to ask me straight out, I was to tell them exactly what happened. He made me promise."

"And why do you suppose he would he tell you to do that?"

"He didn't want me to get in trouble with the police, I suppose. He's my friend, but I'm his friend too."

"Did you notice the state of the bike the next day? Was it dirty? Was there mud on the tyres for example?"

"Yes, come to mention it, I had to give the bike a good hosing down. It was in a right state."

"And when he came back after his stay in Germany, did Bobby say anything further to you about what he did that day? Did you ask him?"

"No, we never talked about it again. Not mentioning it was a kind of ... seal on our friendship. It would have been cheap to bring it up."

Chapter 28

"We've spoken to Andrew Whitfield. He has told us you came and got your bike from his lock-up garage and when it came back it was covered in mud. Do you still deny you were in England on the weekend of the murder?"

Stuart had let Myles deliver this thrust. He wanted to be free to observe Snoddy's reactions.

Snoddy simply sneered.

"*Bien vu, mon petit Myles.* You should take up orienteering. You're a natural. I'd back you to get to at least the second marker. Mind you, I wouldn't want to have too much on you getting there before the others have finished the course."

Myles' 'professionalism' was running thin. He had taken as much as he was prepared to take from this spotty student with his pumped-up ego.

"Listen to me, Snoddy, all we need to hear from you is whether you are sticking with this little fantasy of yours of not being in the country when Stevens was murdered. If you insist on going on with it, you'll be saving us all a lot of time. We can just charge you and then we won't have to listen to any more of this rubbish that you spew out all the time."

"I do think you are getting cross with me, Sergeant Myles. I do like it when you're cross; it brings out the best in your metaphors. The way I see it is this. If I deny that I was in England on poor old Saint Stevens' last day, you will produce evidence that I am lying – and that's going to look bad for me in court. If, on the other hand, I 'admit' – and I use the word at this stage only under the immunity of inverted commas, let the recorder be told – if I admit that I have been fibbing, then that's not going to look very good for me in court either, is it? So it would seem that you have me, gentlemen. I will observe an honourable silence and keep my powder dry for the twelve just men and true – sorry, persons – how naughtily incorrect of me!"

If Snoddy was genuinely worried about his situation, his show of disinterest was deserving of one of the awards for the histrionic art that appear with the regularity of a menstrual cycle on our television screens. It was Stuart's impression that he was genuinely relishing the situation, not just the localised shots at Myles, but the wider, more global parameters of what was happening. If playing the part of the master criminal was central to Snoddy's self-image, his pride would surely have been dented beyond repair by the crude stonewalling he had now resorted to. That he had not been detected before was largely down to chance; Myles' failure to reveal the true nature of his expulsion, Greenfield's reticence and Stuart's predecessor's inability to understand motivations that did not conform to the standard deviations from the main concourse of social compliance. Had he been silly enough, having got away with the first murder, to attempt the second? Surely he must have seen that it was a case of good luck rather than good judgement. And why this persistence with the role of *homme supérieur*? Was he just a silly little clever boy capable of weaving great patterns with words, but unable to hammer a nail into a wall? Perhaps, and maybe that was why he kept up this taunting of Myles – to keep things in a sphere where he was at home and could dominate. But against that, he *had* hammered nails into walls. He had conducted a very effective campaign against Judge Harte. He had been very successful in getting his revenge on Mercer; *he* was now in a wheelchair while Snoddy hadn't even been formally taken in for questioning.

Myles was getting nowhere. Perhaps a change of course . . . .

"You are a Latin scholar, Mr Snoddy. What do you make of the motto: *Ex actionibus veritas*?"

282

"If I didn't know better, I'd say that it was a wise old Roman proverb, probably from the pen of some avant-garde thinker with a name something like *Kierkegaardus*. But I do know better. It comes straight from the hot thoughts of *ego veritabilis*, written in an epistle to a *Richardus Devinius* on the occasion of his backstabbing by an individual known to his enemies as *Inhumanus Ignoramus*."

"Ten out of ten for provenance. What about significance?"

"Oh, I'm sure I don't need to explain that to you, Inspector. You're an educated man. Existence precedes essence and all that. But I'll make it simple for our sergeant friend. When the lion makes its kill, Sergeant Myles, it eats the meat fresh and drinks the blood hot. Then come the hyenas; the best of the meat is gone and what's left is congealed in the blood that has run cold. But they make do. And then it's the turn of the vultures. By this time the meat is almost putrefied and stinks to high heaven. A fresh kill is needed. The truth's like that, Sergeant. Someone ventures into new territory, wrestles with reality and makes new artefacts of truth; then the second string of thinkers come along and butcher that truth and pick out bits and pieces of it and think they are eating of the food of the gods. Then finally the invasion of the *Pöbel* – the *Pöbel*, that's people like you, Sergeant – and they don't even know that they're eating shit. They will take anything as the truth simply because it's there – available and digestible."

"Stevens was a hyena and Kennedy a vulture, am I right?"

"Well done, Inspector! It takes guts to go after the truth and wrestle with it and bring it down. The Stevenses of this world haven't got that kind of grit. They just want to prettify everything. For them truth is beautiful, but they can't see any difference between what is beautiful and what is pretty. They turn the truth into chintz tablecloths and velvet curtains and God, are they house-proud! As for the Kennedys, they don't even look for the pretty; they are the architects of the sixties and seventies and they are as soulless as the buildings they design.

They build plastic cowsheds for the people who have had their souls taken away by the chintz and velvet brigade."

"So you thought a fresh injection of 'truth' was needed – an act of purification to clear the air and rid St Jude's at least of the stench of plastic?"

"I like your equation, Inspector Stranaghan, but why is it you always insist on using 'u' and 'i'? What's wrong with good old 'x' and 'y'?"

This was becoming too much like a home game for Snoddy. Just like his mentor, he was more than willing to be drawn on the machinations of the *Zeitgeist*, but they were not going to get anything out of him that would add to the evidence they already had. Did they really need any more? They had already more than enough to charge him. So why was he drawing it out? There was something niggling, something that didn't quite fit. Stuart had the same feeling about the case that he remembered having when he was a philosophy student. He could never believe that he had understood any philosopher until he could *believe* what the philosopher was offering. It was the act of believing that mattered – after that he could throw his belief in the dust bin. In this case he had not even got to believing yet! He was still unable to see how Snoddy was making sense to himself. Sometimes at university he had had to settle for an understanding in words; Leibniz' theory of monads, all forms of Christian belief in the Resurrection from the 'happy-clappy' to the monastically devout – and now Snoddy's unclever cleverness – or was it Snoddy's clever uncleverness? – they all had to be closed and put back on the shelf marked: 'Comprehended but undigested'. He had got his mouth round it, but he hadn't swallowed.

He left it to an eager Myles to do the honours.

Chapter 29

It took several months for the case to come to trial. Heather had returned from Ireland and life had got back to a comfortable familiarity. There were just as many days without caps on them, but with her there they did not seem to inspire the same sense of agoraphobia. Stuart had returned to his own station and had been back to dealing with the usual run of cases, crimes, that is, committed safely within the standard deviation of behaviouristic predictability. '*Stick-insect mechanicality*' he called it. And depressing it was to feel the pressures of a social universe imploding back towards the point of the great libidinal shriek. The '*I want – I need – Give me*' was getting louder and louder and with the increasing din came a coarsening and narrowing of what they wanted, what they needed, what had to be given them. In one case he had had to deal with an eighty-three-year-old woman badly beaten by two youths who had forced their way into her house and stolen £80 from her – they weren't on drugs, they just needed the money to buy tickets for a pop concert. Such are the modern *Raskolnikovs*! They would of course go through the system; it would be shown that they had been 'let down' by the education system, by the lack of parental guidance, there would be the inevitable show of tut-tutting, initially targeted at the boys but then, almost imperceptively, fanning out to wag a finger at an uncaring but, conveniently, anonymous society. He had lost count of the times he had seen this happen, but he had never been able to bring himself to accept it. Snoddy senior had been served up on the altar to it. The guilt that floats like gossamer in the liberal air is a great palliative, leave it there, let it flit about aimlessly, but try to direct it and it will come down on your head. It's a kind of anti-matter that has all the appearance of matter, but it destroys anyone unsophisticated enough to believe in its substance.

The Snoddy trial opened just after Christmas. He was charged with the murder of Dr Stevens and the attempted murder of Mr Kennedy. The prosecution ground its way through the evidence. Much was made of Snoddy's resentment at his expulsion and the true reason for it emerged, although not the fact of Myles' possession of the truth and his failure to act on it. Judge Harte was called to show how vindictive Snoddy had been in his campaign against him, establishing that Snoddy was not a man to let grievances die in their own ash. The main evidence was of course Snoddy's failure to account for his movements when the murder was committed. He had secretly returned to England and recovered his motor bike, which was in a muddy state when it came back. Not only had he lied initially to the police, but when confronted with the evidence, he had continued to deny that he had left Germany. The second main prong of the prosecution attack was the Walther. The same Walther had been used in both crimes. Snoddy had had such a weapon in his possession; his reason for borrowing it in the first place was shown to be very dubious – he had never previously shown any interest in the weapon – and he had come up with a very lame account of how he had lost it to the proverbial man in a pub. This was the main link to the attempt on Kennedy's life, but there was also the fact that he could not account for his movements and that the mud found on the tyres of his motor bike was rare in that part of the country except in the area around Whinny Way. The letter that he had written to Richard Devine was also produced in evidence, showing his empathy with his former teacher and the threat contained at the end that action would follow. The email message on Kennedy's computer came under intense scrutiny. Dr Greenfield was summoned to analyse it in terms of what he knew about Snoddy's mind set and he was brought reluctantly to admit that what was said was consistent not only with the substance of Snoddy's Nietzscheanism, it was also couched in a style typical of his former pupil. During the prosecution's case Snoddy's council remained passive, one might say lethargic; he challenged very little and had no questions for many of the witnesses. This included Stuart whose evidence went totally uncontested. With such lack of challenge it only took two days to get through the case for the prosecution. Stuart was due back to normal duties after he had given his evidence, but he couldn't think of missing the rest of the trial and had decided to take a few days leave to follow it through.

It was a cold, hard-to-get-out-bed morning. Stuart got up and looked through the window. There were small quiffs of snow in the air and a thin white covering on the lawn with the stubble of a green beard showing through. The image remained with him as he shaved in the bathroom, but his thoughts soon reshaped themselves around imaginings of the case that Snoddy's council was about to present. All these imaginings were vivid in their beginnings, but they tapered off before they got to a middle, let alone an end. In each imagining the defence had something in reserve that they were about to wheel out and use to crush the prosecution case, but the sound would go quiet and the picture dim before the precise nature of this weapon was revealed. Stuart remembered his first chess match for his school. He hadn't thought himself good enough to be picked for the team and although only playing board six, he imagined he was facing a master, an impression confirmed by the nasty little eyes that stared at him from across the board, the kind of eyes that refuse to give up the secrets of the mind behind them. Every time his opponent made what seemed to him a poor move, Stuart had been suspicious of a devious trap and had refused to take the advantage that was too apparently on offer. It was not until all the others had finished their matches and the cleaners were demanding that the room be evacuated that he finally took his courage in both hands and walked into the 'trap', only to find that there was no trap and that his opponent had been totally unworthy of the respect he had accorded him. This incident had come back to him on many occasions in his life, but he had learned to be wary of it, for the boldness and self-confidence that it urged turned out to be infelicitous just as often as they proved appropriate. Neither Snoddy nor his council had 'nasty little eyes', but he was far from sure that there were no secrets lurking.

The third day of the trial opened with the promise which, despite years of bitter experience, the morning light in the courtroom always invoked in Stuart – the assurance that rationality would somehow bring solidity and shape to the primeval social stew. The boldness and clarity with which the tipstaff demanded silence for the judge, the dignified, if stagey entrance of his lordship clutching a file of notes containing no doubt his distillation of what had been subject to his penetrating wisdom in the proceedings thus far, the confident order of his opening remarks, pronounced in tones that inspire a sense of inferiority in all those born without an English spoon in their mouths – all this never failed to suggest a laboratory of the human condition, where with time and patience the deepest secrets of the souls of men would be uncovered and a breakthrough made into a higher realm of fusion between the animal and the angel. Snoddy's council, now in wig and gown, had shed the chrysalis of the cleverness he had shown in the interview room, and transmuted into a servant of the court and its quest. Stuart marvelled at how this fantasy had survived all the distortions and self-serving lies he had heard from legal lips over the years, but in a way he was glad to have preserved his little cocoon of naivety.

The defence began with an attack on the circumstantial nature of the evidence presented by the prosecution. There was no hard evidence linking their client to the crimes, only a series of coincidences which they would reveal as such. But first they would deal with the question of motivation, of which the prosecution had presented a confused, distorted and totally inconsistent picture. For this reason they would call as their first witness the defendant himself.

Snoddy walked slowly and with very deliberate steps from the dock to the witness box. Throughout the trial he had taken great care over his appearance; he wore a brown leather jacket and an assortment of good quality, plain coloured shirts with toning ties – to-day's colour was light blue. He seemed intent rather than nervous as he took the oath. It only occurred to Stuart later to be surprised that he made no show of refusing the Bible. The barrister made the usual gestures and noises that suggest welcome to his client – this always took Stuart by surprise; it reminded him of news broadcasters who thank one another profusely for each contribution, as the news story gets passed up and down the line.

"The prosecution has suggested that you bore a grudge against Dr Stevens for having asked you to leave the school. Was that in fact the case, Mr Snoddy?"

Snoddy looked along the ranks of the jury before making a reply.

"Dr Stevens was acting out of misguided kindness. He was a man who liked to be kind. In fact I would say he was a man who was addicted to kindness. How could I bear a personal grudge against him? What he did was not in the least bit personal."

"Are you saying then that you admired Dr Stevens? Are you asking the jury to believe that you had a high opinion of the man?"

"No. Most definitely not. Dr Stevens was an old mother hen of a man. He was weak and he encouraged weakness in others. Weakness is something to be pitied. It is the job of those who have been charged with educating the young to develop the strength in them, not to glorify their weakness."

"And how did Dr Stevens do that?"

"If you want to encourage children to develop what is best in them the last thing you must do is tell them that they are all equally important, no matter what. That is a big lie apart from anything else. In life we are as important as the importance of what we do. Most people have a little inner circle of importance, but to think that we can extend that circle beyond ourselves and our immediate family on the strength of simply being what we are is pie in the sky. If that's all there was to it, we could leave the pie to rot in its own juices. But there's fall-out. It's not the done thing to admit it, but the stink of sentimentality is not just an unpleasant stench for those who have retained some sense of smell, it's a toxic cloud that is spreading and causing a plague of inertia and underachievement in its wake."

"Let's get back to Dr Stevens. What did he do to make you think that he was an agent in this slide?"

"Apart from his 'style' and the general ambience that it encouraged, he threatened to drop subjects from the curriculum that made pupils aware of their own limitations. Dropping Ancient Greek was one of the first things he did, and he was making noises about getting rid of German and Latin. He wanted to replace them with what he called 'friendlier' subjects such as psychology and sociology. The worst thing he was threatening to do was to change the system of scholarships. St Jude's always offered about a dozen scholarships every year to pupils whose parents couldn't afford the fees. There was a pretty stiff exam and the pupils with the best results were given a place. He was talking about getting rid of the entrance exam and selecting on the basis of what he called 'need'."

"And what was so bad about that? Isn't it a basic tenet of the socialist movement to give '*to each according to his need . . .* '?"

"Our physics teacher, Mr Curtis, once told us that one of the main problems in modern physics is to square our understanding of the way things work when they are very large and the way they work when they are very small. That's exactly the problem when it comes to politics. You see someone down on his luck or someone being attacked by a group of thugs, of course you try to help, or you should do if you've any aspirations to being a human being. But when you try to apply that on a social scale, all you end up doing is 'victimising' the victim, embalming and mummifying him in what should have been only a temporary state. The overwhelming 'need' of people who have a particular need is to be given a fighting chance to deal with it, but it must be a chance where it is they who do the fighting! Our free educational system is exactly that – the opportunity to fight your way through to a life experience that is in some way richer. Anyone who tries to spare you that fighting is denying you the very chance that he thinks he is offering you. Just look at what has happened to the working class in this country. The stuffing has been knocked out of the best of them. Try to raise your children to read and think, try to keep your street free of the scum that pollute it, try to stand on your own feet financially – and what happens? You are classified as being someone not in need of a helping hand and you are punished for your independence; if you attempt to act like a grown-up; it's seen as ingratitude to those who would wrap you in swaddling clothes and lay you in your play pen. The only kind of help on offer is help that demands that you never leave the nursery!

"The vast majority have learned their lesson and stayed where it's warm and safe – and utterly mindless and soulless! It's funny how poor we are at joined-up thinking. It's taken the liberal establishment a long time, but they've finally come to realise that children need a father as well as a mother in their lives. When there are no fathers around to stop them, mothers have this annoying habit of spoiling their children. They can't resist seeing to all their '*needs*'. But how long will it be before it dawns on the proud members of the liberal élite that what's good for the goose is bad for the gander? The whole social apparatus is being run by a great single mother-mind. We've been spoiling – and I mean *destroying* – the working class since we started throwing them out of their factories. It's the new morality. It's 'good' to spoil, for it shows the selflessness of the 'spoiler'. That it encourages selfishness and fecklessness in the receiver doesn't seem to count. 'Good' is acting like a mother – caring, that is. 'Bad' is acting like a father. This of course should not be considered as sexist. Men are not left out. No, not at all! In this *timid new world* fathers are gradually being brought to acknowledge that they are just mothers in disguise. What these self-righteous bastards are doing is giving themselves a moral heave-up at the expense of the people they are doing their so-called good unto. This whole exercise has of course the added bonus of keeping the underclasses firmly stuck in the libidinal mud, thereby perpetuating the legitimacy of the position of the *good* as providers to the needy. The *good* then organise dinner parties – Hampstead is the favourite venue, I believe – to admire each other's halos."

This little 'unpleasantry' failed to produce any reaction among the jury who had seemed bemused and uncomprehending throughout Snoddy's exposé. But Snoddy was clearly not looking for reinforcement. He continued undeterred.

"What is needed is a society that acknowledges that both the male and the female instincts have a place. How they balance each other always remains problematical, but the way things stand at present rules out even the beginnings of an attempt to come to any kind of accommodation. It is now taken as read that people should be saved from themselves; they should not be allowed to become the 'victims' of their own faults ... Faults? Forget I said that. It's taboo to suggest that 'faults' exist; 'weaknesses', that's what they are – and children have 'special needs' – and we appeal to the old code of chivalry – a manly code at that – that demanded mercy for the weak. But there's weakness and weakness. We can all have sympathy for the kind of weakness that describes failure to match up to a situation in terms of strength or know-how or skill. But the other kind of weakness, the weakness that is a catch-all for a baseness of spirit that accepts defeat at the first hurdle should be met only with contempt. A mother loves her child no matter what and will excuse anything, but that is not the role of the father. His job is to prepare the child for the big, bad world outside the nursery. And that might involve injury and pain in the learning, for in the long run if the child fails to learn, neither parent will be able to protect it from the consequences. That is the bottom line. The ordinary working people of this country have been let down by what has passed for socialism since the Second World War. What they needed from people in authority was the help that a father gives; what they got was the over-indulgence of a single mother, and a particularly stupid one at that! And what has been the result? We have allowed a culture to develop that has no resistance to the germs of capitalist consumerism. And – the biggest irony of all – all this has been done in the name of liberal socialism."

At this point the judge interrupted.

"I think we are in danger of losing our way here. Could you please point out to your client, Mr Montgomery, that this is a court of law, not a political debating chamber? I also fail to see how it is in your client's interests to pursue this line of questioning."

"I am trying to establish, my lord, that my client had no strong personal feelings against the deceased, and that while he is not denying having negative feelings, they are of the kind that anyone with his political orientation might harbour."

"Very well, but there's no need to go any further down this line. I think the point has been established."

"I would like now to look at my client's attitude to Mr Kennedy. Do I have your permission to continue, my lord?"

"If you must."

"Thank you, my lord. Now, Mr Snoddy, could you please tell the court about your dealings with Mr Kennedy?"

"I had no dealings with Mr Kennedy."

"You never met the man?"

"No, never."

"But you were heard to express negative feelings towards him. And my learned colleague has made much of a letter you wrote to Mr Devine criticising the unfortunate man and, my colleague would have the jury believe, threatening dire consequences for the action he took against the equally unfortunate Mr Devine."

"What Kennedy did to Richard Devine was despicable. Richard was standing up for the values of the school, whether you agree with those values or not, and he was hung out to dry because Kennedy and the governors hadn't the guts to take on the little minds that have tried to order the world as if it were nothing more than a messy kitchen. Of course the reason why they wouldn't stand up for him is that they are the same kind of people as the ones who drafted all this 'human rights' rubbish in the first place. Rubber-glove men! 'Judge not lest ye be judged' – that's as far as their moral thinking takes them. They are moral emasculates. They can't get it up. They grope around them and can't get enough feel to conjure an 'ought' from an 'is'. What they are constantly in search of is a bit of moral pornography, a two-way mirror where they can watch as others indulge in a bit of moral judgementalism – then their juices are stirred. Once they see an 'ought-not' being given physical expression all that pent-up opinionism is unleashed in an orgasmic fury of self-righteous condemnation. They don't get to a full blown 'ought' of course, but their 'ought-not' response to the 'ought-not' they have '*voyeured*' comes as a blessed relief and a welcome reassurance that their moral manhood is still intact."

"Let us be clear here, Mr Snoddy. Are you telling the jury that you are against human rights? Do you really want them to believe that you are a monster who would support the kind of atrocities that have taken place in those parts of the world where human rights are not respected?"

"My father has been an atheist all his life. He is a good man. He believes in right and wrong, but more important, he always believed in *doing* right and trying to put up some kind of fight against wrong. Yet any time he got into discussion with Christians they almost always ended up claiming him as one of theirs, however much he protested his innocence. There is the same arrogance on the go now about human rights. You can't seriously be against them unless you're a paedophile or a thug who goes around beating up old ladies and stealing their handbags. But if you have decent instincts towards your fellow creatures, then you can be 'saved', you can be brought to the true faith; it's all just a matter of 'education'. The whole thing makes me want to throw up.

"If you want to know, it's civil rights, not human rights that I believe in. Civil rights are not god-given; they are for societies to work out for themselves and are constantly open to change. They must be sensitive to the general circumstances that a society finds itself in and, the most important thing of all, they must be sensitive to the actions of the individual. What you do determines what society does to you. If you are a pain in the arse, then expect to be doused in antiseptic! If this jury finds me guilty of killing the dear doctor, then what right do I have to expect society to spend a fortune keeping me in prison, paying the Danegeld to prevent me from re-offending? It's almost the exact opposite of the Spanish Inquisition. They damned the body to spare the soul from Hell. Nowadays we spare the body but keep the soul in Hell. Ah, I hear you say from behind your two-way mirror – we've got him now; he's talking *punishment!* *Punishment* isn't allowed! I know, I admit it – I put my hands up. It's a fair cop. I've broken the rules; I've lost that bloody stupid game that everybody plays – If you try to argue any case, you have to accept that you're playing '*spot-the-dangerous-word-and-show-how-clever-you-are-ball*'. It passes for politics nowadays. Get on the radio or the TV and use one of these 'dark' words and you're dead meat; you'll be gobbled up by the political Furies.

"Anyone advocating punishment is denying that people have moral immunity from what they do. This is to rubbish the wholesale moral immunisation programme that was carried out – probably by rubber-glove man – about the same time as the National Health Service was set up. It's interesting that we can talk about good lives and wasted lives, we are allowed to talk about good people, but it's not on to transfer the 'wasted' from the lives to the people. It's as if when things go negative we mustn't get personal. What's this mysterious gap between people and the lives they lead? We bloody well ought to get personal! Rights and wrongs are personal things. Have you ever considered what would happen to our moral thinking if we invented a negative to 'rights'? Presumably it would be 'wrongs'. People might then have the 'right' to be treated positively in certain instances and the 'wrong' to be treated negatively in others. Right behaviour would earn rights and wrong behaviour would deserve 'wrongs'. Nothing very exceptional there, you'd say. This is basically the way 'primitive' minds have always thought about justice. But imagine what would happen if the primitive minds got sophisticated and extended the idea to '*universal human wrongs*'. Where do you think that would leave us – I'd say, in just about the same amount of shit that we're in now with rights."

"I think your client is losing his audience, Mr Montgomery. Could we please get back to the admittedly much smaller matter of trying him for murder?"

"I'm sorry, my lord. My client has a very inventive mind and he finds it genuinely difficult to keep it in check. . . . Mr Snoddy, let's return to your relationship with Mr Kennedy. You confirm that you never met the man and that the feelings you had towards him were formed merely at second hand?"

"I do. If I were to attempt to slay dragons such as Mr Kennedy I would be a very busy little knight. The world is coming down with them. They are as common as the muck that's in their heads."

"Thank you, Mr Snoddy. That will be all."

At this Mr Montgomery sat down. There was an almost audible gasp from all those who had experience of court procedures. Was that it? Was he not going to deal with the question of the Walther? What about Snoddy's secret visit to England and his lying to the police? Surely, he needed to offer some form of explanation! The prosecuting council was also taken by surprise. He was an experienced advocate, used to thinking on his feet, but you could see his reluctance to begin his attack before he had geared himself up. His experience saw him through. He got very slowly to his feet and looked around the court. The silence was allowed to brew before he finally pronounced a blessed end to it and the disorder it was harbouring in the mind.

"Your council has been most generous to me, Mr Snoddy. He must think me a very poor hack for he has done much of my work for me. He has established a motivational link between the two cases. Both Dr Stevens and Mr Kennedy represented the enemy, didn't they, Mr Snoddy? And you, in the arrogance that you have been honest enough, or perhaps inadvertent enough, to show to this court, have not shied away from administering what you consider the appropriate punishment."

Snoddy smiled the smile of someone relishing the prospect of a contest he was confident of winning.

"I trust the jury are better at keeping awake than you when people start using long words. Or was it the long sentences that got to you? The central point that was made during your nap was that I did not see my expulsion by Dr Stevens in personal terms and I had not even met Mr Kennedy. As far as I am concerned the two gentlemen were *'walking shadows'* in a society of men *signifying very little*."

"Yes, but you are what passes for an intellectual, are you not, Mr Snoddy? And intellectuals are people who live in and through ideas. What for other people are empty abstractions is for the intellectual the very stuff of life. An intellectual would not need a strong emotional motive in order to act; he would be happy to be in the service of what he considered a great idea. Of course the energies even of intellectuals are not averse to taking sustenance from such *tacky* emotions as rancour and resentment. I put it to you that you were not as high above the water mark of emotion as you would have us believe. You were outraged by what you considered the injustice of what had been done to you and you combined this sense of bitterness with an accommodating *Weltanschauung* to galvanise yourself into an action that was both base and despicable."

"You seem to be asking this court to believe that I would have 'punished' Dr Stevens for merely putting the final touches to an action – both base and despicable I would add – that had been the brainchild of the dependably base and despicable Gillian Sloane. Surely my rancour and resentment, as you put it, would have had her rather than the dreadful doctor in its sights? Yet you have not claimed that I have harmed a hair of that empty head. It's not for me to tell you how to do your job, but shouldn't you have tried to show that I took my revenge on Jezebel? The jury then just might have been brought to believe that I was vindictive enough to turn then on the hapless Ahab."

The prosecutor was visibly angered by this. He was a man, whose stock-in-trade was wounding with words, but he was a hunter of herbivores; resistance and elusiveness was all he normally expected from his quarry. If he was minded to swap blows with Snoddy, he resisted the pull of his anger and appealed instead to the judge, who delivered the standard lecture to the witness to confine himself to answering the questions and, in a gesture of professional solidarity, suggested in tones that dripped with contempt that the learned council had no need of instruction from the likes of him on how to conduct his case. Snoddy nodded in feigned regret at what he had said and assured the judge that he was sure that the council knew his job and would demonstrate it to the court by securing a guilty verdict. The prosecutor tried to appear not to take this in the spirit it was meant, and continued his interrogation.

"Let us now turn to this cock-and-bull story about you losing the Walther you had borrowed from Mr Devine. You claim you were in a German pub, got into conversation with a total stranger and, when he expressed an interest, you handed it over to him in the sure and certain hope that he would return it to you complete with the history of its provenance? Are you sure he didn't offer you any magic beans? At least then the jury would know what fairy tale you are asking them to believe. Let me see, where should we start? We'll leave out the 'once-upon-a-time' bit. Tell the jury what this handsome stranger looked like."

"I'm sorry to disappoint you, but he wasn't a bit handsome. As far as I recall, he had mousy brown hair. He wore it in a ridiculous ponytail. I remember thinking he was trying very hard to show he was a thinking man, someone who rejected but someone who in turn wanted to be rejected by them what accept so that he could be accepted by them what reject. A bit like those old fogies who wear club ties and blazers – you know the type? Of course, they've a different agenda; they want to be accepted by them what accept as people who reject them what reject. Do you know what I mean? It's all a bit sad really – all this belonging stuff."

"I'm sure the jury find that very amusing, Mr Snoddy, but then you are very good at being amusing. That, among other things, is what storytellers do. And you are very good at making up stories, aren't you? To get back to the story, this not-so-handsome stranger persuaded you to part with the Walther on the understanding that he would return it to you when he had completed his investigations into it. Is that the line you are spinning – sorry, taking?"

"No, to spinning .Yes, to taking", Snoddy replied with a broad smile.

The prosecutor was undeterred.

"But Prince Make-Us-Believe never returned and you were left with the cinders of ignorance to rue the day when your innocence had been betrayed by the lure of knowledge beyond your ken. Let me see. Where have we got in this sad tale? We seem to be suspended somewhere in the air between the Cinderella and the Faust stories. In any case, it had an unhappy ending, didn't it, your story? You never saw the not-so-handsome stranger again."

"Alas not. But then the story isn't over yet, is it? Perhaps Prince Make-Us-Believe as you call him will seek me out with the long lost Walther and rescue me from all the squalor of doubt and give me an honoured place by his side in the royal court of truth. There wouldn't be a dry eye in the court, this court I mean, would there?"

The prosecutor engaged in a grin with the jury.

"Let's move to the other fairy tale that you have brought along for our amusement. There is incontrovertible evidence that you left the farm where you were working in Germany and secretly returned to England, took possession of your motor bike which you returned in a muddy state – a state consistent with it being driven in a place similar to where the murder of Dr Stevens took place – and then went back to Germany without anyone being aware that you had been here, except of course your friend Andrew Whitfield, who was looking after the bike. When confronted with the evidence by the police, you simply denied everything. Do you have anything to say by way of an explanation that would fit with anything other than that you came over and murdered your former headmaster?"

"I wish to withdraw my statement to the police. I did return to England and I did take the bike out for a spin. But I did not kill Dr Stevens."

"Why then did you lie to the police? This will have to be very good, Mr Snoddy, but no doubt your fertile imagination will come up with something at least to entertain us."

"I panicked. I did something I was ashamed of that weekend and I didn't want it to come out. That's why I lied to the police. It was a very foolish thing to do, but once I had done it, it wasn't easy to pull back from it."

"Really? And what apart from killing Dr Stevens did you do that you were so ashamed of?"

At this point Snoddy's council rose to his feet and asked the judge for this question to be deferred until later. The defence had evidence that they wished to present to the court, but it was sensitive and they wished to present it in their own way. When this evidence had been brought to light, they were quite agreeable to Mr Snoddy returning to the witness box and answering the quite legitimate questions that the prosecution would want to put to him. The judge was not pleased with this arrangement. He pointed out that the defence ought to have delayed the appearance of Mr Snoddy as a witness until this 'evidence' had been presented, but he would reluctantly agree to a postponement of this line of questioning provided there was minimum delay. The prosecution raised only mild objections and Snoddy was excused. It had been a long morning and the proceedings were adjourned for lunch.

Chapter 30

Stuart had noticed the Devines in court and as everyone was filing out he caught them up and suggested that they grab some lunch together. There was a pizzeria not far from the courthouse that did real Italian pasta. Richard made a half-hearted excuse but Margaret overruled him in the way that wives are able to make the assumption of authority seem like a plea for a treat. They walked the short distance to the restaurant in one of those 'anti-conversations' that is looking for more convivial circumstances to launch itself into the full-blown version. The trouble with such prologues is that they always sample too many topics and spoil the choice available for the main course. He learned from them that Kennedy's condition had remained largely unchanged; there had not been the expected improvement and it seemed that the restriction in the use of his right arm might be permanent. There was no question of him continuing in his post; he had been given a generous retirement package and been replaced on a permanent basis by Mrs Swanson. Evans had put in his resignation and was to take up a lucrative appointment with one of the examining boards.

"And what about Dr Greenfield?"

They had reached the restaurant and were browsing the menu, having ordered a bottle of the house Chianti.

"Bruce never changes. He keeps generating opinions."

It was Margaret who had been doing all the talking. Richard had said little since they left the courthouse.

"He is writing the book he has been threatening us with all these years. What did he tell you it was on, Richard?"

Richard seemed less than enthusiastic to take up his wife's invitation into the conversation.

"I'm not too sure. I think it's about one of his German writers. I don't know which one. He did tell me that it was this Snoddy business that had got him going on it."

"And what about yourself, Richard? Are you safely back in harness?"

"Oh, the news of my humiliation didn't get as far as the criminal justice system then? That's some consolation, I suppose. I was made to write a letter to the damsel and admit that I had acted in a way that was insensitive to her youth and her innocence. Mrs Swanson was quite charming about it, really. She said that she understood my reaction, but that I should not have left myself open to an accusation of physical assault. As teachers it was our job, she said, to show that situations can be resolved by non-physical means and any recourse to physical strength to settle an issue was an open invitation to the violent elements in society to indulge themselves. She had of course nothing against physical restraint when the situation called for it, but this was not such a case."

"You wrote the letter then? You must have found it hard to do that."

"I wrote the letter, Mr Stranaghan. Margaret wanted me to do it. And to be honest, I didn't want to lose my job either. We need the money. And with this hanging over me I might have found it difficult to get another job in a school that bears any resemblance to what I'd call a place of learning. There aren't too many of them about any more. A question of swallowing one's pride, I told myself, and readjusting one's image of what it takes to be a proper human being."

"And have things got better for you at school? How are you getting on with Mrs Swanson as head?"

"I suppose it's still early days, but I'm beginning to regret doing what I did – I mean, apologising to that little madam. Something's gone. How can you explain to your classes how great men have sacrificed themselves to further the great causes of history when you yourself couldn't even summon up the courage to say no when the forces of political correctness came calling at your door? I have a picture of Thomas More in my room in school, Mr Stranaghan. It serves as a reminder to me every day that I have lost the right to prepare anyone for the world of ordinary, let alone great doings. I suppose I will limp on and with time I might even come to forget what a wimp I've been. But I don't think that will really help. I think in a way it will make it even worse."

It was clear that Margaret Devine had shared many hours with her husband in this pit of despair and was anxious to usher the conversation away from it. Stuart would have liked to know if, with hindsight, she regretted urging her husband to do the sensible thing, but he shared in her concern to bring the conversation to higher ground and lighter air. The trial offered itself for speculation. Stuart was non-committal when asked how he thought things were going and Devine had little to say about the level of his surprise at Snoddy's arrest. What did emerge, however, was the news that Devine was to be called as a witness by the defence. He had already appeared for the prosecution – merely to confirm that he had lent the Walther to Snoddy and had failed to get a credible explanation from him for its loss. That's why they were both here to-day. Snoddy's lawyer has called him late last night and requested his presence; testimony would be required from him. No more detailed explanation had been forthcoming. This was all the more surprising, since, when he had previously given his evidence, the defence had not even bothered to cross-examine him. A puzzle for the afternoon to resolve!

They got back to the courthouse leaving themselves only a few minutes to wait before proceedings were resumed. Snoddy's council, Mr Montgomery, stood up looking distinctly more authoritative, one might have said majestic had it not been for the 'protester-academic seventies look', clearly dear to him, which grinned through his counsel's garb.

"My Lord, I would like to re-call Mr Richard Devine. I realise that this is slightly unusual, but evidence has come into my possession which makes it necessary."

Richard's face winced with unease. Over lunch it had struck Stuart that he had been coming and going from the conversation like a foreign station on long wave; Stuart had put that down to his preoccupation with his coerced apology. But obviously he had been suffering from anxiety as well as a sense of loss. He got up awkwardly from his chair and walked with self-conscious resolve in response, one would have thought, to a summons to his place of execution.

"I'm sorry to impose on you again, Mr Devine. Teachers are such busy people, I know, and are charged with such an enormous responsibility. I will try not to keep you very long.

"You testified that you were the owner of a World War 2 German pistol, a Walther P38 automatic pistol to be precise, which, in case the jury has forgotten, was standard issue to the German army. Over a million of these pistols were produced. Tell me, Mr Devine, was there anything about your pistol that could clearly distinguish it from the other 999,999?"

"Yes, it had initials etched on it and there was a two-inch scratch along the top of the barrel. It was because of the initials that we thought there might be some hope of tracing it."

"And what were the initials?"

"It was H-D S. We thought it likely that the H-D stood for Hans-Dieter."

Mr Montgomery turned his back on Richard, went back to his table and picked up a plastic package. He held it in both hands and smiled first at the judge and then at the jury before handing it to the bemused witness.

"I would like you to take a good look at this package, Mr Devine. You may open it and examine the contents."

Richard fumbled clumsily with the plastic. When he eventually located the sealing strip and prised it open, he put his hand inside and retrieved a pistol. He then went through the irritating ritual of replacing his ordinary glasses with his reading glasses before he was ready to follow council's instruction. His examination did not take long.

"This is my pistol!"

"You are quite certain?"

"Yes. There are the initials in that old German script and the scratch has a little twist at the end. Look. No, there can be no doubt."

"Thank you, Mr Devine. That will be all."

Richard's relief that his ordeal was over got him out of the chair and propelled him the first few paces towards his seat beside his wife, but then his curiosity kicked in and he seemed to want to turn back. It was however no more than a hesitation; he walked on. All eyes were on him, but everyone's attention was with the pistol. Mr Montgomery was of a mind to orchestrate their curiosity. Just as Richard was taking his seat he announced,

"My Lord, I wish to call Herr Thomas Metscher."

Two men stood up at the back of the courtroom and moved towards the witness box. The first was a bespectacled man with well-behaved brown hair wearing an expensive grey suit. The second was a man in his fifties with greying greasy hair that was inclined to curl, straightened out like crumpled up newspaper and forced into a long ponytail. He wore a suede jacket that was too short for him and served only to emphasise the hump that the years had developed in his shoulders. But he had an affable look and he gazed around him in undisguised interest. The other man was there to interpret for him. The question and answer session that followed took on the air, appropriately Stuart thought, of an over-an-out exchange between pilot and base in a Second World War Spitfire cum Messerschmitt.

Mr Montgomery began by establishing Herr Metscher's identity. He was a commercial traveller for agricultural products operating out of Freiburg and serving the Black Forest area.

That is where he had encountered Snoddy; they had got into conversation at the bar in the *Gaststätte* where he had been staying in Donaueschingen. Snoddy had mentioned the Walther and his interest in finding out about it, and as he had a friend who was interested in such things, he offered to ask his friend to take a look at it for Snoddy. He was scheduled to be back in Donaueschingen within a couple of weeks, but there had been a family bereavement and his plans had had to be changed. It was some time before he got back to the town and he had lost the address Snoddy had given him, so he hadn't been able to return the Walther. It was with an air that betrayed a little too much self-congratulation that Mr Montgomery concluded:

"The Walther only came into our possession late last night, My Lord, and there has been no time to submit it for ballistic tests, but we are confident that such tests will show that this was not the weapon that was used in the shootings. I would suggest that these tests be carried out immediately and that we adjourn before my learned friend begins his cross-examination of . . . what was it he called him? . . . Prince Make-Us-Believe."

Chapter 31

The green stubble produced by the quiffs of snow on the lawn had turned into a full white Santa beard the next morning as Stuart pulled up the blind and allowed the day to greet him. The boy in him felt instant delight, but the persona that had evolved along with his wrinkles and his greying hair just as immediately registered angst. Heather had said she wanted to come with him, but the arrival of the snow killed off the intention formed the night before in the more favourable climes of her own excellent cooking and a couple of generous glasses of Stuart's best merlot. She had work she could be getting on with. Stuart was not disappointed. There were times when he delighted in bringing together elements of his life that did not know each other, but it was like introducing friends, one needed to be confident they would get on. He was not sure that he wanted Heather to enter the Snoddy world. He had been curious and was not opposed to a meeting, but he was now relieved of the task of acting as her interpreter and he could bask in the idleness and insouciance of mere observation. He was after all on holiday.

The journey to the courthouse was less difficult than antici-pated. He had to pioneer the route along the streets of his 'executive development', but once he reached the main road, the snow had long been humbled into a dirty sludge and human ascendancy had been firmly re-established. He did however share in a sense of solidarity in adversity with the other snow-veterans, when he got into the warmth of the courtroom, but not without a slight pang of conscience at his treacherous admi-ration for the enemy.

The trial re-opened with the announcement that ballistic

tests had confirmed that the Walther was not the weapon used in the two shootings. In the light of this the prosecution saw no point in cross-examining Herr Metscher and the defence continued its case. Mr Montgomery, still smiling in Cheshire fashion, (Stuart wondered if the smile had lasted through the night) declared the defence's wish to re-call Miss Gillian Sloane. The prosecution council jumped to his feet in protest.

"My Lord, this witness has already appeared before you and my learned friend had every opportunity to cross-examine her, but declined to do so. This is the second time that the defence has done this. It is simply not acceptable."

Before the judge replied Mr Montgomery came in.

"My Lord, could any reasonable person interested in justice possibly argue that the truth was not served by the first slight breach in etiquette? I think the court will find this second act of indulgence to common sense even more revealing."

"Very well, Mr Montgomery, but I trust this is the last re-call of prosecution witnesses. We would be obliged if you would produce some witnesses of your own."

Miss Sloane came to the witness box, an apparition from the fashion pages. She was a genuinely beautiful woman. Her natural beauty however was neither enhanced nor diminished by the glamour of her make-up and clothing; it was summarily sidelined as of secondary importance. Mr Montgomery delayed for a moment, presumably to show that he was not a kill-joy opponent of the general stunned admiration which she commanded. When he came to speak, his voice and manner gave a good imitation of respect, but, one suspected, deliberately not just good enough to be taken for the real thing.

"Miss Sloane, in your previous submission to the court you said that my client had made unsolicited sexual advances to you to the point where you felt that you were in danger of being raped. You reported the incident to Dr Stevens and you very generously agreed that if Mr Snoddy were expelled from the school you would let the matter rest there. Is that correct?"

Miss Sloane responded positively to the reference to her generosity and attempted a stoic smile of approval of what had been said. Mr Montgomery continued.

"We will not go through the details of the incident again. I think the court will have no difficulty in remembering your dramatic account. But one question I would like to ask before moving on: Why the generosity? Why allow this disgusting little spotty youth off with a meaningless expulsion – his time at school was almost up any way – why let him loose to go on to rape and pillage the womanhood of academia?"

Miss Sloane was visibly confused by this question. There was a hurried application of her handkerchief to her nose before she replied.

"I thought he had learned his lesson. It's not unusual for sixth form boys to be infatuated by young lady teachers. Dr Stevens explained about his unfortunate background, his father having been to prison and all that. So I decided that he had been punished enough."

"I see, you thought that the father having been to prison was a 'punishment' for something he, that is to say the son, was going to do sometime in the future. I must say, I am intrigued by this form of moral accounting. Is this some new theory of ethics that you are developing – an updating of the notion of indulgences, democratic version? Now it's not the rich that get off with throwing money at the church, it's the ordinary little Joe Bloggs' for putting up with having such sordid little lives and such miserable little genes."

Miss Sloane picked up the tone, if not the substance of what was being directed at her.

"You know perfectly well what I mean. I just meant that I felt sorry for him and didn't want to rub salt in the wound."

"But what wound was this? Surely it was you who were the wounded party, Miss Sloane, not Mr Snoddy. Or perhaps you weren't? Perhaps it was indeed Mr Snoddy who had been sinned against?"

Miss Sloane moved in her seat and looked away, directing her gaze to an indeterminate point somewhere in the top right hand corner of the room; she was not going to dignify the question with an answer.

"You see, I am genuinely puzzled, Miss Sloane. You did not seem to show the same generosity of spirit towards your unwanted admirer when you suffered sexual harassment at university, nor again at your new employment with Mercurial Messaging after you left St Jude's. You seem to attract a lot of harassment, Miss Sloane. Or would 'invite' be a better word?"

"I can't help it if men react that way with me. I am the victim here and you are trying to make it out that I've done something wrong."

"If you were indeed the victim, Miss Sloane, then you have done nothing wrong and the law is there to protect you, but let's move on. Could you tell the court where you were and what you were doing on the day that Dr Stevens met his most unfortunate end?"

"I can't remember. It's a long time ago. You can't expect me to remember what I was doing on a particular day over two years ago."

"Come now, Miss Sloane. That was the day the headmaster of the school where you were teaching was murdered – hardly an everyday occurrence. Surely something that would stand out in the memory even of someone with such an unfortunate history of crime involvement as yourself."

"I'm sorry. I don't remember. I remember when I heard the news, but that was on the Sunday morning. What I was doing on the Saturday is a complete blank."

"Let me jog your memory then ... My Lord, I would like to submit this photograph in evidence. I've had copies made for yourself and the jury."

Gillian Sloane had a moment to consider the photo while

copies were being handed out to the jury. Her face was a confusion of surprise and horror.

"Now, Miss Sloane, could you describe to the members of the jury who you see in the picture?"

"That's me and Robert Snoddy."

"And where exactly are you?"

"We are at front door of my flat."

"And what are you doing?"

"He is giving me a bouquet of roses."

"Could you describe the expression on your face?"

"What do you mean?"

"Are we looking at someone who is pleased to be receiving the flowers or someone about to throw them in the donor's face?"

"I suppose I look pleased."

"So, Robert Snoddy, the man who you say tried to rape you, came along and gave you a bunch of roses and you were happy to accept them. Is that what you are telling us, Miss Sloane?"

Miss Sloane's voice was in need of a sequence of little throat-clearing coughs to keep going above a whisper, but then it revived.

"I was brought up in a Christian home and we were always taught to forgive our enemies. Robert came round to thank me for allowing Dr Stevens to keep the whole matter quiet and make up the story about the cannabis. I thought he was being very grown-up about the whole business and deserved to be forgiven."

"Did you invite him in?"

"Yes, I did. His was a gesture that needed a response, I thought."

"And you weren't frightened he would attack you again? I must say, Miss Sloane, your faith is remarkable. You are a credit to your priest. What happened when Robert came in? You just said some grown-up things to each other and then he left. Was that it?"

"We talked about what had happened and he admitted what he had done and begged me to forgive him."

"And you forgave him."

"Yes, I did."

"And what form did this forgiveness take?"

"I don't understand what you mean?"

"Come now, Miss Sloane. Words are cheap. What was needed was an *act* of forgiveness. He had brought the roses as a token of his contrition – and they did not come cheap by the look of them. What did you do to reciprocate?"

"I didn't do anything. I think forgiving him *was* an *act*."

Mr Montgomery made a token effort at suppressing a patronising smirk.

"I am sure the jury will have no difficulty in accepting your skills as an *actress*, Miss Sloane. But to keep to the point, let us be clear: you are saying that you and my client indulged in nothing other than serious grown-up conversation during the period of his stay? Are you sure you don't want to chalk up another allegation of rape or sexual harassment? This is your last chance and, from what we know of you in the past, you aren't one to pass up on such opportunities."

"We just talked."

"I would like to submit a second photograph to the court, My Lord."

The same ritual followed, the members of the jury showing both curiosity and self-importance as they each received the large A4 sheets. Miss Sloane's face was now in total disarray. Her eyes were flurrying around like a bewildered bird that had just fallen down the chimney.

"Now, Miss Sloane, can you please tell us what we are looking at here?"

"I'm sure the jury can see for themselves – it's a picture of me."

"And what are you wearing? I know, it might be more appropriate to ask what you are not wearing, but I wish to be positive."

"I'm wearing a blue top."

"The same blue top you were wearing in the other photograph?"

"Yes."

"But what has happened to the rather expensive-looking jeans you were wearing? Did they get in the way of the *adult* conversation you were having with my client? Oh by the way, who is that in the mirror on the wall behind you? Would that be my client? He seems to be just as well dressed for this 'adult' exchange as you do."

Miss Sloane was clearly approaching a fork in the road; the choice was between tears and invective. She edged towards tears, but left the other gate open.

"He had no right to do that. Taking lewd pictures of someone without their consent, that's a criminal offence, isn't it? I had no idea he was taking those pictures."

"He didn't take the first picture, Miss Sloane. It was a friend of his who did that. But you're right – he did take the second one. If you take your eyes off, shall we say the highlights of the picture, you can see the mobile phone in his hand."

"The bastard! He made me do it. He humiliated me. He told me that if he was going to be punished for attempted rape he might as well get his money's worth. He said that if I reported the rape I'd get even worse next time."

"Now when exactly did he say that? Was it before you had sex or after? Be very careful before you answer."

"It was before. Of course it was before. What do you take me for?"

"I'd dearly love to answer that, Miss Sloane, but the jury is not interested in my opinions. So let's focus on you. If I understand you correctly, you are resurrecting the old chestnut, the rape allegation. It really is your party piece, isn't it?"

Miss Sloane had given up all thoughts of tears; she was already well down the road of the righteously angry.

"What gives you the right to sneer at me? This court should be protecting me, not treating me in this way, as if it was a crime to be female and attractive, as if it was my fault that bastards like your client, the disgusting bugger, can't keep their dirty paws to themselves."

"Mobile phones are really wonderful things. Do you ever wonder, Miss Sloane, how they have changed our lives? They have so many uses. There's one use in particular they have that is not generally known. Did *you* know that they can do a very passable job as lie-detectors? I'm sure you didn't. If you had, you would hardly have come out with all that claptrap. My Lord, I would like the court to listen to this recording. It was taken by my client on his mobile phone at the time of this second alleged violation of the witness."

A look of the death-facing horror of a trapped animal flashed and then froze across Gillian Sloane's face. Mr Montgomery took his time plugging the recorder into the socket in the floor beneath his table and then adjusting the volume and the bass and treble controls. During this time the silence he was generating was working up for closure.

"My Lord, to assist the jury I have had a transcript made and with your permission I will have it displayed on a screen."

The judge nodded in approval and the screen, already wired up to a computer, was wheeled in. This procedure produced a second span of silence. The witness's face now registered an absconding of the spirit; the soul had evidently abandoned the body to its fate. The recording was short; one could hear a few pleasurable moans followed by gasps, some squeals of delight and then, after a minute or so when only breathlessness could be heard, a voice that was clearly Gillian Sloane's saying in the most caressing of tones that *she was right about him all along; he was every bit the man she had expected him to be!* There followed a short exchange in which Snoddy apologised for his reluctance to make love to her on the earlier occasion at her house. When she came on to him it had taken him unawares and he had 'chickened out'. She in turn apologised for her 'vindictive overreaction'. She knew she shouldn't have gone to Stevens with that cock-and-bull story. But what was a poor girl to do to get her man? They both laughed at her choice of words. Mr Montgomery switched off the recording. He then turned to the simmering Miss Sloane, who would have cut a pitiful figure, had it not been for the obvious anger she showed at her helplessness.

"I assume you wish to withdraw your earlier allegation? I think the court has now a very clear idea of your relationship with my client and, equally important, your relationship with the truth. The only question that remains is when this encounter took place. Could you please enlighten us, Miss Sloane?"

"I can't remember. It must have been just before he went to Germany."

Her delivery was too deliberately casual.

"You remember very well. It was at exactly the time that my client was supposed to be out on his trusty mechanical steed, slaying the first of his headmasters. Only of course you don't want the court to know that. After your sexual humiliation you wanted to get your own back. The very last thing you wanted to do was to supply him with an alibi. You can tell us now or, if you prefer, the court can listen to another piece of recording. We can hear you both discussing his trip back from Germany and his plans to return the next day. Shall I press the button, Miss Sloane?"

"All right, all right, it was the day of the murder. I admit that. The bastard treated me like a piece of meat. He brought me the flowers, and practically got down on his knees and begged me to forgive him. When I let him in, we made love and he got me to blurt out all the feelings I had for him and then, before he left, he suddenly turned nasty – he told me I was a whore, that he had done it just for a laugh and that if I accused him of rape this time I'd be very sorry. This time I wouldn't get off so lightly. I was scared."

316

"But you weren't scared enough to refuse to tell the truth when he phoned you just before he was arrested and pleaded with you to tell the police what had happened?"

"No, do you think I was going to miss a chance like that to get justice for what he'd done to me? You've no idea – he didn't just call me a whore, he made me feel like a whore. I can still feel the dirt clinging to me. Okay, you were right, I did lie, but I did no more than any woman in my place would have done."

"That, my dear Miss Sloane, is for the court to decide. But let us be clear. Do you confirm that Robert Snoddy was with you between 3 and 8 o'clock on the day that Dr Stevens was murdered?"

A faint, but resentful 'yes' was strained out through the teeth. Montgomery then turned his back on the hapless figure and addressed the judge.

"My Lord, in view of the evidence that has come to light I move that the case against my client be dismissed. There is no longer a case for him to answer."

Another silence ensued, a very different silence than before, it was the silence of consensus. The judge however was not of a mind to accept its authority meekly.

"Mr Montgomery, what we have witnessed in this court in the past few days has been a travesty of the processes of law. You and your client were quite clearly in a position to spare the court the expense and the energy of a trial. Yet, for reasons best known to you, you went through the charade of defending the unassailable. The case against your client is hereby dismissed, but I shall require a detailed explanation from you in writing before I decide whether or not to report your conduct to the bar council."

With that he dismissed the jury and removed the restraining influence of his presence from the court room, unleashing a commotion of reactions among those left behind. Snoddy, whom Stuart had been watching as he grinned his way through Gillian Sloane's public humiliation, was accepting the congratulations of his well-wishers with the kind of noncha-lance that seasoned professional footballers bring to their celebrations of goals, things to be seen as the inevitable product of their genius and as such unworthy of naïve delight. Stuart felt the numbness that comes with detachment. It was quite a few minutes before the blood of involvement began to flow again and he started to consider his own position in the affair. Had he been negligent in not bringing these facts to light? Were there other lines of enquiry that he should have pursued? Nothing came to mind, but 'nothing' is never convincing, it just leaves you in the no-man's-land between hope and resignation. Then he remembered Greenfield's warning not to arrest Snoddy. It had been given in a tone of intimacy as a token of friendship, but he had dismissed it as the rhetoric of the occasion. Perhaps Greenfield had after all tried to be a friend to him. But that would mean he had some knowledge or insight into what was to come. At that very moment Stuart spotted the rather stooped figure of Greenfield leaving the court room. The 'coincidence' was perhaps less remarkable than at first sight, since it was probably the unrecorded sight of Greenfield that had provoked the memory in the first place. He had looked out for Greenfield every day of the trial, but surprisingly Greenfield had not shown up again in court after he had given his evidence. He must have come in just after the case had started this morning and found a seat at the back. As he had his back to Stuart, there was no possi-bility of catching his attention without shouting out. But once the crowd had 'uncorked' itself through the doorway there were spaces in between the outpourings in the wide entrance hall for Stuart to catch up with his *friend*. As he did so, it occurred to him that he did not know how to address the academic; he was not comfortable with 'Bruce' and 'Dr Greenfield' did not sit at all well with the unspoken intimacy that had hiccupped between them. That was the problem – he was not sure if the intimacy was real or imaginary. He settled for a tap on the shoulder.

Greenfield turned round and smiled. But there was a hesitation before the smile appeared – Stuart could not be sure whether it followed or preceded recognition.

"Ah, Stuart! Good to see you!"

He offered Stuart his hand.

"This is hardly the outcome you would have chosen."

Stuart scrutinised Greenfield's face for signs of satisfaction. He found nothing incriminating.

"No, I must admit, it has all come as a bit of a blow. There's a lot more to young Snoddy than I gave him credit for."

"I'm sorry for that. I hope it won't have any repercussions on your career."

He was gracious enough not to say 'I-*did*-warn-you'.

"Careers aren't all they're cracked up to be. Imaginary paths leading to imaginary points. When you get to look back at them from our age you see they only put on a show for the young or for those who think they have more ahead of them than behind them."

The thought clearly appealed to Greenfield whose contempt for those who 'had made it' in education had long ago ditched the personal stage of bitterness.

"How about a spot of lunch? I know a little bistro where even the French approve of the wine."

Stuart accepted with an alacrity which he at once deplored.

Chapter 32

Chez Bonnard offered all the rituals that inspire the sense of mystery and reverence for the act of eating – the head waiter with the frown of the sophisticated decision-maker as he chooses a suitable table, the menu laced with the pretentious footnotes of a concert programme and the entrance-test challenge of selecting a wine that will not raise an eyebrow. Greenfield revelled in it all like a returning son. He reminded Stuart of those sophisticated middle-aged playboy actors of the black-and-white forties and fifties, always with greying temples and preferably foreign accents, Charles Boyer or Vittorio De Sica, for whom grand hotels were the natural habitat. Greenfield's rather loud bow tie however was an offence to the prohibition on colour and challenged the illusion.

It was Greenfield who was first to broach the business that both men knew they had with each other.

"You're not too disappointed with the outcome of the trial then?"

"No, I wouldn't say I was disappointed with the outcome. It's me I'm disappointed with. I underestimated my opponent and I was taken for a ride."

"You don't think you simply got it wrong and arrested the wrong man?"

"I certainly got it wrong, but I did not arrest the wrong man. He was the right man all right, but I was wrong to arrest him."

"But how can you say he was the right man? All the evidence proved that he wasn't. He had a cast-iron alibi and the Walther that killed Stevens and wounded Kennedy wasn't the one that he had taken from Richard."

"That's just it. Everything that showed that he was innocent proved in fact that he was guilty."

"Paradoxes. I do like paradoxes."

"Snoddy quite deliberately set me on a paper trail. The Walther was a complete red herring; he borrowed it and conveniently 'lost' it so that it could not be established that it was not the murder weapon while at the same time casting suspicion on him, especially when he came up with the ridiculous story of giving it to a man in a pub. As for his alibi, he could have produced that at any time. Snoddy wanted to be arrested. And he couldn't have concocted such an elaborate cocktail of suspicion and alibi, of poison and antidote if he hadn't orchestrated the attacks in the first place."

"But what makes you think he wanted to be arrested?"

"Two reasons. The main one was the publicity it would attract. Did you see how many pressmen there were in court? It was them he was addressing, not the jury. The whole thing was beautifully stage-managed. It wouldn't surprise me if one of the broadsheets offered him a tidy sum for his story and, of course, with the coverage he's had any book he produces will sell like hot cakes. And don't tell me he hasn't a little volume ready and waiting in the laptop. Earlier in the investigation I was inclined to dismiss Snoddy as a suspect because I couldn't see how he could expect to further any cause he thought he might have by killing Stevens. I don't know if 'cause' is the word – 'revelation' might be better. Whatever you choose to call it, it doesn't run along the usual left-wing, right-wing grooves. But now we all know what according to the Snoddy critique the Stevenses and the Kennedys of this world are doing wrong. And should there be any of us who didn't get the message this time, they will have ample opportunity to catch up on it later. And look! – he has managed all that without having to do the usual martyr-to-the-cause thing and serve his time in prison."

"And the second reason?"

"Much more personal. He wanted to make a public spectacle of Gillian Sloane. This was another thing that puzzled me. Why kill Stevens who was after all what most level-headed people would call an innocent party in the affair and let the real villain go free? Well, he succeeded in doing both. Stevens offended against the gods, Gillian Sloane merely against the person and their punishments were proportionate."

"What about Kennedy?"

"I don't think Kennedy was in the original picture. Snoddy had set the trap for my predecessor, but through one thing and another – not least Myles' failure to tell his boss the truth about the expulsion – we failed to take the bait and he '*got away with it*'. It must have been a great disappointment to him – all that brain power wasted on a common murder and of a man he had no strong personal feelings against. In a way he owed it to Stevens to make good his death. So he decided on a second murder. Actually, I don't think he intended that any great harm should come to Kennedy. The shot, you remember, did little damage; it was the fall that caused all the serious harm. He simply wanted the investigation to be re-opened. Of course, he had nothing but contempt for Kennedy and his ilk, but as he said himself, if he started trying to eliminate the Kennedys of this world he would need to resort to the gas chambers."

Stuart had been looking at his companion the whole time he had been piecing his thinking together, but his eyes had been with his thoughts. Then suddenly he switched to 'visual' and became aware of a broad grin on Greenfield's face.

"But you got to this long before I did, didn't you? That's why you advised me against arresting Snoddy, isn't it?"

"You might say I suspected it. It was certainly in my mind when I went over to Germany to check on Robert. He admitted having returned to England the weekend of the murder, but he assured me he had not killed Stevens. I believed him at the time. However when Kennedy was attacked my suspicions were aroused again and I gradually worked it out. But let's get to the sixty-four thousand dollar question. If Robert didn't carry out the murder, who was it who did?"

Stuart looked at Greenfield and suddenly heard himself speaking a thought that he had certainly not given conscious approval to.

"You did, Bruce."

The response was essentially lexical; it was a pattern of words that popped out rather than a thought; just like an answer you would give to a structured question in a language drill. But once they came out, the words had to fend for themselves and take on responsibility for their own substance. Stuart feared for them. Surprisingly, they fared well; they were not crushed by a storm of protest and indignation or by a withering drought of scorn and derision. They met only a knowing grin, which bestowed on them a status akin to official recognition of their right to exist.

"That's an intriguing thought, Stuart. But aren't you forgetting that it was I who persuaded your sergeant Myles not to spill the beans on Robert? If I had been part of the conspiracy, surely the last thing I would have wanted to do was to prevent Robert's arrest?"

This was not the first time in his long career that Stuart had had to put his mind where his tongue had taken him, but any time he had done so, he had had it confirmed that threat was the mother of invention.

"You misread Myles. You thought that he was straight up and straight down and that your suggestion that he keep the information to himself, far from dissuading him, would have encouraged him to pursue the matter and would lead the investigation to Snoddy. You tried the same thing with me when you advised me not to arrest Snoddy."

"So you think I went out and shot Stevens, and then to stir up the hornet's nest again, I went out again and shot Kennedy? I am flattered that you have such a high regard for my athleticism, and for my aim – especially since I've never fired a gun in my life. And then there's the little matter of my alibi. I'm sure you've already checked it, and no amount of creative thinking on your part is going to change the fact that I was at home on both occasions and I have witnesses to prove it."

"I'm not saying it was you who carried out the actual shooting. That would not be your kind of thing. But what would be your kind of thing would be to mastermind and orchestrate the whole business."

"Ah, I see, you think I got someone else to do it. You think it was a contract killing! Now's there's a thought. Let me see, you think that the bottom had fallen out of the contract killing labour market to the extent that humble schoolmasters can now afford their very own life-extinguishers?"

"Hardly, but how about a contract based on an economy of grievance?"

"An economy of grievance? That's a new one on me. Do go on. I'm intrigued."

"It's very simple, and I'm sure you're quite familiar with the principle. Instead of trading in money you trade in grievances. I have a grievance, you have a grievance. I sort out your grievance, you sort out my grievance. In the middle, matching the grievance-buyers to the grievance-sellers, we have a grievance-bank and of course a grievance banker. I think you, Bruce, are the manager of the grievance-bank."

Greenfield leaned forward and filled Stuart's glass. Then he sat back in his chair and raised his own glass, smiling throughout.

"I love the idea. It's something I might have thought of myself. But then surely, come to think of it, it's an old idea. Isn't that the whole idea behind a criminal justice system and a police service? Swap your word 'grievance' for 'injustice' and there you have it."

"Yes, but can you do that? An injustice is not the same thing as a grievance."

"Agreed, but there is no reason why they can't coincide. Any

324

criminal justice system that forgets that has developed delusions of grandeur. It is trying to get into a dialogue with the gods when it should be addressing the needs of men. It amazes me how our criminal justice system can on the one hand rely on the cloudy thinking of ordinary men when it comes to judging guilt or innocence, but refuses to allow common sense a say in setting the parameters or in punishing the guilty. That, it seems, is a matter for the high priests of the Law who have a better notion of the mind of God. It's mediaeval in its arrogance. We ordinary mortals wouldn't know for example what a life sentence was if they weren't there to tell us."

"So you think that Stevens deserved to die? You think that if we had a criminal justice system worth its salt he would have received the death penalty for his pompous liberalism?"

Greenfield's grin had faded; it was still there, but it had lost its *ad hominem* condescension and taken on a stoical persistence.

"No, I don't think that. I do think though that the liberalism he spouted is profoundly wrong and is leading us into a pit of sentimentality. In appearance it's a gentle thing, but it's far from harmless. It encourages people to think that it is their god-given right to have an uninterrupted dialogue with their libidos. But it's not only the cause of the decadence that is beginning to smell all around us; it's also the reason why those in authority don't take action against it. In the name of compassion the liberal establishment thwarts any attempt to create a system of justice that protects decent people from the kind of people who answer to the libidinal imperative: *I want, therefore I may.*"

"But Snoddy doesn't stop where you stop, does he? He is not content to limit his attack to the addicts, what he sees as the yobs swilling around in their libidinal vomit, nor to the people in high places who refuse to deal with their filth. He wants to attack the problem from the other end as well. He wants to get at the people who spread the plague of sanctimonious paralysis, especially those who spread it among the young. It started when he realised how pathetic the response of the police and the courts was to the plight of his neighbours and how outrageously the criminal justice system reacted when his father took action, while nothing was done against the yobs that were terrorising the neighbourhood. You advised him on that. You told me so. But how far did your advice go? Are you sure it didn't extend to the attack on Joseph Mercer?"

"I will not lie to you, Stuart, but you're not going to get a confession from me either. Let's put it this way. If you were a Platonist you might find me guilty, but no self-respecting existentialist would entertain the idea."

"I'll take that as a 'yes', shall I? – But, of course, so delicate a 'yes' as to wilt if ever it got to court. You put him up to it, but your hands are clean as regards the act itself.

"The big difference between the Mercer punishments and the Stevens punishments is the way the severity shifted from the culprit to the law-giver. Mercer is in a wheelchair for life, but the judge got off with psychological scarring. Poor old Stevens on the other hand lost his life and little Miss Sloane got no more than a humiliation."

"A double humiliation, Stuart. Think of how she must have felt when Robert laughed at her after their afternoon of passion and how that must have simmered over time. But you're right of course. Surely you see why? The balance had changed completely. In Robert's eyes Stevens was the greater offender in the second incident just as Mercer was the main offender in the first. What Gillian Sloane did to him was trivial; he didn't really care very much about being expelled. But, much more important, what she did she did as a rather pathetic individual. Stevens on the other hand was acting *ex cathedra*; his was the hand of God and that God needed to be punished for its contempt for honour and truth."

"But so was Judge Harte. Didn't he do exactly what Stevens did? Or should I say 'didn't do'?"

"That's true. It would seem that Robert's thinking has evolved. He seems now to want to take on the whole liberal consensus with its disregard for justice and its elitist 'ivory-towerism.' It's a curious irony that these sophisticates have so much in common with the Sunday observance society, but instead of insisting that nothing should be done on the Lord's Day, their mantra is that nothing should be done in the Lord's name. They call all moral interventions into the way things are judgementalism, and judgementalism – apart from their own of course – they are constantly reminding us, is a bad and arrogant thing. You heard Robert say as much in court. Looked at another way, you might say they are applying the principles of the free market economy to morality – no interventionism please! The basically decent instincts behind liberalism have been perverted into a philosophy of passivity towards wrong-doing; our pious friends no longer aspire to right-doing for fear that they might get the right-doing wrong. They are proud to announce that it's better to let a hundred guilty men go free, perhaps to kill again, than to condemn an innocent man. The 'perhaps to kill again' they of course very conveniently leave out. By some magic the liberal mentality finds no difficulty in disabling the circuit of guilt between the crimes it allows to happen and the decision to be on the side of the merciful. It is perhaps time for that circuit to be reactivated. And perhaps Robert is the man to do it."

"How does killing the likes of Stevens achieve that?"

"By prising their decision-making out of the safe haven it has found for itself. If they can be made to realise that taking the easy option gives them no immunity, then they might return to the real world and address the problems they are supposed to address – protecting the public from criminals instead of *caring* for the black sheep that have fallen by the wayside; educating bright working class children instead of encouraging them to feel comfortable in the ignorance and stupidity of the culture that is stifling them; saving people from idleness and dependency instead of playing the righteous Lord Bountiful so that 'compassion' can feel good about itself. Robert has seen the effects of this moral *préciosité* all around him. He feels his whole class has been betrayed by it. Who could blame him if he has decided to fight back?"

"Are you saying that you think he was behind the Stevens murder and the attack on Kennedy?"

"'Let's put it this way: it would come as no great surprise to me to discover that he was behind both crimes."

"But that's why you went to see him in Germany, wasn't it?"

"I had my suspicions. When I confronted him, he admitted he had returned to England that weekend, but, as I told you, he swore to me that he had not killed Stevens. He told me all about the business with Gillian, but I knew there was more to it than that. When I persisted, he referred me to a talk I had given to the Thinkers' Club on the nature of policing and I think I got the message."

"Which was?"

"I was looking at the relationship between the public and the whole apparatus of our system of justice. I postulated a society where no police existed. Imagine you are wronged by someone more powerful than you. What do you do about it? You can't take action on your own. The only course open to you is to form a cooperative society and get the group to help you get justice. You in turn have to be willing to do your bit when others get into the same predicament. It's the old socialist principal of *United we stand, divided we fall.* That is the core principal behind policing and the basis of the whole criminal justice system. When Robert Peel was setting up his police force back in the early eighteen hundreds he set out nine principles of policing. Central to them was the notion that the police are the public and the public are the police, the sole difference being that the police are full-time professionals, paid to devote themselves to duties which are incumbent on every citizen. It was very simple – too simple, alas, for modern sophisticates; they want to dress the whole business up and add all sorts of adornments – baroque become rococo. They've turned what is essentially a tool into an *objet d'art*. And now having transformed it into what they think is a beautiful thing, they have become totally obsessed with preserving it in its glorified form – it's out of the question to risk damaging it by actually using it! But the job it doesn't do still needs doing. The people in the greatest need of policing and justice are those at the sharp end of society; it is they who suffer daily from the excesses of laissez-faire-ism. What are they to do? Grin and bear it? No, why should they? Why should they subsidise liberal aestheti-cism? If they want to live their lives free of the oppression of the yobbism that the *bien pensants* seem willing to tolerate on their behalf, they are driven to re-invent a force which addresses their needs. That is what Robert would seem to be doing. You saw the beginnings of it in his hounding of Judge Mercer."

"So you are saying that I'm right and that he *has* formed a citizens' cooperative, a band of brothers who look out for each other when they become the victims of crime? I can see that you approve, but who gets to decide what constitutes a crime and what the appropriate punishment should be?"

"You seem to be missing the point. It's not the failure of the police force that is the core problem. That's just a symptom, albeit a very serious symptom. The problem is rooted like a virus in the liberal establishment. The whole criminal justice system is rotten to the core. It has evolved into a cabal of conscientious punishment-objectors. It's like an army that refuses to fight for fear of killing the sons of foreign mothers. This might show a great generosity of feeling, but any such army would have forfeited the right to call itself an army and it would have no moral authority to object if others took on the duties that it refused to discharge."

"But what has this to do with Stevens and Kennedy? They had no connection with the criminal justice system."

"No, but as you yourself pointed out, they, and people like them are part of the virus. Dear old socialism used to believe in the alleviation of poverty. But it defined poverty not just as lacking the wherewithall to fill your belly; it was also not having enough to fill your mind and your spirit. Education was the great hope of the socialist movement – a process of discovery that could bring the sons and daughters of the working class to share in the great cultural treasures of cerebral endeavour. St Jude's played its small part in this with its system of scholarships. But over the years the ideal has fallen in love with itself. It's exactly the same thing that has happen in our system of criminal justice. Rather than put minds through the rigours of a great journey, the educational establishment has turned the whole adventure into a package tour. It is open to everyone, the fit, the flabby, the willing, the will-less. All very fair and democratic, you might say. Fine, but what is the point of everyone going somewhere where everyone already is? The whole point of the journey was for the traveller to be transformed and enriched, but the journey that's now on offer guarantees painless exploration for all without anyone having to leave the bus. Success is sure, but it's empty; what now passes for education has set itself the target of getting everyone there – but the 'there' must have wheelchair access. The main thing is for everyone to be able to say that you've been there and done it and they're given holiday snaps to prove it. Just as we have criminals back on the streets having '*paid their debt to society*', having served their '*life sentence*' for taking a life, we have school leavers with A levels bulging in their pockets, who seem strangely unable to make any worthwhile contribution either to themselves or to the country as a whole. But we can't complain, we 'know' they are educated; after all they have the 'holiday snaps'. It's a classic case of good intentions falling in love with themselves. The great thing about sentimentality is that doesn't need to know anything about the object of its fixation; it's the fixation that counts.

330

"The *bien pensants* are very quick to point the finger when 'backwoodsmen' naively demand direct action against crime and anti-social behaviour; '*Shame on you*', they say, '*You really must learn to take these things less personally. Take a more sophisticated, more objective approach and look to the root causes.*' Well, maybe Robert has taken their advice to heart. Maybe he has found that there's not enough fear of consequences in the criminals or in those that insist on emasculating those consequences. You may well be right. Perhaps he *has* decided to tackle the problem from both ends."

"This 'cooperative society', I find it very hard to imagine he could have managed to get it up and running without the help of someone like yourself."

"That's a question you need to ask Robert, although he's hardly going to give you an answer, is he? I'll say one thing to you, Stuart. Don't make the mistake of underestimating him again. It will not just be a bunch of his cronies that you will be dealing with. Robert understands the power of the random. If it exists, this band of brothers, as you call them, will be hard to trace. For every proxy pardon issued by the surrogate saints of the justice industry, you will find men and women being denied the justice and protection of the Law. Look to those people. Many of them, of course, will bend the knee to the 'higher wisdom of the Enlightened' and do absolutely nothing, but some will have the guts to raise their fists in defiance. They it is who will want to reclaim the roles of policeman, judge and jury. And it looks likely that Robert has taken it upon himself to show them how. None of these people will be called upon to mend their own injustice; that will be done for them by others; in return they will be asked to right the scales for yet others. There you have it, Stuart – the founding principle of community policing, the synthesis of the personal and the objective. If I'm right, your net will need to be cast very wide indeed."

Stuart marshalled his forces for one last push of insistence.

"If I am to believe you – and I don't say I do – how can you justify your involvement in all this? At the very least, you knew what he was doing all along and still you said nothing."

"I've said plenty over the years, Stuart, and who has listened? There's a lot of me in Robert, a lot more than there is in anyone else. Why should I betray him? I am in total sympathy with his outrage. But when it comes to stepping up from the accountant's role of balancing the books of justice to the top job of managing and directing, I get squeamish. It's not that I've any objection in principle to the taking of a human life, but I do like the victim to be personally guilty of a crime that my conscience – not necessarily the law – can square with the punishment. As for those who have committed the crimes, I have not the slightest problem in going along with punishment that the law has signally failed to impose, but as to the authority figures, those who blindfold themselves with the rules and conventions of our sentimental society and refuse to have any dealings with the messy business of keeping justice alive in a world that is bleeding from its absence, there, I do have a problem. In terms of effect, theirs are the greatest crimes. And I do see that if things are to change, these are precisely the people that must be targeted. Is that a virtue or is it just feeble-mindedness on my part? If you listened to conventional wisdom, I should doubtless be commended for my restraint – it would be deemed to show that I have not lost touch with my humanity – but I'm not so sure. A lot of innocent people were killed in the war with Hitler, but that failed to persuade many of that generation to resist their pacifist instincts. In the end I did exactly what my dear friends, the dreaded good liberals always do – I did nothing, and, you know, it works – I didn't get even the slightest shock of guilt."

Chapter 33

It was quite late in the afternoon when Stuart parted from his companion in front of the restaurant. It was a good three-mile walk to the station. He had the car, but the hour that it would take him on foot offered greater sanctuary. Superintendent Winkworth might 'share his pain', but then again he might not; from what he knew of the man, it was more likely that he would delight in it. He had shared Stuart's failure, but this morning's disaster in the courtroom would let him climb out on Stuart's shoulders. Stuart's own sense of failure had little to do with what had happened in court; he had had the most interesting case of his career and he had settled for what looked a simple three-no-trump game when a slam was on in a minor suit. The fact that the seemingly straightforward game had gone down was of little consequence, the missed slam was where the ache was. As less and less distance cushioned him from Winkworth's reaction he saw that his feet were avoiding the cracks in the pavement – no penitence would be too great to earn a second swing at the grand slam.

Lightning Source UK Ltd.
Milton Keynes UK
UKOW05f1319120114

224392UK00002B/25/P